Dollarbird

RAINY DAY RAMEN AND TH[...]

Gordon Vanstone is a Canadian living and working in Singapore. *Rainy Day Ramen and the Cosmic Pachinko* is Vanstone's first novel and is an ode to the country which captured a piece of his heart during his eight-year stay in Tokyo as an international school teacher.

Praise for *Rainy Day Ramen and the Cosmic Pachinko*

'Vanstone's protagonist takes the reader on a debauched, alcohol-fueled spiritual quest through a hallucinatory Japan of cursed *gaijin* houses, seedy hostess bars, a Beatles-themed McDonalds, mysterious internet café denizens, and one seriously pissed-off cat. Grab yourself a couple of cans of Chu-hi and join him on the journey.' Isaac Adamson, author of *Tokyo Suckerpunch* and *Complication*

RAINY DAY RAMEN

and the

COSMIC PACHINKO

GORDON VANSTONE

Dollarbird

Dollarbird

First published in 2021
by Dollarbird, an imprint of Monsoon Books Ltd
www.dollarbird.co.uk
www.monsoonbooks.co.uk

No.1 The Lodge, Burrough Court, Burrough on the Hill,
Melton Mowbray LE14 2QS, UK

ISBN (paperback): 978-1-912049-82-0
ISBN (ebook): 978-1-912049-83-7

Cover design by Cover Kitchen.

A Cataloguing-in-Publication data record is available from the British
Library.

Printed and bound in Great Britain by Clays Ltd, Elcograf S.p.A.
23 22 21   1 2 3

Dedicated to
tanuki everywhere

Contents

COSMIC PACHINKO Part 1: Notes from the Netcafe   11

RAINY DAY RAMEN Part 1: Okinawa (Soba)

  1 Bus to Nowhere   63
  2 Unmasking   76
  3 Gertie and the Manky Peach   92
  4 Amorous Amphitheater Apparition   104
  5 The Sun Moreover Ascends   122

COSMIC PACHINKO Part 2: Man from the North Country   143

RAINY DAY RAMEN Part 2: Ocean (Shoyu)

  1 The Ferryman Speaketh   183
  2 Dallas From New York   197
  3 Message in a Bottle   214
  4 Octopus Balls and Tanuki Nuts   227

COSMIC PACHINKO Part 3: The Tale of Gaijin   245

RAINY DAY RAMEN Part 3: Tokyo (Tonkotsu)

  1 Hachiko on Earth (aka Tokyo Love Letter)   271
  2 Tatsuya, Machiko, and the Emo Fascist   280
  3 Dallas in Detention   286
  4 Devouring The Manky Peach   298
  5 Cosmic Pachinko   304
  6 Rainy Day Ramen   313
  7 Lost Letters of Eleanor Rigby   325
  8 End of the Line   331

COSMIC PACHINKO Part 4: Molotovs of the Mind   345

EPILOGUE Rainy Day Ramen and the Cosmic Pachinko   377

Cosmic Pachinko

PART ONE
Notes from the Netcafe

No man or woman born,
coward or brave,
can shun his destiny.
—*Homer,* The Iliad

Reflected on a whisky sheen, the pixels burn. I type. I drink. Paragraph by paragraph warped puzzle pieces fall, and syllables stretched through silence struggle to connect blurred ends. Submerged in this indigo incandescence, I mash keys, aimless and seeking. The ferryman told me music lived in the air between notes. Perhaps, it's in the space between the letters where I'll be found.

I've been holed up behind the half-length navy-blue curtain of this cramped cubicle since returning to Tokyo a week ago. Though I'm beginning to suspect, in some sense, I've been in hiding and flight going back much further than this.

Curls of blue-grey cigarette smoke have been caressing corneas since morn. Eyes, red and sore, I rub into the palm of each hand. Black characters blur then come back into view on the glowing screen in front of me.

Hours spent, day and night, as I try to make all this coherent; memos entered on soggy coasters, drunkenly written emails sent to self, notes scribbled on the inside covers and margins of battered paperbacks. Fuzzy memories, spawned by abused cells, strain to fill gaping holes between scattered fragments. I'm unsure whether I'll find any meaning in it all. I'm uncertain there exists any meaning in these records of scattered and fragmented living.

Sometimes you just have to scream into the abyss, if only to hear your own voice echo back.

***

My long journey back culminated when I wandered into Shinjuku and stood beneath a photon waterfall. I gazed into the vortex of Shinjuku's fluorescent night, a point I'd hovered in visions delivered during those waning Okinawan days when, after tracing the red thread of my mind's eye, found myself hundreds of feet up awash in Yasukuni-dori's synthetic kaleidoscope sky.

I had no reason to give the whole episode with its thread, and where it led, any more credence than a simple trick of the imagination. Nonetheless, I followed the inebriated, half-sleep daydream, in reality, from the small island of Okinawa, up the Pacific, over Honshu and into Kyushu – to arrive here, back in Tokyo.

Anticipating something consequential to happen, I stood still, arms spread, palms out. With my neck craned back, I tried to pinpoint the exact spot where I'd traversed the dark void, and floated in the artificial dawn. I hoped the answers I sought lay there.

Scanning an ever-exploding chaos of movement all around, I awaited my burning bush or other such sign. Listening through beat ears as bebop blasts of the metropolis night blew through the dark like a frenzied jazz orchestra; I lingered, expectant, for some change to come over me, but none did.

What now? I unleashed a shuddering yawn – *a place to lay my head*.

Set to exit the perennial pandemonium, I turned, when a phantasmal vibration underfoot, like a distant locomotive approaching through an endless black tunnel, carried a strained sensation. I froze. A gust channelled through the canyon of high-rise *depāto* and karaoke towers, stroked Yasukuni-dori's long stretch of pavement, hit me sidelong, and hissed with a feline ferocity: *Ah'm nay done wee ye yet*.

The words rang with an eerie familiarity. Along the wide sidewalk, I weaved away from my supposed prophetic point, seeking their source and contemplating cats. Businessmen in black blazers brushed past toward midnight trains to solace, while my eyes scanned the cement for any mangy white strays, yet I embodied the only one in sight.

In Ebisu, there are tons of stray cats, I remembered. I'd even asked a date about it once. 'It's an affluent area, so nobody eats them.' I winced, and she laughed, having a go at the gullible foreigner.

Urban legends aside, Ebisu was too far in the wrong direction to trek to that night. Even with no destination in sight, I knew this much. No matter, with my monkey mind going apeshit, Shinjuku held plenty of stimuli for arboreal locomotion; leaping at tinctures and clinging to harbingers. And sure enough, looking up, a string of red lanterns pulled me into Kabukicho, Shinjuku's entertainment district.

Barely down the first backstreet, the sweet sound of stiletto heels tapping pavement drifted to my waiting ears. Agog eyes glanced up to see a slim hostess in a pink mini-dress tottering past.

'Good evening,' I said, expecting to be ignored. She gave me a sideways glance and half-smile.

'*Kimoi!*' she squealed, reached across the space between us and squeezed my forearm with delicate fingers and elaborately embellished nails.

A rat the size of a chihuahua scurried across our path. Pleased my leering glance was not the object of her revulsion, I watched the rodent disappear into a wall-cast shadow.

'*Gomen.*' With an embarrassed smile, she retracted her hand.

'It is okay. Scary and gross, yes?' I gestured at the alleyway where the rodent had vanished.

'*Sou desu.*'

'Though through no fault of its own – we can't very well change the role we're cast in.' I'd switched to English but made little more sense than if I'd tried to express the same with my limited Japanese. 'It is what it is. Unable to transcend its essence ... A rat is a rat ...' I blathered on, unsure whom it was spoken for, or for what purpose.

She replied with a quizzical look. Before I could progress our one-sided chat any further, the hostess gave a small well-manicured wave by her hip and disappeared into the narrow entrance of the next bar.

I'd been drinking all day, yet not until that brief human contact did I finally feel drunk.

Steeped in the wooziness I'd been craving, I looked into the window of the club lost in a fantasy born of bottles.

The door flies open. I burst in, brush past a doorman in a dark three-piece suit standing to tell me this is a private club, 'No foreigners welcome.'

Seated solitary on a black couch, reclined against the arm with legs crossed high, she tosses her silky black hair over a petite, bare shoulder. I advance with one hand extended and propose, 'Come away with me from this place. We'll start a new life together.'

She reaches up, our fingers interlock, and I pull her toward me. Stood, torsos touching, I reach an arm around her slender waist and draw her to me tighter. Head tilted, I near her red, moist, parted lips ...

The door swung open, and a red-faced salaryman came tumbling out. I was back on the street, in mind and body. The momentary high brought on by our red-light interaction dissipated. Only the reflection of my unshaven and dishevelled form, brushed in neon luminescence, was thrown back from the tinted window of the *kyabakura* club.

I continued to study the figure staring back at me, hoping to recognize a semblance of the man who once occupied his form. A plain white T-shirt stretched out and dribbled with drink stains, hung atop baggy, low-slung jeans. With a backpack over one shoulder, I looked very much the skater kid persona briefly inhabited in younger days.

Yet, there I was approaching thirty, caught in this perpetual adolescence. In another time or place, I would've overthrown tyranny, fought in wars, faced death and known life ... It was then a salient thought struck; *the portrait of my youth, far from that of an artist as a young man, is nothing more than an amateurish finger painting of a clumsy toddler.* In reflection, I stood – existing still in the absence of any swift, savvy brush strokes.

My shaggy, dirty blond hair was styled using my palm at a public bathroom sink, parted on the left and slicked back on each side. Our eyes met – mine and the familiar stranger staring back – they were glassy, with pupils like piss holes in the snow circled by irises of icy blue-grey. The bluish eyes and blondish hair, I'd come to recognize as my bread and butter, a sort of currency adore here in Asia. This perhaps was what eclipsed my loser circumstances, and allowed me to deludedly emit the remaining shreds of an ol' cockiness, as I ogled each passing bar butterfly – and doing laps in the liquored vibe, projected desire onto downcast, mascaraed eyes.

Into the mirrored glass, I attempted a smile that looked like a small cornered animal baring its yellow teeth. I closed my lips over the plaquey grin. *A brush, a shave and a good night's sleep, and I'll be back in top form.*

After the extensive once over, I convinced myself there was maybe a hint of genuine interest in the initial half-smile from the high-heeled hostess. This was followed by a realization the window was only reflected on the one side. That patrons inside could have been observing this vacant foreigner's meticulous inspection of himself, prompted me to move on, embarrassed though slightly buoyed.

I walked in fading memory of the *kyabakura* girl, and *that touch – there was alchemy in that touch.*

Bars sprung up seven stories on either side. I imagined in those blocks the thousands of young women; slinky dresses clung to tight bodies, languidly draped in the dark clubs. Hostesses abound throughout Japan but are at the highest density in Kabukicho. Modern-day geishas, without the strict etiquette training, and text messages instead of pillow books – they sing karaoke, light cigarettes, and pour whisky mixed with seltzer water for salarymen patrons who hope to carve out an oasis in their desert of toil and banality. While the hostesses aspire to capture a fancy, and be rewarded with gifts of Prada or Louis Vuitton, badges of honour adorned of their feminine wiles.

I pushed on, deeper into the labyrinth, passed male hosts in imitation designer suits with exceptionally gelled hair, roving in effete gangs of three or four. There was a smattering of *yakuza* bars where low-level thugs smoked in front of tinted-window, black Mercedes sedans, awaiting the evening's orders and misdemeanours. In brightly lit pachinko palaces, lifelong punters and bored housewives sat chain-smoking and dropping ball bearings, blithely ensnared in noisy doldrums of fugitive dreams.

With a freshly lit cigarette, I stopped and spun a slow revolution. Drawing one long drag, I took it all in with an orange ember embrace. *Seven stories, three cars, two parlours, one rat and no cats ...*

Neon tracers dissolved from view, stood there in the middle of the street, the night congealed around me once more. *It ain't adding up ... subtracting and dividing, plenty. Conundrums multiplying and answers ... well, any numeral multiplied by zero produces zero ...*

I gave my head a shake and started moving again. *Numbers can get fucked! Save for counting syllables. To compose haikus.*

From behind me, a young woman's cackle, and exalted banter milled through the air like prayer wheels spun. It broke my rumination, a reminder that this night, like all of them, was sacrosanct with lust, madness, passion and hope.

Om, mani, padme, hum.

My eyes settled on the stretch of Hanamachi street which lay before me and I blinked three or four times to make sure I wasn't seeing things. Yet even after the head-clearing ritual, the phantasmagoria remained. There, on a shoddy corner of the sleazy street, a rotund man in chequered polyester pants wobbled to and fro, flying a kite.

The night was starting to patch together like some messed-up mescaline trip. Though, under honest appraisal, my life of late had morphed into one long psychedelic ride. Or perhaps insanity was just one's way of making the mundane more palpable.

I crossed from one brick sidewalk to the other. Past doll-faced babes on billboards, an all-night conveyor-belt sushi buffet and adult arcades, I closed in on the Kabukicho oddity.

I lingered a comfortable social distance away from the misfit and studied his actions with a cool curiosity and persistent disbelief. 'What are you doing?'

'Fly my kite.'

Well, you ask a stupid question ... 'Yeah, I see,' I said with my best disarming smile. 'But like, it's a strange time ... a strange place.'

'*Hai.*' Thick-rimmed granny glasses on a bulbous bald head magnified his wide-set eyes. With a flat broad nose and thin lips plastered in an amphibious smile, he looked like a contented bullfrog as he fiddled with the kite string in carefree concentration.

He was *dasai* in a *kawaii* kind of way and I couldn't help but speak to him with the condescending demeanour you'd talk to an imbecilic child. 'I've only ever seen people flying them in the parks and stuff, in like the daytime.' On our lily pad slab of sidewalk, I crouched down to his five-foot stature. 'How'd you get it up there, buddy? Must've been difficult, yeah?'

'When the wind whispers "it's time",' he confided in a hush-hush tone. 'Then, we run so fast, catch an updraft in wait, and above the pavement and buildings we soar.'

I smirked imagining the little butterball waddling down the narrow side street. The grin faded as my glance shifted from the sex show signage reflecting off his shiny scalp, to his fingers tugging at the white line. The thread turned fuchsia under Hanamichi's persistent glow, as I followed it up.

'Now, I keep moving, always moving, and it fly through sky.'

His wonky grin tilted upward, as he watched his handiwork dance a gentle ballet above the parlours and bars.

The kite was nothing special, a classic diamond shape. Underneath it was the darkest blue, almost invisible against a midnight sky. I couldn't see the other side, the design which projected into the cosmos beyond.

'Can I have a go?' I asked. The question, half in jest, but at the root was a very real desire to connect with the childlike innocence of the act, if only for a moment.

'No, no, no,' he croaked in an apologetic chuckle.

I shrugged, gave him one last supercilious smile and bid farewell. 'Okay, have a good night.'

'*Hai*, I'm glad you could make it.' For the first time, his eyes strayed from the hobby at hand and landed on me. With the same static simper, he scanned my form. Behind those Coke bottle glasses was a twinkle of pride in his eyes.

I did a double take at him but figured the phrase was ill-plucked from an English textbook shelved long ago. He turned his attention once more to the diamond in the sky as I walked away.

Down the block a ways, I glanced over my shoulder. He remained, the strange little man – seams stretched, crammed into his 70s leisure suit – pulling on string, and caressing the night. Pedestrians passed by, but paid him no mind, the same as when I'd approached and during our short exchange. Though avoiding anomalies and the unwanted attention acknowledging them could cause, I'd noted, was a common cultural trait.

I'd been in motion for fourteen hours straight as I zig-zagged across Kyushu, transferring trains and trudging pavement, seeking a path to contentment but only arriving at forked junctions with no signage for Nirvana nor Hades. The long journey collected in the muscles of my legs and back. I stretched under the street's neon rays like a tree reaches to kiss the sun.

My escape from Kabukicho's grip lay a convenience store, love hotel and noodle shop away. With another long yawn and upward stretch, I fought off the temptation to circle back for one more pass through the flame. As I exited the scorching blue backstreets and notorious alleys, a memory struck.

The family's finest white tablecloth covers the dining room table of my childhood while red and white pillar candles glimmer in the centre. The smell of turkey and family chatter wafts in from the kitchen beyond. I kneel on my chair's cushioning, peer over the barred backrest and study with detached curiosity a small nativity scene, in keeping with dictates of the season erected on an oak cabinet. The mother, Mary, I choose as victim for my childish antics. Plucking her from where she knelt beside the crib under the gaze of three sage men, I turn to face the table and lean over so I can reach the flame burning atop a blackened wick. An idle hand dips her blissful stare into the pool of melted red wax. It hardens rapidly around her form, after which, I peel the imprint from her face and place it on the print of my tiny pink index finger. The first pass is quick. I study the finger cut through the blaze, watching it bend, break, and smoke before reforming to flicker and burn on. I repeat the same movement slowing it down each time, experiencing the heat on approach build to a searing warmth. The veil melts in blood-red drips, hitting the white, wax puddle as soothing pink swirls. Until finally, it is gone, consumed by fire and insouciance. I edge closer, drag my finger in slow, steady increments for one final sweep; warmth turns to heat, the nerves of my fingertip register a sharp scald, and I retract.

'Fred Buchanan, stop that right now! And get down from there, you're going to get wax on the tablecloth. Or burn the goddamn house down!' My mother's voice barks from under the alcove entrance. Chastened, I slump and sit sullen with my bum on the dining room chair, the virgin tucked between my legs.

In a sense, I'm still playing such games. There remains an attraction to the flame, and any voice of reason is muted by an ocean's expanse.

The tempting warmth of chaos diminished as I crossed a four-lane thoroughfare. Shin-Ōkubo, at the ass-end of Shinjuku's Kabukicho, is where all the seediness and debauchery of the district is shat out, leaving kernels of raw indecency and the stench of alienation. If you go out partying in Kabukicho and end up in Okubo, you either took a wrong turn or are steering to satisfy deeper transgressions.

With the glow of Shinjuku's red light fading to a tenebrous burgundy, in front of a low-end, nondescript love hotel, I neared a gaggle of streetwalkers.

'You wanna get a room, handsome?' beckoned a husky voice. The first hooker in a row of four lining that dark stretch stepped out from the shadows to proposition my path.

I studied her: broad shoulders, strong jaw and taller than your average Asian, though the six-inch heels helped. 'Thanks, but not tonight. I just got back into town. Gotta find a place to stay.'

'Stay with me, baby.' She grabbed my wrist, softly, but with a discernible manly grip.

The big hands and hint of Adam's apple confirmed my suspicion. My all-too-eager lady of the night was, in fact, a ladyboy.

'We'll have a good time,' he added with a suggestive smile.

I twisted my arm free of his grip. With a nod and polite, if not flirtatious smile, I said, 'Sorry babe, maybe another time.'

The next two in the androgynous row hung back in the shadows and lay in wait for riper fruit. But the fourth tossed her smoke and lunged to my side. I could feel the perky fake tits rub against the bare skin below my sleeve.

'You're just as much a whore as any of us,' he came on, more aggressive than the first.

'Huh?'

'An attention whore,' he clarified. 'You're getting off on our advances. You fucking love it. Don't pretend like you don't.' He seductively whispered the accusation up into my ear.

It sent a chill. Was it arousal or fear? Fear of arousal? Or plain panic, he'd seen right through me.

'Suck my dick!' I lashed out confused, tired, and exposed.

'That's the whole point, honey.' He unleashed an uproarious laugh, hoarse and affected.

Despite myself, I lit a smoke and lingered, studying the tranny. A part of my brain, or something lower, told me to ignore the obvious and entertain the offer, as this one was in the guise of a very attractive young Asian lady.

'Where are you from?' I asked, disarmed by his quick retort, curious to know how he'd seen through my initial kabuki.

'I'm Filipina, and the other three here are Thai.' The fact they weren't Japanese was a given. The locals don't engage in streetwalking, and I'd never come across a Japanese transsexual. His English was good, with just a hint of accent, sounding a bit Latina through the forced femininity.

'So, why'd you say that?' I asked, suddenly meek. 'That I'm an attention whore, getting off on this whole exchange.'

'Was I incorrect?' He raised a thin painted-on eyebrow.

'Not entirely, I guess that's why I'm standing here rather than down the block by now.'

He had me dead to rights. My motivation for engaging so courteously, I'm inclined to misrepresent as some unorthodox form of altruism. '*Hey, I respect your identity ... hold no prejudice ... am accepting of all who cross my path, blah, blah, blah ...*' But that's bullshit. It's pure self-indulgence. This one saw that and called me on it.

'You're right,' began my confession, 'I was feeding my ego, craving contact, lusting after lust ...' Then I asked the million-dollar question, 'but how'd you surmise all that so quickly? How'd you see my intentions so nakedly?'

'Shit honey, I been around,' he said with a confident air. 'You walk down this alley then veer toward our post as you pass, the anticipation of one of us propositioning you was written all over your handsome face.' He stroked my cheek with long, painted nails atop thick sausage fingers. 'And honey, I'm quite gifted when it comes to all things, nakedly.'

That fake girlish giggle was becoming more convincing each time he unleashed it. 'Yeah, you're a perceptive one.'

'Here, honey.' He handed me a pint. 'Take your mind off all this inane introspection.'

I inspected the label. Nikka Black clear whisky, the cheapest the convenience stores have to offer. I knew it well.

I wiped the lip with my shirt, immediately realizing the faux pas. I felt a pang of guilt and took a long haul, hoping to wash away the insensitive slight. Wiping the bottle's mouth again before handing it back, I figured might conceal my earlier indiscretion. 'Thanks,' I said with downcast eyes.

He accepted it back with a staunch silence, brought the bottle to his mouth – paused, looked at the glass lip, shot me a cold stare, then took a long, meaningful swallow off the pint.

I'd tainted the moment. 'Well, thanks for the drink. Nice meeting you, but really, I gotta be finding a place to crash for the night.' I shifted my weight from foot to foot, anxious to leave.

'Sure thing, dear. Don't be a stranger.' He placed a meaty hand on my shoulder, and as I turned to walk away, let it slowly caress down the length of my arm.

Halfway down the short street, she called out, 'and honey, don't you worry … we're all driven by self in the end.'

I smiled an acknowledgement and left just as I had come; some weird white cocktease, a lookie-loo, lurking those 1 am backstreets.

Near the bottom of the small avenue, round the corner came a bespectacled salaryman, mid-forties with his collar up and head down. He passed, averting his gaze. I looked over my shoulder to see him grab the arm of the second streetwalker and escort her into the dim-lit entrance of the love hotel.

At least someone has a destination in mind, I thought, as I rounded the same corner onto Okubo-dori and continued to wander. Under the street lamps and away from the backstreets was a collection of Japanese language schools, K-pop memorabilia shops and Korean BBQ restaurants. Despite the almost theme-parkish vibe Shin-Ōkubo had recently acquired, the low-rents and dark alleys meant it remained a haven for outcasts and down on their luck expats.

Minutes later, loitering out front a local convenience store, a *shōchū* highball in hand and hiccups with a citrus burn, I sensed I'd arrived. Heavy eyelids shot open as a flash of fur streaked through the 7-Eleven parking space.

'There you are! Ya little fucker ...' I proclaimed to myself. My head jerked violently to the left, and I gave chase. The grapefruit Chu-hi splashed onto my knuckles as I flicked a lit cigarette to the sidewalk and sped up to close the gap.

The tom slowed to a light trot but darted forth at intervals like he was consciously keeping me at a safe distance. The cat's stubby tail bent at a right angle as if telegraphing his next move. His cream-coloured fur was dirtied by back-alley living, and if I squinted, could make out an arced scar down its back haunch. Half a block ahead, he turned and looked straight at me. The eyes glowed two hues of yellow, reflecting underneath a light pole. '*Ah'm nay done wee ye yet,*' came the same refrain.

It hit the back of my psyche like a charging sumo wrestler, and I stumbled backwards three weaving steps. Message received, the feline looked away and cut down the adjacent side street. In hot pursuit, I came to the rounded kerb and swerved into the narrow road. My eyes darted to every dark corner and hollowed nook, but the cat was gone.

When I looked up, I was stood under a sign which advertised in red-outline, black block letters: Genki Internet Café, 2F, open

24 hours. I walked up the carpeted steps and checked in for the night. I've been extending it in twelve-hour slots ever since. At nine hundred yen a night, like a couple of pints at the pub, it's the cheapest accommodation going.

* * *

Faux wood panelling lines the partition walls of my cubicle. The black leather chair fully reclines, allowing me to get some partially horizontal repose when needed. A knapsack containing all my belongings is stuffed under the desktop which holds the monitor, an ashtray, a few empty cans of beer plus the one I've got on the go. There's free soda and ice for highballs and even a shower room for when the cramped living space starts to reek of stale tobacco, bathtub gin and what I'd like to consider my manly musk but to others is just plain stank.

I'm not the only one who calls the Genki Netcafe home. There are mostly the comers and goers; gamers, lovers, manga fiends and the like, but I've identified at least three other residents. The first, I met the morning after my long jaunt through the Tokyo night.

I awoke and went straight to the communal men's bathroom to piss out the previous night's delights. The Accountant, as I've termed him, was adjusting the knot of his tie when I arrived at the sink to wash my hands. He centred the knot just right with the top button of his white collared shirt and smoothed his black blazer with brisk strokes of his palms. Satisfied with his appearance, he turned to me, smiled, and gave a formal morning salutation, '*Ohayo gozaimasu.*'

'Good morning,' I replied, still wetting my hands in the lukewarm stream. With my bloodshot eyes and four-day stubble, I looked altogether unworthy of that much respect from this go-getter.

'*Ganbatte.*' He wished me luck for the day as he turned on his heels and exited.

'Yeah, good luck.' I leaned against the sink a tad dumbfounded. *Have I woken up in the same internet café or somehow come to at Mitsubishi headquarters?*

As the washroom door swung closed, I watched him briskly march toward an open curtain, bow low to an empty cubicle and enter officiously.

I checked the clock as the door shut with a click. It read 7:59, just on time. *Hey, whatever you gotta do to get by.*

In my newfound privacy, I felt vomit rise and puked yellow bile into the basin. I splashed water on my face then tilted my head to drink from the faucet, rinsed and spat.

Back in my cubicle, I'd planned to get another five or six hours' sleep, but the chubby little eager beaver must have inadvertently inspired me. I got my shit together and checked out; unbeknownst that I'd be back, and back, and back again.

I set out to assess for what purpose I'd been summoned back to Tokyo. The best way to accomplish this, I figured, was to throw myself upon the city; see people in action, in purposeful movement, heading in some decided direction.

I would submerge myself in the metropolis, and perhaps through osmosis, come to understand why it beckoned my return.

***

All human traffic flows toward the station during morning rush hour.

A green and grey Yamanote line train arrived and I crammed in. Bodies pressed together so tight it was hard to know where your own appendages ended and someone else's torso began. Like the Tom Waits song, 'I'm big in Japan', but purely in the literal sense. At over six feet, my head was clear of the crush. Below my nostrils, though, a salaryman's barcode Brylcreem comb-over and mothball mingled suit jacket secreted a combined odour which assaulted my senses and made the vomit rise again.

The next stop was Shinjuku. Doors opened, bodies flooded out, and impossibly more people packed into our cattle car. Station attendants in immaculate uniforms of polished brass buttons and pristine white gloves pushed against the mass of bodies so the doors could close.

When they finally slid shut, we were jammed in all the more densely, and I struggled to inhale a full breath. In the ensuing melee, we'd been involuntarily reshuffled. To my benefit, I'd been reassigned to a petite office girl. The scent of lavender and wildflowers wafted from below. With the pleasant shift in scenery, I had to fight against some sort of olfactory arousal that was setting in. With the constant squeeze, some unsuspecting commuter would surely be struck by the rising action.

At the next stop, the flow of bodies in exit carried me off onto the platform. To re-experience the rush hour train was both exhilarating and exhausting. I stayed off and exited Yoyogi station. I made a stop at the 7-Eleven for two tall cans of Chu-hi; a grapefruit six percenter to ease the queasiness and calm the nerves, then a nine percent Chu-hi Strong to bring on a morning buzz.

In Yoyogi Park, I sat on an empty bench and drank. It was fairly barren on that weekday morn. The odd straggler passed hurriedly to catch their morning commute.

I remembered the last time I'd drunk in Yoyogi. It was with my American friend Dallas, Gertie, this tough Irish chick I'd known from my first moments in Japan, and Akiko, a uni student I'd been dating a little and sleeping with a lot.

Whisky, beer, and Chu-his, emptied and unopened, were scattered all around the blue tarp we had laid out to mark our territory. We were surrounded by other revellers having similar celebratory afternoons under the cherry blossom trees.

It hits from mid-April to early May, *hanami*, when the cherry blossoms bloom. In droves, the residents of Japan flock to parks and riverbanks to bask under the white, pink beauty of the flowering *sakura* trees. Under canopies of adorned branches; eating, drinking and laughter abound.

'Fuckin love this time of year,' Dallas declared, standing as if holding court while we sat on the tarp drinking in contentment.

'Aye, it's the craic,' Gertie concurred.

'For like two weeks, all these uptight office drones let loose, hit the piss and live carefree. Pretty much like Fred lives twenty-four seven, three sixty-five.' He gave a snort while gesturing in my direction with a sloshing beer can. 'They ought to call it a Fredami.'

I laughed along and drank from my whisky and Coke with satisfaction. Not in agreement but pleased, they'd all bought the act; swallowed whole, the portrayed outer image.

'In the spring air, inebriated they stir. From shopgirl to CEO, petty differences recede, and pure bliss succeeds, under a *hanami* sky.' I punctuated the verse by sculling my drink and pouring yet another.

'A couple of whiskies and he thinks he's Dylan feckin Thomas,' Gertie teased.

'Yo, throw a beat behind that shit, and we got your first single, Freddy B.'s dope ass *hanami* rap.' Dallas proceeded to provide an amateurish beatbox as he danced, and the plastic tarp crackled.

With my arm around Akiko's shoulder, I pulled her down beside me. We lay, looking up at the cloudless blue sky through a tranquil floral frame. Sweeping her bangs to one side, I planted a kiss on her forehead. 'You having fun?'

'It's perfect,' she said, then turned her head away, adding in a whisper to the treetops, '*demo*, too brief, *ne*.'

The words barely penetrated. We lay in silence under the pinkish umbrella while blossoms above burst like fireworks. I wondered if that was why the name for fireworks, *hanabi*, was so close to *hanami*; flower viewing. There was probably some shared *kanji* character, or they were formed by similar strokes or something.

I puzzled the language like that sometimes but had done little to actually learn it. I thought of asking Akiko, the expert beside me; instead, I lay in inaudible ponder.

A breeze passed through the branches, they quivered, and petals fluttered downward like a first snowfall. I raised off my back and stuck out my tongue. A single leaf landed on the tip. I bolted to my feet and jumped around, pointing to the pink petal that had stuck there. Unable to enunciate, I said, 'OOK ... I Aught it on ay UNG!'

Everyone laughed at my overwrought elation and clownish carrying on but mostly were caught up in the contagiousness of simple joy.

***

I picked my morning drink up off a wooden plank of the weathered bench we rested on. An autumn wind blew, the desolate branches above my head rattled in the emptiness. I took a drink, set it down on the green chipped paint and thought it strange, if not inspired, a memory with that cast of characters should visit me then.

Stranger yet when I contemplated the seemingly plain, incidental events which had led me to that park bench. Pushed off the train at Yoyogi station, craving a drink which drove me to the nearest convenience store and finally to wander into the park as sanctuary from the station crowds, where I could sip and smoke in solitude. It was as if each act conspired to draw me there and conjure that specific memory.

That *hanami* party was one of the rare occurrences where all three of those relationships were together in one place at the same time. Though, during my first year in Japan, a separate and special bond had formed with each.

Gertie, a confidant, like a big sister, she watched over me and attempted to steer me right. We saw each other through ups and downs until I couldn't pull her out of the final fall. Dallas, my partner in crime, as we tore up the town. Together, we selfishly sought kicks, unapologetically indulged in satisfying our base instincts and, though the shovels dulled, dug life. And Akiko, the lover, who gave pleasure atop my simple futon, and many other desired environs. In those arms, I found warmth and comfort, before breaking from the embrace, leaving her holding only betrayal and pain.

Like the sequence of events directing me to that park bench, on a grander scale, I couldn't escape the feeling that all three of those people were fibres in the thread which drew me back to Tokyo. In half-drunk waking dreams or strange hallucinogenic visions, each had strolled through the landscape of my mind, calling out in cryptic communications.

As I sat swigging grapefruit *shōchū*, my mind raced to connect the dots. *The innocuous memory of that joyous hanami day, is it some kind of ethereal intervention? Coordinates to whatever I'm seeking? Those fallen-by-the-wayside relationships, are they keys?*

I shook my head to clear this rush of realizations and then wrote them off as implausible suggestions.

I finished off the first Chu-hi with a steady hand and opened the strong. It kicked a little on the way down. Inhaling cigarette smoke and taking another hard swallow, I submerged myself in a comfortable fog.

* * *

I usually carried a paperback to keep my thoughts from wandering too far into burlesque reflection or fantasy. I'd not brought one with me that day. With my second can to consume while I waited for rush hour to clear, I wanted something to occupy my mind other than those unfiltered thoughts.

At the next bench along the path, a retiree sat reading the paper. I saw him finish a section and set it down next to his brown slacked thigh.

'Sorry to bother you. Can I borrow?' I gestured to the folded section with my hand, having exhausted my Japanese vocabulary in the request.

'Yes. Can you read Japanese?'

'No, but is okay.' I gave a self-deprecating laugh and shrugged. He smiled back.

I picked up the section and returned to my bench. I skimmed the pages, registering the pictures and then inventing stories to accompany them by splashing together what little knowledge I'd garnered of Japanese culture and current events.

There were three pictures of fugitives on the front page. Probably the same I'd seen plastered on wanted posters outside police huts throughout Japan. They were members of the Aum cult who carried out the Tokyo subway sarin attacks back in 1995. Here, fourteen years later, it looked like they had caught one of the last remaining members. The photo below the wanted picture depicted a figure hidden from the media with a black jacket thrown over his head, handcuffed and being ushered into a courthouse. *A small healing on a deep wound to the psyche of the nation*, concluded my draft.

I flipped through a couple more pages, most had pictures of suited officials either posing for photos or taken candidly. On the last page was an old brick building. It was placed at the back of a large grassy courtyard, with well-manicured hedges lining a concrete path leading to an arched entrance. Like an Aztec tomb, the building proceeded upward from each side in two-storey tiers, at the centre it shot up seven stories from the gothic embowed opening below.

At the top of the tower was a clock – *the watchful eye*. I imagined the building with protest banners hung out of shattered windows and Hideki shouting rallying cries to the crowd below. I knew it well, the clock tower at Tokyo University. It was the centrepiece for Hideki's story, where he'd put on his mask.

The old man in the Okinawan park had only crossed my path briefly, but I had to think he was part of the reason I was back in

Tokyo and there in Yoyogi park not even two weeks later.

With only the single picture, I wasn't able to figure out the story. My slipshod contrivance wouldn't suffice, so I stood and walked back over to the man seated down the path.

'Sorry again ...'

He looked up and gave a diminishing polite smile. His glasses had transition lenses so I couldn't decipher if he was annoyed by my pestering, but felt as if his eyes gave a disapproving glance at the morning libation dangling from my right arm.

I held out the paper with the picture of the Todai clock tower facing him, 'What say this?' I asked in broken Japanese.

He grabbed the paper and quickly read the blurb. 'It say forty year ago today,' began his reply in English, much better than my pidgin Japanese. 'There was protest when student in Tokyo University fight with police. One student die. This story say, today is ceremony to remember the protest and student.'

'Thank you,' I said as he reached to hand the paper back. I waved it off.

* * *

Rush hour had passed. As per usual, the train had standing room only, but we were not shoulder to shoulder, and I enjoyed the personal space as it headed east.

At Ueno Station, I followed the path from Ueno park to Tokyo University that Hideki would have taken when he led the protesters back in '69. While I walked, a picture formed of Hideki, flanked on either side by Tatsuya, head of the campus Zengakuren and Tatsuya's girlfriend, Machiko, another prominent member of the group. *'Yankees go home', 'No More Vietnam' and 'Remember Nagasaki, Murder No More' blast through a bullhorn while a throng of student radicals swarm the concourse and storm the clock tower for the great siege.*

I hung back on the university grounds while the small ceremony was conducted in front of the spidery tracings of vine stem crawling over the bowed entrance to the auditorium. Western oaks and olive trees bookended the building and peppered the foliage around the grounds.

As I studied the building's façade, more details of the old man's recount came to life. The windows repaired and intact now, I imagined breaking, one after the other, while heads of the rioting mob pressed forth to shout victorious and drape banners over the red brick.

I couldn't see into the clock tower, though my mind depicted giant interconnected metal gears and a system of supporting cables surrounded by wooden planks for standing, something like Quasimodo's humble abode.

Hideki, with his bundled banner tucked under his arm like an oversized rugby ball, heart racing, bounds up the stairs, as if breaking down the wing for a game-winning try. Arriving first in the tower, he kicks out the window and watches the shards fall to the steps below. He sets to untying the twine around his banner when Tatsuya arrives. Sweat pouring and adrenaline pumping they struggle with the ties, look up from their efforts, and smile wordlessly, still panting from the climb.

Below, the man in a tweed coat and thick-framed glasses droned on into a microphone. I didn't understand his words, so continued to play out Hideki's version in my mind. What was now the serene lawn of the concourse, I let the old man's words enliven with the chaos of that day.

'Our amplified speeches roused the conviction of our comrades below. As their wrath reached a fever pitch, the first three police vans pulled up to the campus gates, unloading black-helmeted and trench-coated riot squad police. They took their posts as a succession of vehicles followed. When the force was a hundred strong, the cops marched in formation onto the university grounds. Our righteous

army clad in thrift store camo jackets and white helmets scrawled with kanji protest slogans, pulled bandanas over their faces and readied for battle.

'The first round of tear gas was fired into the concourse crowd. A wall of cops long and deep with shields up and night-sticks drawn advanced as a totalitarian tsunami. Our side answered back hurling bricks and insults into the police bloc, but were unable to disperse their formation. When opposing groups collided, the assailing protesters met with punishing blows. They fought back gallantly but to no avail.'

Fixing my eyes on the clock tower again, I pictured the three 60s Japanese youth – Hideki, Tatsuya and Machiko – shouting encouragement to their bloodied and bruised compatriots below.

'Later, the building now surrounded, it was the police's turn at the bullhorn demanding our evacuation. Tatsuya and I answered back with vulgarities and slander of their conformist minds and hearts. We lit ends of cloth and hurled gasoline bottles at the fascist sheep below. The riot squad hit back with tear gas shot through the windows below but were unable to reach our tower. They turned the water cannons on us, and the Zengakuren leadership were hit by powerful streams knocking bodies into bodies in the enclosed space. Unable to breathe in the painful confusion, we had no choice but to begin our descent toward the hand-to-hand combat awaiting us below.'

I looked up and squinted, wondering if the midday sun hung above was the same Hideki peered into, as the blows rained down and he was beaten unconscious.

The official at the podium must have wrapped up his remarks as a polite clap rippled through the crowd.

The article I felt had been a pretty clear signpost, but it seemed only led to a quaint pictorial tour of the old man's rehashed story. I left, no more clued into my purpose for returning to Tokyo than before. I don't know what I was expecting. After all, it wasn't my history, it was Hideki's. At least if I ever saw him again, I could tell him I'd visited the grounds of his alma mater – the scene of his great triumph, before the fall.

A part of me thought I might find his friends Tatsuya and Mariko at the ceremony and fulfil a promise I'd made to him. Silly of me to think it would be that easy.

I stood back from the lawn and swallowed the last drops in my can as the ceremony closed and the crowd dispersed.

As I lingered, two men in their mid-twenties walked by, both wore black jeans and canvas jackets. I hadn't seen them in the audience. They too must have been hanging back beyond the fringes of the official gathering. They shot me synchronized stink eye whilst walking past. One of them slowed up and spat on the grassy ground at my feet.

Too stunned, I didn't react. In China, say, such behaviour might be par for the course, but here in Japan, this level of open disrespect was unheard of. They didn't laugh afterwards; it wasn't done as a joke or dare. I could only imagine the motivation was pure detest.

Still puzzling out the spitting incident, I boarded the train. By the time we hit Akihabara, I was halfway through a fresh can of Chu-hi and had forgotten all about it.

From the Yamanote line window, the Sega store, like a big red Lego brick stood on its end, signals Akihabara's approach. Exit here for cosplay gals, gamer nerds, otaku kids, and the manga scene. Socially awkward with a misogynist lean, here's your maid cafes, tried it once but wasn't my scene. Further on is Takadanobaba, where Waseda University students congregate for school club piss-ups, culminating in sloppy, ceremonial, circular bows goodbye; we're social animals, eh! At least we struggle to be. Or on Sunday afternoons die-hard noodle fiends line up around a *Baba* block to eat in some sought-after hole-in-the-wall. And then, Muted Mejiro, an oasis of serenity like a silent bank along an ever-rushing amphetamine stream. Its repose broken by an Ikebukuro roar, with its tough-talking street thugs and bustling red light, not as iconic but every bit as sex-crazed as Kabukicho's own. It was my first taste of Tokyo, tethered to Yorii on opposite ends of the long Tobu-Toju line. Then there was Shibuya … Mecca for any horn-doggin *gaijin*. Women, women and then some, beautiful and stylish, *genki* and young, not quite down to every last one, but for sheer density and numbers, it's rivalled by none, moreover for a night on the grog … goddamn, it's fun.

I rode for hours, got off here and there, finally concluding: *the city's a smorgasbord for all appetites and warped desire.*

That first day after arrival, I did four complete circuits of the Yamanote line. I peered through the windows as the train completed circular loops around central Tokyo, absorbing it intravenously, stop by stop, in small drips, replenishing my soul.

***

Back at the Genki Netcafe, I checked in for another night and made my way to the fountain pop machine for some Coke to mix with my whisky. There, I again met the Accountant.

'Ah, *otsukaresama desu*,' he greeted with a bow. It was a formal workplace greeting, which means something along the lines of, 'thank you for all your hard work today'.

Obviously, he'd no idea I'd accomplished nothing that day or was bound by social protocol to recite the line.

'*Kampai*,' I replied, raising my cup in his direction, giving the international sign for cheers.

His expression remained static with a simpleton's smile as he turned and walked back to his cubicle. He was dressed identical to how he'd greeted me that morning, only the top button of his dress shirt undone and tie loosened, to denote the workday had elapsed. When he arrived at the open curtain, he failed to bow, but instead uttered, '*Tadaima*' or 'I'm home', which one usually says when returning to their actual residence after a time out.

'Fuckin freakshow,' I exclaimed under my breath. Clearly, he was deluded and considered this small internet café closet both his workplace and home.

I pulled closed my own curtain without ceremony and plopped down in the chair. Another pop-up appeared and three rows of airbrushed beauties donning a variety of cosplay outfits blocked my screen. *Why do they blur out their eyes?* I wondered before hitting X.

This prompted two more boxes to open. These girls wore different coloured bikinis and their mouths were blurred instead. *Is it to create an air of mystery for the customer or to protect the identity of the girls?* I pondered anew.

Before I knew it, I had nine screens offering me a melody of unknown services. It was a moot point, as I didn't have the money to shell out on call girls, nor did I imagine they would entertain me in an internet café. Nonetheless, I theorized, I'd go for the one in a pink bikini, with a tincture of a smile forged on her face and eyes of amber-gold. There was some mystery I'd have liked to uncover there.

My mouse like a water snake slithered across the pad and devoured all nine nests of sexy sparrows and their offers of sensual ministration.

In an attempt to fix the problem, I deployed the only IT skills I've got and turned the computer off and on. The reboot began with a whirl of the internal fan as the hard drive fired up. A green bar crawled across the screen.

I should go to the front desk and request a new booth, I thought to myself. Though, judging from the clientele I'd seen come through, they were all likely riddled with viruses. Plus, sadly, the musty cubicle had begun to feel like my own.

Besides, if it was my tale I sought to tell, perched there on my black leather chair, then the distractions were fitting. For mine is that of a wanderer, a restless soul, in body and mind, blown off course time and again.

A tilted bottle over clear, glistening rocks, poured caramel coloured and burned just as sweet. Mouse clicks, snores and muffled voices crept over the three walls and in through the low open ceiling of my room. *One last dance with John Barleycorn,* my head chimed in before a hearty swig. Though when it kicked, setting a tingle the nerves of my fingertips and toes, I knew we'd grind on through many long nights and silent songs to come. As inebriation approached the sublime crescendo an immortal feeling set in.

Now speak muse.

***

A low whimper grew into a high whine like a wounded calf, interrupted by human-sounding sobs, choking on despair.

I turned up the volume on my headphones and mixed myself another whisky and Coke but still couldn't block out the cries of this suffering beast. His wailing kept me up until 4 am, when again, he repeated his commotion the following night.

After my second sleepless night, I saw the pitiful creature. He wore grey jogging pants like you'd expect an unemployed and partially homeless individual to sport, but tucked into the elastic band was a rumpled white dress shirt. It was as if he'd incompletely cocooned; bought the sweatpants at the local Don Quijote discount mart, but rallied, resisted and refused to fully give into this regression.

His lanky frame staggered to the communal water boiler where he pressed the top and steaming liquid filled a cup of instant *ramen* noodle.

Ice fell into my glass with a light clink. *Blasphemy,* I thought, looking at his Styrofoam container. 'Hi, how are you doing this morning?' I began softly, in my best approximation of compassion.

He looked me over with bloodshot eyes and hung his head.

I worried about setting off the waterworks again but pressed on despite myself. 'Listen, the crying ... It's, uh, bothersome. Can you stop it, or do it more quietly?'

Again, he looked at me with red, watery eyes. His bottom lip trembled. '*Sumimasen*,' he muttered and performed a dejected shuffle back to his booth, both hands cradling his meal like a monk carrying an alms bowl.

I knew I should've shown more empathy but also felt his troubles were no greater than the rest of our lot. Lack of sleep had made me irritable; plus, why should we all be subject to the reverberations of his frailty.

I figured I knew the score; salaryman loses job and for fear of losing face, dresses up in suit and tie and pretends to go into an office each day. This charade continues until it collapses under the weight of mounting bills or his own lies and guilt. Kicked out or too ashamed to go home, Weepy ends up here, sobbing loudly in his sad, little cubicle each night. That is, until he decides to get his shit together, sack up and get back out there, or makes an unscheduled appointment with the third rail of the subway tracks. It was a common Tokyo tale.

I hoped my frankness would push him toward the former rather than latter, but naturally uncompassionate and fucking tired, it didn't much matter to me at that point.

Despite the twinge of remorse I felt after the confrontation, it seemed to have worked. Sobs could still be heard that evening but soft as if muffled by a pillow or sock.

* * *

On my many trips to the drinks machine for ice and mixer or to the bathroom and back, I'd noticed a cubicle bursting with human possessions. A stack of clothing, photos, books, toiletries, plates and kitchen utensils crowded the small space. It was often empty, though passing by on one occasion, I'd observed the occupant from behind; close-cropped salt and pepper hair and broad, slightly stooped shoulders under a pilled and moth-eaten army-green cardigan.

That figure was Brooks, the third resident of the Genki Netcafe. I nicknamed him this after a character from a famous prison movie, the old man who'd spent his whole life inside and was thus 'institutionalized'.

Our Brooks didn't look that old. From behind, taking into consideration posture and shit, I guestimated him to be in his mid-forties or early fifties. And clearly, he'd been calling that closed computer console home for many days and nights now.

Two days ago, I finally met him face to face. He's why I'm sitting here, eyes blurry and well tipsy, typing all this shit.

I'd been out doing my regular *tour de conbini* around West Tokyo, a term which makes it sound far more glamorous than it actually is. Essentially, it's where I buy a drink and smoke in front of one convenience store before moving on to the next and doing the same. Subconsciously, I think, I was hoping for some revelation to come to pass as I walked and stood, drank and smoked – but nothing happened.

Well, something happened. I slid idly into a blissful ignorance, like an old man at the local *sentō* into a warm wooden tub – until I forgot I was hopelessly lost in life, unemployed and living in an internet café.

To say I was killing time would be putting it lightly. Slowly and sadistically disembowelling it was more accurate.

Returning to the netcafe at dusk with a tall boy in my left and a smoke in my right, I passed a row of vending machines, lit-up and fighting off the waning day. At the end of the row slouched a slightly dishevelled yet oddly dignified-looking chap. The moth-eaten cardigan made me think it must be Brooks.

'*Komban-wa*,' I ventured.

'Good evening,' he answered in English. 'Returning from a day's meander, are you?' He, too, was equipped with a can and a cigarette and took a taste of each while waiting on my reply.

'Pretty much, was hoping it would turn into something more substantial, but ...' My thought trailed off with no excuses on hand. I slipped my empty drink into the plastic receptacle. The machine to his left was illuminating Chu-hi's and various beers. I indicated towards it and asked, 'Another?'

'Always,' he answered with a sly grin. I instantly felt a kinship with the man.

I fished out the correct change from a pocketful I'd accumulated during my *tour de conbini*. 'Beer?'

'Yes.'

So, I got us the same as he was working on, a tall can of Sapporo. I handed him the cool offering and pointed down the street. 'I think we stay at the same internet café.'

Brooks nodded. 'Yes, that's the place. I stay there.'

I cracked my drink open by the pull-tab, it foamed over due to the trip down the shoot. I sipped at the head, then looked from the Genki Netcafe to Brooks. 'Umm so, how long you been there?'

'I'd say a few years now.' He shook his head, grimacing in disbelief at his own words.

'Fuck me, how'd that come about?'

'It just sort of happened,' he said. 'Is a long story, I'll be sure to tell you sometime if you stick around.'

I began to suspect he wasn't local. The accent was off, lower and more hollow than typical Japanese, like a block of wood being struck at different angles.

I extended my hand. 'I'm Fred.'

'Jae-hyun.' He reached out and grasped it. We shook. Again, clenched in his hard, rough grip, I was self-conscious. Aware that my long slender fingers and soft uncalloused palms marked me as an interloper, a middle-class fraud, unworthy of these alleys and park benches I favoured, and dubious to those who dwelled there.

Jae-hyun, Korean? The out of place accent now made sense. Looking at his face, I could see the flatter, broader forehead, strong jaw and pronounced high cheekbones. Finally, the taking refuge in Shin-Ōkubo – it all added up.

'So, you're Korean.' And then went with what I thought was a clever crack, 'North or South?' Right when I was about to bust out a smug smile and revel in my geopolitical understanding of Asian relations, it backfired.

With no hint of play, Brooks replied, 'North.' Unoffended, he continued, 'But again, that is part of my journey, which perhaps I'll share if it is of use to you someday. And yours?' He crouched and placed his empty can next to a well-worn brown loafer, and opened the one I'd given him. 'What ended you up in the Genki Netcafe? You've been there over a week now, correct?'

'Yeah, I just arrived back here. I was working in Okinawa for a few months, but it didn't work out as planned, so I'm back here.' I gave him the abridged version.

'Okinawa is beautiful, I hear, can't imagine why you'd leave there to come back to the hustle and bustle of Tokyo.'

'Tokyo's electric! The buzz produced by this city is unmatched,' I explained with an uncalled for conviction, feeling a bit put on the spot to justify my reasons. 'But yeah, I guess the true reason for my return is unclear as of yet.'

He nodded. 'So, you came back here for what?'

'That's also unclear,' I said, head down, blowing smoke toward the pavement.

'It seems there is a lot in your life that is unclear.' He cracked a thin sympathetic smile. 'Don't fret, most of us don't end up living in a netcafe when we have it all figured out. As you've probably noticed, our regulars don't exactly fly in on the wings of victory.'

I assumed he was talking about the Accountant and Weepy, probably past residents as well. While he was clearly not a man of means, he seemed to be more together and mentally sound than those two. *Where do I rank on the desperate and pathetic scale*, I wondered; *me, the gaijin.*

'I just got some shit to figure out.' It felt like my explanation of my situation, much like life itself, was going nowhere fast. 'It's like I was pulled back here, by like ... these strange events and odd signs. But ya know ... I might've been looking for an excuse to leave.'

He sat with this confession and sipped his beer. 'I guess you've got to decide if you are running away from or toward something.'

'Decide? Or discover?' I inquired.

'Hmm, yes.'

After a ponderance, where he looked through hooded eyes at nothing in the distance for some time and I wondered why so many I'd encountered these days had been moved to do just so, he committed to an allocution.

'Sounds like your plight is destinational in nature. When we think of a destination, we assume arrival at a physical place. Yet, you've arrived and are still lost, *ne*?' He looked to me for confirmation of his summary. 'Sometimes, we arrive at our destination and are only halfway through the journey.'

'Like?' I urged him to continue and lit another cigarette for stimulation and in hopes of inhaling those insights.

'Like destiny.' His gaze shifted from the distance to my face, which likely bore an awed expression.

'Tokyo being my destination, and my destiny still unknown?' I slumped against the vending machine, my shoulder lighting blue and orange the various buttons while the female computerized voice rejected me with commands barked in Japanese.

'Not just Tokyo, I don't believe it works in such vague determinations. Here!' And he pointed forcefully at the ground we stood on. 'You've been brought here – to this street, to the Genki Netcafe, to drinking and smoking with me in front of these vending machines at this evening hour.'

I took a long, frustrated haul of crisp, hoppy Sapporo. We'd gotten trapped in a revolving door of fallacious logic, and I once again was figuring nothing out. 'Yeah, but this all brings me back to my initial quandary, why?'

'Aye, there's the rub!'

A semi-homeless North Korean quoting Shakespeare on the fly; *this Jae-hyun cuts quite an engrossing figure*, I concluded.

He tossed the burning butt of his cigarette into the empty can. It hissed as it extinguished in the ale dregs. Brooks, or Jae-hyun, gave a parting nod and delivered some final baroque thoughts on the subject before he walked onto Okubo-dori and turned left.

Where he was going, I had no idea ... perhaps, chasing a destiny of his own.

***

I followed in Jae-hyun's footsteps and blew right past our netcafe, then straight through Okubo and into Kabukicho's seedy maze. As I threaded underbrush in a neon jungle, my mind munched on his abstruse directions to discovering one's destiny. '*We overrule necessity and surrender ourselves to the irresistible flow – that irrepressible force of events shaping our path.*'

Surrender ... What more ya want? I'm living in a fucking internet café. Besides, what about free fuckin' will? I continued debating the middle-aged Korean man in my mind.

The little existential crisis was making me thirsty, so I reached into my pocket for a handful of change. A one yen coin slipped through my fingers and fell beside a sidewalk crack. A yen doesn't land like other coins with that sharp clink of urgency to be retrieved. It hits soft and faint – *oh, so futile and useless*. I was tempted to just surrender it to the street, though I've always had an affinity for the useless and futile, both in possessions and pursuits. I bent to pick it up, stiff and groaning, as if I'd aged by decades, not days, since leaving Okinawa – *not the most ergonomic lifestyle I've fallen into*. Added to my palm, it proved a worthwhile trip as I eyeballed 148¥.

Posted up outside a FamilyMart convenience store, I sipped my aluminium companion, cylindrical escape for 148. Glowing signage at every doorway stretched skyward, offering a hodgepodge of host and hostess clubs, sex shops, soaplands, massage parlours, love hotels, beer halls and whisky salons. Manoeuvring all around the neon battleground were Shinjuku's soldiers of the night, armed only with sins and sorrows, they waged war on loneliness and despair.

Over a Marlboro's glowing cherry, I continued to watch the stream of life flow past. Washed up on that embankment, I lingered like a cultural Peeping Tom. The blue radiance of the awning and silver standing ashtray, the bushes behind which I lurked, and peered through the assorted windows of those far-flung lives in passing. I viewed their actions and indiscretions, but they didn't see mine – when they looked back all they saw were their own skewed and distorted reflections. No one was expecting me to adhere to their strict cultural norms, I was a spectator with no skin in the game. This, the great freedom of my expat existence, which I could choose to transcend or exploit. I passed through their world as an aberration – *a gaijin* – translation: outsider.

Transitory tranquillity, I've found in this translucent existence.

I emerged from my desultory trek through the scarlet gloam at the outermost corner of Kabukicho. In the vicinity of Yasukuni-dori and Seibu-Shinjuku station, I basked in the big city cinder, still believing the oracular location owed me a celestial nudge.

The after work crowd spilt from the station exit and into the Shinjuku night. I decided to hold my own little happy hour at the McDonald's across the street. I ordered a Coke, went into a bathroom stall and poured a double whisky highball – only a hundred yen and always on special.

When I arrived at the fourth-floor smoking section, I spotted her, alone on a stool by the window. She was one who rejected the conventional Japanese beauty myth of a milky white complexion and had gone instead for the sunkissed pecan tone, my taste preferred. Her hair curled in elongated waves, shimmering with blonde streaks like morning sun off a spring brook. Long permed lashes and makeup touches caused her eyes to appear larger and rounder like anime, or what some locals considered more western. She had the style of an understated Shibuya *gyaru*, but like she'd recently blossomed out of the popular youth subculture. Anyway, I was immediately taken.

The smoke and mirrors of her overall appearance worked for me, also, I'm a sucker for delicious thighs. She wore brown suede thigh-high boots, what we called 'hooker boots' back home, but were fortunately everyday fashion for the young women of Japan. From where the boots ended emerged a hand span territory of bare thigh before a navy blue miniskirt began.

Some god was smiling on me, as the red-topped swivel stool next to hers was empty. I took a mammoth sip of my whisky and Coke. My throat had gone dry from eyeballing her, and a little shot of liquid courage advisable for approach.

'*Riter, kudasai*?' I asked. It was a weak opening line but enough to catch her attention and gauge interest.

She handed me a pink lighter with a tilted head and smiling eyes, I took as an invitation to proceed. The key, I knew, was to launch right into conversation and hold her interest. It'd been a while since I'd worked a proper *nampa*. Chatting up chicks used to be my favourite Tokyo pastime, but I was out of practice after Okinawa, where motivation sapped, I fell into a kind of sexual anorexia. Anyways, *nampaing* this beautiful woman in a Shinjuku Macdonald's, plotting to feast on those dark, savoury thighs, seemed the ideal opportunity to overcome the anorexia and revitalize my vigour.

I lit my smoke deliberately; head tilted, hand cupped over the flame to throw an orange glow across my face in a mimicked James

Dean style. 'So what are you doing tonight?' I asked using the Tokyo slang, which tainted most of my limited Japanese.

'After, I go to work,' she said, a stifled smile for this foreigner's rough-edged dialect.

That worried me. *Hostess?* I conjectured. Not that the job bothered me, only they were tough nuts to crack, especially for a lowly *gaijin* such as myself.

'What is your work?'

'*Baru, desu.*'

I went momentarily silent, disheartened as I saw my chances slip away.

'Are you living in Tokyo?' she asked me, in pronounced perfect English. The follow-up question and fact she was open to transitioning the conversation to English were positive developments. With the Tower of Babel fallen at our feet in blessed rubble, my outlook brightened.

'Yeah, I stay nearby, in Shin-Ōkubo,' I answered, omitting, of course, it was in an internet café.

'That's nice, and what do you do tonight?'

'I'm looking for my Yoko Ono,' I said with a wink. It was a cheesy line and gamble as to whether she would have any idea what I was fucking talking about.

Now, most would be wondering why I would choose to say something so oddly arbitrary, and possibly construed as racist, to this pretty lady I was hoping to impress.

See, this particular Shinjuku Mickey D's randomly has a Beatles theme. I guess the franchisee happens to be a huge fan. Many Japanese are still mad for the Fab Four. Downstairs, erected beside the ordering quay and sealed inside protective glass casing are life-size statues of John, Paul, George and Ringo on the iconic crossing next to Abbey Road studios. The walls are adorned with black and white photographs of the band's visits to Japan and Beatles music plays through the restaurant's sound system 24/7.

'Well, I'd hate to break up the band.' She played along. I was instantly elated my cheese was accepted, ingested, and batted back in good form.

'No need to worry, I've long been a solo act.' I felt a rising confidence and swagger emerge.

'Well, that's good to hear,' she replied, seeming to blush, though it may have been an effect of her voguish makeup.

'I'm Fred, by the way.'

'*Hajimemashite* Fred, I'm Yukie.'

I extended my hand. After our limp shake, I didn't want to let go but allowed my soft grip to slide over her slender fingers. The out of place custom effected a delicate twitch on her lips, a smile maybe. She took a sip of her coffee and looked out the window, though I sensed she was inspecting my reflection in the glass. I lifted my chin and clenched my jaw, in an attempt to project a strong profile.

After my moment of vanity, I lit another smoke and placed my blue lighter on top of the pack. Yukie's gaze fell upon it.

Busted, I thought.

'Good, you found your lighter?' she said with a kittenish smile.

'Oh yeah, look at that.' I reached over and under my cupped hand, lit the cigarette that rested between her lips.

We exhaled and shared a cosy uncomfortable laugh.

The banter was refreshing, and I did my best to keep it going. We smoked and finished our respective beverages. She must have caught a whiff of my highball because she asked what I was drinking. I produced the mickey with a contrite smile. It was not a good look to be drinking dirt-cheap whisky on the sly, alone in a McDonald's early on a weekday eve, but she just smiled back. It didn't faze her, we wrote it off as me testing the slack on that long *gaijin* leash.

* * *

By chance, well not so much, I met her the next night, in the same smoking area around the same time. I'd correctly guessed, black coffee and Beatles' tunes were part of her nightly routine – and our short flirtatious conversations between long cigarette drags, I'm determined to make part as well.

On our second encounter, we talked and got to know each other a little more. It was then I noticed her nails. Well, her nail.

At one point, she was texting away at warp speed. She had one of those newfangled smartphones that were all touch screen, though it was the speed with which she typed, despite the inch-long, heavily laden nails, that impressed me.

'How do you do that?' I asked.

'Do what?' She continued tapping the screen.

'Text so fast, even with those crazy cool nails?' I gestured with my eyes at the nails. In keeping with her Shibuya gal style they protruded long, painted and bedazzled with glitter, studs and rhinestone beads.

She giggled and held out her hand, fingers together and extended like a bride-to-be would flaunt her diamond engagement ring to a group of envious spinsters. Studying them and perhaps wondering herself, she said, 'I don't know, am a girl, so just can.'

With each of her digits lined up side by side, the nail of her left index finger stuck out in its simplicity. It was painted with a black ellipse which had a sapphire blue stud in the middle, like a single unblinking eye.

'Why's that one …' I began to ask, as she balled her hand into a fist and placed it on her lap under the Formica countertop.

She smiled at me sweet and shy, and I smiled back, letting the question fall by the wayside.

Outside of the curious incident with the understated nail, we spoke of general topics as two people might on a first date. Though, I'd hate to categorize it as a first date. I know I'm kind of down and out, but am definitely planning something a bit better than the smoking section of McDonald's when I eventually asked her out.

I learned she liked hair, makeup and fashion. I didn't like those things, per se, but I liked she did. One look at her showed it worked in my favour. Far from being hobbies of mine, I indeed was planning on making Yukie and all her beautifications my preferred diversion.

On a slightly more personal level, she told me that in high school, she'd visited Nebraska as an exchange student for six months. It was there she'd picked up her English.

'Oh, big sky country,' I said, even though it sounded a meaningless thing to say.

She sighed and said longingly, '*Hai*, such a big sky, and at night, so many stars.'

I sipped whisky through a plastic straw and mused; it had been the right thing to say after all.

The manner in which she stared through the window into the Tokyo night made me feel as though there was something more there. She was suddenly a million miles away. Nebraska. Some event or experience had inexorably altered her there – between the prairie and the panhandle.

I looked sidelong at Yukie, still lost in thought peering into the twinkling metropolis as chromatic photons tripped along the darks of her eyes, and my mind formulating all kinds of designs on this chick with the kaleidoscope eyes.

'What brings you to this Macdonald's each night?' she asked, snapping out of her reverie.

You! I thought, but managed to hold back the candid burst. 'I just love Beatles music. Can't get enough of it! Now, some may disagree, but I would argue when John penned most of it, he had meant for it to be listened to just like this, in a Japanese McDonald's.' I wore a bratty smirk as I rattled off my smart-ass answer.

Her glossy lips tightened in a pink purse. 'In that case, I should leave you alone to enjoy your music in peace,' she said with an audible sigh.

I realized then, I'd better get somewhat honest, sometime soon.

I explained I'd just travelled back from Okinawa after 'quitting' my job and was living in an internet café over in Okubo, while I figured things out and searched.

Even the sugar-coated version seemed to throw her. She stroked her heart-shaped chin. 'Search for what?' she asked, hair falling as she tilted her head with minor intrigue.

'I don't really know yet. I guess I'll know when I find it. But like in a general sense – meaning,' I said, sounding hokey as hell, as honesty often does.

'Hmmm, well that's good.' She looked away and seemed to ponder something for a split second, then looked back at me as if she had settled the matter. 'I could help you. I mean, if you want any help in your search or quest or whatever it is.'

'Quest, ha, I like that,' I said, smiling and shaking my head. 'Makes me feel like Don Quixote ... the literary character, not the store, eh.' My companion scrunched her brown button nose, confused by my sudden nervous babbling. I drank from my whisky-Coke to centre myself. 'I wouldn't give it that much weight. But yeah, definitely, I'd love that. As it stands now, I'm actually pretty lost.'

'Okay, *kuru*,' she said and laughed with a nervous edge. I guess the offer had surprised even her. Maybe, she wasn't prepared to drop her wall and let me in so easily either. '*Eto* ... if you want a change of scenery some night and can listen to music other than the Beatles, we could go to a bar or disco on my night off.' Despite the bargirl exterior, her voice rang high and soft, chaste and angelic, like church bells or the Vienna Boys Choir. It could have been put on, as is often the case, local dudes dig the feigned naiveté. Cynicism kicked in and I wondered for a second, *Is this a honey trap? Am I getting played?*

I shook my head, and chuckled inwardly, mocking my nutty notions. Of course not. In my circumstances, I'd be the worst target in all of Tokyo for such a scheme. Plus, I knew from somewhere deep inside, a warmth in my head, and tingle in my crotch, that despite the odds, I'd ignited at least a spark of unalloyed attraction in this beauty.

'Sounds like a plan,' I said with a breezy blasé and looked to my cigarette as excess ash fell with two taps. But if she could read beneath my carefree pantomime, I was beaming like a schoolgirl asked to her first sock-hop.

***

The next day began like most others, crossing paths with the Accountant and exchanging office pleasantries as he headed into his cubicle to conduct whatever fantastical work kept him busy all day in his imagined position at some fictitious company.

'*Ganbatte,*' I called to him out the bathroom door, with the exaggerated *genki-ness* coming naturally to my delivery that morn.

I returned to my computer to finish off last night's whisky and masturbate like a mouse. The netcafe, I'd come to realize, could fall somewhere between a porno theatre and brothel at times. Still, I tried to keep my self-gratification as discreet as possible within these thin half-walls – a wheely chair, leather squeaks, the strangled groan, and only a pulled curtain to hide my shame. The job got done, with a loose grip and legs braced against the vinyl floor. Aided at first by promiscuous pop-ups, then, eyes closed, visions of adorned nails raked down a bare back, and her body bent over a Formica countertop, flushed faces reflected in the fourth-floor glass, and the city beyond all flickering light, in envy of the night.

I lit a cigarette and poured what remained of my whisky. It went down with a single gulp and a dry-heave. With watery eyes, I looked at the empty glass and decided it would be my last. *I'm off the sauce*. Then another voice chimed in and suggested I'd been rash, best to wait until tomorrow. I paid at the counter for another twenty-four-hour stint and left.

Taunted and egged on by the loose change which jangled in my pocket, I tramped through Shinjuku streets and Okubo alleys. Perched at the precipice of convenience store kerbs, I awaited the next inescapable sign or preordained event to light my way. Until at dusk, I surrendered to the squander of another day.

A cyclops-eyed finger had undulated in sinuous curls through my mind all day, beckoning to the source. In the end, I avoided the McDonald's and another chance fast food encounter in case my showing up night after night was giving off too much of a stalkerish vibe. Besides, with only a cursory physical attraction and fragile curiosity to work with, I decided it best to play the long game. At least until I figured my shit out a bit.

On the Kabukicho sidewalk, a long luminous tube ignited above my head. It brought no new ideas, except to find Jae-hyun.

There was no sign of Brooks in front of the vending machines we'd first met, so I cut down the next road leading back to Okubo-dori and Shin-Ōkubo station. Small shops grew into four- and five-storey apartment blocks and entertainment buildings; chock-full of bars, massage parlours and soaplands. I spotted Brooks drinking a can outside a pachinko parlour, past the lit signage showing off the talent working at a Pink Salon on 5F.

'Hey, been looking for you,' I said, catching my breath.

'Look no further,' Brooks replied. 'Seek and ye shall find,' he added with a wry raised eyebrow.

'Well, I sought all day and found nada.'

Plinks, plunks, rings and *dings* blared onto the street from the parlour's side entrance. Caught in an overwhelming stench of stagnant second-hand smoke, I lit a dart to freshen the air.

'You play?' I pointed a thumb over my shoulder toward the deafening noise, thinking this wasn't the most peaceful place to chill out and drink.

He shook his head. 'It's comforting. It immerses me in a past that was both my salvation and enslaver.' Brooks dropped that heavy nugget on me then pointed toward the 7-Eleven across the street and asked, 'Drink?'

'Yeah, what will you have?'

'No, no, it's my shout,' he pointed out and walked toward the sliding glass doors. I followed, happy to escape the pervasive clamour of the pachinko palace.

I waited outside the shop and wondered about his use of 'my shout'. *Where had he picked up that English expression?* I guess I was not the first *gaijin* to cross his path and employ his wisdom.

'*Arigato gozaimasu!*' The clerk's salutation followed Brooks out the automatic doors as he exited with a plastic bag. He handed me a tall can of Chu-hi and took the beer for himself. The plastic clung to the condensation of two more cans.

A two tallboy chat, I thought, reassured I wasn't imposing on my new acquaintance. *Friend, confidant, teacher, priest?* I searched for a more accurate definer and ended up back on acquaintance.

Brooks gripped the can's rim in his right hand, hooked the tab with his middle finger and pulled the beer open single handed. He'd performed the same odd ritual the other day while his left remained in a pocket.

'So, pachinko, do you sometimes play or just like the parlour atmosphere?' I asked in an attempt to crack this riddle.

He pulled his left hand out of his pocket and held it up in explanation. It had somehow morphed and frozen in a grotesque claw. Wincing, he attempted to move the fingers, only managing to manoeuvre them mere millimetres while his face turned red with pain and exertion.

'How'd that happen?'

'Arthritis coupled with carpal tunnel,' he blankly stated, curiously studying his own disfigured appendage like it belonged to someone else.

He was only in his mid-forties. The damage done from the play of a simple seated game seemed extreme, to say the least. 'From pachinko?'

'*Hai*, seems impossible, *ne*. But twisting and turning the little knob, directing those silver ball bearings down into the money slot – fifteen sometimes twenty hours a day – it did the damage.' A twinkle still played in his eye while detailing this peculiar obsession that had all but crippled him.

'Speaking of unhealthy fixations.' He smiled in my direction.

My cue to state the purpose of my visit. 'I've been thinking about this destination and destiny shit we talked about yesterday. And how it applies to my predicament ...'

'Let me interject, don't think of it as a predicament. It's just life. All life is a predicament.'

'Yeah well,' I began, watching office drones, students and night workers stream from the station as a river of predicaments. 'Where do I go from here?'

A couple of salarymen milled around and smoked near the convenience store entrance while Brookes and I huddled near the standing ashtray like bums around a dumpster fire.

'You want to take action, *ne*? Deposited here, stuck in the mire, you sense your journey is far from over yet unsure where to turn next.'

That about summed it up and I nodded my agreement.

'Hansel and Gretel,' he said.

'Huh?'

'After I defected, I arrived here with no Japanese and no English. Like a toddler, I learned to read and speak from simple nursery rhymes, then fairy tales and built my way up to great works of Shakespeare, Shikibu and Twain,' he said, with clear reverence for each name spoken.

'Well, yeah, your English is great.' I threw in the complement I'd been saving for the right opening.

He gave a head bow of appreciation with a red-faced, wide grin. 'Your life, where it is now, makes me think of that old Grimm's fairy tale.'

I scrunched my eyebrows. 'Then, who's the cannibalistic witch? Where's the confectionery house?'

Brookes extended his arms and turned in a slow circle, a full three hundred and sixty degrees. 'Your gingerbread house, lured by all the treats your heart desires.' He gestured with his Kirin canned hand to the buffet of dissipation, all forms of escape, splattered throughout our immediate vicinity; toward the sandwich board with pics of tarted up Japanese schoolgirls in a cosplay massage parlour, toward the lit signs stretching seven stories of pubs, snacks and hostess bars, toward the pachinko parlour packed to the hilt with gamblers steering their ball-bearing dreams, toward the love hotel adjacent an apartment block and the high-heeled hostess making her way to work, toward Kabukicho where all this abounds more fervently and towards the convenience store's stocked fridges and whisky-laden shelves.

'And, the cannibalistic witch …' He gestured this time with his eyes, to my right hand from which a cigarette dangled and my left which gripped the half-drunk Chu-hi.

I took in his analogy with some offence, yet hid it under a contemplative look. 'And so, my way out?'

'Breadcrumbs.'

'Breadcrumbs?' I took a drink and laughed. 'Listen, I like ya Jae-hyun, but what the fuck are you on about? You've totally lost me.'

He reached around my waist toward my ass. I flinched and might've even cocked a fist. *Had his kindness come at a price? Was he grooming me? … As I believe the expression goes.*

'Don't flatter yourself,' he said with a grunting laugh, 'you're not my type.'

I felt the paperback I was carrying around slide out the back pocket of my jeans. Brooks studied the front cover then flipped it over to the blurb.

'Good read,' he said, as a statement rather than a question, referring to the copy of Dazai's *No Longer Human*.

'Yeah, it is.' The cover was separating from the binding, the pages dog-eared and stained. It was a light read in length, but heavy in subject matter. I'd been rereading as I made my way from *conbini* to *conbini* and park bench to park bench those past few days. It was beginning to hit a little too close to home.

'Good selection, very apt,' Jae-hyun continued like he'd read my mind. He stared down at the book held awkwardly in his arthritic claw, fanning the pages with his good hand. 'But your answers aren't there,' he stated. 'These are Dazai's breadcrumbs. You won't find your way out in here.'

'Yeah, I know.' But I didn't. I was still stymied as to his directions.

'Your breadcrumbs are in here.' He tapped my head at the temple with a crooked index finger, 'and in here.' He put his hand on the left side of my chest.

I was less flinchy with the physical contact this time around, even finding it strangely comforting after the defused confusion over the earlier reach around.

'You think I should write a book? That will help me discover … ya know, whatever?' I enquired, both flattered and daunted by the assignment.

He shook his head, smiling at my simplicity. 'Words will suffice. Written records of your path, those are your breadcrumbs. Hell, you live in a netcafe two feet from a keyboard. Perhaps that's how you'll find your way. It's merely an idea, though.' He finished non-committal, like my scourge of uncertainty was contagious.

After that, he went silent. I went silent. We sipped our drinks and sucked on yellow-brown filters. Brooks handed me my novella. I slipped it into my jeans.

The pachinko parlour's clangs and bangs pushed across the pavement, provoking my desire to know more of this man, his journey, his damaged hand ... his breadcrumbs. But it was comfortable in the hush between us, so I didn't bridge any of these subjects.

'Thanks,' I said and deposited my can into the recycling bin on the FamilyMart stoop.

'Wait,' he called as I turned to walk back to the netcafe. 'Here.' He handed me the second Chu-hi from the plastic bag. I accepted the chilled can, while the simple gesture warmed my heart.

'See you around,' Brooks said; an aluminium can clenched in his good hand, a smoke poking out of his gnarled paw, a halcyon smile upon his lips.

I left him there. Maybe he'd go back to the deafening clatter of the pachinko parlour, to take from it whatever it was he got, basking in that chaotic noise.

I cracked my Chu-hi and ambled back to the netcafe while Mother Goose of memory, cross-legged on a colourful carpet, tried to recall details of Hansel and Gretel from childhood storytime.

In contemplating breadcrumbs, my stomach growled. I detoured into Yoshinoya for a rice bowl. The ticketing machine had pictures so I could roughly decipher the dishes, and it was a little less a shot in the dark what I'd get served. Still, as I handed the attendant my order on the one-inch-cardstock ticket, it was enough of a mystery yet to keep me intrigued.

***

Ice melts into a whisky highball and my deemed inspiration dilutes, as the pixels burn. A cursor blinks, mocking my endeavour, and I question the acumen of an acquaintance's advice. Symbolically stood on the cliff's edge, I ready to dive in and swim the depths in search of vague answers to undefined questions.

I hear a soft muffled sob. It must be around 3 am.

It passes quickly. Maybe my harshness, in a contrary way,

helped Weepy.

Am I capable of helping anyone, even myself? Can I be any more than a sprawling gadfly on this earth?

Perhaps I'll find out, following the analogous breadcrumbs and their syllabic trail. The pixels burn, the yeast rises, and I rip the first morsel clear of the loaf. I struggle through muddled memory for a prudent place to drop.

I remember a quote that deposits me on the concrete outside a far-flung convenience store. On a muggy morn, the winds of discontentment blew gale-force against my back. Braced against that pseudonymous push, on a Thursday morning outside a FamilyMart was where shit began to get fucked up. That's where I drop the first breadcrumb.

Pinched fingers hover and slowly spread, releasing the nothingness. A single finger falls to rest in the concave of a square, black key. Against immense pressure of unknown origin, I push downward.

Rainy Day Ramen

PART ONE
Okinawa (Soba)

Even those people who have no sorrow of their own often feel melancholy from the circumstances in which they are placed.
—*Murasaki Shikibu,* The Tale of Genji

1// Bus to Nowhere

The cat was back.

I'd just settled in by the delivery entrance behind a FamilyMart convenience store. Having lit my smoke and cracked my drink, I was looking forward to absolute solitude while I hid back there and slid slowly toward oblivion, but then the fucking cat came slinking around the corner.

I swallowed hard, unsettled by his arrival. Somehow, we'd become locked in this bizarre interspecies turf war since I'd washed up on those Okinawan shores a few months back.

He stalked toward the steps, jumped up on the concrete platform leading to a rusty delivery door, and began to consume the catnip some do-gooder staff or neighbour had left out for him.

I had a nip of my own, off the freshly opened Chu-hi while watching him enjoy his free ride. No freebies for me, I had to purchase my treat, a hundred and forty-eight yen a pop for that cool metallic warmth.

He finished his snack and looked up with cold recognition: the other neighbourhood stray. Locking me in his gaze with those dysfunctional eyes, one of icy blue and the other a sinister yellow, as if by telepathy he sibilated, 'Fuck off, mate!'

Not this time, you feline fuck, I thought defiantly in attempt to communicate back. *I was here first*. I stepped toward him, thinking it might scare off. On the contrary, he arched his scarred, dirty white spine and challengingly poked his nasty little face forward. Bearing marks, evident of a lifetime of back-alley brawls, I should have known he wouldn't frighten so easily.

What have I done to this moggie fucker? Is there not room for both of us here? I puzzled at its natural disdain for me.

Having been evicted from my alley perch after our first meeting over a month back, the creepy cat had stuck in my consciousness. I'd maundered the backstreets drinking and pondered its history, its purpose and meaning.

There, once again locked in our power struggle, I resurrected one of my theories. *Is it Soseki reincarnate?* You know, 'I Am Cat'. *But what beef would Soseki have with me?*

I looked at the inside of my calf below the beige cargo shorts' hem. *Could it be the tattoo?*

'*Sokuten kyoshi,*' a quote from one of his books was tattooed there in *kanji*. It roughly translated to 'discard egoism – follow heaven and god'; or so I'd been told by the eccentric and alluring first year Lit student who hoarded manga comics and liked each of our sexual encounters to play out as a rape fantasy. A routine which rapidly downgraded from kinky, to amusing, to annoying.

After being taught the quote by that little minx, I incorporated it into the conceived design of Japanese koi swimming in a sort of yin-yang pattern around the four characters. At the time Hiro-san inked me in *Zugaikotsu* Tattoo, it seemed like apt guidance, a summation of some sort of Zen living philosophy I fancied pursuing: '*sokuten kyoshi?*'

Yet here I am, all ego and spiritually bankrupt.

And yes, there I was, driven purely by self; self-indulgent and self-seeking, my very existence an affront to Soseki's words. Standing there in judgment before what I was presently considering the great writer reincarnate, his disapproval was palpable as he bore sharp incisors and hissed.

The tom took a step toward me. I took one back. My heart raced, I was jumpy and on edge as the days' drinking had just begun, my raw nerves yet to be saturated. I felt another transmission, stronger this time, or perhaps I was becoming more unhinged.

'Fuck off, ya cunt! Tis my stoop so ye can jus' feck right off, you pat' etic fuckin' piece of shite!' His voice, the way I heard it in my head, was that of an angry working-class northern Englishman. Contrary and for no conceivable reason, I know, but who was I to nitpick the inconsistencies of a fragile mind currently engaged in a telepathic pissing contest with its feline foe.

Does he despise me because I'm a foreigner, because I've invaded his sanctuary, or does he perceive me as a pitiful pisshead to be kicked around?

The island of Okinawa has a collective disdain for foreigners. Too many years of too many American military on their soil and all that comes with it. On the other hand, every time our paths crossed, I had a drink in one hand and smoke in the other, so the pisshead shoe fit snuggly.

'Fuck you, you fucking cat!' I blurted back – the only retort I could muster, my voice cracking nervously. I said it out loud but low, for fear any passerby might hear me arguing with the back-alley tom.

The thought of splashing my drink on him crossed my mind, but those would be precious drops adding to a mouthful lost for my own consumption. Instead, I stomped my foot and gave the weak growl of a self-conscious guard dog. That tough bastard didn't even flinch or blink one of its mismatched eyes. Instead, he arched further, emitted a chilling hiss and bared more of his brownish-white fangs.

I gulped, turned and walked briskly away from the convenience store onto a quiet residential street. A quick look over my shoulder showed the cat had returned to his snack on the stoop, entirely nonplussed by our most recent battle of wits.

Well, to the victor go the spoils. I trudged into the late morning sunlight, my drink half-empty and warming, another day's defeat under my belt.

An obese charcoal cloud lay in front of me. While I walked in sunshine, the cumulus approached with a wall of rain. I gawked at the meteorological anomaly until the fat grey fucker overtook me.

I ducked under a red awning and into the restaurant attached. The distinct starchy aroma suggested it was a noodle shop. I ordered Okinawa soba. By the time a massive steaming bowl was set in front of me, the rain had unfortunately passed. I'd miss the accompanying solemn beat of droplets as I ate in the quietude. I dug into the thick white soba noodles, they took some of the bite out of the broth, but the sizeable chunks of meaty pork were a pleasant addition in this regional variant of the dish.

How have I ended up on the opposite end of these chopsticks? I mulled over with a mouthful of pork belly.

Simply put, I'd slid down the hollow centre of a pipe dream. The dream had hovered around a deep magenta for a while until finally fading to black. This left me in a state of suspended animation; up-down, left-right, forward-back, not a clue where to turn and fearful of the rigor mortis of life setting in. Stranded there, I paid my bill and exited.

Down the block, I leaned against the cool metal of a bus stop pole. An old city bus came to an abrupt halt and the doors swung open with a hiss. As it lurched forward, I dropped change in the box and weaved my way to the rear of the vehicle aided by headrests and silver rails.

The bus was pretty much empty except for a few locals in their seventies with shopping bags at their feet. I slumped low, peered out the window and pulled the tab on one of the beers bought for the ride. The bus would put some distance between me and my workplace, my apartment, and the judgmental glances of the neighbours, grocery clerks and roaming retirees. It promised movement, a passing landscape, escape.

Calm ocean breezes rock me gently in a hammock, tied between two palms. A swell comes up, so I set down the Mai Tai, grab my board and paddle out. That was where the hazy exhale of the pipe dream was supposed to deposit me.

Teach for a year, save my shekels then open up a surf shop slash beach bar, was the plan. The Beaver Dam, carved and painted on pale driftwood under a palm frond roof. Bob Marley and beach bimbos; six-packed and shirtless, the tanned, dirty blond owner kicks back with a blunt and a beer as a midday party ensues.

Invites all around: old friends, new friends, strangers, schoolmates, co-workers, and acquaintances. Even those I secretly resented – especially those I secretly resented – just to show 'em all, in my own contrived bohemian way, I'd made it all happen, and I did it *My Way*.

Obviously, too many pseudo-salaryman drunken nights belting Sinatra through the karaoke mic had given me delusions of grandeur. My way had landed me sipping beers on a city bus at noon.

Arriving in Okinawa, the generic daydream started getting picked apart. Swells only hit the main island when a typhoon approaches. The job would barely provide enough for the reggae albums and dope, let alone beachfront property. Most glaringly, I was a beginner surfer at best and wasn't getting any better.

I snapped out of my reverie as we headed out of Uruma and into Urasoe. Through water-spotted windows, I observed the sparse city streets. Most of the shops were closed indefinitely, shuttered with rusted metal roller screens. Although Okinawa had a reputation for being the Hawaii of Japan, you didn't need to stray too far from the beaches and five-star hotels before signs of hardship began to blemish the cityscape. My gaze wearied. It slipped somewhere between the glass streaks and city streets, where my reflection in the bus window projected onto each rundown boarded-up shop flashing by, my being cast along the barren, desolate sidewalk.

The passing scenery provided a striking contradiction to the Manza Beach Resort I'd sat at poolside a week and a half earlier, sipping a slushy orange beverage with an unnaturally red maraschino cherry on top.

The day began with a visit to Cape Manzamo, one of the tourist spots responsible for giving Okinawa the island paradise reputation it enjoys. From a grassy bluff one looks over the shrubbery to view intricate carvings of erosion on the cliffs below; the white froth of breaking waves, sweat of the perpetual sculptor, moulds the rock wall ever so patiently and delicately.

I looked out toward the East China Sea where the large hollow of a protruding stony arch allowed the sparkling water's surface shine through. Shifting my attention from the hole to the rock, it looked like an elephant trunk dipping into the ocean below as if to drink of the azure blue.

Of course, since it was shaped like an elephant head, the stone also resembled a large flaccid cock. When this realization hit, I snickered to myself and looked around for someone with whom to share my phallic observation. All I found was the stirring of a feeling so persistent as to be almost imperceptible and my immature grin fell to ground.

This protrusion was clearly the pièce de résistance for the crowd of mostly Chinese bus tourists who jostled for position and have their pictures taken with it featured prominently in the background.

Looking through the crystal-clear waters at the shadowy coral reefs below, I puzzled out the mesmerizing illusion in the ombre hues of blue-green effused. A tentative voice broke my stupor. 'Sir, very sorry, can take photo us, yes?' One of the tourists held out an expensive Nikon.

The man and his wife stood shoulder to shoulder. I centred them in the viewfinder with the stony trunk and sunlit sea in the background. Right before I clicked the photo, a collection of grey swirls materialized, swishing through the sky behind the unsuspecting couple. Squinting, I fought to make out the strange apparitions. Faces revealed themselves, Japanese men, women and children, forlorn and faded, the type one might see in black and white photographs from a bygone era.

I clicked the picture and looked to the sky behind the couple. It was again clear and blue. Handing back the camera to the man, I showed him the image I'd taken, at the same time looking over his shoulder for evidence of the smoky illusions.

Although viewed only briefly, those faces of despondent and tormented souls cast on the soaring grey streaks unnerved me. I was left with an ominous feeling that there, behind the beauty of the wide green bluff, still lingered some distant and lurking devastation, a great tragedy of untold thousands.

The aura of the place had shifted. Maybe I'd previously read or heard something about the cape. I don't believe in ghosts, per se, but the mind is most definitely a haunted place.

Thirty minutes later, I was sitting outside a large, ellipse-shaped hotel. Under its bright white reflection, I shaded my vision with a single cupped hand and peered across the small bay to the bluff. Something about the scene reminded me of Gatsby's East Egg and West Egg, though I couldn't say why.

An older lavish hotel, the Manza Resort at the end of a thin, jutting, rocky point; I guessed would be East Egg, but wasn't sure how. While awaiting the twenty-dollar drink I'd ordered from the cafe, some spoiled brats frolicked in the pool, and a dapper, older gent in a tanned summer suit walked by with a trophy wife or mistress on his arm. I felt like an imposter.

The drink arrived, and I took a sip. It tasted of syrup and artificial fruit juices but almost nothing of alcohol. With the girlie drink in hand, a wicker chair substituted for the hammock swing, and elevator jazz instead of reggae; an optimist could say I'd gotten halfway there, with my one-pack, farmer's tan and dark-blond, unwashed hair.

It was a beautiful spot, yet it dawned on me, *I don't belong here*.

The cliché fantasy which I'd chased across the five islands of Japan, well below the southernmost tip to that cushioned poolside seat was never going to materialize. More importantly, it wasn't what I wanted anyway. I'd just needed something to hold on to, some elusive image to follow. But right then, I let go. I gave up the childish pursuit of that juvenile fancy. In that moment, I took the cushion from my seat, put it over the face of those yellow umbrellaed, daiquiri dreams and smothered 'em.

'Sir, would you like another?' asked a smiling cafe waitress as she leaned over my chair, blocking the sun to cast a soothing shade across my face. Full breasts plunged forth the white fabric of her blouse. My eyes strayed to a gap between buttons and the crevasse of flesh below.

'No, thank you, just the bill.' I forced my eyes away from the cotton peephole.

'Certainly, sir, are you enjoying your stay here in Okinawa?' Sunshine played through her lightened hair, and it shimmered a candy tangerine.

'Yes, it's beautiful.'

'Oh, excellent. Business or pleasure?'

'A bit of both.' With a simulated smile, I handed her my glass.

She walked away framed by the pool, its surface reflected off the lobby glass and an ocean backdrop in the distance. I watched her flexed, dimpled buttocks swish back and forth, and thought, *Ah, sea-nymph you hold no power over me anymore*. But like so much of what comes out of my mouth or into my mind, it was bullshit. Overpowered I was, by her beauty and grace.

'Or pleasure?' she asked. I hadn't even had a crack. Seven months it'd been since I'd kissed and known the soft embrace of the fairer sex. At first, it was a decision, sobriety and celibacy – a cleansing ritual, or penance, or something, after too many debauched Tokyo nights. The island, The Beaver Dam, and all the fleecy indulgence of my shallow make-believe were meant to be the grand break from that self-inflicted piety.

Getting back on the booze was a piece of piss. I swung open the door of a fifth-floor bar and the small bell over the entrance jingled to alert of my arrival. The mama-san, a forty-year-old Filipina in a tight dress, smiled and brought over a 26er of whisky – bottle service with a cartoon keychain hung around its neck. While the bottles, bill and drawn black lines changed often, my trusted Doraemon keychain remained, night after night, the same.

Unlike my sobriety, the chastity had hung on with more vigour – less by choice than circumstance. Ego's at the heart of everything and too many competing suiters, in the form of young buff Marines, had stifled my confidence, stolen my swagger. While it was easier to blame the island then look inward, the result was the same and loneliness like a parasite devoured from within.

A breeze rippled the waters of the pool. It was lust and wanting that blew me here, perhaps the same would blow me back

After leaving the swanky poolside, I picked up a full bottle of whisky at half the price of my hotel drink. At least you could taste the booze in the mixes I made. Sat on a low brick wall of Onna's public beach, I stared out at the massive expanse of sea and felt both lost and liberated.

I came to with the sun on my face and sand in my crack. At some point during the night, like Humpty Dumpty, I'd fallen off the wall and slept sprawled out on the sandy beach below. The lids of my eyes opened with great effort as if they'd been glued shut. The first sight I spied was the whisky bottle lying on its side in the sand, a castaway's castoff.

I raised myself to a seated position, picked up the bottle, placed it in my mouth, and tipped the base skyward. Remnants trickled into my mouth and down my throat. It was a quarter shot, at most, but just enough to revive me.

My phone was dead, and I had no service anyhow due to unpaid bills. Squinting into the sun, I guessed it was around 10 am.

'Fuck!' I was supposed to be standing in front of a class of pre-pubescents teaching them English two hours ago. 'Dammit, Shit,

Motherfucker!' I swore to the heavens. *There's an English lesson for 'em.*

It itched like sandpaper between my butt cheeks with each sweaty step down the coastal road. My hangover had a hangover as I went through a Rolodex of excuses to explain away my no-show at work, but came up with bupkis. Food poisoning, family death, flu; they'd all been deployed since starting back on the piss.

I felt woozy during the slow walk in the blazing heat. A chain convenience store, like an oasis mirage, appeared in the distance. I sped my pace, feeling it advisable to acquire a few drinks to perk myself up and wash away the accumulated worry.

I entered through sliding glass doors to an electric ding and the clerk's tepid call of *irasshaimase.*

Once again, my eyes struggled to open. They took in darker, sterile surroundings. A tube filled with a clear liquid inserted into my vein ceaselessly dripped. I sought recollection of any events between the *conbini's* automatic doors opening and the IV in my arm, but lost focus on the liquid-filled bag hung from a smooth silver bar overhead.

From what the doctor would tell me later; I had come out of the washroom with my pants around my ankles, babbling something incoherent about sandpaper, before I collapsed on the floor. The shopkeeper called an ambulance, and I ended up there, in my curtained gurney, fucked.

Dehydration and vitamin deficiency was the diagnosis and suspected cause of my fainting spell. When they said they wanted to keep me overnight, I had them contact the school I worked for. At least I'd found my excuse.

'We will release you today, Mr Buchanan,' a young doctor informed me late the next morning, 'but you need to take better care of yourself.' He said in a serious tone, with just a hint of genuine care.

'What's the issue ... am I going to live?' I asked with an

uncomfortable laugh, the question being only half in jest.

Exhibiting a strong command of formal English, he proceeded to quiz me on my lifestyle. How many cigarettes a day, how much alcohol consumed, what was my diet and how much sleep did I get?

Of course, I answered in massive depreciations so as not to arouse any suspicion and be let out as soon as possible, but still, my diminished responses were sufficient to concern him. Likely, the blood they took helped him see through any attempt to whitewash my unhealthy habits.

'We'll need you to cut down on both the drinking and smoking. Overall, you need to take better care of yourself and begin eating better,' he finally prescribed.

I loved that about Japan, they would never think to tell you to quit smoking or drinking, full stop.

'So, with my clean bill of health, are you gonna release me back into the wild, Doc?'

Although his English was technically sound, he obviously didn't understand the colloquialism and looked at me with a confused expression.

'So, can I get out of the hospital now?' I rephrased and attempted to sound less jovial.

He cleared his throat. 'And, what is the sound of your mind?'

That's some zen shit, I thought. *It either clamours like a four-storey pachinko parlour or drones monotonously as if a lone vending machine on a desolate street corner in the pastoral night*. Was the answer I never gave, but instead fidgeted in my seat, reluctant to reveal anything incriminating. 'Huh?'

'I'm sorry, what about your soundness of mind?'

'Oh. *Hai, ii desu*,' I blurted out. Clearly, they thought me a suicide case. 'I'm all good.'

The young doctor eyed me sceptically. 'Yes, well then, we'll prepare your bill. Clear that downstairs, and you are free to leave. But please, look after yourself, Mr Buchanan,' said the young doctor as he gave me an amiable and concerned parting smile.

Of course, a goddamn bill! It hadn't crossed my mind that I'd have to pay. I figured I was covered, but only partially. Any such financial request, no matter how small, was well beyond my means right then, like asking a beggar to loan you a twenty.

A plump, rosy-cheeked attendant in a pink smock handed me the bill. I took a number and sat in the waiting area to pay. Seventy thousand yen, just under a thousand bucks. A month's rent, double my unpaid bar bills, a fourth of my salary or about a hundred bottles of cheap whiskey I'd be needing to fuel my resilience. Having crunched the numbers, I stood up, walked out of the hospital and trashed the bill in the nearest bin.

All of the nurses and white-coated men couldn't put me together again. On weak legs, I headed to the nearest convenience store to quench a terrible thirst. I bought two Chu-his to pour through my cracks, avoiding eye contact with the cashier as I paid in loose change mixed with sand and tobacco. A plastic bag slung around my wrist, I exited through sliding glass doors, into a new day.

Sat on a park bench I sipped off the rim of my second can of grapefruit Chu-hi and contemplated the state of things. I don't know if I willed it, or if it were just dumb luck, but the short stint in the hospital had given me the perfect alibi for not showing up to work.

I was given an inch and immediately attempted to stretch it into a mile. I used my 'ill health' to take off the rest of the week. But come the following Monday, I had no motivation to return. I woke up with a ubiquitous, paralyzing fear. The thought of standing in front of twenty pairs of dead adolescent eyes only drove me to the payphone to inform that I still wasn't feeling up to par.

The next morning, the image of taking attendance in a voice weak, shaky, and densely layered with the previous evening's wine, women and song, kept me in bed until noon. Following that, the thought of shirking from an unmoving clock, facing my failure to have formed any real connection with the students and of no longer knowing why I'd come there or what I was working toward; kept me away each successive day. I had stretched that inch a little too far, and it snapped.

Reaching out to the secretary after a week of flimsy lies and sorry excuses, she cheerfully said, 'Okay, Mr Buchanan. Please come in to see us when you feel up to it and have time.'

It was just a little too blasé and distant, like an ex-lover who'd clearly moved on.

Fuck it! I'm free, I told myself as I hung up the payphone and walked away, carrying cold cans in a plastic bag, and a pit of guilt in my stomach.

The bus pushed on through bleak city streets where the only swells I rode were asphalt ones. Those recollections befell to a soundtrack of an inordinately loud engine, grinding transmission, and whining brakes of the old bus playing in the background. An olfactory B-side of faint diesel, paired with the taste of room temp ale in tobacco tainted swigs, completed the city street symphony.

Sapped of spirit, strength and vitality, I languished in this constant calypso and sipped my beer. Periodically, the bus halted at designated stops to let off and pick up more passengers. I didn't know where I was going, there was no destination in mind. Those trips I'd been taking almost daily were never about going anywhere, merely an attempt to get away from it all.

A thought descended – *I've ended up in limbo*.

With the easy disposal of my ersatz dreams, the low set wooden bar had disintegrated. Arched back and unsteady on wobbly legs – frozen, suspended in existence, and unable to clear the infinite air – I found myself bracing for a fall.

2// Unmasking

Sufficiently far enough away from the cankerous combo of my flat and former employer, I pressed the buzzer and disembarked the city bus. Even as the bar signs snoozed in an afternoon shade, it was unmistakably Goya.

Months ago, on my first bus ride through, Goya's seediness sung out to me the ol' sirens' song, its chorus the red neon silhouette of a pole dancing woman advertising the Amazon Gentleman's Club. Near one of the island's American military bases, it had all the accoutrements off-duty soldiers craved, namely cheap bars and easy women. Though they be dormant then, the area had the kind of geography where a man of my ilk could waste away an afternoon roaming backstreets alone with his thoughts, and bludgeon them to death.

I purchased whisky for six hundred yen. Two doors down I procured a medium Cola from McDonald's and ducked into one of my much-fancied alleys to mix. I dumped out half the Cola and topped it up to the brim with rotgut. A quick stir with the yellow plastic straw, I took a sip and enjoyed the soothing burn as it slid down my gullet.

While threading the alleys sipping my poor man's cocktail, I passed a small, inviting park with a couple of benches, two or three trees, and a grassy patch. There were five or six old men in the park either seated on spread-out newspapers or leaning against tree trunks. They drank from jars of *sake* or tall cans of beer and unanimously smoked. Other than the age difference, it looked like my kind of crowd.

I took a seat on an empty bench and pulled out the paperback I carried around to occupy me during those hours of solitude in which I was still able to digest words. I opened to the dog-eared page. The man seated on the bench next to me did a double-take at the cover.

I began reading and sipped at the straw.

'Are you in the process of taking off your mask or putting one on?' asked my bench neighbour in near-perfect English.

Jostled to attention, I looked up from the page.

'Always,' I replied, raising the empty mickey in a 'kampai' motion with a bratty smile, not really knowing or caring in the least what my response meant.

'Hmm, well, that's not really an answer, is it?' he identified. 'And, well, yes, you're drinking is, in some form, likely an act of putting on a mask, as much as it is stripping one off.' He spoke like a learned professor, unwilling to accept my cavalier response. 'But my question was more broadly based. Here in Okinawa, in this stage of your life, and with whatever events have brought you to this park; is it part of a process of shielding or unveiling your true self?' His words were measured and deliberate as he dragged me down his deep-rutted path of self-examination. 'Or like Mishima, are you hiding your latent homosexual tendencies behind a manufactured epitome of masculinity?'

Ah, now he's just riling me into engaging. I laughed nervously, as the loaded question had thrown me. It wasn't the conversational opening I'd expected from one of those bums in the park. 'I guess you've read your Mishima?'

He nodded a neutral expression and waited.

'Well no, and clearly I'm not pursuing any ideal of masculinity.' I held out arms lacking any definition and gestured at my developing paunch.

The old man just stared at me with a self-satisfied smirk and an aura which seemed to say, *go on*, in a long drawn out voice.

Newspaper rustled and a sparrow chirped. I dropped my guard and looked inward with some serious thought. *How the fuck ... did I get here?*

'Shit ... well, I guess I'm putting on a mask.' I looked at my cup and rotated the straw counter-clockwise, second-guessing this assessment. 'No, actually ... the mask I wear has been firmly in place for some time now ... long before I got to this park, and well before I arrived in Okinawa.'

My tattered Adidas kicked at the dirt and I bit my lower lip. 'But I guess the nagging feeling I've been having is this sense that the mask is slipping off, you know? ... And it's like, I'm not ready for it to fall, 'cause I have no fucking idea what's underneath. So every day I'm struggling to hold it on. Nonetheless, it keeps sliding down against my will and waning effort.'

He lit a smoke, as did I. We inhaled in unison. I took a long sip of my whisky and Coke, feeling exposed. It appeared I'd been conned into joining this curious Goya book club after all.

'If the novel is truly autobiographical as most think it to be,' the old man orated, 'then Mishima began to construct and wear his mask in adolescence and was never able to take it off. This mask evolved over time, but Mishima was unsuccessful in ever fully removing it. His inability to confidently remove the mask, all the while feeling it paradoxically fastening tighter and sliding off was his plight. It contributed to Mishima's demise and finally suicide by *seppuku*. As you may know, many considered this novel his veiled suicide note.'

Shit, not again. 'No man, I'm cool.' I sucked my drink through the chewed straw. 'It's just I like his writing. Don't read too much into it or anything.'

'Please forgive, I'm not saying that you will suicide. That is very much a Japanese answer, or say solution ... no a cultural phenomenon.' His pristine English faltered somewhat, but he recovered well. 'We are particularly fascinated with this form of escape. Let's attribute it to the fact that our society stringently requires us to wear these masks.'

'Sounds about right.' I dismissed this with a shrug though remembered a stint living on the Chuo Line in a Tokyo which earned the darkly comic nickname 'Chuicide line' thanks to the many jumpers and disruption to service, announced always to the waiting passengers as 'track maintenance'.

'Yes, in fact, many masks, in all areas of our lives. The consequence of taking them off can be dire: shame, isolation, banishment. Since you are *gaijin*, you will not have this experience, at least not with the intensity of a Japanese. But it remains that you will never find the ability to exist comfortably until you can remove your mask and be at ease with exposing what is underneath.' He paused there, drank from his can, and let his words sink in.

I pondered his little sermon. Undoubtedly, there was truth in it, but I couldn't connect how it applied to my circumstances. *Did I put a mask on anywhere? Wasn't I born wearing a mask, aren't we all?* I hacked up a wad of phlegm, held it in my mouth for a second, then swallowed. *What a bunch of bullshit.* In retrospect, he offered concrete advice, but it didn't immediately penetrate my scepticism and arrogance.

Our little literary conversation had gotten a bit too personal a tad too quick and I figured I'd turn the tables – *see how much this walking Mishima thesis knows personally about putting on and taking off masks.*

'So, is the man I'm speaking to in this park today wearing a mask? Or are you maskless?' I asked, a snide sneer commandeering my lips.

A smile crept up one side of his face like he'd been expecting this line of confrontational questioning. The old man took a long swallow of his beer, he looked over the little park, beyond its limits, and further.

'I was born in Yokohama, right after the fire-bombings of Tokyo subsided. The war ended, but the American troops stayed on, and then on. At first to ensure the imperial tendencies of Hirohito would never again rear their head, and then because we were not allowed to form a military of our own. Even now, they stay to protect us. How very philanthropic of them, *ne*?' He chuckled, in such a way as to convey all the sarcasm loaded into his sentiment.

'But of course, it was only a strategic occupation, part of their military-industrial complex.' He took a drag of his Seven Stars cigarette and drank again from his tall can of Kirin beer like he was settling in for a long fireside chat.

I polished off what was left of the whisky and visibly set the empty mickey on the bench, figuring, *if you're going to hang around small city parks with the wounded weekday warriors, you'd better damn well qualify.*

'My father inherited a small *izakaya* after he returned from the war,' he said. 'Due to its proximity to the Yokota Air Base, it was frequented by soldiers and over time became somewhat of a, how would you say ... a honky-tonk bar. In fact, you still see these relics in Goya with neon Miller Light signs, Budweiser on tap and a jukebox in the corner playing Hank Williams.

'In my youth, I spent many nights in that bar, clearing tables and serving small plates of food to accompany the army men's beer. I observed the soldiers as they laughed and smoked, got drunk, and sometimes violent with each other. The punch-ups were fun to watch. Seeing the men's knuckles crack against cheekbones and then watching as they drank with red welts forming on their faces as they went back to their drinking and laughing, it taught me a bit about toughness and what constituted surface wounds as opposed to those that run deep.

'And then, of course, were the slurs. Overheard night after night as the men commented on their Jap neighbours, Jap girlfriends and my father – the Jap that served their drinks, cleaned their glasses and prepared their meals. They spat out their vitriol in the same nonchalant manner with which they spat saliva on his barroom floor.'

As he spoke of these servicemen from that bygone era, most in their graves by now, I could see a resentment still simmered inside him. Perhaps, I thought, he'd mistaken me as an off-duty soldier and was looking to needle me until I lashed out.

'I'm not American military,' I stated.

'I know,' he chortled.

I guess something in my appearance or demeanour cleared me. I'd let my hair grow longer; mostly out of laziness and finances, but partially to avoid being confused as American military who made up the bulk of Okinawa's foreigner population. Of course, beyond that was the situational aspect of drinking alone on a park bench in the middle of the day. I could've been AWOL, though he probably would have dug that.

'As I said, growing up around my father's bar, if it taught me anything, it was how to be tough. I excelled at rugby, which got me a scholarship to Tokyo University. I majored in political science, as it was a playing field on which to exercise my burgeoning beliefs.

'In the late 60s our student protest movement was reaching full boil. I had one foot in the door before I'd even arrived on campus, and became a fully-fledged member of the Zengakuren from day one.'

'Sounds like Berkley in the 60s,' I said, warming a little to his story.

'*Hai, onaji.*' He briefly slipped into Japanese – throwing me a softball, 'yes, same.'

'I loved the thrash of bodies in a rugby scrum,' he continued. 'But as the students and cops clashed with kendo sticks and tear gas, as all my harboured indignation of youth congealed into a coherent ideology, as everything I was and believed came crashing together in one beautiful, violent symphony, I found my true passion. I was a dissenter, an agitator, a rebel,' he pronounced, and a smile spread from cauliflower ear to cauliflower ear.

Just then, on that still thick neck, atop those only-slightly-slumped-by-age broad shoulders, you could see the old rugger in him yet. In the fire that ignited in his eye as he shared his tale, I could see an old rebel still stirred.

'We fought for various issues such as liberalizing of our education system and land rights, but the one dearest to my heart was that of anti-American imperialism. I became one of the louder evangelists for greater statements of resistance and rose up the ranks. At the same time, I was excelling on the rugby field. By my junior year, our squad was poised for city championships, and I was an assistant captain.'

I looked around our own minuscule park at the bedraggled old men who sat around socializing or drinking alone and pondered if each had his own story to tell, and what carefully placed artefacts would lead them to share it.

'It started off at Ueno park – ' began the old man's description of his protest. The energy in the air that day and details of taking the campus clock tower animated my bench mate as he spoke with increased intensity and eloquence.

'The tower had six of us now, all top-ranking members, Tatsuya and I hoisted the banner out the window and watched it unfurl, the black *kanji* letters spelling out our message: "End American Occupation of Japan and Vietnam Now! Death to Fascism!" A cheer went out from the crowd below. Hundreds maybe thousands who couldn't fit into the building as part of the occupation blanketed the concourse. There was undeniably art in our destructiveness ... a language to our violence.' He drank and smiled inwardly.

I doubted if I'd ever had a moment like that. A memory of pure bliss, where I knew I'd arrived exactly where I belonged and was entirely in my element. I drank whisky-Coke through the yellow plastic straw, hoping it'd fill the hole.

'"ARE YOU READY TO FIGHT?" I felt the words rip through my voice box. A roar went up from the group below which shook the clock tower's concrete walls. As if on cue, the first police vans arrived.' His hand – knuckles white, clenched in a tight fist – rested on his right thigh.

Battered out of the clock tower, he began his descent. 'I pulled a red and white rising sun bandana over my face and dashed down the stairwell filled with smoke and tear gas. Through the embowed entrance I burst, running toward a scrum formation of waiting uniformed officers. Behind me, I heard Machiko scream as she was nabbed. "Die pigs, get your idiot hands off her," Tatsuya cursed as he was also taken down.' His Kirin can splashed onto a tuft of grass as his excited hand gestures attempted to capture the action of that day.

'I swung a short club and caught one of the cops under the helmet on his left ear. Before I could rear back and strike again, a shield struck me hard. I stumbled and fell. Boots and nightsticks rained down on me as a swell of bodies converged to take their parting shots.

'Through the bodies and blows, I saw the last sliver of purple dusk before everything faded to black. The final strikes delivered unconscious with a beatific smile inscribed upon my face.' His fingers rubbed across his forehead and down his cheek, tracing his jawline as he read like braille the old battle scars; then he repeated the motion, like rubbing a slate clean ... or putting on a mask.

The reminiscent smile which had played on his lips up to that point, as a palm proceeded over his lips, was erased and replaced with a straight-lipped, regretful frown – a sign his tale was about to turn.

'I awoke in a cell, bruises and welts covering my whole body. I touched my forehead where a gash left residue of crusted blood below a hastily fastened bandage. My classmates were released one after the other as they paid bail, and paperwork was filed for court dates. I, however, remained.

'The next day, I was called to a questioning room. They had identified me as a ringleader. I faced charges of conspiracy to incite a riot, assaulting an officer, and destruction of property. I was asked to give the names of my "comrades", but refused to cooperate, so was returned to my cell.'

'You didn't rat. Good on ya,' I said, expecting it was the encouragement he wanted to hear. It wasn't. His head turned and looked at me cold. However, the vexation was directed inward rather than out.

'In the early evening, I was led again to an examination room for more questioning. This time the two officers were not alone, they were backed by the Dean and Coach Hirao-san. Dean Aihara raised my downcast eyes to meet his warning glare, and began to speak; to formulate the lie that was to be my story.'

Assuming a nasal voice of what I'm guessing was his view of the stuffy old Dean, he continued. '"We know the protest was planned by a Mr Tatsuya, Mr Daisuke and Ms Machiko. Mr Tatsuya was expelled last year but continues to be a campus agitator. His punishment will be legal in totality. Ms Machiko and Mr Daisuke are facing expulsion in lieu of criminal charges. We think you got caught up in the movement of bodies which brought you into the clock tower with the organizers. You're a participant who ended up in the wrong place at the wrong time." The old bastard paused and gave me a condescending once-over like I was a pitiful schoolboy caught scraping in the yard.

'"Since this is the case, you will continue to be a student of Tokyo University, and as long as you are involved in no other instances of disorder, you will be permitted to graduate. This is the case, Mr Hideki?" It was a statement, wrapped as a question, and presented as a gift.'

Hideki, that's his name. We'd never even introduced ourselves and yet there I was, so deep into his life story. I made a mental note,

I was likely to wash away somewhere along the way.

Sparse grey-and-black stubble sprinkled Hideki's jawline. A jaw which pulsated rapidly, as it clenched against the decades' old frustration. 'What was expected of me was to agree the mostly fabricated story was affirmative. The Dean stared at me urgingly, angered to have been brought to the station and toss me this alibi. When I looked at Coach, he wore a meek grin and nodded enthusiastically, being the one who'd orchestrated this intervention. Coach was a nice guy, but he was, like all of us, motivated by selfish ends. He saw our chances at the cup slip away if I was expelled and unable to play. Without thinking much of the consequences, I capitulated and said, "*Hai*".'

'That one word ...' he shifted his weight on the hard park bench. 'That single utterance was all it took for me to lose myself from that day and for a long, long time.'

'So that was the mask?' I inquired.

'Yes, that is where I believe I put it on, or it was inadvertently thrust upon me. I returned to classes, and what I thought was my old life. But I'd changed, everything had changed. We lost our semi-final match of the Rugby Championship, so it was all for nought, even for Coach. I returned once to the Zengakuren headquarters, only to be met by cold stares. They assumed I'd grassed. Whether I had or hadn't, it didn't matter. I'd shown no solidarity. I had turned on our cause, on my principles and with that single syllable "*Hai*", I erroneously shifted the course of my life and irreparably damaged the content of my character.' Hideki exhaled a long breath and looked to the treetops and overcast sky beyond. Searching for what, I didn't know.

'With all my supposed fringe and radical ideology, I ended up working a low-level municipal job at the Shinjuku ward office. I'd gone from being an aspiring guerrilla in the student protest movement to a pencil pusher and paper shuffler in the very government we'd set out to overthrow.

'How did I deal with this change of fortune, this mockery of a life I existed in? As any weak man would ... I turned to drink and women.' He raised his can in a 'cheers to that' motion and raised an eyebrow to effect a knowing look that communicated, *'you get it, ne!'*

'And Shinjuku was the perfect ward for these distractions, our office itself situated on the outskirts of the infamous Kabukicho district. The hostess bars and gambling dens all wanted to cosy up to ward politicians, no matter how insignificant. We oversaw the regulatory licenses, issued fines, ordered inspections and handled taxes. Us ward officers were all on the take, and I was no exception.

'Your typical salaryman, living and working in a salaryman wonderland; up at 6 am and sat behind a desk for 12 hours with frequent coffee and cigarette breaks until we broke around 8 or 9 in the evening and patronized hostess bars to drink and sing karaoke until last train. The whisky was comped, and women encouraged by their *yakuza* handlers to sit and flirt with the ward officials. This routine became so ingrained I hardly remembered I was living a lie, my existence a farce of my true self.

'I married one of the hostesses as she was on her way out of the bar circuit. At 29 she didn't look a day over 38, as the lifestyle will do to a lady. She'd gotten out of the game with a couple of pairs of Manolo heels and a Gucci handbag to show for her misspent youth. She was still attractive though, in a worn and spent kind of way. I was no catch either, beer-bellied and balding. I still had my broad rugby shoulders, and she those smooth, long dancer legs, but what we shared most I'd say was our misery. The disillusionment of having wandered so far off the path we were meant to be on and the dismay that we were too far astray to ever find our way back.'

Somewhere along Hideki's journey, I'd edged closer to the orator. I'm guessing it was when it turned dark, like macabre drivers who slow up to observe the carnage of a wreck. I was practically falling off the park bench, as to not miss a moment of his described demise.

'We weren't married long when I discovered that mistreatment of my wife was as good an outlet to redirect my self-hatred as the bars and bottles. Exchanging favours at the local gangsters' establishments, I'd seek counterfeit comfort with their whores in the backstreet love hotels or extend lines of credit to gamble away our savings in black market betting dens. When my wife would question my activities and the lack of money for her to run the household, I would curse her, pull back her ponytail and smack her face. Afterward, while she sobbed into the silence, I drank whisky and watched the red welts form on her cheek, like those Yankee soldiers in my father's bar. The worst of it all was I felt nothing, no remorse and no shame.' He turned his head to the left and stretched it backwards to crack a stiff neck. Or was it to shun his shadow?

'I convinced myself I was making her tough for the harshness of life, but truth was, she was already tougher than me. The government was cracking down on corruption. Soon my gambling debts and lustful nights extended beyond any and all favours I could provide in my position at the ward. I found fewer and fewer outlets of escape for my disgruntled soul.

'On an early morning in July '85, I waited on the Keio line platform. It was humid, and I was hungover. I felt only slightly lower than usual, but that extra depth was enough. As the train was approaching at speed, I went to take a step over the yellow cautionary line. I stepped, but my leg didn't move. It wasn't fear that paralyzed me, I'd made my decision and was resolute to end my monotonous merry-go-round life. Though the right leg I'd naturally lead with wouldn't budge.

'I looked down and saw a sweaty heavy-set man beside me, standing on my untied laces. He followed my stare down to his foot and observed his shiny black shoe pinning my shoelace to the platform. "*Gomen*," he apologized with a small bow and jolly smile as the train came to a stop and the doors opened.

'I said nothing. Mouth agape, I watched a single bead of sweat travel southward from his forehead down to the tip of his nose, where it hung briefly, and fell onto the platform cement. The doors closed, and the man was gone.

'I remained there, frozen, then got down on my hands and knees and rubbed the darkened circle where the sweat droplet had landed. I lifted my index finger and inspected it, yet all that was there was dirt from the platform cement. I wanted to capture it, that single droplet. In it, there was everything; it was the nectar of my rebirth.' A tincture of a smile formed across his previously forlorn face. He cleared his throat, then took a hearty drink of his can.

'I got on the next train but didn't go to my office. Instead, I transferred and rode to Ueno Station. It was my first time back on the campus since graduation, and I was unsure how I would react. The answer came swiftly when I fell to my knees and vomited in the grass. Through blurry, watering eyes, I looked toward the clocktower, like a small child staring up at his mother's disappointed and scolding face.

'On all fours in the grass, head cocked, squinting into the sun as it manoeuvred behind the tower and white fluffy clouds floated by, a spittle of vomit drooled from my lower lip – I was utterly defeated. The red-brick tower and cyclops eye of the clock stood guarding the heavens beyond, it stared down upon me in judgment while I sobbed and silently repented.

'A week later, I had quit my job and with a single bag waited at Haneda Airport. In Okinawa, I found voices of resistance still alive, perhaps muffled and at times no stronger than a whimper. Still, they called to me, and I knew my survival depended on answering. Here, the anti-base movement has the same basic dictum; to end the American military presence in Okinawa and throughout Japan.

'So, I've found my way home in a way. At certain times we show our distaste for US foreign policy, though our true revulsion is reserved for every time they spit on our floor, a middle-aged cab driver gets stabbed by two servicemen, a girlfriend strangled to death by her marine boyfriend or the gang rape of an adolescent schoolgirl.'

My stomach churned with white guilt. I contemplated going on the defensive and throwing Nanking at him, but it was a false equivalency. Plus, I'd gotten to like the old dude, no point being a dick.

He looked to my silent face, almost like he was waiting for my challenge. When I remained listening, he continued. 'The passion of our movement is no less voluminous, although our actions tend to be more muted. The raging fire of rebellion that was the 60s has faded to a flicker; sit-ins and peaceful marches, political rallies and petitions are the norms now. Although, I've found occasion to throw a few more bricks and end up in a few more cells.' He took a satisfied swig and lit a fresh Seven Stars cigarette.

I considered if he expected some sort of congratulatory remark. Instead, I played the shit disturber, 'Get rid of the US military from Okinawa, and you'll likely be next on the list.' I guess I felt like being a bit dickish after all.

'Hah, you are a quick study of Okinawan culture.' He said in a good-natured smirk. '"I'm not Japanese, I'm Okinawan!" I assume you've heard more than once. There indeed are many here who would be happy to be rid of all who do not have generational ties to the Ryukyu Kingdom. So maybe you will be proven correct, not likely, but possibly ... and I couldn't judge if that is to come to pass. As for now, I'm enjoying my island life: finding purpose, awakening the warrior and, *hai*, having removed my mask.'

I looked to the caked dirt and trodden tufts of grass at my feet. As far as I could remember, I'd never turned my back on my convictions. *Had I ever had any to turn it on?*

Once, I'd carried a sign and wore a T-shirt – the iconic image of Ali shouting over a KO'd Liston with the words, 'I ain't never caught no flak from the people of Iraq' written underneath, back when baby Bush had ordered the trumped-up invasion. But, I wasn't at the protest march because of any deeply held stance it was an unjust war. Like always, I was there rapacious and seeking. It had simply seemed a cool scene to smoke weed and try to score with some dreadlocked, wild bush, hippie chicks.

The moral philosophy which most informed my actions would probably be hedonism, although less by choice than instinct. A self-proclaimed instant gratification junky, if it feels good do it … and if it feels really good, do it over and over again. Who doesn't crave escape when mediocrity suffuses and discontentment strikes?

Loss of faith was not my struggle. It had never been me in the corner, in the spotlight, losing my religion like an emancipated and closeted Michael Stipe or Dostoevsky's Ivan brooding in the vestibule. My Canadian Protestant upbringing was akin to being raised agnostic. I'm told I was baptized, although I'm not too sure what that even means, something about being allowed through the gates of heaven. Like a handstamp which lets you back into the celestial nightclub? Faint and faded are memories of Sunday school with the requisite bible readings. So there must've been some church goin' when I was young. Then, I don't know, we got better cable? But nothing about any of it penetrated. There was no visceral response the first time I laid eyes on Jesus in his crown of thorns, nails driven through palms and feet, dying on the cross. Jesus seems like an alright guy, great abs too – but Jesus on the cross included, all that symbolism and ritual of religion, it merely washed over me like lukewarm water. Nothing stirred within – I had no real faith to lose.

As a largely apolitical agnostic, it was hard to grasp a straw by which to show due deference to the old man. Hideki went to all that effort to tell it, I wanted to indicate that his story hit on some profound chord, although at the time, it would've been a lie. Not that I had anything against lying, but something told me he'd have seen right through it.

Looking up from the ground, I said, 'Perhaps, I'm not so much wearing a mask as a hood. Like those hostages tied to chairs with sacks thrown over their heads, I'm existing in total darkness.' This, unfortunately, was all I had to relate to him.

'Maybe, but even so, you need to find a way to remove it.'

I shook my cup to confirm it was dry and signalled to my bench companion the same, my cue to leave. I stood up with a slight sway, gave a feeble foreigner bow then walked out of the park and into the backstreets of Goya.

3// Gertie
and the Manky Peach

Sometimes you speak to a stranger, it could be as brief as ordering a coffee or a more substantial conversation as I'd just had with the Japanese Abbie Hoffman-san in the park there. The after-effect leaves you with this distinct, indescribable lightheadedness and warm tingle, pleasant in nature. It's different than being drunk or stoned. The numbness of the mind is similar, but there is something natural, pure, almost divine about it.

When this feeling descends, seemingly without rhyme or reason, after contact with certain individuals, I am always left wondering, why? Why that person? Why that innocuous exchange set off this reaction in my being? And do others experience it, or was it just me?

I can't help but believe it is some sort of extramundane communiqué. Despite the meaninglessness of the words exchanged or contact had, there was something there, something to take note of. The most plausible explanation I can arrive at is that in the tapestry of life, specific people weave together the scenes – those people who were the mysterious catalyst for this buzz, they are the thread.

The buzz wore off, as they are wont to do, and left my head more or less swimming. Beyond the fog, the old man's story marooned me confused and searching still. I tried to recapture the comfortable numb which had followed my exit from the park and saunter down the first few backstreets, but the stitch was sewn, its meaning unknown.

I settled on a final conclusion, simple and evasive, *he could spin quite a yarn.*

The street, in those last licks of daylight, carried a collection of nihonjin-Rockwellian scenes. A baby in a peach sling pressed to the bosom of a young mother as a dapper gentleman walked his Akita pooch in the opposite direction. Behind him two boys in matching school uniforms sauntered along engaged in some serious talk on the state of things. I smiled at their oddly adult manner. My mind slowed it all down to a snail's pace, and awaited a lacuna by which to slip in.

A blizzard blew through my observing eyes, and the world around me erased, replaced by four white walls. A red string spread across the room's white floor, unravelled from a small ball of origin in the absolute centre. Pieces overlaid each other or looped out alone in wild departures. A single strand led out of the room, into a dark unknown.

I viewed the static scene from above. My ceiling perspective left me unable to grip and follow, though I desperately wanted to see where the thread concluded.

A cat entered, the scarred and scraggy stray from the convenience store stoop. He walked to what remained of the balled yarn and batted it powerfully with his dirtied claw. It rolled across the white floor, unravelling its entirety. The white feline looked up with those menacing mismatched eyes to where my presence observed from above. Jaws spread open wide and he gave a single, vicious hiss.

My eyes opened with a start, my back against the brick wall of a FamilyMart and ass on the pavement. A metal cylindrical smoking ashtray stood next to me, and the cigarette between the fingers of my clasped hands still burned. Elbows rested on each knee, like caught in a foxhole prayer.

To avoid passing out entirely in front of the convenience store, I stood and picked up my can. For inertia, I took a long drink of the carbonated grapefruit-flavoured *ōchū* and was a body set in motion.

In the settled dusk, back on Goya's main drag, predatory women emerged from darkened doorways like hungry grey eels. I veered toward their nests on approach, seeking a grab of the arm followed by offer of massage, nude show or companionship over drinks. In different forms, the elixir's the same: women and booze, the potion producing momentary escape from melancholy into madness. While tempted to indulge, experience and a few grand has taught it's little more than a band-aid on a bullet wound.

Having turned down all offers on the short gauntlet of lust and libations, it'd have been unfair and a little embarrassing to tease my way back. So, in that mood and milieu, I gave up my quest for revelry and settled for electronic companionship. No, not one of the infamous Japanese sex robots – the local internet café.

Closing the half-door, I sat in the leather recliner and opened a fresh can. With a burning cigarette resting in the ashtray, I settled in to indulge in familiar TV shows and old movies, comfort food for the mind.

Hours later, I was awoken by a light knocking on the plywood door and lilting voice of the cafe clerk mispronouncing my surname. 'Bu-Chan-San … *Sumimasen*, Bu-Chan-an-san?'

'*Hai*,' I replied in a hoarse voice, struggling out of the chair to attend to the uncommon interruption. The computer menu bar read 4:25 am, so my twelve hours were far from up. I slid open the door and peered through bloodshot eyes at a young female clerk who looked embarrassed to have disturbed me.

'*Denwa*, ahh, telephone.' She indicated, pointing toward the front desk where the receiver of a landline lay upright on the counter.

Confused and sock-footed, I walked down a small aisle to the phone. Snores and rustling came from the occupied cubicles and the single thought of *who the fuck knows I'm here* raced through my mind.

I gripped the receiver by the moulded handle and held it to my ear. 'Hello.'

'Aye, Fred, ye drunk cunt!' came a jovial greeting, delivered in a thick Belfast accent. 'Been a while mucker. What about ye?' she continued.

'Huh, who ...'

'Nay time for banter, mate. The oul church clock is ticking, and I gotta tell ye the score. It goes back to when we were mates in the Big Peach Gaijin House. Ye remember the boggin spot, aye?'

'Gertie? Shit, is that you, Gertie?'

'Fuckin' took ye long enough to catch on. Now shut your gob, let me give ye the lowdown. Ye acted an eejit back in the day, but we also have a good craic, more often 'en not. Ye a good fella, Fred, jus' got too langers all the damn time. But now ... yer fucked, ain't ye.'

'Yeah, kinda ... how do you know where ...'

'Remember tha night we got back to Higashi Koseki Station after a good lash?' she cut in. 'Aye, I don't reckon you do, you'er mashed cunt! I had to 'elp you out the train you 'ere so pissed.'

She was right, I didn't remember, sounded like hundreds of nights we'd had.

'But once on the platform, ye toss off me 'elpin arm. And ye fuckin' walked slalom down the empty platform. Stumbling to the edge, you'd catch ye'self right before ye fell right on the tracks. Then ye go stumbling the opposite direction and smash a pole or tha oul wall ... It would've been a laugh if I didn't think ye're gonna kill ye'self, boyo.'

I pictured myself in this state, in that scene, and was disconnected from it all.

'So I tries to 'elp ye again, and ye told me to "fuck off, cunt". I know ye, not a tough guy, and I knows you were trying to take the piss ... but I gave ye North American arse license to use the feckin expression, and done told ya ... Ye never use it on a woman! Your mate or not.'

Yeah, she had warned me of that rule. So many times, I could practically picture her eyebrows, thick and dark like Guinness stout, drawn together in a pissed-off V as she rehashed the abstruse memory.

'With that, I figure I was feckin' done with ye. I walk ahead and leave ye there ta drag ye own arse home. Thing was, I thought we were on the last train,' Gertie said, 'but then I 'ear another one comin'. It barrels into the station, as your feckin' oblivious arse went stumbling back toward the open track.'

This, I felt, I should've remembered.

'Leading with ye head, ye goes right over the yellow line, and a millisecond before yer about to get decapitated by the oncoming train, you stopped and reared back, arching yer back 45-degrees, like some pisshead contortionist. I thought ye were goin' keel right over but jus' as suddenly you righted yer'self and stood straight up,' she recalled with astonishment.

What was she on about? After ... what was it, over a year, since we last spoke or saw each other?

'Ye walked in a completely straight line down the centre of the platform. Hammered and impervious to me and to the fact ye just cheated death, ye ambled right past where I stood with me mouth agape in wonder. I swear, Fred, it was like the 'and of God reached down, grabbed ya by the 'air on the back of yer 'ead and yanked ye back from Márbh.' She laughed with a nervous edge. 'Fuck the luck of the Irish, this jammie bastard's got somethin truly preternatural goin on. And I thought to meself, "Aye, he acts soft that one but by god, he's a survivor."'

After a hesitant snigger, I imparted one of my favourite lines. 'God watches over drunks and fools ...'

'Well, ye a double blessed cunt then,' she said. Her sardonic chuckle through the static, made me smile. 'But I might've been wrong after all, about the luck and shite,' Gertie returned to a more serious tone. 'I mean, jus' look at the state of ya, all pissed up an' banjaxed.'

'But you can't even see – '

'Fact be, don't go cursin' yerself,' she interrupted hurriedly. 'Ye didn't tip the bin ... ye probably nudged it a couple times, but ye didn't topple it. Now, I imagine you away with the ferries and off yer face somewhere, but ye need to get back. No hand of God ta yank ye this time, ye gotta save yourself, salvage what was lost and what was stolen ... there's a train a'comin ...'

'What do you mean, go back? Back where?' I pleaded for more information.

'Where they made a hames of us all, the feckin' Manky Peach,' she said patently.

'The Gaijin House? Are you there? Where are you calling from, Gertie?' A dial tone was the only answer I got as my flurry of queries trailed off in a whisper. I traced my finger around and down the black coiled cord one final time, then hung up the receiver.

Soft voices floated up from the headphones draped around my neck when I awoke back in the internet café cubicle. Grey ash and residue rings dotted the counter and keyboard. I rubbed my aching head, got up, and grabbed some ice and Coke from the fountain pop machine. A quick glance sideways at the reception area and the black landline sitting on the counter brought the memory of Gertie's call rushing back.

Both hungover and still drunk, in my ever deteriorating circumstances and unhinged mind, it was becoming more and more difficult to decipher dream from reality. Sick of questioning, I went to the front to find the girl who woke me for the call, but there was a young man at the desk. She might have gone off shift, or maybe was never there at all.

Beside the keyboard, I topped up my cup with what was left of the previous night's whisky. I sipped the highball, closed my eyes, and thought of Gertie.

I'd landed at Narita airport after a thirteen-hour flight where I'd done more drinking than sleeping. I was a tad tipsy taking my first unsteady steps on Japanese soil but found the 196 bus stop outside the arrivals area. I was, of course, dying for a cigarette and dragged my suitcases over to the smoking booth. The very Japanese contraption was an enclosed glass cube with suction fans on the roof, and clean silver ashtrays implanted throughout.

Two men in black suits carrying no more than briefcases smoked and spoke in their native tongue. I understood not a word. The foreign syllables wafted in my ear, bounced around my brain and then exited, confirming I had arrived in this exotic new land. It set anxious butterflies aflutter in my gut.

How'd I get here? was my next thought. The answer that came was simple really; *I'd applied, been hired and flown over by the recruiting company to teach ESL at a local junior high school.* I checked my facts, and they were solid. But actually being there, it felt somewhat surreal.

With three beers in a plastic bag for the ride, I returned to the post. The bus idled, so I put my larger suitcase underneath the carriage and made my way down the aisle, passing sparsely seated Japanese as I went.

She was the only white girl, sat three seats from the back row. Very white, of a bred-under-overcast-skies pale complexion and raven black hair, which was unkempt, shoulder-length and cut in no particular style. Unlike the young Japanese women I'd seen throughout the airport, who had taken every effort imaginable to touch up their appearance, this woman seemed to have made none. Nonetheless, she sat there cool and confident, reading a book and drinking a beer.

I pulled out my own book and beer, cracked both, and began indulging. It was inevitable that we would soon be speaking. What with us sticking out like two sore Caucasian thumbs. But more so because our actions mirrored each other too perfectly.

'I tried to read that once. Too difficult, so I gave up,' I said, glancing at her novel's cover.

'Aye, is for me too, I jus' keep givin' 'er a go. Got to accomplish somethin' in me life.' She forced a tired smile. 'What ye reading there?'

I showed her the cover.

'Aye, read that, Kerouac is a real misogynist cunt, and his mucker Cassidy is even worse.'

'Yeah, I'm re-reading it. I loved it the first time, but now a lot of it seems like meaningless ramblings, of a hopped-up hippy,' I offered in feeble defence of my book choice.

'Aye, but it speaks to us, especially you blokes, at a certain time of our lives. Most books don't stand up to the second or third read unless they're truly great. Or it takes at least that many reads to make 'eads or tails of it all.' She held up her copy of *Finnegan's Wake* as an exclamation point.

'I'm Fred.'

'Hiya, I'm Gertie.' We reached across the aisle of the moving bus and shook hands.

In the ensuing conversation, we discovered that we were off to work for the same company in the same small town, in what I thought were the outskirts of Tokyo. Turned out it was well beyond there.

'Yorii desu,' Gertie announced as we disembarked, weary after our respective flights and the two-hour bus ride shooting the shit the whole time.

The memory of our first meeting faded into the fabric of my cubicle walls. Almost three years ago ... *Fuck, has it been that long? Adrift here on this foreign soil.*

'Gertie', I typed into Google. It returned millions of unrelated results. After wading through dead brain cells of trial and error, I perfected my search and, on page 10, found a synopsis of an eBook self-published under Gertrude McCafferty. The story was not recent, the post made before she would have arrived in Japan. From what I could preview, it was well-written, young-adult fiction. A bit raw for the genre, but that may just have been how they rolled in Northern Ireland. Before Gertie had come to work in Japan, she'd worked at a sort of detention centre or halfway house for wayward girls; drug addicts, alkies, suicide cases and teen pregnancies who'd been kicked out by strict Catholic parents. The story was written in the narrative voice of a troubled girl and perhaps born out of her experience working there.

After reading the book sample, I remembered, near the end, Gertie was writing again. At first, I assumed it was related to her new job, but later revealed itself to be more of a pathological manifestation. Locked alone in her room for days on end, those tapping keys signalled the death rattle of our friendship.

One night, I decided to check in on her. The plan was to drink whisky, chain-smoke, and shoot the shit as had been our thing, though even before knocking I had an inkling it wasn't going to work out that way.

She answered my knock looking frayed and dishevelled. The dull light of the smoky room shone off her tangled and greasy black hair, which mustn't have been washed for days or even weeks. She'd fallen into a funk after losing yet another teaching job. A thick Northern Irish accent was a devalued currency in the Asia English teaching game. Her students had complained that they couldn't understand *Eigo Sensei*, so she was canned again.

'It's total fucking bullshit,' I'd said to sum up nicely the injustice of it. Gertie knew the score; in the end, no matter how well you taught or strong your work ethic, American English or upper-class British were what the customers wanted. We commiserated together, and Gertie perked up after she got a new gig writing online content for one of the big chain schools. Her resurgence in gumption proved short-lived, though.

Looking over my listless friend, I asked, 'How you been Gertie? How's the writing coming ... you working on a lesson?'

'Sorry yeah, I'm stuck in on me writin', can't be 'anging out tonight.' All the confidence had drained from her voice. It was mousey and evasive, so unlike the Gertie I'd gabbed with for hours straight on that long bus ride. There was no more taking the piss, schooling me on UK politics and punk rock, or arguing about literature. I missed it.

'I'll only stay a little,' I said, producing a bottle of whisky and pushing my way in. Her eyes darted from me to the door, to the window, like she was searching for an escape route from her own room.

The ashtray was overflowing with butts. A plate with brown, black crumbs gave evidence she was eating if only plain toast. There was a mug with a teabag sitting next to it on the floor. I tossed the bag and poured whisky. Rummaging through the mini-fridge under Gertie's unnerved gaze, I found an open can of Coke. I poured the flat soda into the mug and handed it to Gertie who flinched before reluctantly accepting.

Edging toward the small frosted window, I slid it open to air out the stuffy room, which stank of stale cigarette smoke. Then, I lit one myself and exhaled out the open window, instructively. Gertie remained standing and shifted nervously as I put on a relaxed air, hoping she'd settle and I could get some straight answers about what was going on with her.

White rectangles were stamped on the yellowing walls. 'You took down the posters. Planning on moving out?'

'Aye, thinking about it,' Gertie answered, emotionless and lost gazing into her discoloured wall.

Where I'd posted up by the window, her computer screen was visible on the small desk each guesthouse room came furnished with. I could see a single chunk of unbroken text taking up the whole page and discerned it wasn't one of her lessons. I tried to read some of what was written on the sly, as we uncomfortably occupied the small Gaijin House room ... *puss oozing walls shrieking sinister screams, they moan, they curse. Lucifer's excrement, placenta and piss spray forth ... wash over me ...*

Not sly enough, I'd peered too long. Gertie gripped and kneaded the corner of her bedspread. 'Um, I ... I got shit to do. Ye gotta feck off now, Fred.' They were familiar words, spoken in an unfamiliar deadpan tone.

'Is this your lesson?' It was my last play. I needed to gather more evidence of what was going on in her head before she kicked me out. 'Let me have a look. I'll give some useless feedback, eh.' I added a phoney laugh in an attempt to sell the ruse.

I reached over to the computer and began scrolling, pages upon pages, block and blocks of unbroken text. I had little time to take in much, but the snippets that penetrated pelted concern like dark hail pellets. *Maimed, mutilated, through bleeding ice picked eyes ... The ceiling drips battery acid, blackened burning holes in alabaster breasts ... flesh rips from flesh, blood pours ... amputated cunts, curse their cancerous walls ... shit ... fuck ... murder ... death.*

Gertie lunged across the room, slamming shut her laptop before I could absorb any more twisted, tourette's twitching prose.

'Get out!' she screamed. 'Is, you! Ye jus stood by and let it all 'appen!'

'Gertie, what's going on, I just want to help ya. What's all this shit? You're not alright, just let me ...'

'GET OUT! GET OUT!' She cowered in the corner with her laptop cradled in her arms like it were a child some authoritarian regime was trying to rip from her bosom. I backed out of the room with my bottle of whisky and pint of dejection.

Walking across the hall and two doors down to my own small room, the little voice in my head that for some weeks had been whispering 'flee' surged to a scream. I grabbed my suitcase, packed my shit and spilled out the door.

Bag in one hand, bottle of whisky in the other; I'd never been one for necking spirits straight from the bottle, but it came on naturally and burned poetically. Outside the exit of the Big Peach

Guesthouse in the zero hour, I removed the inverted bottle and matching tears streamed down each cheek.

That was the last I saw or heard from Gertie until the inexplicable phone call arrived at four twenty-five earlier that morning. I scoured the World Wide Web, but like a walk in the season's first snowfall, she'd left no footprints.

4// Amorous Amphitheatre Apparition

After eight hours of drinking, dreaming and reminiscing in an internet café, I wandered home on uneven sidewalks, under tangled nests of telephone wire and past boxy little Kei cars going elsewhere. At the foot of my door waited a store-bought *bento* box, a note slipped under the elastic band which held its plastic lid to the base.

The *bento* had tempura, hamburger steak, seaweed salad and a side of rice with an *umeboshi*, sour plum, on top. The note attached read:

> Dear Mr Buchanan,
> We hope you are well. Please eat and take care of yourself.
> Contact us for your release from the school and anything
> we can do to help you get home safe.
> Dr Ito
> Tomodachi English School

I sniffed the food, then bit off the end of a tempura shrimp. I put it down and pushed the bento away, feeling lashed by kindness, racked by guilt and seized by fear, and though I was too sick to eat, my paranoia was dining out heartily.

I sighed, threw the note on top of the uneaten bento and lay back on my futon. Surely, the next note at my doorstep would be an eviction notice. The hamster wheel of my mind was spinning full throttle; the furry little fucker running like he'd shot a speedball as I considered my mounting problems.

I'd need money to escape the island but had little to none. *Where am I to go?* The note from the school indicated they would steer me home and by that they meant Canada, I assumed. *Well, that is probably the smart play, but I can't go back there – not in defeat.* Bad symmetry, since that's how I'd left.

After graduation I bummed around my province for year or two; got a DUI, was hired and fired by a couple of ESL schools, and smoked a ton of weed. I'd dated a pothead then a pillhead, and started a poem and short story or two, all of which were more uninspired and uninspiring then the last. As I peeked for purpose or my million-dollar idea at the bottom of the next bottle or bong bowl, the worried voices of friends and loved ones seeped through. It was concern, but I heard only disappointment. I was loved and cared for, and therein lay the problem. The pressure of expectations from others, no matter how minimal, has always scared the shit out of me. In the end, I ran as far away as possible, 'to find myself' as they say. Besides, what else was I going to do with a Comparative Lit degree?

The hamster wheel slowed, thoughts trailed off, and I stared into the cream-coloured ceiling until I was cognitively whisked away.

A shift in perspective lands me on the floor of the bare white room. My forearms and hands are all I can see of my form. They reach down and begin to gather up the unspooled red yarn, untangling knots and crosses, wrapping it back into a ball until all that's left is a single strand leading into ripples of stygian blackness. Mesmerised, I gather and wind, slowly, carefully as the line gets shorter and shorter, the clandestine destination beyond the darkness closer and closer.

Pausing at the entryway, I can hear nothing beyond the obsidian wall. The gathered ball in my hand carries surprising heft.

My other hand grips the visible end of red thread, suspended in the air somewhere between taut and slack, it stretches for half a foot before penetrating the dark void.

I reach beyond the frame through the darkness. A strong wind blows at my forearm. Against the gathering gusts, I fish around, finally grabbing what feels to be the frayed tip, at the end of the line. With one bounding step, I've reached the other side.

The noise strikes first; horns and traffic, voices belting out through loudspeakers and the rustle of thousands of bodies in movement below.

As my eyes adjust to the drastic change in scenery, I find myself a hundred meters up with a bird's eye view looking down a stretch of Yasukuni Boulevard.

Through the caliginous portal I've arrived, suspended with a dangling piece of red yarn in hand, afloat above it all – aglow in the permanent dawn.

In terrified anticipation of the imminent hundred-foot fall to the pavement below, I found myself instead bolting upright on a soiled futon. I lift my hands. Not a thread nor skein they held.

My eyes closed tight in attempt to recapture the prescient point, high above the street, after where it underpasses the Seibu tracks – a spot my mind had coined 'the place of permanent dawn'. A chasm of *izakaya*s, bars, karaoke palaces and department stores form a collection of neon signage pulsating so brightly it affects a sense of dawn in even the deepest midnight hour. Emerging upon this spot during many a sleepy train ride, I'd have to check myself to ensure I hadn't misplaced yet another evening in a Celinesque attempt to 'Journey to the End of the Night'.

The vision had served its purpose and decreed my destination. It was a hasty decision, made like a cornered beast looking for any direction in which to flee. Yet it was all I had.

I surveyed the room. My apartment was dry, so I took to the streets.

I assumed my usual afternoon aimless meander, yet on that day, my ambling thoughts had an oblique destination. Through my headphones, a rapper spoke of his money problems. *True dat*, I thought. Contemplating financial woes, I rounded a corner, and there he was: my furry nemesis, the flea-bitten tom, Soseki's stray soul, the fucking cat.

This time, we forgo the pretence, no sizing each other up or staring down. We got stuck right in.

'Well, well, look at who t' fuck is back in me ginnel, tha daft cunt!'

'This time, you're the one who's leaving, you homeless, piece of shit.' I dropped the exercise in telepathic communication and babbled aloud at the cat.

'Ahaha, 'at's rich comin' from the likes a tha. 'Omeless! I may be, but ah manage jus' fine with the cards stacked against me. I got a little somethin' calt street smarts,' spat the cocky cockney cunt. 'You on t' other 'and … jus look't state of ya. Homeless if tha ain't already, tha will soon be, lad.'

I wasn't hurt, per se, by his mangy words. Even so, his mere presence and manufactured speech, scratched away at any dignity which remained to be exposed.

'We'll see who's going down hard, asshole.' I ran toward him with a raised right hand. The cat held his ground. Without much of a premeditated plan, I swung an open hand – what a Jersey pimp might call his 'bitch slap'.

Just as I unleashed the slap, he sprang and swiped too. I felt the tear of flesh down my right cheek as his claws made contact.

A southpaw, eh, I noted through the sting.

Following through on my own swing, taking twice as long to make contact as his, I finally caught the little bastard behind the ear and down its neck. Knocked sideways, he spun around 180 degrees and landed on his feet, as they do.

For good measure, I splashed booze from my can at the tom.

A few drops landed on his back and face. The rest was lost to the pavement. Still, it carried more effect than my laboured slap. He scurried off a few feet then turned and stared. Raising a shoulder to touch my cheek, three red parallel lines stained the fabric.

I lifted the can to take a drink, and my arm convulsed with adrenaline. The Chu-hi splashed over the edges and onto my knuckles. I got the opening to my mouth and drank heartily.

'You little shit, I win!' I declared.

'T'ell yeh do, y' cunt,' he answered.

'Call it a draw,' I conceded.

'Call it whatever t' 'ell tha like. Tha be fuckin off'n no time, and ahm back on my steps.' He slinked a semi-circle to face me square. 'Yet, I si thi 'round … ye daft cunt.' He finished with a Cheshire grin.

The tom was right. The walls came crashing down, and I could see myself as I must've looked to outside observers; drinking, smoking, pacing, and trading barbs with a stray cat. I felt a trickle of blood slide down my face. I spat in the feline's direction, walked toward the convenience store and straight into the bathroom. The scrapes were two inches long, red around where the skin had broken and bleeding. I took a handful of toilet paper off the roll and dabbed the cuts. One hand gripping my can and the other pressing tissue to my face, I continued to walk the neighbourhood.

After a block or so, I took the blood-blotched wad and put it in my back pocket, so I'd have a free hand to light a smoke. I pulled a Marlboro out of the pack and spun the lighter's spark-wheel. Smoke got in my eyes. I blinked repeatedly until they watered and cleared.

The first object that came into view after my eyes focused was a familiar statue halfway down the street. It was off the sidewalk on the edge of a property that accommodated a rundown ironwork studio. I'd seen it before though only took a passing notice. Something about it on that afternoon told me to give it a good once-over. I approached with heightened interest and looked at the brass bull, head down and pushing forward with its horns aimed at an imaginary foe.

The artefact led me toward the most curious relic I'd come across in deference to these Okinawan bullfights. I hoped it would prove a fitting atmosphere for which to hash out a forming, inchoate plan.

At first glance, Agena Park looked much like any other rusted playground and patch of grass coupled to constitute a sorry excuse for a city park. But if you penetrated the exterior, past the parking lot, over the grassy field and through the cluster of trees behind, you were rewarded with casting your eyes on a tucked-away gem of Okinawan history and culture.

I emerged from a small path and looked down upon a defunct and ancient bullring. Grass grew in patches on the dirt floor of the circular ring while metal corral fencing marked the perimeter of the fighting area. Tiered seating went up in rows; each flat circular patch of green larger in circumference than the one below, forming an impressive amphitheatre. Low walls of carefully stacked stones separated each successive grassy tier. The parakeet blades were long and overgrown as if the archaic stadium had not held an audience in many decades, though an odour of manure in the air suggested there was a stable of bulls nearby, if not to compete than to train within the old ring.

Ruins of a 14th-century Ryukyuan fortress created a most spectacular backdrop to the old ring. Boulder piled upon boulder crawled up the hillside, forming a massive crumbling wall. Shrubs sprouted out of the crannies between rocks, and a cluster of trees grew on top like a foliage toupee. Studying it, I couldn't quite imagine the structure of the castle proper from what had survived.

Though, I was able to envision something clearly.

On the second rung, she was bent over, arms extended, supporting herself against a ploughing body behind. Small delicate hands gripped grass beyond the rock wall, her head thrown back with silent screams written across her face. Both bodies were stark naked with no shed clothing in sight, as if they just existed that way – the first or last people on earth.

Not taking my attention off the action below, I reached under my waistbands and felt for the forming erection. It'd been a flaccid few weeks since I'd had one of those to play with. It heartened me to see a lustful imagination could still fuel the blood of excitement flowing. A brisk scan to ensure there was nobody in sight, I undid the top button of my jeans and unzipped.

In the unfolding spectacle below, I tugged back on the vision's shimmering, shoulder-length black hair. With her chin raised, in profile, I recognized the carnally panting face. Akiko, her svelte form arched like a bowing courtesan to graciously receive each lance.

I threw my chest upon her back with a final thrust and burrowed my face against her neck, whispered a heavy exhale in her ear through drapes of fallen hair, and finished. Blades of grass ripped from the turfed seat supporting our eroticism poked through the tiny fingers of Akiko's clenched climaxed fist. They floated soft and lush to earth in the aftermath of our release.

In the masturbatory matinée concluding below, I came inside Akiko. But in the reality recommencing above, I'd cum in my boxer shorts. Taking the blood-spattered tissue from my back pocket, I wiped away liquidy jizz.

The vision of entwined lovers evaporated, I was left alone in soggy shorts, observing from the uppermost region of the amphitheatre seats, the figure of Akiko evanesced. As was often the case after blowing one's masturbatory load, I felt empty and lonesome. I lay back on the grass, lit a smoke and thought back.

The scene played out in my fantasy below, partially borrowed from memory, was reminiscent of my first time with Akiko. In the open air, bent against the trunk of a Japanese elm, I'd entered her – my first tryst, first frolic, first fuck in the land of the rising sun.

I'd met Akiko sometime after Gertie and I disembarked from

our fateful Narita airport bus and began working as assistant language teachers in our respective schools. Being an ALT was about the fucking easiest job on earth, but it was also wholly unfulfilling. Essentially, I was little more than a glorified tape recorder.

The job was a joke, and while the Japanese countryside had its charms, it didn't offer the anonymity and chaos I craved. After work, I'd stroll down the gravel shoulder of a two-lane road back to the house shared with Gertie and three Americans. The Americans would come home, cook hamburger helper dinners, and go to bed early so as to be fresh for their next day's lessons. Gertie and I would raid the local convenience store of technicolour canned cocktails, local beers and cheap whisky. We'd return to the house and stay up late listening to the Stone Roses and Stiff Little Fingers while we shared about past relationships, told old war stories, and pontificated on what it meant to be denizens of this mad realm.

When one of our flatmates would sneer and say, 'I see we're starting the party again.'

We'd raise our cans, force smiles and exclaim, 'You know it. Wanna join?'

Gertie wrote it off as them being American. It was the end of the Bush-era, and she was rife with a bit of anti-Americanism herself. Whereas, I spied and castigated through my Holden Caulfield lens the airs they donned. At times, Gertie didn't mind Caroline, the other girl. But I thought she was the worst of the lot; a mousy, midwestern Christian, a worrywart and jumbling ball of judgment and nerves.

It was Caroline who spoke up first for the American delegation. 'We are trying to do our best here. We'd like a little more civility and respect in the house. You can drink on the weekends if you must, but on the weeknights, we think it best we all concentrate on our profession.' She folded pipe-cleaner arms and pursed her thin lips.

First off, I thought referring to the job of assistant language teacher as a profession was rich and totally confirmed how out of touch this chick was. I was all set to tell her off when Gertie said, 'Aye, we can oblige. Nay more bevvies on weeknights.'

I assumed she was placating Caroline to get them off our backs, then we'd turn around and continue our perpetual piss up. But Gertie's word had more honour than mine, and when she turned to me after and said, 'Ach, is for the best,' I could see she'd made a genuine promise.

After that, when the ennui of Yorii living became too much for me, a 45-minute train ride on the Tobu-Toju line deposited me in Kawagoe. With a Starbucks, department store, and bars that had clientele under the age of sixty, it was a bustling metropolis in comparison.

On a well-manicured lawn just off the main shopping promenade, I carried a cold Asahi. Out of the corner of my eye, I picked out a slim, scantily clad Asian girl with heavy make-up and dyed blonde hair. I posted up next to her and cracked my drink. '*Atsui desu, ne.*' It wasn't – it was a comfortably cool spring day.

She giggled and continued talking to her friend while they glanced furtively in my direction. I'd struck out, I figured. Oh well, as Gretzky once said, you miss ninety-nine percent of the shots you never take. I fished a cigarette out my pack in an attempt to look undaunted. While I searched my pocket for a lighter, the friend of the blonde walked over and handed me hers.

'*Arigato*, umm, *onamae wa nan desu ka*?' I said like a dyslexic first grader reading Moby Dick, and that about exhausted my command of the Japanese language at the time.

'I'm Akiko, and this is Naoko,' said the understated friend. A long smile, stretched wide across her face, revealing a straight row of shiny white teeth in a slight overbite. Crescent moon dimples formed on each cheek as she tucked shoulder-length hair behind a long, elegantly formed ear. Tomboyish and enticingly elfin, her breasts hid as small round mounds beneath a buttercup-coloured lace halter top while taut brown thighs protruded from a pair of daisy dukes.

Akiko extracted a dart of her own from the box and put it to her mouth. She lightly chewed on the filter, took the cigarette out of her mouth, and then inserted it back in between her lips before tilting her head and lighting. With that, I lost all interest in the friend and turned my attention and intentions to her – beauty shaded with a mauve pastel.

Three days later, we met in the same Kawagoe park and walked to one of the cell phone providers where she helped me buy my first *keitai,* a simple au flip phone. Our phones flipped open, we lined up infrared ports on the back, pressed the right buttons, and swapped numbers in an act Akiko called *sekigaisen.* 'Pretty cool,' I said and hoped further sensory exchange was in store as the night wore on.

As we strolled down the promenade, Akiko's phone buzzed and she answered. '*Moshi moshi*!' I imitated the informal Japanese phone greeting in the same high, feminine voice I'd often overheard. My childish humour extracted a big toothy smile. A few blocks on, we entered a restaurant she selected.

'*Sumimasen,*' Akiko threw her arm in the air and screamed through the *izakaya* to grab our waiter's attention.

Shit, how very un-Japanese, I thought of the uncharacteristically abrasive act. Though I couldn't have been more wrong. While a strict politeness protocol governed most social interactions, ordering in an *izakaya* was a rare albatross, where the desire to enjoy food and drink was permitted to be expressed with unbridled exuberance. I would come to appreciate and even cherish this beautiful glitch in the system.

Her small frame taken into consideration, Akiko could put the beers back pretty good. She smoked about half as much as me, which was still a lot, and continually performed the bijou ritual of chewing on the filter and teasing her lips with the cigarette before lighting. It became even more endearing, almost sensual, each time – though I couldn't proffer why.

Akiko took care of the ordering and delectable little dishes began arriving on a rolling basis, placed in the middle of the table tapas-style.

I was devouring a thin fish when Akiko inquired, 'Do you like the Unagi?'

'Yeah, it is fucking delicious,' I said of the freshwater eel, charcoal-broiled and brushed with a sweetened soy sauce.

'Is Kawagoe's local speciality dish. For man, makes strong,' she informed me, with a mischievous smile.

'Oh, yeah?' I caught her meaning and liked what I heard. 'I'm pretty strong as is, but I'll take help wherever I can get it,' I said with a wink. I tended to wink a lot, especially on dates. Even more so on first dates. I think I picked it up from my father. He used to wink when he outwardly told an inside joke, but his timing was better. I guess I thought it was charming, yet I tended to overdo it, and then it looked more like a nervous tick than a subtle flirtation.

'Why did you want to come to Japan, and why choose Yorii?'

'I don't really know why I came here.' I really didn't. I mean, I wasn't a Japanophile like many foreigners. I wasn't obsessed with manga, J-pop or other popular elements of Japanese culture and they hadn't grown on me since. Great writers, but I hadn't discovered that yet.

'You know, I guess I wanted to put an ocean between myself and everything I knew or was.' It was the first time I'd explored the question and was answering more for myself than the person who asked.

'Like, nothing happened that forced me over here, nor was I pursuing anything.' I straightened on my chair and gripped the table's edge with a free hand as if to brace myself against the admissions to come. 'I kinda never felt like I belonged anywhere; not in my family, not amongst shifting groups of friends, not on teams joined or jobs worked. Others didn't sense it, I'm pretty sure of that. I was great at playing the part; could blend in and assume an appearance of confidence and belonging no matter the group.'

I returned a cigarette to my lips and inhaled introspectively. With a windy whistle, I exhaled, contributing to the *izakaya*'s sinewy blue haze, and continued my rambling answer. 'Then I figured, if I were always going to feel out of place, even where I was most adept and suited to belong, then why not push it to the extreme? Move to a completely foreign land, that way when I felt the old discomfort and displacement, there was no mystery or confusion as to why. I would be a stranger in a strange land ... and so feeling strange would finally make sense.'

I'd been staring into the amber circle in my mug during the soliloquy. When I looked up, I expected to see a bored or confused look on my companion's face, but Akiko was looking right into my eyes, her soft features rocking in a compassionate, knowing nod.

Popping *edamame* out of its mushy, warm shell and into my mouth, I asked about her life; Kawagoe, school and hobbies. When we landed on her family, Akiko seemed comfortable enough talking about what sounded like an uncomfortable situation. She lived with her dad, ailing grandparents and had been largely responsible for raising her two younger siblings. Now that she was in college, the boy middle school-aged and sister in high school, they could mostly look after themselves. Money was usually tight, with her dad in and out of work as a truck driver, on the road a lot and when he wasn't, he enjoyed placing a bet or spinning the pachinko wheel.

'What happened to your mom?' I asked, hoping I wasn't prying.

'She moved to the mountains about seven years ago.' Her eyes trailed away from me and settled at no specific spot over my shoulder. I sensed not to press on, but after a drink of beer and lighting a smoke she offered up more. 'She moved there after having emotional problems. I think is called in English, *eto* ... nervous breakdown?'

With my mouthful of beer, I tipped my glass in her direction to signal she'd been correct with the phrase.

'Before her troubles, she was a good mother,' Akiko stated with conviction. 'When I was young, she would prepare my lunch and make hearts or smiley faces on the rice using seaweed and ham and even *hana ninjin*, which is cutting the carrot so it looks like a flower. It is kind of tradition in Japan, so when you open up your *bento* at school, you're reminded how much your mother cares. Also is like competition. It sounds silly, but the son or daughter with the most extravagant design of their lunch box must be loved the most.' She blushed and wore a reminiscent smile. 'After my mom left, I tried to do for my brother and sister, only on special occasion like sports day and festival time. It takes a lot of time and effort, so I appreciate even more, she do every day for me.'

'That's really cool,' I said. It didn't accurately convey how impressed I was with her unselfishness. I left it at that, anyhow.

'When I start middle school at twelve, my mom begin to change. I think, maybe it started before, but for us she hide it. How long, I don't know? Then she couldn't hide it anymore … her energy ran out.' It was Akiko's turn to stare transfixed into her glass, eyes swimming on the ale's surface.

'She would be crying in the morning when she made our breakfast and not change out of her nightgown all day. My dad, he didn't know how to handle. At first he tried to help her, but not for long, then the yelling start. Japanese walls are paper thin.'

The woeful little snippets of her crumbling home pricked at my unsentimental sensibilities. It was like emotional acupuncture from which I was moved to feel a deep empathy. On the verge of betraying my trained cool exterior, I attempted to hand her an out. 'It's okay, I get it … I'm really sorry she up and left you guys.'

'She didn't really leave us and move to the mountains,' Akiko corrected. 'The mountains were where the sanatorium was. The breakdown got worse, her depression led to taking many medications, but none worked, they only made her worse. She would spend whole days in bed.'

'During October, when the days were getting shorter, she was caught in three attempted suicides,' Akiko stated matter of fact.

'Shit,' I blurted, but meant it sincerely.

'The first, she was acting erratic at Kawagoe-eki. A woman in sandals and nightgown pacing the platform, it raised suspicion. The station security led her off the platform and into a local police stand. She never said she intended to jump, but also wouldn't say she didn't. Two weeks later, we were called again, she'd been pulled out of the Arakawa river. I went with my dad to the station. We found her dripping wet and shivering with a blanket wrapped around her frail shoulders. What struck me was the blank look on her face. There wasn't sadness, fear, or even regret – it was totally empty.'

'*Beer-ru, futatsu*.' Akiko ordered two more from a passing waiter.

And I thought, *Good call*!

'Finally, her creativity gave out. What I mean is; she wanted to do what she was going to do – the suicide – away from our home … so none of us might find her. But that energy ran out. Returning from school one afternoon, my youngest brother discovered her unconscious on the bathroom floor. Alcohol and pills.'

It was ill-timed, but I took a hard swallow of the freshly delivered beer.

Akiko didn't seem bothered and went on, 'They pumped her stomach and kept her overnight in the hospital. I visited with my dad. He said if we bring her home, she will keep trying, and the next time may be successful. He found the mental institution in the mountains and would drive her up the next day. I wanted to go up to Gunma-ken with him, but he said I have to stay and look after my brother and sister who were still kids then.'

She'd been telling her story somewhat detached but here her demeanour changed. Hazel eyes of juniper and almond drifted to the surface of the *izakaya* tabletop and her voice lowered. 'Lying in that hospital bed, a barren branch tapping against the windowpane in a late autumn wind, her hair frazzled from the friction of the bathroom floor and hospital bed pillow, all the colour and all the endurance for life drained from her face ...' She paused, her eyes downcast and wandering, as if painting the memory on the stained wood surface.

Akiko cleared her throat, 'That's the last clear image I have of my Mother.'

'And you never saw her again?' I asked.

Almost startled, she looked up and said, 'I asked to visit her once. I was told they had to get approval from the patient. My request was denied. I don't blame her, maybe she did it for me, or maybe she was doing it for her. After that, I never requested again. She might still be up there in the mountains. Maybe she got better and was released. I don't know, but she never came home.'

Perhaps I was to take the story as a warning – to treat her heart with kid gloves. Perhaps she struggled through and told it to me in entirety for just that reason. Unfortunately, the stoic face she bore at the end left me feeling she was more resilient than she actually was.

I topped up my drink, then hers. I told her how I thought it was amazing she balanced looking after her siblings, college and a part-time job. A demure smile hid behind her waiting cigarette. What I didn't voice was how petty I now felt, talking of my discomfort and need to escape. Here was this young woman facing her problems head on and shouldering the burden of fate's shitty hand. All I ever knew was to cut and run.

We drank a couple more beers and steered the conversation to greener pastures. From there on, I did most of the talking. Every once in a while she'd do the thing where she brushed back strands of hair to expose a listening ear. Her smile even brighter, in the pain it washed away.

'*Okaikei onegaishimasu.*' I yelled into the air and beamed at my newfound fluency. The cheque arrived and I paid up for our feast.

Her face was flushed from the booze and heat of the *izakaya*.

As we walked in a spring breeze and talked freely, the redness subsided. We held hands, our arms swung with a steady ease, and for a fleeting moment there was a brazen purity about us.

We cut through a park. The ground was hard-packed dirt with a low iron fence around the perimeter and a couple of leafy ginkgo trees. Akiko pointed at an apartment building that bordered the lot and said that she lived there. It seemed this was where we would part ways. I leaned in and kissed her. She reciprocated, parting her lips and tilting her head. We were both good and sauced, so had our tongues working and hands ferociously groping body parts in no time.

I became hard and pushed the bulge up into her denimed crotch. She took the bait, reached down and undid my belt. Her hand was soft and cool on my cock. Down her abdomen and beneath her waistline I roamed, fleecy black hairs brushed against the buried knuckles of my exploring hand.

Bow-legged against denim handcuffs she received me. A chill evening air on my bare ass parlayed off her warm envelope while Akiko pawed at the tree bark of a supportive trunk. The exhilaration of getting caught in that public display of ultimate affection overtook me quite suddenly, and my arousal rose to a rapid crescendo. I let out a long breath and threw my head back, looking skyward to the leafy canopy above and scattered stars beyond.

As I returned my attention to feast my gaze upon the exquisite contours of Akiko's back, a figure at a window in the bordering apartment building stole my focus. An elderly man in boxer shorts was observing our act; mouth agape and drooling in addled absorption. The little self-control I'd been clenching, slipped from my grasp with the old man's demented stare. I pulled out, spurting juices of passion on the small of her back.

In a silence of peaceful accord with the night, we pulled up our jeans and undergarments, buttoned, zipped, adjusted and shared a gentle kiss of overlapping lips. I whispered a goodbye that reverberated in her twinkling eyes.

I stopped into a convenience store for my requisite two beers and missed the final train heading toward Yorii by ten minutes. Sated, I drank in front of the station, replaying our semi-exhibitionist sex on the insides of my eyelids like a Times Square peep show. Then, with no other choice, I lay back to pass out on a slab of pavement outside the shuttered station gates.

Laying on my concrete bed, looking up at the infinite space above, I felt like Magellan, though couldn't say why. Spent and buzzed in a foreign land, it just came and seemed right enough. I counted stars, and though none fell, before I lost consciousness, wished to retain the night upon awakening.

Sometimes we'd meet in Kawagoe, and others, she'd train out to the house in Yorii. We'd punch and kick holes in the rice-paper frames of my sliding *engawa* door. Our smashy game of fornicating tic-tac-toe ending with spilt cum on tatami floor. Afterwards, laying on my futon in embrace, the superfluous glare from a rural pachinko cathedral shone over the highway, reached across the communal garden and through the slightly ajar sliding door – cracked to let in the fresh night air and out the odour of our sweating bodies and post-coital cigarette smoke – finally, illuminating Akiko's face in a deep blue, rendering it wistfully beautiful.

'She's a good lass, Fred. Treat this one right, will ya,' Gertie warned in parental tones after her and Akiko had gotten to know each other and gotten to like each other. They'd bonded fast over alternately laughing and commiserating over dealing with my drunken antics.

'Yeah, yeah, I will,' I replied like a spoiled child with no intention to follow through on his hollow promise. I'd oblige, as long as circumstances, or more rightly constraints of countryside living persisted.

'Nay enough potency in the ether for me here, nay more.' Gertie confessed to me one evening as we sipped Cocktail Partners outside the local Lawson and watched the sky crimson at dusk. 'Found a wee *gaijin* house in Higashi Koseki, found a job and the like, yeah. Lots of free rooms. Ye should consider moving down with me, Fred.'

I took a sip of my Cassis Orange. 'That's cool.'

It was two weeks later, as the dogs howled forlorn cries of yearning throughout the Saitama countryside, I arrived at Obusuma station and boarded the Tobu-Tojo line for one last long ride. Straight through Kawagoe the tracks carried me, and onwards to the other end of the line; the abounding station of Ikebukuro. Then it was on to my new abode, the Big Peach Guest House.

I stubbed my smoke out on the ground beside me and stood in air subtly tinged of sex and bullshit. I took a last look at the ancient amphitheatre, shook off the plethora of aroused memory, and made my way up a rudimentary path. A trickle of semen dripped down my inner thigh as I stepped up the stony staircase, remnants of the old castle.

Arriving atop the inner bailey, I looked down and imagined the men and women of the old Ryokan Kingdom in *yukatas*, colourful *kimonos*, and *geta* clomping up and down the steps of the amphitheatre far below.

Houses, low lying apartment blocks, schoolhouses and baseball diamonds scattered the Uruma landscape to the southeast. To the west, thirty or so simple, white family-unit housing blocks of Camp McToureous were placed orderly on a large patch of Okinawan soil. The dichotomy between this relic of a fallen kingdom neighbouring the barracks of those modern invaders had an ironic taint. I touched below my right eye where the claw marks began and thought of the old man in the park from the previous afternoon, his vengeful mission and eye for an eye philosophy. All of a sudden, everything made just a little more sense.

A half-hour later, I wandered down the path and out of the grounds having formalized my flimsy plan.

5// The Sun Moreover Ascends

A collection of items to sell were piled in the corner, the rest of my apartment empty save for a backpack, futon and pillow, which I lay upon to rest my head. In no time, I was asleep.

A hospital gurney wheels down an antiseptic hall. Tube lighting flickers and flashes past and voices babbling in foreign tongue criss-cross above me. On my back, I'm rushed through the corridors as if it's an emergency, yet I feel no pain. Can you feel pain in a dream?

A right turn and I'm wheeled into a dark room and abandoned in silent solitude. The gurney has transformed and I lie on a low cot. Grabbing hold of the metal frame, I drag myself up, swing my feet onto the floor.

The linoleum is dark blue with white stars of various size. In places, patchy black cigarette burns bore through the linoleum like astronomic sinkholes. A television sits atop a mini-fridge in the corner of the room. It flashes on and static plays before a face appears. A gurgling command is voiced in Japanese with an authoritative tone. I open a door and step into a hallway, silencing the TV head's low hypnotic drone.

The hall's frosted windows have lower halves painted with designs of low-lying treed hills. Between each window is a large painting of indigenous mythical beasts. A green amphibious demon emerges from a river, the Kappa's viridescent, muscular human torso and tortoise-shelled back drips circles of cyan watercolour.

Then a hairy humanoid with a simian face stands on its single leg, a tail hangs below the knee and a single wide and wild eye stares out.

A deep inhale – the musky odour carries an opaque sense of recognition of the place, which does nothing to quiet my trepidation. The sinister atmosphere grows heavier with every step. The light flickers on and off, and masked, hidden figures lurk behind the jungle growth on the painted window panes.

I pass each room's red door and lean in to hear sounds of sexual congress multiplying from within. The screams grow and shift from passion to pain and terror as if the act has turned violent and victimizing. As I pass more doors, there is no need to lean in to hear the cries of rape and torture emanate from inside. They permeate the once silent hallway.

I quicken my pace. The painted creatures' eyes follow as I pass and a green scaly arm of the Kappa and single hairy appendage of the simian beast reach from their frames, grabbing at my hospital gown. The linoleum's white stars morph into shards of glass on the night sky floor. I'm forced to pick my way through the perilous path.

I stop in front of a door which looms larger than the rest and square my shoulders to it, the hallway fallen silent and still once more. At eye level, gold numbering is painted over the red base – room number fourteen. I reach down to turn the handle. It's hot. I don't feel the heat but smell sizzling flesh. My hand retracts. I reach forth to try again, when something suddenly seizes me from behind and I'm yanked with violent strength off my feet and away.

My eyes shot open. The air-conditioner blared, but I could feel the futon dampen with sweat under my back. I threw off the blanket, rolled onto my side and began to shiver.

The street outside was vacant of living souls as if the whole town had died in some unseen apocalypse. I imagined myself as the last waking survivor able to roam free of past and consequence.

Bare white walls and a white floor, the room was devoid of

furnishing and decor other than a soiled futon, single sheet and scattered cans. Grey metal slats stretched across the windows. A streetlamp shone through and cast a play of light and shadow to effect a tangerine, black-barred square on the middle of the floor. It struck me; *this place looks like an asylum*. I was unsure if it looked that way because I felt like I was losing my mind, or I felt like I was losing my mind because it looked that way.

I stood and paced the floor like a caged hyena. After the demoralising incident with the cat earlier, I'd vowed to put the plug in the jug, get it together for whatever came next. Fifteen hours on and my heart beat with rapid irregularity, my skin crawled with sharp-toothed fleas, and my mind short-circuited, scurried with grim imagery projected somewhere between nightmare, hallucination and memory.

Wildly scanning the room, my eyes landed on a half-full whisky bottle, stoically standing as the sole surviving soldier in the centre of a recyclables battlefield. *Incarcerator and emancipator*, it brought me back, reminding I wasn't actually locked in a mental ward cell.

I ceased traipsing in my troglodyte existence and sat at the foot of my bed. Ash dotted the space between cans and along the futon's edge. *I'm fucked*, I thought, knowing I couldn't not drink.

I free poured the whisky and topped it up with Coke, a generous half and half. It was still dark outside, and the dawn seemed a little ways off, as it was not yet darkest. Cross-legged on the futon, I tried to recapture details of the lucid dream, to plough deeper into the subconscious symbols and grasp the implications. I closed my eyes tight and received only jumbled scraps of black, brown burns on an evening sky, and a faded number 14 scrawled in flakes of gold on an ominous red door.

When I opened my eyes again, morning had broken. The melancholy mood of the previous night evaporated with the rising sun. Struck by rays of the Okinawa sunshine, I left my apartment with a surfboard under one arm and guitar in the other. The items artefacts of annulled aspirations, negligent tools of misguided character renovations. The vessel, rudderless and dilapidated, frequently stalling to re-adjust the load whilst he juggled a lit cigarette and Chu-hi can in either hand.

A long-dormant optimism awakened at the prospect of exodus and I was feeling remarkably buoyant as I arrived with my first load at the local recycle shop.

Back in my flat, the futon and a few scattered cans were the only signs left of habitation. I counted my bottom line. Twenty-two thousand nine hundred and fifty collected from my ambling bazaar, coupled with the withdrawal of every last yen from my account, gave me over fifty thousand yen – about five-hundred bucks.

A few Chu-his took me through my last night on the island. I awoke with the dawn, tossed cans weighed down with soggy cigarette butts into a plastic bag, set an empty glass on the counter next to the apartment key, threw my pack on my back and left, not exactly like a thief in the night, but pretty damn close.

It was about a forty-five-minute walk to the Ishikawa Dome where the bullfights were held. I ambled in that general direction and arrived at the stadium two hours early.

In a Hemingway state of mind, the bullfights of course, I wanted to find an outdoor cafe and order absinthe without sugar in a dripping glass or knock back a couple fine à l'eau. There were no outdoor cafes in Okinawa serving booze in the mid-morn, so I made do with a less literary whisky and Coke on the kerb outside a Sunkus *conbini*.

As noon approached, I paid 2000 yen and entered the stadium. Cement bleachers went all the way around a circular reddish-brown ring, a mixture of sand and clay. The seating scaled upward to an impressive dome-shaped ceiling. At scattered openings, natural light shone through, giving the arena a cathedral-like feel.

As I made my way up the stairs to find a seat, someone grabbed my arm, jolting me and halting my ascent.

'Ahh, the masked man,' said my companion from the park, sporting an old prospector's grin. 'Come for the bull sumo? You are in for a treat.'

'Yeah, thought I'd check 'em out. Take in a little local culture before I depart,' I said, vaguely touching on the reasons for my attendance.

'I suspect you are still parading through life with your mask on.' He put his hand up to his face as if miming someone holding a mask to their face and did a little sidestep dance from one foot to the other.

I was sick of the analogy but answered with a polite smile. 'Yeah, guess so ... we'll see.' Running into the familiar face unsettled me and I proceeded to shift uncomfortably as my eyes darted throughout the stadium for empty seats.

'I thought you weren't an American soldier?' It was rhetorical, a set-up, he didn't wait for my reply. 'Then, why does it look like you've been out raping and pillaging!' he blurted, then unleashed a loud bar room guffaw.

I had no idea what he was getting at, then remembered the cat scratches on my face and forced an abashed smile. Hideki-san seemed off that afternoon, so different from our first meeting. The callous jokes, his chummy demeanour – *ah, he's sauced.*

He was indeed in high spirits with his face beet red and glistening from booze and pre-bullfight excitement. Well, at least he'd developed a sense of humour since the day we spoke in the park, albeit a dark one.

His companion, a man of similar age with a gleaming scalp protruding from outgrown horseshoe hair eyed his convivial friend inquisitively, and me suspiciously. One of his Okinawa comrades, I figured.

As drunk as he was, Hideki picked up on his friend's disquiet. His incarnadine head turned to address him and, to my surprise, launched to my defence. '*Gaijin wa* (the foreigner is),' some gruff

Japanese I couldn't pick up, 'not American and was teacher,' more gargled Japanese, 'we talked when he drank in the park and read Mishima.'

It was the drinking in the park reading Mishima that seemed to sway the court of public opinion and his friend nodded politely toward me with a neighbourly smile. He offered the seat next to them. They sat, and so now did I, in the second row right next to where the action was about to begin.

'Hi, I'm Fredrick.'

'Ah, Fledlick, *hajimemashite*. My name Junichiro.'

'He is *hentai ojisan*!' My drunken acquaintance laughed uproariously at labelling his friend, 'a dirty old man'. It was a common friendly dig amongst Japanese men of any age.

'You can just call me Fred,' I told him. Junichiro's English was clearly not on par with his pal Hideki and I thought this might be easier on him. It was a relief really; *at least I won't be getting any in-depth psychological analysis from this one.*

'Ah, Fled, *hajimemashite* Fled.'

'Nice to meet you too, Junichiro.' I was plenty used to the mispronunciation by that time, and 'Fled' was proving to be a fitting moniker. I had fled Canada, fled Tokyo, fled my apartment that morning and in a few hours would be fleeing Okinawa.

I told Hideki my plan to retrace my steps back to Tokyo. He reacted flattered, crediting his story in the park as the impetus. If he felt his wise words were acting as some grand guiding light, I didn't want to spoil his self-satisfaction and so swallowed the whole story as to how I was being pushed out as much as pulled back. Besides, I couldn't explain the reasoning even to myself. Instead, I got down to pressing matters, 'Hey, can I bet on these?'

'Ha!' He loved that. 'You want to place bets? Okay, I can help you. They won't take your bet, because *gaijin* ...'

Say no more, I thought

'But I can place bets for you before each match.'

We went through the form outlining the day's matches, there were seven of them. Hideki explained that bulls in heavier weight classes, and of greater prestige, fought later on the card. I decided to bet a small amount on the first bout to get my feet wet and then scale up from there.

The first match he told me was between bulls called Fighting Good Luck and Warugaki Taketora. Neither really spoke to me, but I went with four thousand yen on Good Luck since I felt I could use a little from the onset.

I handed money to the old man, and he left to place our bets. In his absence, Junichiro and I struggled to converse. Every once in a while, he would nudge my shoulder with his elbow and gesture to a female spectator across the ring, uttering something in Japanese I couldn't quite catch, a devilish grin upon his face.

The old man returned and distributed three One Cup Sake from his pockets.

I peeled back the pull-tab top and took a sip. One Cup Ozeki is the cheapest drunk going, even more economical than the Chu-hi and grain whisky I leaned towards. It's favoured amongst homeless, down and out salarymen, pinkiless punters and blue-collar *ojisans*; between one and two dollars for a 180ml jar, and tasted every yen of it. I took a haul and picked up flavours of sweetish rice wine with a hint of cinchona and black liquorice – rough, like a ride on one of those bulls.

'You want to hold the ticket?' Hideki held out a piece of torn lined notebook paper with black *kanji* characters written across it.

Ticket? That? I was thinking but dug how ghetto the whole scene was. With a wave of the hand, I declined, not wanting to put my karma on it.

Men in blue and red *happi* coats threw rice and sprinkled *sake* around the ring. I took this purifying ritual as an indication the first match was about to start. Two bulls emerged from tunnels at opposite ends of the ring. They were led by their owners or coaches on a leash, nonchalantly, much like you would walk a well-trained dog.

They were massive, even though I was told these were the lightweights, weighing in at around 800 pounds. The old man pointed out my bull. The creature looked determined.

The referee lined the bulls up snout to snout. They clinched by locking horns, and the match began. A single twist and push were all it took for Fighting Good Luck to disengage from the clinch and run toward the fencing. The other bull gave chase but not much, just enough to ensure the retreat was in earnest. Within seconds, like that, it was over.

A chuckle and cheer rippled through the crowd. Caught up in the excitement, I clapped as well, before realizing I was out 40 bucks. Turns out his name was a misnomer. He wasn't much of a fighter, nor, for me at least, was he good luck.

My bull was led out of the ring, a few jeers hurled at his hide for lack of moxie. The winner was given a small ceremony where a colourful blanket was thrown over his back and a wreath of flowers placed around his neck. A petrified child was placed upon the winning bull's back as a few photos were snapped in perpetuity.

I lost the next two matches as well. The fourth I won but received only a small payout with my bull being the odds-on favourite. I was one-for-four and down half my cash or 15,000 yen. As discouraged as I was, the ol' gambler's spirit kicked in, and I figured the only way to get even was to go big or go home. The realization I now lacked the latter to go to penetrated the stadium's celebratory mood.

The final middleweight fight was Takoshi Tiger versus Matsumura Guardian.

'Ahh, Matsumura,' exclaimed Junichiro nodding with approval.

'Yes, it's a good name,' agreed his friend, 'maybe, a clever bull.'

'Why is that?' I had to ask, desperate for some inside information, anything that could sway my fortunes.

'Is Okinawa legend,' Junichiro began, but then ran out of

English.

'In the ancient Ryukyu kingdom, there was a king who wanted to know if any of the great warriors was skilled enough in combat to defeat his fiercest bull,' Hideki took over. 'Bull sumo was already a popular event in the kingdom, but never had there been man versus bull. Everyone wondered who would be brave enough or crazy enough to fight the champion bull.' The old man reverted in tone to that of the aged professor I'd become accustomed to in the Goya park.

'Is it a true story?' I asked rapt like a kindergartner during storytime.

'*Hai*,' Junichiro nodded enthusiastically, wanting it to be beyond fable as much as me.

'Hmmm,' the old man mused non-committal. 'A young farmhand stepped forward and said he would fight. The king was pleased with the young man's spirit and promised that if he survived the life or death match, he would prove worthy of being the king's chief bodyguard. The highest post in the land for any warrior.'

We all three, sipped from our most recent *sake* jars before Hideki continued. 'Matsumura requested two weeks to prepare for the showdown. The king gave his permission, and the next day at dawn, Matsumura went to the bull stables ...'

It was very much a Pavlov's dog little scheme Matsumura had concocted. He conned his way in, telling the stable boy, 'I must perform a ceremony to make peace with the bull's essence. After defeat, he will not begrudge my victory and its spirit will not haunt me in the afterlife.' The stable boy bought this real old-timey spiritual shit; hook, line and sinker. Then it gets a little sick. Matsumura certainly had a ceremony planned but one of a different nature. He'd take off his cloak and rub it over the bull's face to imprint his scent on the bull's psyche. Then he'd remove a small sharpened bamboo spear from his trousers and proceeded to poke the bull's scrotum and testicles. The bull did not enjoy this, to say the least, but as he was in a corral, he could not attack the young farmhand.

'No PETA, eh,' I interrupted, at that point, my lone chuckle met by blank looks.

According to Hideki's retelling, Matsumura returned to the stable day after day and performed the same ritual of rubbing the bull's face with his self-scented cloak, then poking it in the nuts. The poor beast became very demoralized in its inability to thwart his tormentor. And so, as the fight grew nearer, the mere scent of Matsumura or sight of his bamboo stick caused the champion bull to cry with fright.

'A great crowd occupied the newly erected bullring the day of the fight,' Hideki proclaimed as if he'd organized it himself. 'Matsumura wore his trusty cloak and his oldest, dirtiest fighting clothes, permeated with his odour. Instead of the small spear, Matsumura entered the ring carrying only a red bamboo fan. He had no weapon to speak of.'

'Hai, eto, Matsumura wa yumi toe ...' Junichiro jumped in excitedly with a flurry of Japanese. Hideki shot him an annoyed glare for trying to hijack the climax of his story, then put a gentle hand on his shoulder to silence him.

'Matsumura bowed to the crowd, then bowed extra deep to the king. The crowd roared and the bull was released. He ran to the centre of the ring with rage in his eyes, ready to fight. Matsumura showed no fear and walked calmly toward the great beast. The bull turned to meet him but was met first with a familiar scent. His nostrils flared. The smell sent a shudder of fear through the animal. When his eyes focused on the figure in front of him, he saw a familiar bamboo stick in the man's hand. The same little tool which had brought him so much displeasure in recent weeks. The bull turned and retreated from battle, giving a calf's bawl. Matsumura opened his bamboo fan, and coolly waved it in front of his calm, composed face.' Hideki cracked a wide yellow smile in conclusion.

Junichiro, his little friend, even though unable to understand the English version, knew the story by heart and was beaming at this point while drunkenly miming fanning himself.

I smiled politely my approval at the outcome and the cunning Matsumura. 'Well, this is a no-brainer then.' I'd counted out my remaining bills during the telling and handed them to Hideki. 'Put me down for 10,000 on Matsumura to win.' I added, 'hope no one has been fiddling with his balls!' miming a stabbing motion with an invisible little stick.

Junichiro laughed. Despite the language barrier, I'd picked up that he was, in fact, a bit of a dirty old cunt and enjoyed some bawdy humour.

Hideki must have recognized that I was disappointed with my previous payout and knew I was in the red on the day, so he gave me a little pointer. 'You can bet the winner ... and the time of the fight. It is much more difficult, but if you get the duration of the fight to the minute, you can win a big payout.'

My eyes lit up at this new information. 'Oh yeah?'

'You want time?' he asked, stood waiting to go place the bets.

'Yeah, definitely.' My mind raced; *2 minutes, 5, 22, 10*? It really was a total crapshoot, the previous fights had lasted between 5 seconds and 25 minutes. I closed my eyes and let my mind go blank. When I opened them, I said, '14-minute mark, Matsumura wins.'

Hideki returned with three cans of Kirin beer and our bets. Once again the bulls were led into the ring by their team of handlers. A single handler, or *seko*, led each bull to meet in the centre where the referee issued a swift downward chop of his arm and started the match.

Snorting furiously and frothing from their prodigious nostrils, the magnificent beasts smashed forehead to forehead, reverberating a sound like two-by-fours smacking together. They retreated briefly to survey the damage, bloodshot eyes fixed menacingly on their opponent, assessing if they'd weakened the other mentally or physically in the initial clash. Then, once again, the bovine battering rams reared back and walloped each other. After this test of resolve, seeing that neither was going to concede through lack of grit, they locked horns for a more tactical approach.

The sweat-soaked beasts turned and tussled as each tried to gain an advantage. As they strained against the other's tremendous weight, muscles quivered beneath silky black hides.

The handlers were a vocal bunch, and Matsumura's man was really letting rip, 'hi-ya!, Hi-Ya, HI-YA.' Both bulls seemed to be in a contented clinch and leisurely pushed against their foe like a slow waltz.

Next to me in the stands, Hideki was shouting his own instructions at the bulls. '*Hai, Momi-Komi*', '*iie, chatsurii ... Hira Hira ...*' I was most impressed with his technical understanding of the sport.

Matsumura made a bold move and exerted sudden upward pressure, managing to lift Takoshi Tiger's front hooves off the dirt flooring. He was trying to throw his whole frame to its side in an epic takedown, but the sheer mass was too much, and the hooves landed back on the ground kicking up dust and mud. I feared the exertion would leave Matsumura vulnerable, yet it seemed the effort to force himself down had left Takashi Tiger fatigued as well. They returned to the dance, a steady push to and fro.

Tiger delivered a '*tsuki*', his horns striking Matsumura above the eyebrows. Like a good jab in boxing, it rattled Matsumura some. It rattled me significantly.

Matsumura answered back with a skilful move of his own, rotating his horns around the neck of his opponent in an attempt to throw Takoshi Tiger off balance. Judging by the screams of '*kake, kake, KAKE!*' from my companion in the next seat, I guessed this was an established move ... called the *kake*.

I squinted to the far side of the ring where the clock counted the duration, just over eleven minutes had passed. I began to fret as neither bull appeared to be slowing down. With each strike and manoeuvre, a great cheer erupted from the crowd, drowning out the constant instructional chants of the trainers flanking their bulls dangerously close to the action.

Takashi mustered from within a reserve of strength and determination. Matsumura was getting steadily walked back the length of the ring, pushing into the dirt on his haunches to resist the advance, but with each rippling resistance of the hindquarters, the mighty shoulders of Takashi Tiger flexed and drove Matsumura backward inches more. His drive toward the elevated dirt and fencing at the ring's perimeter became more rapid. It was there my hopes died.

A meter from the ring's edge, Matsumura ducked his head and, like a rodeo bull, powerfully bucked his hips up and to the left, shifting his weight just in time to escape the forward pressure. Takashi Tiger, powerless to stop his own forward motion ploughed forward, leaving his right side exposed. Matsumura, seeing the opening, drove head and horns into the unprotected flank. In no time, Takashi Tiger was pinned against the sloping dirt at the edge of the ring.

I jumped to my feet and cheered with sheer exhilaration. Hopping up and down, I threw both arms around my elderly friends who were celebrating wildly alongside me.

In the excitement, I'd forgotten the most pressing aspect of the win. Squinting my eyes, I read the clock. Closing them tightly, opening and squinting to focus again, I confirmed what I'd seen the first time – 14:14.

Elated and impatient, I awaited delivery of my winnings. The fourteen seconds didn't make a lick of difference but certainly added a bizarre twist to the divination. My eyes lit up as Hideki handed over a thick wad of cash. I shoved the bills into an emaciated wallet, which now bulged and barely closed at the fold with the welcomed nourishment and new girth.

Before I had a chance to squander my good fortune, I said my goodbyes to Junichiro and the old man with who I felt a renewed, more profound bond after that day. I thanked him profusely for his kindness and hospitality.

'Thank you, young man and good luck to you on your journey. But please remember, while place can play a part, the true power to remove your mask comes from a journey within.' Calmed down after the afternoon's excitement, Hideki's spoke in a tone even and serious, with a hint of genuine affection, I had no idea I'd affected.

'*Arigato*. And I mean it, if you are ever in Tokyo, we should get together … go bet the ponies.' I attempted to add some levity to the farewell as sincerity made me uncomfortable.

'Much appreciated, but I won't be going back to Tokyo, that life belonged to a different man,' he said in sober voice and stance. 'But you could do me a favour. If you get the chance, look up Tatsuya and Machiko.' He wrote down their full names in the correct *kanji* on the fight bill then folded it around a stack of yen, and handed it to me.

'Really, I can't accept! You've been too kind already,' I said.

'You must accept. Trust me, you earned it. I rode your bet on Matsumura down to the minute! I'll be drinking Yamazaki tonight,' he explained with a sly grin.

I took the money with both hands and a bow. 'And what should I say if I manage to find your friends?'

'Tell them …' he paused, contemplating. 'Tell them, "Hideki has found his way." I am not sure whether they will remember, whether they will care, or even if they will understand. But for some reason, it's essential I try.'

I shook Junichiro's hand and then bowed more formally to Hideki in a rare display of deference and gratitude.

On the mostly empty bus, I took out my winnings. Holding the money, counting the money, smelling the musky scent made me positively high. Endorphins reeled off in my head like a boon time stock ticker. After the count, I was a hundred and ninety-five thousand yen richer. I put half the money back in my wallet. The other half I distributed; placed in different portions of my backpack, stuffed between the pages of books, slipped into the pocket of a spare pair of jeans. Diversifying my assets, I believe they'd call it in the world of finance.

I looked out the window. Old and infirm shuffled by or limped toward their destinations in the late afternoon. I'd heard that Okinawa was famous for its centennials, more per capita than anywhere else on earth. Perhaps that was all that was on display out the window those many bus rides; a parade of the ageing and ailing.

On defeated days, feeling battered by life, my fragile mind teetering on the brink, I'd imagine the island's water had been poisoned by some unknown and nefarious source, for some unknown and nefarious reason. Yet on that final ride it hit – *the delusion was a scapegoat*. With the creation of this ludicrous, diabolical plot, I didn't have to own the havoc I'd wreaked. On that afternoon's ride with escape in sight, I saw only elderly souls pushing on.

The bus pulled onto a coastal highway; there was a marina out the right-side windows and the sea beyond. We travelled over the Tomari bridge where a small harbour lay as the long-standing entrance to Naha city. I knew we were getting close, so dinged the bell for the next stop.

I headed down a bending footpath that led to what appeared to be a floating pontoon, where the terminal building, like a two-storey mini-mall, stretched across a concrete berth. Inside, I bought a second-class ticket. A first-class doubled the price, and my recent windfall wasn't going to hold out long.

In a small gift store, I collected in a plastic basket a bottle of Awamori, cans of Chu-hi, and a couple of packs of cigarettes. Even though I was far from a departing tourist, I felt obliged to buy some memento of my time on the island. Okinawa was like so many women I'd coveted over the years, with a longing to bathe in its beauty and mystery. Yet, after achieving entrance, an inevitable disenchantment set in, a realization, it too was unable to fulfil the quixotic expectations laid before the mantel. Left wanting, I turn around and blamed the very thing I'd thirsted for.

In an act of acquiescence, I accepted I was as much to blame as the island and searched for a small memorabilia of the good times we had. A sphere-shaped bead similar to a fishing float hung from a keychain. I didn't own any keys as I had nothing to gain access to. The bead, however, in how it almost radiated light and contained little misshapen bubbles as alluring imperfections, caught my eye. The tiny globes came in various colours though the turquoise, like the sea that would be my road away, spoke to me most. I bought the *chura-dama* with my other necessities and left the terminal building.

A plastic bag around my wrist, I walked past the looming front hull, and ended up on the far corner of the dock. To lighten my load, I opened one of the Chu-his and lit a cigarette. Puffy marshmallow clouds floated leisurely by, I inspected them for silver linings or connotative shapes. Two ospreys soared overhead. They swooped a criss-cross pattern and flew off in opposite directions.

An ocean breeze washed over me. It momentarily stilled my restless soul. Excitement and fear butted horns in my stomach. It wasn't the flutter of butterflies, more like a pterodactyl gang bang. I pondered what awaited me on the road ahead; *certain disaster or fortuitous emerald pastures, perpetual retreat or discovered resolution, serenity or madness?*

I breathed in the briny air. 'Buy the ticket, take the ride,' I mumbled to myself, quoting the well-known gonzo guru.

Done and doing. And really, what else can one do?

In the distance to my right, low lying apartment buildings, all off-white and grey, clustered the port city. I scanned their plain façades and flat rooftops, and longed for the vitality and glittering opulence of Tokyo's streets.

My head swung a hundred and eighty degrees. I gazed out

toward the sapphire blue seas the island was famous for, and yet I'd never even set foot in. Too much idle time frittered away on buses to nowhere, barren rooms and barstools, park benches and convenience store kerbs. For many, the island was considered a paradise, but I'd made it a purgatory.

A foghorn blew, gulls mewed and the wind harmonized a maritime calypso. I bent backwards, my drink in one hand and smoke in the other, and shimmied under the imagined bar of my mind's eye. Righted from my arched pose, I stared over quavering waves, in search of ...

Finally, I turned away from the ocean expanse that would be my faithful companion for the next two days.

I'd only taken one step toward the gangplank when I froze awestruck in my tracks. A tabby cat sat directly in my path, staring up at me with big pale green eyes.

It was an odd place for him to be hanging around. He looked clean and well taken care of. He stood and trotted toward me. I didn't move.

'Hey, little guy,' I cooed, thankful when no answer came.

The small feline pressed his head against my shin, then rubbed his burnt orange striped body across my calf and through my legs, purring as he repeated the friendly gesture on the opposite leg. The charitable contact was assuaging.

I wanted to pick the tabby up, tuck him in my backpack and take him along with me but I knew I couldn't do that. The Okinawa chapter of my life had begun a solitary one and would end a solitary one.

Cosmic Pachinko

Even a fool learns something once it hits him.
—*Homer*, Iliad

I guess you could say my writing has proven cathartic. It has even slowed my drinking; I start the day with beers, move on to Chuhi, and don't get into the spirits until after dark. Today, I've fallen into a bit of a grey area, having written the night through aided by nicotine and whisky. Now the sun has risen and I'm sat with a smouldering cigarette and half-glass of hooch.

What's a roll of film if never developed? I consider when discouraged by lack of progress. *Just moments lost to time.*

My travels, dreams and memories the roll of film, this cubicle my darkroom, and pressed keys the chemical fluids. But as morning comes, a question lingers like so much stale smoke – *can I trust the developed prints?* Or is it all trickery, like an Escherian enigma.

A few of the events recorded, I've interpreted for dim insights pointing me in dawdling directions. I've been reticent to act. My interpretations previously have brought me here; unemployed, possessionless, living in an internet café.

But, what else can I do but push on, lulled into a flimsy sense of optimism by this tip-tapping of keys.

* * *

Each blink lingers into sleep. Yet, I'm forcing myself to stay awake. In a half-hour the Accountant will be up and going through the ritualistic motions of preparing himself for whatever pursuits it were that occupied his days. After an esoteric convo with our mutual acquaintance Jae-hyun the other day, I've become rather obsessed with figuring out precisely what it is that makes the Accountant tick.

This came about as Brooks loitered inside a small laundromat upon my approach. He wore joggers and a grey T-shirt. A pair of jeans, some socks, underwear and shirts were on spin cycle. We talked and drank over the slosh and rattle of the machine.

I told him I'd been 'dropping breadcrumbs', documenting what events had come to pass to lead me here. To which he nodded his approval. I'd hoped he'd show more zeal for my running with his suggestion. So, a little contemptuous, I started airing my grievances.

'It's like, if I just sit in that cubicle writing much longer, I'm gonna lose my shit. I'll end up fucking nuts, like what's his face, the Accountant or whatever.' I smirked, but Jae-hyun looked at me blank, unfamiliar with my nicknames for our small brood of netcafe dwellers.

'You know; cheap salaryman suit, head like a *ni-man* yen square tomato, the self-satisfied grin of a chronic masturbator and pre-recorded pleasantries ... Well yeah, I'd rather not end up trapped in a delusional existence like him, the Accountant.'

'Oh yes, Kai,' he confirmed. 'Perhaps, all is not as simple as you have made it.'

'What, like he doesn't pretend to go off to some imagined job every day, sit like a vegetable and later sign off to return to the same cubicle which he then considers some kind of actual abode?' I finished off my elaborate backstory with a smart-assed snicker. *Simple my ass.*

'Yes, for a start.'

'So, he's working an actual job from that cubicle every day?'

'Not so much a job, I believe it is much more substantial than that, what Kai does,' he answered, staring through heavier hooded eyes, in the profound ponderance he was prone to.

'Well, like what? Is it something illegal? Government?'

'What Kai does is not governed by the laws of this world,' Jae-hyun assessed. Indicating, I guess, it was neither government nor illegal.

'Does this mystery job, or whatever it is, have a name?' My

voice betrayed me and rose with agitation.

Jae-hyun thought for a long time, perhaps to test my fraying patience. During this lull, he sipped from his can and pointed toward the laundromat door with an unlit cigarette. We stepped into the street. It was quiet as usual, only a cyclist and a couple of pedestrians gone past.

Jae-hyun leaned against the corner of a vending machine. He lit up and took a long drag. Exhaling, the smoke instantly consumed by the blue-white background of a Boss Coffee advertisement decaled on the vending machine's side, he finally said, 'You might think of him as a puppeteer.'

'A puppeteer? In that cubicle?' After my retort, I lit my own smoke and puffed on it rather frantically so stubby clouds carried across the narrow street.

'You're thinking too literally,' he said. 'It's more like in his mastery and manipulation of sentient beings.'

'How do you know this about him?' I counted out change and bought a couple of Sapporo tall cans. They fell with a soft clunk. 'The Accountant … or Kai, sorry. Have you spoken to him? I mean, beyond the formalities he regurgitates. Seems like he's not much for conversation.'

'Well, you're mostly correct there. Kai was here when I arrived. At first, it was the same routine you've observed; "Good morning", "Thank you for your hard work today" and so on.' Jae-hyun broke into a sentimental smile, remembering his initial interactions with Kia. 'I felt there was something more there, something undiscovered. I sought to scratch below the surface of the chubby, suited man.'

I handed Jae-hyun a beer. He smiled a thanks.

A solitary salaryman walked briskly by swinging his briefcase with each spry step. Instinctively, Jae-hyun and I fell silent, giving this whole Kai discussion, and Kai himself, an added air of mystery.

As the man's black blazer receded in the distance, Jae-hyun started up again. 'After a period of being met by the same standard salutations, I tried a different tact. You see, I'm quite a strong chess player.'

'Oh yeah?' I said.

'Yes, I learned from a young age, one of the few luxuries afforded us in the North. Anyways, on a spring afternoon, I invited Kai to play in the park.' He pointed to a dirt lot with a couple of trees up the block, on the other side of the street. 'He defeated me easily in seven moves. The next time I managed to stave him off for twelve. We still play once in a while, and I've never won, never come anywhere close,' he concluded with a sheepish grin.

'He's a good chess player, eh,' I said, my voice flat and eyes drifting over the row of vending machines.

'Do you know what makes a good chess player, Fred?'

Something in the question's phrasing or delivery struck me as condescending. I casually shrugged my shoulders, but when no reply came, offered up a half-assed answer to play along. 'Knowing which way the pieces move.'

'Hmm,' Jae-hyun countered with an exasperated look.

I took a swig of beer, thought, and gave a more vested answer. 'And of course, protecting the king while moving offensively to capture your opponent's pieces.'

'Well, that's basically it ... for a basic player,' Jae-hyun said, more satisfied with this inaccurate response. 'No, a good chess player thinks four, five moves ahead at a time. They're not playing your last move, or even your next ... and the most sophisticated, or greatest players, are guiding your moves with each of their own, luring you into position well in advance ... Right to where they need you to be.' He nodded as though pleased with his explanation and however it was to enlighten me.

I ruminated on this in an oblivious stupor, beer can hovering right underneath my dangling lower lip.

'I'm a good chess player, Kai is supernatural in his abilities!' he added for good measure and shot me a weighty look that said *believe me on this.*

I brought the aluminium brim to my mouth and took the waiting drink. 'So what'd you learn?' I asked, chasing the point.

'We talked a little during these matches. Well, I talked,' he said.

'He speaks,' I blurted, like a remedial student regurgitating the only fact that stuck.

'Yes, he can communicate,' Jae-hyun continued, 'but not as you and I, not as other humans interact with chosen words and connected phrases. I suspect, not because he's incapable, but because it's beneath him ... our banal thoughts and ideas. He would, however, I realized shortly into our matches, answer a direct question in the affirmative or negative.'

I pictured Kai, still donning his jacket and tie, sat on one end of the weathered bench while Jae-hyun in jeans and tattered sweater sits at the other. A chessboard and contemplation teeter between them. Kai moves the queen's pawn to D4, under an afore shed *sakura* while Jae-hyun studies the board and probes his opponents' world with carefully curtailed questions.

'Once I'd deduced this, it polished my pursuit,' Jae-hyun cut in, and my vision of the men sat in that somnolent park vanished. 'Still, with defeat imminent, I was under a time constraint to extract as much information as possible with my yes or no questions. So in a way, two chess matches were happening each time.'

'And so this was how you cracked the conundrum that is Kai?' I asked.

'So that was how I was able to garner a vague notion of what it is Kai does,' he clarified. 'Though on second thought, puppeteer doesn't quite capture the essence of it ...' He shook his head and smiled. 'I can't believe the analogy never occurred to me earlier ... It'll seem trite now but ... Yes, Kai is a chess master.'

He let the proclamation hang in the air. I scanned all that was life in seemingly random motion around us and tried to interpret the substance of what was said.

'So as the old maxim goes, we are all just pawns in the game?' I said, voice flat, eyes downcast and despondent.

'*Hai,* for the most part.' Jae-hyun offered up as little or no consolation. He looked down the street to the sign at the entrance of our internet café, took a deep breath and exhaled, 'And then there are Kais.'

'None of this makes any fuckin' sense,' I sulked, showing little regard for the insights I'd requested and graciously been handed.

'And what sort of sense did it make before?' he replied, back in his element. 'Ask yourself honestly, does it make any more or less sense now – your life, life in general, the tilt of the earth, and the turn of our lives?'

'Well, shit …'

So yeah, my interest has been piqued, with Kai's strange demeanour cast in a whole new nebulous lustre.

***

I timed it perfectly and managed to catch Kai as he finished fixing the knot of his tie at the communal bathroom mirror, a double Windsor no less.

To start us off, he gave the obligatory '*ohayo goziamasu*' in a singsong voice of office-protocol exaggerated *genkiness*.

The game is afoot, I thought, feeling cocky and crafty. 'Things going well at the office?'

'*Hai.*' He nodded, his chubby cheeks blown out with a closed lip smile.

'What are you working on today?'

He shot me his stock polite smile but offered nothing more.

Shit, that was an informational question. I recalled Jae-hyun's instructions and realized there really was some strategy involved.

'You'll be finishing up around seven-thirty or eight?' I inquired.

Again, he answered in the affirmative and nodded. It was a

throw-away question to put him at ease. Unfortunately, it'd be my last of the day.

He ran some water over his hands and pushed them through either side of his middle part. Satisfied with his appearance, he bowed short of forty-five degrees and wished me good luck for the day.

Discouraged that I'd gotten so little out of the morning exchange, I concocted a new plan of reconnaissance. I cut down Kai's aisle, crouched and veered toward his cubicle, getting as close to the entrance as possible without disrupting the curtain. The partitions were about six-foot high and one-inch thick. On the fringe of where Kai's cubicle began, I went up on my tippy toes and began to gradually creep the five-foot width. Head cocked to the right, I peered in.

The shiny black hair on the back of Kai's head was the first sight of him sat with stringent posture in front of the system console. I held my breath with each short step. Despite my caution, he must have sensed my presence. Kai's head swung around. Our eyes met. The polite grin vanished, and his face bore the damning scowl of one whose privacy has been rudely violated.

I dropped to the balls of my heels and hurried back to my cubby. Once inside, I reviewed the gathered intel. On all three interior panels were photos, news clippings, documents and notes connected by coloured string to form an intricate web, like a frenzied detective's wall in an old cop show.

On the computer screen, he had been frenetically sequencing a stack of electronic cards, but I was unable to decipher what was on any. The general activities aligned with the woolly disclosures of Jae-hyun, but also to my more pragmatic presumption that he was no more than an insurance adjuster or something mundane and befitting such as that. Specifics, details, were what I was after, though garnered none being busted so quickly.

I was left with an odd sense of guilt, having invaded this strange little man's strange little space. Yet, a far deeper sense of awe and bewilderment pervaded. In the dying milliseconds after his face spun around and met mine, before my eyeline dropped below the curtain's edge, I believe Kai mouthed something with a surly tinge. After multiple attempts to decode the movement of his lips, I could swear they declared, 'Fuck off, cunt!'

***

Once the chemical blue smokescreen clears, I tend to secure little glimpses in. Using what's viewable, I spit forth syllables in hopes some marker will materialize and lead me out of these woods. Those moments, I have to grab by the balls, so as not to be entirely inactive during my sojourn in this netcafe.

The orange Chuo line departs Shinjuku station and runs through the place of permanent dawn as it curves toward Nakano station. I'd labelled the spot thus as I rode that very train back to my guesthouse room in the wee hours of the morn or heart of the night. A neon burn radiating through the train window would cause me to come to in a stupor, feeling I'd arrived at some surreal electric sunrise.

The beer I had for breakfast wasn't bad, so was enjoying another for dessert while riding that Orange Blossom Special with Sunday morning coming down. Thirty-five minutes later I got off the train at Higashi Koseki station. Outside the west exit, I gathered my bearings. There was a small realtor's office to my left and the 100 yen shop, where I used to pick up cheap beers and instant curry, on my right.

I walked past a *koban*, or police box; a small cabin-like structure which houses elderly and out-of-shape community cops. It stoked the dormant fear which had often groped at me passing by on rough mornings, the previous night's blackout binge having left a foreboding imprint on my psyche as an added aftermath to the common hangover.

A new brick sidewalk was much nicer than the concrete slabs I had previously stubbled down. At the Idemitsu gas station, I took a left onto a smaller tree-lined lane. From there, I was looking for a short residential stretch which ran off to the right.

Nothing. I doubled back and went up the next block and then the previous. Every empty lot or newly constructed housing unit became a potential site for the vanished residence. But when I surveyed the surroundings, it was never the right spot. Every time I felt I was getting closer, I simultaneously felt I was drifting further away. After hours of zig-zagging Higashi Koseki blocks, my can of Chu-hi empty, feeling weary and defeated, I wandered back toward the station.

A mini-truck cruised by at a snail's pace. Licking flames from an oven built onto the hatch illuminated the falling dusk. A baritone warble called into the silent evening, 'Yaakkkiiii-immmoooo ...', advertising the sweet potato treats.

The first time I heard the gravelly chant seep through the window of my newly occupied guesthouse room, it sent shivers down my spine, summoning images of a barbaric cult sacrifice. It has become far less threatening over time.

Sweet smoke billowing from the chimney wafted over my path, the first fragrant sign of fall. The jissom smell that accompanies the fresh blossoming trees of spring had long since passed. The cicadas screaming their maddening chorus in the sweltering humidity of summer had died, their exoskeletons fallen and faded. Only, crisp, buttery-scented air comforted my autumn walk to the station.

'Japan has four seasons.' I recalled the science teacher informing me flatly as he settled in a plastic chair of the staff smoking room.

'Yes, I know.' It was not our first time through the routine. Every conversation we engaged in as we puffed away, began and ended with an observation on the local weather. I often wondered if he was nursing dashed dreams of being a meteorologist.

'Summer, Autumn, Winter, Spring. Four seasons. Only Japan!'

This was where the point of contention arose, this prevailing belief Japan was unique somehow in having four seasons. The idea was introduced to me by that science teacher in the rural junior high school, but I'd heard it professed with just as much conviction by many others.

I tapped my cigarette and ash fell. 'Canada also has four seasons. Our winters are very cold.'

It went in one ear and must have been blown out the other by a late August typhoon. 'Japan very special, it have four seasons.' He leaned back and opened a golf magazine which lay on the table, thus concluding the day's conversation.

Caramelized in the scenery and aroma of my autumn saunter, I was inclined to agree with the science teacher, then more than ever, *Japan and its four seasons are very special*.

I pondered the day's search as the Chuo line chugged on, dispersing and collecting passengers at stops along the line. Baffled by my inability to locate the residence, it wasn't only that it had disappeared, the whole block leading to it seemed to have vanished.

The rooftops of Tokyo suburbs flitted past; flat, gabled, shingled, tarred, aerialed and lifeless. They stretched on endlessly like the surface of the ocean. I imagined myself bounding atop them, jumping from roof to roof until I finally fell through one of the crevices, lost to the concealed streets below.

Could the Big Peach Gaijin House up and evaporated into thin air?

The receding buildings outside the window stretched higher, engulfing the tracks, as we approached Shinjuku.

Maybe it never existed at all. A chilling thought, the repercussions of which I'm not prepared to tackle.

***

7:14 pm and 16 degrees, the LED clock on Studio ALTA informed as I exited Shinjuku's East Exit. High-octave vocals and digitized two-dimensional sex rained down from its seven-meter screen when I peeked at the commotion above a twenty-foot Koda Kumi gyrated to her most recent J-pop single.

Further down, I halted in the permanent dawn and lingered long enough to fight off the urge to sob. Nothing had been delivered, no matter how often I stood underneath the dark portal's egress. *And I threw away everything for this wild fuckin' goose chase*, I admonished myself. Though to be fair, it'd already been discarded, in bits along the way.

A drizzle of fluorescent jellybeans fell like acid rain of self-deceit. I scoured the bright building façades enveloping me as if trapped at the bottom of a glowing glass well. Closing my eyes, light burned on the insides of my lids – diminishing dollops on a noir palette. *How was I to get up there beyond the highest blazing bulb?* If only I could climb those polychromatic raindrops like a ladder to the sky.

I slinked away as a disembodied head afloat a black umbrella sea and travelled not through the flame, but in its warmth, on the outskirts of Kabukicho beside the station and elevated tracks of the Seibu Shinjuku line. Ahead, a neon blue saxophone blazed in the night. Small jazz bars are sprinkled throughout Tokyo, but I couldn't recall ever frequenting one. That night felt as good as any, if not better. I entered the place, passing a placard by the door, 'The Blue Jazz' it read.

'Double rum and Coke, please,' I ordered over the long oak bar.

'*Hai*,' replied the bartender as he set to work chipping a perfect sphere out of a block of ice. He set the globe in a wide rim glass and free-poured white rum. He topped it up with a splash of Coke and handed me the expertly made drink. I paid him 800 yen and felt it should have been more for the artistry involved.

I looked the room over. About half the tables were occupied with drinkers; men in business suits or middle-aged couples. There was a stage, empty except for a single microphone stand and, to the back, lounged a baby grand. Blue velvet curtains were pulled back, leading me to believe a live act would soon replace the canned music that was playing some instrumental jazz song I didn't recognize.

I sat at a low, circular table, mid-room. In the centre, a candle burned in a red glass holder. I set my drink next to the vase and gazed at the naked flame. It was serene the way the natural light danced its reflection on the highball glass. This reprieve from Shinjuku's neon barrage lulled me into a peaceful trance, broken when the first chords were struck on the piano, and a hauntingly beautiful voice flooded the bar room.

The singer's eyes fixed the entrance door as she languished through a possessed version of 'My Funny Valentine'. Her long, burgundy gown draped the floor while she writhed a stationary sashay. As the final note trailed off, the songstress's eyes dropped to the hem of her dress and remained there for a brief eternity before the piano started up anew.

Again, she stared longingly through a blue haze of exhaled smoke and settled her gaze on the bar room door. Her body stood rigid, but voice quavered in each intone of the initial notes. With her preserved porcelain skin, she evinced a graceful beauty, timeless and enduring despite her sixty or so years. But those eyes ... when I focused in on her eyes, I'd never seen pain and yearning bore so deep into one's core.

The silky gown clung to her thin frame; yet, it felt as if she was performing a kind of striptease as she emoted from the stage, revealing not her flesh, but deeper – a naked and scarred soul.

I reached forward to ash my cigarette and saw goosebumps running up my forearm. A strange feeling crept in; I knew this woman.

I sought the root, but couldn't reach it. I knew her, but we had never met. I was familiar with her pain, not personally, yet from somewhere that faintly allowed me to understand its origin. It was as if her form were the embodiment of a tale told.

Stripped bare and vulnerable, she sang the final lyrics of, 'Good Morning Heartache'. Wordlessly she stepped down from the stage and glided through the crowd.

'Naomi,' I called out as her body carried past on an ocean breeze.

As if broken from a long spell, her head jerked back stunned by the unexpected address. All the blood drained from her face and she stared, pale and ghostly, right through me. She voiced nothing, but mouthed words, I interpreted as, 'Kaoru, my love.'

With this inaudible utterance, she turned and walked away through the exit. For a moment, I observed her illuminated under the blue saxophone gleam as if she were sinking in a luminescent sea. The neon flickered and she disappeared.

I downed my drink and rushed to the street. I looked in both directions, up and down the block, but she was gone, much like the ferryman, Kaoru, her star-crossed lover who had preceded her.

Headed toward the Genki Netcafe, along the way, I kept a look out for the songstress in the red gown. My encounter with the ferryman, whom I met making my way up the Pacific, misted through my mind as I drifted home.

On the deck, he spoke of how he'd come to find himself a ferry worker and his love-hate relationship with the sea, which had held him hostage on those waters for decades on end.

The way the name had fallen upon my lips, and her reaction when I blurted it out, it must've been Naomi. But in Kaoru's story, Naomi was dead – hence his sequester at sea.

I ran through my memory of the story; his rise as a prominent jazz musician, the two young hipsters falling deeply in love, their relationship forbidden by Naomi's powerful father and then her death in a botched love suicide.

Yeah, suicide ...

'He'll never let us be, the defiance would be too much for him,

and there is nowhere to run, he's too influential.' Naomi lays out the facts for her lover. 'There is only one way for us, Kaoru ... to be together for eternity.' A young Naomi with wide watery eyes declares – prologue to her dark solution.

Kaoru looks beyond his love, follows the narrowing path of moonlight off an inky sea and concludes she's right; they could never return to Tokyo. Apart, it would be too painful, and together, he would surely be killed for his disrespect.

They settle on the only option their young hearts can fathom and enter into the timeless love suicide pact.

In the approaching twilight, Karou and Naomi walk to a modest harbour on Enoshima Island, steal a small dingy and row out, until the shore disappears from sight. There they embrace and kiss their final kiss, before plunging into the frigid waters. Kaoru clings to her in the chill as the boat drifts away.

First light breaks over the horizon, they look into each other's eyes and sink together; under the surface, toward their eternal darkness.

Encased within our celestial dome, the ferryman had relayed his tale of woe with an agony in his eyes equal to none I'd ever seen. Until, that is, of the songstress performing her short set earlier that night.

I took a drag and swig of beer. It caught on a lump which had formed in my throat. For I knew, the pact was broken – not by choice or cowardice, but cruel fate. Through the glass behind me, a salaryman read manga comics at a convenience store magazine rack like it was the local library. Eyes half closed out front, turning to the dog-eared page, I read again, the narrative written on my memory.

'My lungs burned as I held my breath against a cry for oxygen. Naomi broke from my grasp; she flailed and inhaled a lungful of water. I fought to hold on, but everything began to blacken before I felt her slip away, descend and drown.

'The darkness and tranquillity became all-encompassing,

leaving me in a great peace. In moments, Naomi and I would be waking in our imagined eternity together. Hand in hand, in a smoky jazz bar where Coltrane occupied the stage and blew all night.' He had laughed there, despite the darkness, proud still of their imagined afterlife.

But he awoke alone on the steel flooring of an inner hull, no Coltrane, and no Naomi.

Voices of concern float in as he regains consciousness. When they see he's awake, his rescuers flood him with questions; was he alone, what had happened, his name and where he was from. He answers none, just mutely sits and watches as the shoreline nears, alone in that world Naomi and he vowed to leave behind as one. While the outboard motor cries out his desperate longing for death on the seafloor.

'The fisherman dropped me ashore to a waiting ambulance, wishing this strange sopping mess they'd caught at first light, "the best of luck".' Here, Kaoru had knitted his brow and looked toward an invisible horizon in the dark night, then relaxed. Relieved, I presumed, that on that night there was no land in sight.

Replaying the events in my mind on a dim Shinjuku sidewalk, I experienced the same pit in my stomach as I had on the ferry deck, with an added weight of unease, contemplating my ghostly meeting with his fair Naomi earlier, and the immaterial quality of it all.

* * *

An elongated diamond skirted over rooftops a couple of blocks beyond my convenience store perch. With my eyes peeled to the sky, I tracked the camouflage kite's rhythmic sway in the night. Under the mechanical waving arm of a neon Santa, I broke into a wide grin. The comical wordplay of the Ho Ho Love Hotel I'm sure was purely accidental and escaped most who booked in at hourly blocks for their illicit rendezvous. I pondered how they might express the yuletide theme inside, as I walked down offshoots of backstreets I didn't recognise, pleasantly surprised I could still get lost in that nine-block radius. *Tokyo's own little sordid Bermuda triangle.*

I found my bearings, and three doors down cornered my prey. He wore a full-on lime green leisure suit, with bright white shoes. Despite standing out like a Key lime disco ball, no one even looked in his direction, not even to snigger or gawk.

'How are the winds blowing tonight?' I asked, staring skyward at the navy blue patch on the night.

'*Komban wa*,' he said with a friendly familiarity like maybe he recognised me from the first time. But who knows, crazy is hard to read.

'You're in a different spot.' We stood between a Yakiniku restaurant and a small, wood-fronted restaurant-bar called Heartbeat that looked like it belonged more in the Klondike than Kabukicho.

'*Hai*, tonight here.'

'The updraft, right?' I confirmed.

'*Sou, sou ...*'

'Cause it spoke to you, yeah.' A self-congratulatory grin broke for my accurate recount.

He too seemed moderately impressed giving a slow nod, and slight turn of his face, to reconfirm maybe, who this *gaijin* was. '*Nee*, to find the right place in the sky.'

'Right place? So why is here, tonight, the proper place?'

'Com ... mu ... nic ... ation.' He sounded out the word with great care and concentration.

'Huh?' *Like flipping pigeons in tha hood? Was he sending signals amongst yakuza gangsters? Doesn't fuckin' look the part.* 'What are you trying to say?'

'Oh, nothing nothing.' His wide thin-lipped grin stretched toward quiet-bulging eyes. Even more the contented bullfrog, having caught me in this riddle. A quick pull on the string and the kite ducked then rose. His glistening, bloated face turned to me and said, 'It's listening.'

I again followed the line from his hand, tonight painted yellow from a noodle-house sign. I followed it up like Dorothy's yellow brick road, then back down, like a dehydrated hangover piss. And I landed back on his hands – slender, elegant and nimble; an antithesis to the rest of his form.

'Come on bro, give me a go?' I laughed half-heartedly along with my vain attempt.

'*Iie, iie*.' He grinned into the night.

I almost wanted to snatch away the string, like a schoolyard bully. Though I was strangely intimidated by the hobbyist pursuit. An inkling in the aura that intimated; it was more than I could fathom, and beyond my control.

'Okay, have fun, eh.' I left him there in the jaundiced light, straddling the pavement and flying his kite.

Moments later, at a skewed little intersection, another mirage crossed my path. This one more pleasantly presented in heels and short skirt. She tip-tapped past pylons and a parked bicycle when I arrived at her side.

'Hey, I thought that was you,' I said, a lecherous grin sprawled across my inebriated face.

'Oh, Fred …' Yukie wore a deer-in-the-headlights look.

I threw my arm around her shoulder, oblivious as usual, and said, 'Great t'see ya, let's grab a drink.'

She squirmed away from my slapdash courtship and wedged an appreciable space in our crisp locomotion. 'Err, not now. I can't, I'm going to work.'

'Kinda late, I thought you woulda started already?'

'I got request from customer in another bar.' She clutched at her purse and continued the brisk pace.

'Oh, somebody's Little Miss Popular,' I said, thinking it playful. But hearing it now in electric ink, it was delivered in a surly slur, like it'd come from a spiteful place.

The steady beat of heels, stopped dead. Yukie turned to me, her annoyance and discomfort illuminated in the centre of that Kabukicho street. 'Fred, I can't be seen with you now. *Gomen*, it's just if my boss, or customer at bar sees, I'll get in trouble.'

'Oh yeah. Of course. No, I get it.' I bumbled through, her words and intentions. 'Shit, sorry. I'll let you go.'

I was waiting for the final brush-off and Yukie to scurry away. But she hesitated for a second, which hung like a pleasant eternity.

'You don't come to Mac anymore,' she said with a small, illegible smile.

'Yeah, been busy getting everything in order, settling in, house hunting and job hunting and shit.' My evasive inventions felt at home in those alleys, amongst plastic trash bags, blackened brick walls and scampering rats.

'That's good, I hope everything works out okay.'

I shoved both hands in the pouch of my hoodie and stared down at the pavement. 'But I missed our hanging out, our little talks and all, these last few days,' I said, with a little more authenticity. Like her beauty was a kryptonite to my drunken bullshit and prefab conceit. 'But I was planning to show up tomorrow night. If that's okay?' I looked up from the pavement to skim her expression.

'*Ii desu.*' Her chin tilted upward, and off she trotted into the night. She looked back once, maybe to make sure I'd stayed put, then took a right.

Left alone in the alley my mind retreated to its neurotic boudoir. *Why' so standoffish? Going to a bar or maybe something else? A love hotel? Does she moonlight? An escort? A mistress?*

I retired to a local Brit-themed pub. In the familiar atmosphere of the basement bar, I pulled out all the stops to bury my thoughts. Pints of lager and doubles of vodka Redbull immersed me in the bedimmed haze of chatter and laughter. Then, I set to work in my old hunting grounds, bumming lights from and buying drinks for coquettish college girls and plump secretaries. I prowled around with a salacious smile smeared on my face, peppered the joint with snap-happy winks, rested hands on denimed thighs and whispered microwaved words through curtains of hair. When the ugly lights came on at 3 am, I stumbled up the stairs alone with no more than a name and number on a ripped coaster to show for my efforts.

My hand braced against red brick outside the entrance as a stream of urine splashed the wall. A face reflected in a picture window, a whispered smile, and the Shinjuku night absorbed by her kaleidoscope eyes flashed on the insides of my half-closed lids. My wall – bricks of fleeting flirtations, erected in haste with fearful intentions – she'd breached easily, and once more occupied my mind. I zipped up and walked home more discombobulated than usual.

* * *

In my cubicle the drinks continued to flow. I stared through the blurred lips and blurred eyes of scantily clad girls on *delivery health* pop-up ads to see if I could recognize any as Yukie. One minute they all were and the next most definitely not. Until, after a while, their shapes clouded and the whole panel became one fleshy, brunette haired mass.

Fuck it, she's just a piece of ass, I told myself so I could log off and get some sleep. When the booze was strong in me it seemed to work, but I sensed the old defence mechanism wearing thin against her enduring allure.

The constant glare of the console screen, I took refuge from by sauntering out to the ice machine. The fizz on a freshly poured Cola dissolved, as Kai exited the bathroom hair combed and suit buttoned, which singled I'd been up all night. I didn't say anything and wasn't expecting him to either.

'*Ohayo gozaimasu*,' he recited, his cheery tone untarnished by our recent run-in.

'Oh … *Ohayo*,' I replied, caught off guard, and searching him for a motive or some lingering animosity toward me. But he'd fallen right back into character; the chipper little go-getter living blissfully in his cubicle world of make believe.

When Weepy arrived, I was relieved. His lanky form leaned over the water boiler, like the drooping branch of a willow tree.

'*Ohayo gozaimasu*,' Kai fired the phrase loaded with its standard *genki*ness at Weepy this time.

'*Ohayo*,' He said, steadfast in his Eeyore enthusiasm. '*Kyo wa nani o shimasu ka?*'

Wow, a real chatterbox today, I thought, of Weepy's burst.

'*Ah, shigoto, shigoto. Cho isogashi*,' Kai responded.

I observed their exchange with a scrambled scrutiny. Something about it struck me as off, other than the usual, strange mannerisms of the two men. *The split second eye contact, was something communicated there?*

Weepy stirred his instant coffee while Kai marched back to his office.

And wait, it was an informational question, and Kai answered in full? That's not how it's supposed to go …

A great fatigue descended upon me, but I couldn't sleep. I searched for apartments, none of which I could afford, even the lowly *gaijin* houses. Then I job hunted which turned up the usual part-time teaching jobs. Nothing else I was qualified for except maybe the ones looking for a Caucasian mall Santa for the coming Christmas season, and another for a white dude to play the minister during the western ceremony at Japanese weddings. *Got the requisite whisky breath for a mall Santa*, I figured, *probably for the priest as well.*

The console screen reads 5:14, I missed a whole day of Vitamin D and have been up for thirty-one hours straight. Afraid to recline in my black leather chair, I swivel upright, earphones on while the

Pixies play. But, *hey*, I'd better unleash these chains, and go try to meet her. Shit, shower, shave and I'll make my way to a Shinjuku McDonald's for a 7 pm rendezvous, drawn by a promise and power beyond my ken.

One last long swallow of whisky and I'm gone.

***

It was 3 pm on a Wednesday. I stumbled down the sidewalk drunker than usual. I'd imbibed less, but the grog could be unpredictable like that.

In a fortuitous turn, I saw Jae-hyun chilling in the run-down park off our netcafe's street. Maybe it was just a vacant lot someone had deposited a park bench in. I dunno – anyways, I meandered in.

He drank Jinro *soju* from an emerald green bottle with Hangul scrawled down the label. A big shambolic smile scrawled across his lips, he waved me over. His face was ruddy and glistening. I detected he was pretty sauced too – must've been something in the air that day.

I sat on the far end of the bench, a deserted chessboard between us, the pieces packed away in a brown cloth bag with the beige lace drawn and tied.

'You been playing?' I asked. 'With Kai?'

'*Hai*,' Jae-hyun replied. 'You're not going to ask who won?' He said with a modest smile.

I laughed, remembering his assertion of Kai's prowess on the chessboard. 'Hey, did he say anything about me?' Thinking of my impertinence the other morning.

'No, should he have?'

I went on to explain my tip-toed infringement on Kai's personal space. Jae-hyun listened with both curiosity and disapproval.

'And?' he asked in a neutral tone.

'And yeah, it looked like you could be in the right ballpark with your assessment.'

Jae-hyun eyed my assurance through a monocle of scepticism.

'But you know, I only gotta quick peek,' I continued. 'Besides, I'm starting to realize; meaning, like a greased-up sumo wrestler, is a difficult thing to grasp.'

'Hah, true dat!'

It was an out of place idiolect, which bristled an ambiguous association. But I was drunk, and supposed just hearing shit.

Reaching into the plastic bag at my feet, I pulled out one of the Chu-his. Nashi or Japanese pear was a seasonal flavour for autumn. I liked the taste and drank them, quite literally, like they were going out of style, never knowing when they might be pulled from the *conbini* shelves.

'You want to play?' Jae-hyun asked, gesturing to the board between us.

I had four Chu-hi's left in my bag and no pressing plans. 'Sure, set 'em up.'

I moved a knight to F3 for my opening move. 'Big balls,' Jae-hyun teased.

I knew, I was outmatched, but figured if I played aggressive and unpredictable, I could prolong the inevitable. I drank to the soothing distinctive crinkle given off by a Kirin Hyoketsu can as the world went by in a lazy haze. I waited for Jae-hyun's first move, sporting a dopey grin while a rare sense of satisfaction clung to me, like an aura.

'You seem in good spirits. Have you had a breakthrough?' Jae-hyun pushed a pawn out to B4.

'Nah, more of a roadblock.' I shrugged. 'But it's all good, time will tell.'

'Hah,' he voiced with gleeful surprise. 'Quite a transformation from the perpetually restless young man I usually meet. It's either the liquor or a lady, and since you've always had the liquor, methinks, it's a lady that's gussied up your spirits.' After having his fun in old-timey wordplay, he put it to me directly, 'A woman capture your fancy?'

I thought about just nodding the affirmative like Kai would have, but I liked to run my mouth too much. 'Well closer ... Yeah, that may be it Jayzhyun, I'm still figurin't oot,' I slurred.

'Again, with this!' he said, animated in playful frustration. 'Why so much energy figuring everything out. If there is a place for cerebralism, it is most certainly not matters of the heart.'

I let out a soft sigh. 'I wasn't always like this, I'm actually a pretty easygoing guy.' I looked to Jae-hyun who nodded recognition of this. 'I don't know when the weight of life took on such unmanageable mass.'

'Well, you whistle Dixie in the dark long enough, you're going to hit a wall ... or it's going to hit you.' He looked up from the board and met my eye with an arched eyebrow.

Chewing the inside of my lip, I turned the battlement of my rook and contemplated my next move.

'Fuck it,' he said, with a wave of his good hand and gleeful spittle falling on the board. 'Just enjoy and let the pachinko ball fall where it may.'

I wondered if this was a regional variant on the common expression or if it were pure Jae-hyunism. Nonetheless, it was that kind of day. So yes, *fuck it!*

I mirrored Jae-hyun's previous move and pushed my pawn out to G4. He nodded approvingly, though I couldn't say why, so I knew I was hooped.

'Tell me about her. Is she a good lass?'

Lass? Again, the nomenclature threw me. I did a double take at him but wrote it off as just Jae-hyun and his miscellaneous patchwork of provincial and antiquated linguistics.

'Yeah, she's cool and beautiful,' I began and went on to describe her appearance and the ease with which we talked.

I mentioned my concern that she worked as a hostess. To which he replied, 'So? You, my friend, don't work at all as far as I can tell.' We had a chuckle over the obvious there. 'It's not like she's in an alley turning tricks,' he added.

'And there's something both formidable and alluring about her that I can't put my finger on.' I drank from my can in hopes my finger would land on it then and there over the chessboard. It didn't. I served up a muddled interpretation instead, 'Like she's harbouring some deep secret or scarred past.'

'Aren't we all?' Jae-hyun put plainly.

I liked that about Jae-hyun, he always knew what to say to bring me down to earth, make me right-sized. I tend to swing wildly on a fraying vine between extremes in a jungle of self; an egomaniac with low self-esteem, the most affable piece of shit in the room – clashing dispositions of my immiscible existence. My inner self clad in a coarse wool jumper, itching madly – of true contentment, I knew little.

Jae-hyun went out of his way to keep it real and call me on my shit. We couldn't have been from two more different worlds, but in that moment, I knew we'd become unlikely friends.

The mellow surroundings and concentration on the match sobered me some. I was beaten in about twenty moves. I'm gonna say distracted due to the discussion of my burgeoning love life, but that's bullshit.

As the loser, I reset the board. When finished placing all the pieces, I spun the square so that I was now black. Jae-hyun smirked at my petty disposition.

'Like a chakra,' I said. 'Isn't that what the yogi's call it?' I continued describing the one understated fingernail and how it, for some reason, fascinated me.

'Hmmm, interesting ...' Jae-hyun said with brow furrowed.

He pushed out his far-right pawn to start the match. I noted he did so, as with all his moves, using his maimed hand. He'd use his thumb to push the index finger into the ring finger and pinch the piece, pick it up and drop it, not unlike the claw machine in an arcade. I wondered, normally the hand hung nullified by his side. Yet, here he deployed it, controlled and manipulated the pieces with the mangled manus, his former pachinko hand.

'So we left the McDonald's and were walking to find a bar I'd come across. A little jazz joint I thought she'd dig, or more importantly thought might make me look cultured and cool,' I recollected. 'This was, pretty much our first real date, so I wanted to impress. As we walked, I laid the compliments on pretty thick. But that nail kept flashing through my mind. I held her hand and said something schmaltzy like, "you look even more beautiful than usual tonight." Then as part of a two-pronged ploy, I brought it toward my face to plant a kiss on the back of her hand.'

'Smooth,' Jae-hyun said with a smattering of sarcasm.

I winced to concur. 'So, I kissed, and with her hand now held up to my face, I say, "Your nails are stylish. This one though, it's so different. Is there a reason … like what's the meaning?"'

'Curiosity killed the horny cat,' Jae-hyun slipped in, gripping the top of a bishop.

'Yeah, pretty much,' I agreed with a soft chuckle. 'She pulled her hand away and slipped it into her pocket, "My shoes, my hair, my nails. Are these tips from a pick-up guide or something?" She said it like teasing and all, but clearly embarrassed and a little bit pissed-off.'

'"No, is there a guide? Perhaps I should read it, looks like I'm coming off kinda transparent." I said back to her playing along but also kinda ticked-off, embarrassed and insulted.'

'Not bad,' Kai said. 'And her rebut?'

'"We're all a little transparent when you get close enough and look from the right angle." But, like, she was musing, not talking to me or anyone in particular.'

'Hmm, sounds like an interesting woman you've met there.'

'Yeah, so far so good,' I replied, in my typical non-committal fashion.

'And the second prong of your hand-kissing plan, Romeo? '

'Oh, yeah. Basically, testing the waters with a little physical contact.'

'Which were?' He knew the answer but perhaps wanted to see me squirm.

'Frigid.' I hid a humbled smile behind the tilt of my Chu-hi can. 'No worries, I'm warming 'em up,' I added, lowering the can with a big cocky grin.

'How was the jazz club?'

'Oh yeah. We never found it. I walked the same street and adjoining alleys two or three times, but never came across the blue neon sax that hangs outside.'

'That's odd. Maybe you were just intoxicated,' he said, with a dismissive shake of his *soju*.

'Yeah maybe, but I'm sure it was there. You wanna know the fucked up thing? That's two buildings in two days that upped and disappeared on me, like the locales were anonymously swallowed up by sinkholes.'

Our second match ended with me being suckered into a queen sacrifice. I took the bait and found myself in checkmate two moves later. I'd played my fair share of stoned matches in city parks and dingy basements throughout the years, but had never developed into much of a player. Something about thinking multiple moves ahead ran against my natural inclinations. I prefer cards and games of chance.

I racked up the pieces for a third match, no spinning the board or switching colours this time. I was pretty much resigned to my fate at that point.

'What about you?' I asked Jae-hyun, only then realizing that most all our conversations revolved around me and my troubles. 'You got a woman in your life?'

He laughed uproariously. I sniggered a little as well, caught up in the intoxicating mirth, though I didn't think the question that amusing. 'I'm forty-five and live in an internet café. I have a crippled hand and am from North Korea,' he said as the chuckling subsided. 'So no, the women are not lining up around the block to date me.'

'Yeah but you're smart, you speak fluent Japanese and English …' I started to build him up, worried my question had dispirited or ridiculed him. 'Plus, you're a good-looking guy in relatively good nick. I'm sure you can find women to date.'

'I get sex,' he said very matter-of-fact, head held level.

'Well, that's good news!' I flashed an impish smirk.

A weak grin hobbled across Jae-hyun's face, then he fell pensive. 'I'm not at a place where I attract your entirely all-together Japanese women. These days, my romances are relegated to the odd desperate and broken housewife or random women of the night. It's just coitus. I've squandered the rest.'

'How'd you end up here?' I asked, shifting topics, but hoped it ended up explaining the self-sequestered isolation he alluded to.

My rook got captured, and he began. 'I was born in absolute darkness. At night, the North Korean countryside has virtually no artificial light. Exiting my mother's womb into the pitch blackness of this world, how was I to know I'd even been born at all.'

I thought about the glow produced by the Tokyo night, how bright it must shine, like a north star to a satellite gazing down on earth. *Had he sought this illumination from even those first breaths?*

'We were potato farmers – poor, yet no poorer than all others in the land. We grew for the Republic and ate little else than the starchy earth apples.' He drank of the emerald *soju* bottle, a long swallow as if to kindle the memories. 'At 17, I was conscripted into the army and sent to the DMZ. All-day I stood armed with my AK-47 and looked across the expanse of the demilitarized zone at a matching South Korean soldier on the other side. I was supposed to distrust him, to hate him; that was my duty … even my birthright.'

'Did ya?'

'At first, I wanted to do as taught. The army was my way off the farm and maybe even into the higher echelon of society,' he admitted, guilt registering on his face in a disapproving frown.

'Sometimes, tourists would walk through the South's camp. Whites, like yourself mostly, and some Chinese or Japanese. I hated them more; aiming their cameras at us, pointing and trading jokes, like we were exotic safari scenery. Over time though, I started to look more closely. Through my stern, trained glare, something began to penetrate ... empathy. They knew something about my life, which I'd never been told and never been permitted to learn myself – it was pitiable.' He chuckled to himself at this long-ago realization, and I couldn't tell if it was to mock his own naivety or awe at the mechanisms which kept so many in the dark

'After that, I focused the same perceptive glare on the Southern guard across the Military Demarcation Line. Usually, I saw equivalent despise in their eyes as had been programmed into mine, in other cases, sheer indifference. Around seven months at my post, a new South Korean private was assigned. It was in his talced stone expression, in his warm brown eyes, that I found the compassion I needed to enact my perilous plan.'

I lumbered my knight into capture, stone drunk, and wrapped in his story. 'Which was?' I sputtered as he took the defenceless stallion.

'For about three weeks, as we stood to attention and stared across the barren grassy stretch of the DMZ with our guns slung across our chest, one hand ready on the butt and the other fixed on the barrel, I sent messages to my counterpart.'

'Were you allowed to do that?' I asked, sensing that it was a major break in protocol.

'Not verbal messages, and not any form of gesture. Telepathic.' He raised an eyebrow punctuating the word. 'I didn't even know if telepathy existed, I still don't know if it does. But for eight hours every day, I directed thoughts with all my concentrative power to the young guard fifty yards across the way.'

Jae-hyun paused, looked up from the board. When he caught my glance with umber eyes, I was pinching the mitre of my remaining bishop. I altered my tactic and castled my king instead. Jae-hyun nodded his approval and cracked a wee wry smile. I cleared my throat and asked, 'What did you say? Um, or think?'

'I kept it very simple: "I want out", "I come peacefully" and finally asking, "will you let me out?" I repeated them over and over in my mind while fixing the man with a beseeching stare.'

'And he answered?' I jumped in, voice cut with an anxious edge.

'To this day, I can't be sure. It may have been no more than wishful thinking. But late in the afternoon of the third week of my exercise, I received a reply. It started soft, then resonated across the expanse like a sonic boom. "YES." I stood straight to attention as a good soldier would, but when the answer hit my consciousness, I was knocked backwards off my stance. I took no time to question the validity of this sign, I just acted. It was likely a suicide mission, but I crouched and lay to rest the heavy rifle on the ground, then rose to a standing position. My hands were up, not all the way over my head like "I surrender" but more adjacent to my ears as if to say, "I come in peace."

Jae-hyun mimicked the movement on our small park bench. It looked comical with the *soju* and a smoke, in either hand. *Oh, the places you'll go.*

'I crept over clumps of dirt and grass which scattered the desolate space between North and South. I never took my eyes off the soldier on the other side, and he never took his eyes off me nor his hands off his weapon. As I trudged that formidable path, I continued to direct my thoughts, "I only want out, I mean no harm, don't shoot". My eyes fixed on his, the familiar face getting closer and closer, I gauged if I'd eroded enough his stone-faced stare and sweated that he wasn't merely waiting for a clean shot.'

I knew he made it out. I mean he was sitting across from

me, kicking my ass in chess. Still, my heart was in my throat as he described his defection. Then, the mangy white tom with the mismatched eyes flashed to mind and out, like a startled cockroach.

'I arrived to face my foe-cum-saviour. We exchanged no words or greeting. I marched on, and he fell in line behind me. I was taken to a barracks and jailed, but not for long. They held me around the base as a free man for months afterward and interviewed me for intel, hours on end each day. I don't think I offered up much, being young and of low rank. When they figured they'd gotten all the information they needed, I was released into the heart of Seoul with only the clothes on my back. I got by washing dishes and other odd jobs. Along the way, I met Joo Won who was to change everything.'

'A friend?' I searched his distant gaze for clues.

'*Hai*, a friend,' Jae-hyun confirmed. 'But sometimes it's our friends who inadvertently set us on the most fraught paths.' He stared sombrely at the chequered board before moving his pawn into a defensive position.

'Joo Won was another North Korean defector predating me by several years. He'd come to the South on assignment as a propagandist for the party. During this short stint to gather material from which to slander the capitalist and democratic South, after having a small taste of freedom, he decided he didn't want to do that, nor go back. So, he sought refugee protection.'

Jae-hyun's *soju* had run dry. I worried that would cut his divulgence short. Like me, he seemed to rely a bit on the boozy fuel to keep the motor running. My fear unfounded, Jae-hyun pulled a sly stashed tall can of beer from the pocketed travel vest he wore over a grey tee.

The pull tab resounded with a rousing crack followed by a sweet soft hiss.

He went on to explain how Joo Won tipped him off about work in Japan. He was to meet a fishing boat the next day that would take him via the East China Sea and drop him off at the Tsukiji fish market a few days later.

'Early the next morning, I was on the dock with a small sack of simple possessions,' he said. 'I'd left everything I knew once, what was it to do it again? The boat rolled over waves and currents for three days. I never got seasick. Maybe I was a natural for the seas. It was the first time I'd ever seen the ocean and her vastness both inspired and humbled me. I stared wordlessly out at the blue-grey horizon and was heartened I'd walked across the line, if only for that moment.'

My lips curled into a smile which Jae-hyun mirrored, like tides rising on opposite shores.

'Equipped only with the address in my pocket, I made my through the Tokyo labyrinth, ending up here, Okubo. It was the mid-80s, the Japanese bubble was rapidly expanding, and I set to work learning the ropes of the pachinko business.' He beamed even at the mention of the word 'pachinko'. It was odd, how the silly game still brought such evident jubilation like reminiscing an old flame. I hoped that the parlour game itself was not the lost love intimated earlier.

Jae-hyun lifted his hand and counted off on crumpled fingers the ins and outs of his job. 'How to upkeep the machines, managing the clientele, spotting cheats, training up the touts; over the years I worked my way up until I was managing my own parlour, then two and three.'

'So you were making good coin?' I threw in, hiding my surprise as well as I could.

'*Hai*, I was not always broke and inhabiting an internet café cubicle. I lived the high life for a solid decade. Until the contingencies of my success were too much to shoulder.'

'Must've been nice,' I said. Sounded though, like he was heading toward a 'mo money, mo problems' pivot, like the famous Biggie line I could never quite swallow.

'Yes, it had its advantages,' he agreed. 'It was after I made assistant manager of the first parlour that I met Eun-ae. She was pure grace. Like a Korean Audrey Hepburn, or a young Kim Ji-mee.'

My blank expression must've revealed I hadn't a clue who that was.

'I was a year in the South when I went to my first cinema. In a dark afternoon matinee, Kim Ji-mee lit up the screen with her big doe eyes.' He smiled like a smitten teen. It was weird to see the middle-aged Jae-hyun transported back there swooning on his own words. 'When I laid eyes on Eun-ae in a small Korean BBQ shop, I was overcome with the same majestic feeling. She was my waitress that day, handing me raw meat and kimchi, and I made sure she was my waitress each day after until she was mine.'

'Did you marry?'

'Almost, we were engaged. Then came the crash.'

I hoped the crash was metaphorical. Meanwhile, he had my king on the run. I was in check every second move. It was just a matter of time before it was captured.

'You see, it's a massive enterprise ...' Jae-hyun detoured into an in-depth explanation on the intricacies of Japan's pachinko pastime, as my monarch fled. Ties to the underworld, machine fixing, addicts, pros, loan sharks and all the flimsy workarounds Japan's strict gambling laws; but most interesting were the strong, well-established North Korea ties.

'Believe it or not, Japanese pachinko raked in thirty times what Vegas cleared in its casinos. And millions of that was going back to support Kim-Jong's regime. We Zainichi went from forced labourers to isolation and discrimination when the war ended. Though a few lucky ones, like my employers, found their way into the early days of the pachinko business. It was seen as unsavoury work, perfect for the subjugated Korean class. Little did they know it would become a billion-dollar industry they were handing over to these "inferior people".'

He'd trapped me. I conceded by leaning my king horizontal on the board. We didn't set up another game, it was unspoken that the afternoon was coming to a close.

'I knew what was going on long before I did anything about it. I preferred to be an ostrich with his head up his ass.'

I smiled at the misused expression, but suspect Jae-hyun knew he was taking poetic license with the idiom.

'I enjoyed too much the comfortable living, the gangster ties, the nightclubs and fine clothes. Mostly though, the lifestyle allowed me to lavish upon my dear Eun-ae. Then the news reached me. Bygone and horrible events ... I should have pieced them together years earlier, perhaps my reaction wouldn't have been so extreme. I hadn't though.'

The chess finished, with both hands we drank and smoked freely. He talked, I listened. A grey chill cloaked the park, street, and its backdrop of buildings; presage of winter.

'The Pyongyang regime upon getting word of my defection had tracked down my mother, father and little sister, Bo. They murdered them all, in cold blood. A single bullet to the temple for each.' Two twisted, tremulous fingers touched Jae-hyun's forehead in gruesome simulation, and his face hardened.

'Money I was making in my shops went to my bosses, whom I could no longer ignore, were sending it by the bucketload back to powerful ties in the North.' He choked back rage with a hard swallow of ale. 'Maybe I should have up and quit, but it wasn't a clear conscience I was after. No, now it was revenge, in the impossible design of bringing down the whole system.' Jae-hyun shook his head at this long passed madness which had consumed him wholly. Though it would seem, he registered no regret. He'd followed his heart, a heart full of fury.

'I fixed the machines, on the sly, every last one in all three parlours. In a few days they were paying out in fistfuls, and patrons lined up around the block for the loosest machines in town. A sure thing is always popular with gamblers. The parlours lost hundreds of thousands before my overlords caught wind of the scam and came swooping down to stop it.'

'Did they catch ya?' I asked, thinking maybe since he was still alive he'd gotten away with the grift.

'Of course they caught me,' he answered. 'You thought they would have killed me, *ne*? Yes, I was expecting the same. Almost hoping for it. Yet, that would have been too easy. They had a more sadistic plan for me.'

'Eun-ae,' I uttered, each syllable a barely audible whisper.

'Yes, but not what you're thinking, again too exact, too uninvolved. Instead, they lured her away with riches, and I'd like to believe, though could never confirm, threats; to family or maybe to me.' He said, conflicted, still to the day. 'I have to believe her abandonment was not only for filthy lucre. I returned to our apartment one day, and she was gone with all her possessions. The engagement ring left on my pillow with not a note nor teardrop as explanation.'

His eyes welled up. This threw me as Jae-hyun was always so controlled and analytical in manner.

'If I wasn't before, on a suicide mission, I certainly was then. After they stole my Eun-ae, the pursuit of revenge became even more manic. I was determined to break them, to bring down the house, as they say in your Vegas jargon. But it was an impossible obsession, especially now that I was in a weakened position.'

'You'd lost your queen,' I threw in thinking it quite congruous.

'*Hai*, and was reduced to a pawn,' he said in concert. 'Still, 20 hours a day I snuck in and sat, turning the little nob, directing the ball bearings of the vertical pinball machine. I won a bit and lost bits, here and there. It became clear I wasn't even making a dent. If anything, the overlords were enjoying watching my compulsive demise. I switched tack and cheated. Magnets used to steer the ball, but even though I knew how to do it well from my years in the trade, I was caught after a time. My hand was smashed with a mallet. Bandaged I returned and played through the agony. Only to be crippled by shame, by fear and by defeat.' He held up his mangled hand. 'And just fucking crippled.'

I winced, studying the knots and lumps at each joint, pondering what was more powerful: *love or revenge? Regret or redemption? Or are they two sides of the same coin?*

'One afternoon, into my fourteenth hour of steering pachinko balls through the house set pegs, the final one fell ... one slot left of centre. It was my moment of clarity. I surrendered. I exited the parlour leaving behind my basket of shiny silver balls for some other player to claim.'

'Where'd you go?'

'I went home,' he said, 'only to find there was no home left. A padlock was on the door and an eviction notice pinned to the peephole.'

'And you ended up here?'

'*Hai*, here is where I ended up, the Genki Netcafe ... four years ago, for a short recess.' He chuckled at the absurdity of it now.

'Sorry, if it's too prying. But why have you stayed so long? Like aren't you sick of living there, don't you think it's time to move on?' I asked, my eyes following cracks in the dried dirt below.

'It is where I need to be,' he answered, placid and poised. 'I may not like some of the detours along the way, but every step and sidestep, every rut or painful shard stepped upon; it is what it is, and was what it was. I accept it today, the path that led me here. It was necessary and absolute. I'm here now. When it is time to move on, I'll move on.' Jae-hyun, stretched his neck from side to side. I got that. The partially upright slumber of the netcafe left one with many kinks to work out.

I opened the empty plastic bag and silently collected up our empty cans, crushed butts and *soju* bottle. Jae-hyun put the pieces back in the brown cloth bag, he folded the board in half and drew the string tight.

'Thanks for the game.' It felt as if I should say more yet couldn't find any other words.

'My pleasure,' Jae-hyun gave as his cordial reply.

I took slow, stiff steps toward the darkening side street.

'You're here for a reason too,' Jae-hyun called after me from the bench where he still sat smoking.

'*Sodane*,' I muttered to myself before I turned my head, nodding a half-hearted acknowledgement.

***

Tonight I drink my whisky straight and write with a renewed fervour. Since my Higashi-Koseki excursion and roadblock, I've been stymied on my next move. I thought of widening my search, but the prospect of another afternoon in futile searching wasn't appealing and, from all assessment, completely redundant. I guess all I can do is reflect in front of this monitor and drop more breadcrumbs, fuelled by the motivation to not end up four years on in this same cubicle. Sorry Jae-hyun, I can not 'accept' that!

'Fuck.' Raw whisky spits from wet lips as the curse sails out of the stuffy cubicle into a hushed cafe.

Keep writing ... Eyes peeled, Fred ... Spot it! Any sign, whether it be directional or off-ramp indication.

I'm an urban refugee. I assuage myself, thinking it sounds kinda hip and bohemian.

No mate, you're a fuckin bum. Reality kicks in. *Get a job, get laid, get a proper apartment, get your shit together!*

I can't. Not yet.

Then you're fucked, mate.

The conversation ends in the same hushed, harsh-defensive tone it began. Part pep talk, part dressing down; these dialogues have been cropping up in the solitary cubicle when night has descended, and the day seems a fair distance away.

You're here for a reason. Jay-hyun's parting words from the park bounce off the four melamine masked chipboard walls. I pour more whisky over smooth melting ice cast in the blue glare of the monitor screen. Reclining back in my black cushioned chair, letting the aqua luminosity of the console wash over, I'm transported back to the deck of the A-liner, a passing sea speeding by below.

I sit up abruptly. *The ferryman … a faded tattoo … Dallas … the malcontent house … Akiko … blood-speckled stones … Gertie … tortured souls and tattered hearts* speed past my mind's widow, like scenery from a runaway *shinkansen.* Names, memories and symbols – people, places and things – flood the small cubicle. I touch keys, look deep into this waiting screen as if seeking movement beneath a water's surface, and see beyond my ocean voyage.

Rainy Day Ramen

PART TWO
Ocean (Shoyu)

Real things in the darkness seem no realer than dreams.
—*Murasaki Shikibu*, The Tale of Genji

1// The Ferryman Speaketh

The gentle rocking of the ship lulled me into a foggy stupor. A quarter bottle of Awamori contributed much, to be sure.

It was certainly no leisure cruise. I sat atop a thin mattress laid over the tatami floor of the communal sleeping area. I'd been reading *Catcher in the Rye* for the umpteenth time, but my stomach began to churn from the motion and concentration. So I just sat cross-legged and drank, contemplating whether I were possibly a psychopath.

A group of young guys, probably university students, played cards and nursed beers while they talked and joked in a subdued timbre. A couple of older men slept soundly already. They wore the loose grey slacks and coarse button-up shirts of factory workers or maybe truck drivers. I was blithely ill-equipped to identify any as phony.

Chapman, Hinckley and Bardo, all with dog-eared copies, even the homegrown Ichihashi read Salinger and *Kafka on the Shore* in a ladies dress during his years on the lam. But those killer Caulfield fans read it all wrong. They'd taken to the bank truisms in his disillusioned view of a society self-indulgent and shallow, yet missed the underlying innocence, a childlike curiosity at the core. They failed to realize; the wonder was at war with the cynicism.

I dog-eared the book at page 107, put it away in my backpack, then took another slog of Awamori in an attempt to stack the odds. Insouciant, I concluded I wasn't likely to off a Gallagher ... *he's no Lennon, anyhoo*. That said, I've been known to murder a version of

'Wonderwall' a few hours into a karaoke *nomihodai*.

Earlier while exploring the ship's amenities, I discovered only that the voyage promised to be a long, monotonous one. The boat had a small dining area, although there was no food being served, so it was a collection of bare wooden tables surrounded by vacant chairs. A minimalist design throughout, hints of oak or spruce on the pillars and railings gave the interior a sort of East meets Scandinavia vibe.

There were a couple of vending machines where one could buy cup noodles and chips. There was also, of course, a beer vending machine. These machines I viewed as a real novelty when I had first arrived in Japan. If you put beer in vending machines back home, they would be pried open and pilfered on a nightly basis, not to mention all the bleeding hearts who'd protest their existence as fuelling underaged drinking and contributing to societal decay. Here, they just glowed on abandoned street corners throughout the country, unmolested, beacons of Japanese civility.

I fancied a smoke before attempting sleep, and the fresh ocean air would clear the gathering Awamori mist. Heading out on the lower deck, a strong wind kicked water into my face with an exhilarating sting. Shoving my head into an alcove, I managed to light a cigarette. The glowing ember burned rapidly not from my inhalation but mother nature taking some wicked hard drags.

My arms crossed and held tight against my chest, I rounded the back of the ship where the wind died down. I found a simple metallic bench to sit and finish the smoke. Looking into the night sky, I had one of those moments of awe where you are struck by the vastness of it all. Thousands of stars peppered the Pacific ceiling. On Tokyo nights you're lucky if you see even one, and even luckier if it doesn't turn out to be a satellite or passing plane.

Stars reflecting off the black ocean surface triggered thoughts of the cosmic-patterned linoleum floor in The Big Peach Guesthouse. The ferry wake that ripped through the illusion tantamount to the cigarette burns wreaked – minuscule consequences of passing out on my cot with a still-burning dart dangling from the end of a dead-to-the-world arm before the inevitable crash and burn on a linoleum sky. Then it hit ... *In my barren Okinawa room, ravaged by the horrors, the static screen and haunted halls which led to a golden number fourteen ... the setting for my waking nightmare ... it was The Gaijin House.*

I unscrewed the lid of my Awamori and took a swig straight, it went down with an earthy char. I fished another smoke from a soft pack of Marlboros. The flick of my lighter illuminated an approaching figure. The silent form neared, cloaked in darkness. I could track its movement by the glowing orange ember of the cigarette between their lips. Behind the approaching tangerine gleam, I made out a heavy navy blue jacket and slacks to match, underneath he wore a lighter blue collared button-up shirt. I recognized it as the ferry workers' uniform, not a captain, but one of the labourers or general staff.

'Good evening,' he spoke first, unsurprised to see someone else on deck and not fazed in the least that it should be a *gaijin.*

The oversized uniform hung from his thin body like a child playing dress-up in their father's clothes. Perhaps, I thought, the heavy coat was acting as an anchor so the small frame he inhabited wouldn't blow right over the liner's railing.

As he brought the cigarette to his lips for another drag, I noticed that he held it between the ring finger and thumb like you'd smoke a roach. This oddity of form drew my attention to the rest of his hand. Nothing extended beyond the knuckles where the middle and index finger should've been, and the pinkie ended in a rounded nub at the first knuckle. Careful not to get caught staring at the minor deformity, I quickly looked away.

I extended the bottle toward him.

He waved it away, explaining, 'Work.'

Shit, this one must've fucked up royally! I thought,

contemplating the hand, assuming his missing digits originated from the quintessential *yakuza* punishment.

'You go to Kobe?' He asked, slicing through the silence.

'Yes,' I said, 'Is that where you live?'

'*Iie.*' He walked over to the bench and sat in the space beside me. With a sweeping motion of the hand toward the black sea beyond he exclaimed, 'I live here.'

'So you live on this ferry fulltime?'

'No, I work on the ferry, I live on the sea,' he corrected, emphasizing an imperceptible difference.

I didn't have much to say about that existential obscurity. Since I was drunk, and therefore blunt, I cut away social niceties and asked, 'What happened to your hand, sir?'

He looked at his hand then turned it over as if until I'd mentioned it, he had no idea there was anything off about it. He smiled and was missing about twice as many teeth as he was fingers. 'It is a long story, young man. Though, it does explain how I came to live on the sea. I can tell you if you'd care to hear.'

I wondered what it was about me that attracted these old boys (as well as other assorted strangers and nutjobs), and made them want to tell me their life stories. I figured it was less about me and more my being a situational anomaly; always alone, always with time on my hands, and generally looking bewildered in life – perfect fodder for their fare.

The last one worked out well, I figured, if not in the story itself then the fortuitous meeting at the bull sumo. *Who's to say this ferryman isn't needed stitching in the patchwork blanket of my existence.*

Persuaded by my own logic, I acquiesced with a nod, lit up another smoke, and leaned against the cold metal of the bench.

'The women of my home were always clucking, "Kaoru, he is such a handsome boy but always looking sullen. Why so sensitive?"

'You see, I grew up in a house of all women. Aunts and older sisters banded together to support my young widowed mother.

'While pregnant with me, my father was called off to fight in the Imperial Navy. He was a gunner on the behemoth battleship *Musashi*, when torpedoes struck from above, sending my Father and over one thousand Japanese soldiers into the Sibuyan Sea at the Battle of Leyte Gulf. My father never got to look upon his son's face. I never got the opportunity to stare into a father's prideful eyes.

'I was cared for well by the women in my house, if not pampered and coddled more than a boy should be. Perhaps, I was sensitive and sullen, though it was they who, um, sow the seeds.'

His facial bones of cheek, jaw and brow were barely contained by the thin weather-beaten skin stretched over. Burrowed in the skeletal face were dark brown eyes, soulful and searching – and still, after all those years, sensitive and sullen.

'One surety,' Kaoru continued in a syncopated whisper, 'was my lack of understanding of the world. I didn't know how to react to people, so mostly I observed in a near-catatonic state, looking as if I were on the verge of tears. But I wasn't on the verge of tears. I wasn't sad at all. It was actually intense concentration from trying to puzzle it all out.

'What confused me most, maybe even terrified me, was how to react when confronted directly by others. Luckily in a house of women this rarely happened, they tended to occupy and invest themselves in their own concerns, and I was free to sit back and observe, in unending uncertainty.

'That was how I existed in the world. Until I was thirteen, when one day, a record came home with my sister. Before, my mother and aunties had absolute control over the music that continuously breezed through the house. It was uniformly *enka* or classical. While it didn't bother me in any way, it also had no effect over me whatsoever. It was just more of the white noise that was life.

'That afternoon though a sound was produced on that circle of vinyl that would prove to be different ... life-altering. As soon as the needle dropped the very first notes penetrated whatever force field had surrounded me up until then. Something in life suddenly made sense, I understood, I felt ...

'It was jazz. Magnificent chaos; instrument piled upon instrument, intersecting and overlapping, and that horn stoically carrying it all. The sax spoke to me most clearly of all. I understood precisely what it was saying.

'I picked up the album jacket; an African American man stared downward bathed in blue light, the spigot of his instrument penetrating the frame. In *romaji* characters, it said "Coltrane" and below, "Blue Train".

'Earlier that spring, I'd started middle school. In Japan, every student is expected to join a club. I never had any desire to join anything, so I'd been putting it off. For most of the boys it was usually sports, but I didn't play any sports. Hitting or chasing a ball, it didn't make any sense to me. Though now, I'd been instructed. The next day, I walked up to the band teacher and told him I wanted to join.

'"Oh, I am happy to hear this. What instrument do you play, Kaoru-chan?" I was asked.

'"I don't play, Sensei. But, um, bu', I would ... I want to play ... I mean, I'd like to ... learn ... the saxophone."

'It was the first time I can remember ever requesting anything for myself. It was the first time I ever knew what it was I wanted. It felt strange and uncomfortable. But the next day, when I held the cool brass in my arms, then nothing ever felt so right.

'A few years later, I dropped out of school and moved to Osaka. I honed my skills in the small jazz clubs that were cropping up around the city, usually playing backup for more seasoned musicians. I was told I had a great ear so I could riff well off the lead of others, but my sax had yet to develop its own voice.

'After blowing in these second-rate jazz clubs through my teens and early twenties, some cats told me the real scene was in Tokyo. If I ever wanted to be a bandleader and cut an album, I needed to go there. I hopped a train the next day.

'It was the early 70s and the scene was blowing up. I immersed myself in it from Kichijoji to Roppongi and Shinjuku to Ikebukuro. I gigged in all the joints: The Velvet Violin, The Pitless Inn, Quartets and The Pharaoh's Dance. When I wasn't playing, I listened. A note would hit, and I'd hold on. Depending on the note and how it was blown, it could take me anywhere, past, present or future ... to heaven or hell and back. Then I'd trip on the next one, on and on, until the ragtime morn.

'Somewhere along the way, my sax found its voice. I was composing original songs and leading a band on the horn. The culture also introduced me to weed, then opium and *hiropon*. The dream stick became a new dark instrument in my life which in no time superseded even my passion for the sax. The pipe was between my lips anytime the spigot wasn't. For years, I drifted from club to club, through Tokyo nights, in a jazz-fuelled hallucinogenic haze.

'Somewhere along this trip, Naomi was thrown into this muddled mix of muse and master.

'"Man, you really can blow! I liked your set." I heard a sweet voice say after an early gig at the Velvet Violin in Roppongi. I turned to meet those words and like that, she had me ... like boarding the "Blue Train" all over again.

'Women often approached me after my shows, and I often slept with them. "Kaoru is such a handsome boy," as my sisters and aunties prophesied. But still sullen, still sensitive, still closed off to a world that confused me as much as ever. So, none of them ever penetrated. They left me feeling empty and alone. That is, until Naomi dropped on me, like the needle. As soon as she spoke, I knew there was something different, like those first notes of Coltrane; I understood, I could hear ...

'Awaking the next morning with Naomi in my arms, it was the

same comfort I felt holding my first sax back in the middle school music room. We were inseparable from there on out; she at every one of my gigs front and centre, then afterwards we drank and smoked weed in my apartment while I softly played solo compositions for only her aphrodite ears.

'Then, when opium came on the scene, together we chased the dragon down a rabbit hole, from which we could never emerge.

'From the outset, bandmates and fellow musicians warned not to get close to her. "She came from a dangerous family," they said, "it wouldn't end well for me." The warnings came too late, removing her from my life was an impossibility. I was hooked. The cocktail of intoxication had become too much for me; Naomi, jazz, the dope – I needed all of them to cope in this world I'd never quite adjusted to.

'Soon, the warning of my friends came to fruition. Coming out of a gig one night, I was grabbed and torn from Naomi's side. She screamed out to me and cursed the dark-suited men by name. I was thrown in the back of a black Mercedes, driven to a smoky room in the back of a small bar, and found myself sat in an oak dining chair looking at a man of sixty with a thick head of slicked-back jet-black hair. He had a dark tan and heavy eyebrows which were furled as he peered at me, not in malice, but cold calculation.

'On each side and standing back from where he sat, were solid, rectangular men wearing matching black suits and dark sunglasses. Arms hung by their sides with a visible gap, their chests inflated, even in natural pose.

'The older man lit a cigarette and stood. Between us was a simple wood table with an ashtray and glass of whisky on his side. In the centre, a large Sakai Takayuki knife lay perpendicular. He paced in the dense silence. Exhaled smoke curled and collected under a low-hanging lamp, suspended at the table's centre. It cast an ominous glare over the waiting knife.

'I studied him through the indigo mood as he circled back and forth like a caged panther waiting for the feeding hour. Finally, he spoke, "You are fond of my daughter, Kaoru-san!? And she is fond of you!?" These were posed as questions, but oddly, also stated as facts by the elderly stranger.

'"My daughter has tried to hide her relationship with you from me. I do not appreciate this. I do not appreciate that you have made my daughter lie to me. Please, do not be angry with her, she has not yet confessed of your affair. She has great honour."

'He chose his words tactfully and with great care as he continued, "But I became suspicious of her activities and so had my subordinates follow her. They have seen her coming and going from your shows, your apartment, and even your drug dens! So, Kaoru, you have not only turned my daughter into a liar but also an addict and a whore. For this, I cannot forgive you." His tone broke as he spat those final words with sheer malice.

'He stopped pacing the length of the table and glowered down. The way his eyes burrowed, I was unsure whether he was awaiting my answer or daring me to answer.

'"I love your daughter, sir," I began, "and I would have come to you for approval, but Naomi never mentioned ..." I attempted to defend our relationship, but could sense it was useless.

'"I understand you are a musician," he said, all but ignoring my reply. "My daughter is only a girl of twenty-three, she is impressionable and idealistic. She has talked of your music as genius, but I fear it is far from that. It is a kind of black magic, that has cast some wicked spell over my dear Naomi. Tonight, I break that spell!"

'As he droned on, I stared my nemesis in the eye – a misguided attempt to conquer his charge. I failed to notice his goons had walked behind, and before I could resist, my forearm was pinned to the oak surface. Trapped, the *wakagashira*, or first lieutenant of the Inagawa-Kai organization, or as I now knew him – Naomi's father, picked up the knife that had lain motionless on the tabletop, suddenly animating it with malice intent.

'"This can happen in one of two ways," the *yakuza* lieutenant explained in a practised tone. '"I give you the knife, and you cut off the last finger to atone for the dishonour you have brought upon my daughter and myself. In this way, you save face and show at least a shred of manhood. Or I take the finger because you are too much the delicate and decadent artist for this last-ditch nobility." As he composed this ultimatum, the knife was set down and handle slowly spun to face me square on.

'With my free right hand, I reached across the table and grabbed the handle. A perverse smile spread across the *wakagashira*'s face. I rested the blade on the bottom knuckle of my little finger. With eyes bulging, froth of fury and hate forming at my mouth's corners, I looked into the eyes of my tormenter and applied all the strength I could muster.

'The blade cut through flesh, cartilage and bone. The drawn-out "I" of "Naomi" still circled the room, after I'd screamed her name in longing and defiance to stifle the slice.

'The finger was severed, but I still pressed down the knife with all my might as if trying to cut through the oak of the table itself. A twitch beneath each cheek as Naomi's father's jaw clenched was the only indication I'd penetrated his cold exterior. A white cloth was handed over my shoulder by one of the goons.

'"You will never see my daughter again," was my departing warning as they dragged me to a waiting cab.

'By the time the taxi had dropped me off at my apartment, the towel had bled through in patches of dried burgundy and fresh scarlet. I struggled to fetch my key and open the door with only a single hand. As the door swung open, there was a profound sense of both yearning and dread, Naomi would be waiting inside. Both unfounded, I was met only by silence and sorrow.

'I knew I should go to hospital to have my finger attended to, but first I reached for the pipe. Something to sand the edges off this jagged reality I'd landed in.'

Kaoru took a pause here to light a cigarette. He then reached over and grabbed the awamori bottle by the neck, tipping it toward me in a gesture of permission. As I well know, reminiscing can be a thirsty business. I nodded my approval.

Many inhales and exhales of the soporific smoke later, the phone rang. He went to her; stoned, low and aching.

Naomi grabbed his arm and drew the clothed hand to her face. She began gently unwrapping the bloody rag. Her tears dried as she performed the action, ritually, like unfurling a *yukata obi*. It was the first clear glimpse either of them had gotten at the maimed hand, dyed in patches of claret and coral while the wound site of the sever still oozed red, radiant blood.

'Oh, Kaoru, you will never play again,' Naomi declared, detached, in a state of shock and terror. Then it hit him, *he would never play again*.

'I did this to you! I did this,' she wailed.

The love suicide was her idea, but Kaoru never fought it. At the shoreline in Enoshima with the great Buddha of Kamakura at his back, once again in the embrace of his beloved, plunged to the nadir of their union – it seemed their only route out.

Naomi sunk to the cold ocean depths and perished. Kaoru, by some cruel fate, was lifted from the waters and survived.

'Attended to in the hospital, under morphine coercion, I cooperated,' Kaoru began his explanation of the aftermath. 'Looking at my freshly bandaged hand in the late afternoon as the morphine waned, I put on my still damp jeans, grabbed the sweater resting off the back of a chair, and snuck out of the hospital ... adrift in the world once more.'

'I snuck back through Tokyo and on to Kansai, collecting my meagre possessions as I went. I made the drug dens of Osaka my home for a few weeks but even when I took to mainlining H, it was not enough to remove the agony of life without Naomi.'

I knew he was clean when he told his story, been that way for a long time, but still, he wore the withered frame of an opioid addict. The muscles of his jaw pulsed with each word and pause, the tendons in his neck flexed and fissured with each smoke and swallow.

'However, the heroine did dull what should have been a screaming physical pain, and so an infection of my neglected amputation spread through my hand and ended me up in hospital again. It forced the removal of these next two fingers.' He held up, for my perusal, as exhibit A, three uneven fleshy stubs on his right hand. Moreover, his forlorn expression communicated that during those dark days, a deeper infection of loneliness and self-hatred had spread through his being and amputated something more.

'The ocean depths which had so cruelly rejected me, still called out day and night – taunting me, scorning my failure. When I boarded this ferry in Kobe more than thirty years ago, I counted my losses on phantom fingers; Naomi, Jazz, my father, and any worthwhile connection with the world.'

He had intended to jump off halfway to Okinawa. Escape from life was not going to elude him that time. It wasn't ideal, but he'd go it alone and perhaps his Naomi would be waiting for him on the other side.

'Drunk, I went to the railing and rested my foot on the bottom rung. As I was about to throw my leg over and let my body follow to the waters below, I heard the sound ...'

Naomi, was my immediate thought.

'The sound of the sea,' he corrected. 'Like those first notes of jazz, I understood it absolutely. Where the drugs couldn't, it silenced the uprising in my heart and made the minutest mend of my soul, but enough. Enough for me to hold on.

'I swung my leg back over the top rail and stepped down upon this very same, grey deck. I couldn't return to land. There was nothing there for me any longer.

'This great ocean took a father I never knew, and the lover I knew only too briefly.' Despite his words of loss, a calmness had replaced the earlier grief which had plagued his timbre and expression.

'In the early days, I would sometimes cry out in anguish, "Why?" But of the many things she has taught me, one is forgiveness.' Lids heavy, his sage eyes stared through slits to his watery mistress writhing in the night below. 'My purpose here is not to question, only to listen. To find solace in whispers from the past. To be devoid of verdict and conviction, of appetite and acquisition, of malice and obsession. I was lured here as my fate to reflect, comprehend, and exist in serene simplicity.'

'Until when?' I found my voice and asked in a sleepy mumble. My eyes focused on the dark ocean, all black invisible waves like music in motion, and his disembodied words arriving through a vacuum.

'Until it's time,' he answered. 'With hushed heart, I patiently wait and listen for my master and sensei to accept me in finality. When she does, I will go with peace to meet my father and be with my love once more.' He stubbed out his cigarette and deposited it in a small black satchel he carried. With no words, only a composed nod, he stood and walked away.

As if awaking from a slumber, I suddenly became alert, stood, and rushed to catch him. I'm not sure why; to offer one more haul off the Awamori or maybe for confirmation?

He'd already rounded the corner to the starboard, or port, or whatever. I arrived the leeward side as a vague grey form receded, blending into a thick descended fog toward the entrance door of the ship. I started to call out, but he disappeared into the haar before I ever saw him enter.

His tale read like a paperback novel; as Willie would say, 'the kind that drug stores sell.'

I was perplexed by how his English had gotten so good, or

was it my Japanese which had drastically improved? Honestly, upon reflection, I have trouble recalling which language the story was even told in.

When I think back to that evening on the deck and how the mysterious ferryman appeared from the darkness and vanished into the fog, it plays like a hallucinatory extemporization. The whole interaction lives in my mind somewhere between memory and imagination, apparition and illusion.

2// Dallas From New York

When I returned to the common area, the lights were off. A chorus of deep breaths and snores filled the room. I managed to pick my way through the scattered bodies in the darkness to locate my patch of mat. I plonked down on the blanket with a thud and took out my wallet, cigarettes and serviceless phone; placed them on the tatami and moved the half-empty Awamori bottle by my hip, ready, like a sheathed *katana*.

In no time I'd joined the choir in sounds of sleep. Through the depths of this slumber, a ringtone penetrated. It persisted, so I groped beside me and by instinct answered my dead cell phone.

'Hello,' I said in a groggy voice.

'My man, Freddie-B! What up, you with a fine lil' chica? Got a *bijin* bent over? Hope I'm not interrupting you on the job, ol' buddy.'

'One second, I can't talk here,' I whispered.

I raised my body unsteadily and made a clumsy traverse out of the common area, kicking the feet of two passengers as I went. They groaned and stirred. '*Sumimasen,*' I offered in apology, hoping I hadn't woken them.

Out in an empty corridor, I found a seat by the window and looked at the clock on my phone. 4:29 am. 'Dallas? How'd you reach me?' I spoke tentatively, reluctant to believe anyone was on the other end. 'My phone hasn't had service for months. Plus, I'm in the middle of the fucking ocean.'

'Shit man, you on a cruise or something? Fucking, grab some

biatch and do tha Titanic thing off the front, yo. These chicks eat that shit up. Then haul that dress up and really give her what for.' The laugh that followed was unmistakably Dallas'; full-throated, brash and carefree.

'It's a ferry. I'm on my way to Kobe. Why are … how are you calling?'

'I missed you, man. Jus wanna be chillin wit' my Canadian homie, "from old blocks, and old crews". Scored us an eight-ball in Roppongi last night, gonna see if you were down to do some lines and hit the club, like back in tha day.'

'It's four o'clock dude, and like I said, I'm on a ship in the ocean.' I had to reiterate this to myself more than Dallas; to refute, feebly, the surreal phone call.

'Yeah aweright, I'll jus go solo.'

'Where are you, man?' I wasn't going to let him go without some answers. 'In Tokyo still?'

'Yeah, you know me, I'm still illin' in tha TKO.'

'This is really fucked up, how you're calling out of the blue. A couple of days ago I got a call from Gertie. I was at an Internet café in Okinawa …'

'Gertie, huh. How she doin?'

'Don't know, she sounded the same, good actually, like before the … you know. Anyway, she had some kinda message for me. I guess it's maybe why I'm heading back to Tokyo … to find out what she meant … to figure shit out.' I was still half asleep and dazed, mumbling gibberish off the tip of my tongue.

'Yo, you coming back? Cool, make sure you look me up. We'll hit the town.'

'Yeah, yeah, sure. Hey, are you still living in the guesthouse … Big Peach?'

'Fuck, no! That shithole was fucked. I mean we had some good times there, but you couldn't live there long, it'd drive ya fucking cray-cray. No point goin' back there. But we need to talk, so find me.'

'Yeah, cool. Hey, find you where?'

'Just find me ... Later bro.'

'Later ...' He'd hung up, but there was no dial tone, only dead air. I pressed the little, red hang-up button anyways, out of habit.

I didn't feel like stumbling back through the tatami mat obstacle course of sleeping bodies. The call was a total mindfuck that left me baffled. Plus, talking to Dallas kind of made me want to pull an all-nighter, stay up and watch the sunrise.

I had a pocket full of change, so fished some out and got a can of beer. In the smoking-room, I bought a fresh pack from the vending machine and rummaged through my jeans for a lighter. The lounge had a long bench with three standing ashtrays set in front. A glass wall faced the boat's empty lobby; encased by this large observation window felt a little like being on display in a zoo exhibit after visiting hours.

I checked my phone, but no record of any received calls showed, and of course, no bars, which confirmed the impossibility of it all. In the pervasive soundlessness, I needed some music. I threw on Gang Starr's 'No Shame in My Game'. It transported my thoughts back to the Big Peach Gaijin House on a Saturday afternoon shortly after I'd moved down from Yorii.

A door was open a crack and old school rap blared into the hallway, the beat blast was refreshing. I like to describe my music taste as eclectic, but have a particular penchant for 90s hip-hop. Like grunge, it belonged to my generation and there wasn't much else of value we could lay claim to. I knocked lightly, to compliment the inhabitant on their musical taste and maybe expand my social circle beyond Gertie.

'Yo, come on in,' came a confident, booming voice.

I opened the door and was met with a friendly smile. A man about my age, late twenties or early thirties, wearing a tank top and shorts, looked as if he was finishing up a workout. Faint freckles dotted flexed biceps and shoulders as he gripped the corners of a face towel draped around his neck.

'Hey, heard the music when I was walking by, good tune. Gang Starr, eh.'

'Hell ya, Gang Starr tha shit. Threw down some of the dopest rhymes of their day.' He said jovially, with almost comical cultural appropriation.

I was to find Dallas had more of an encyclopaedic knowledge of hip-hop than any white guy I'd ever met. With correlated dress and speech, it'd be easy to think him an absolute poseur, if there weren't an unmistakable authenticity to it, like a method actor gone too deep, lost forever in the role.

'Yo, boooy. You been livin here long?' he asked.

'Almost a week now,' I replied, wondering when he was going to drop the act.

Though it wasn't an act. He was just a product of his environment, which happened to be a far more interesting environment than I was produced in. I'd considered Gertie's tough working-class Belfast upbringing more compelling as well, and for that matter most everyone else I'd ever met.

'Dope. I'm Dallas. Beer?'

'Fred. Yeah, I'd love one.' We shook hands. He had one of those uber strong grips, but not in a dickish way like he was trying to exert dominance or anything, just enthusiastic and naturally strong.

'Fred? Sheeet, not like that mo-fo Durst I hope. Fuckin, rap-rock is an abomination, cept The Beasties, of course!'

Dallas swore about as proficiently as anyone I knew. Though strangely, I would notice, then learn, he would never curse 'motherfucker'; 'mo-fo' yeah, but 'motherfucker' never.

This derived from some light childhood trauma stemming from his name. His mother's name was Deborah, commonly shortened to Debbie. As he explained, it was in fourth grade that one of his classmates became aware of this and even though still young, was worldly enough to connect his name, Dallas, and his Mother's name, Debbie, to the iconic 70s porno movie, 'Debbie Does Dallas'. Hence, Dallas endured the later years of elementary school being taunted by this association and the apparent juvenile taunt that he was, in fact – a mother fucker.

'Fuckin' ten year old can make the goddam connection. Why my Mom and Dad didn't when they fuckin named me in eighty-three is fuckin beyond me.' Dallas lamented one night when we were drinking at an Irish bar in Shibuya.

Gertie was with us and laughed. Not at him but with him, she liked that story. 'It shows the cocky bastard's got some humility,' she'd explained.

Our initial connection was over hip-hop, but chasing vice would prove to be where the substance of our bond was forged. I always harboured a slight conflict of conscience when I got blind drunk and womanized. But Dallas embraced his vices wholeheartedly, never once questioning whether there was any other conduct which may behove him better.

I think even Gertie, with her feminist views, respected Dallas for his unwavering traits, no matter how flawed they were. Never once did he kowtow his sexism or philandering ways to appease Gertie's sensibilities. Consequently, they had some epic rows over politics, gender, and just basic decorum. But Gertie enjoyed a good row, and Dallas was always up to give her one.

She and I shared a somewhat pessimistic view of human nature, a belief that the world was full of phonies and fakes. Deep down, I believe, she held some affinity for the way he caroused through life so unapologetically. Crass, sexist, shallow, *hai*! But he fuckin' owned it.

If anything, the reason Gertie didn't like Dallas was that it devalued her view of me. When she observed the way I carried on with Dallas, she probably thought I was a little phony myself, and she was probably a lot of right.

I'd always played the chameleon. Carrying a deep need to

be accepted and having no clear concept of who I really was, I'd assume the appearance of whomever others wanted me to be in any given situation.

When Dallas parroted a raunchy rap crew and said: 'I like to get down and have a good time, ain't nothin but pleasure in my rhymes', I could get on board with that. Just as when Gertie would quote, 'I am no bird; and no net ensnares me: I am a free human being with an independent will'; I dug that shit as well. *Eclectic and accepting or apathetic and fake? Who fucking knows.*

Point being, I liked them both. Although I'm confident that there was an unidentifiable affinity between the likes of them, I was rather unsuccessful in bridging it. So during my Higashi Koseki days, I had these two friendships fastened on like skis that were continually getting crossed.

'You got a ho on the go?' Dallas inquired as we sipped our beers that first afternoon.

'I met this chick when I was living out in Yorii. Nice girl, we've been hanging out and hooking up, but I'm not sure where it's going now that I'm in Tokyo.' I downplayed my relationship with Akiko more for my sake than his.

'Cool, my advice; don't bring sand to the beach.' He said with a wry smile and sipped his beer. 'What ya doing tonight? Hit da club?'

I was supposed to head to a local bar with Gertie, where she was friendly with the bartender. But clubbing, Tokyo style, sounded way more appealing.

'Nothing,' I said.

'Nice, Shibuya it is. Fuck bro, you bring them boy-next-door good looks, I'll bring the muscle, and we'll fucking crush it wit dem bitches.' He laughed assuredly and gave a playful punch in the arm. It was a trained jab and stung.

An ex-boxer, I'd later learn, Dallas had joined a Brooklyn gym to quell the tide of 'Motherfucker' taunts received during elementary school. Irish-Italian roots marked him as good fighting stock, 'The next Great White Hope,' as Dallas joked with a dismissive scoff. He got tough and he got good, put a stop to the bullying and then rose up the amateur ranks. His big break came at 19 with an undercard fight in Madison Square Garden. 'I got my ass kicked, bra,' he explained. 'Wish I could say some mobsters paid me to take a dive, or it went the distance and I lost by decision. But straight up, I got knocked the fuck out in the second round. Next fight, I got knocked out in the first. I hung up the gloves.' He'd pointed to a pair of red boxing gloves, quite literally hung up and dangling from a hook on the back of his door. 'I had the skill in me, but lacked the fight.'

'Shit, shower, shave and I'll meet ya back here at 8 pm, aweright,' he'd instructed that first Saturday.

I was back at the red door of Dallas' *gaijin* house room at ten after eight.

Dallas was clad in a Knicks basketball jersey, gratuitously to show off the definition in his biceps and shoulders. He also wore a gold chain, and baggy jeans belted mid-ass, with a pair of Jordan's, the Japanese designer kind rather than the functional basketball shoe. 'Like a chachi, two-bit pimp,' was how Gertie described it when he wore the same outfit a few weeks later as the three of us headed out somewhere.

'Gangster, gangster at the top of the list,' I joked, handing him a cold can of Asahi.

'Yo, you know it homeboy. You've kept the skidrow look, that's cool,' he said without a hint of irony or insult.

I looked down at what I wore. I did rock a skid look, pretty much always had. Ripped jeans, a plain white dollar-store Tee, battered skate shoes, and a hemp necklace to highlight my bohemian inclinations finished off the attire.

'It's all good, yo, we got a whole "Ebony and Ivory" thang goin on, it'll play well.'

I failed to see who the ebony was in our duo, but I'm 99 percent sure Dallas was referring to himself.

With his infectious optimism at our backs, we headed out on the town. Dallas' pursuit was relentless, talking to girls on the platform, in the train, outside Shibuya station; like a fat kid in a candy store with an insatiable sweet tooth, he pilfered the shelves.

Carried through Shibuya crossing on rapids of bodies and confectionery expectations, up Centa-Gai, we surged past fashionable shops and blaring arcades. Brightly dressed beauties like spilt Skittles scattered all around. Couples, hearts-a-flutter, walked hand and hand while conquering consumers milled about carrying their acquired wares. Intersecting through an electric air like ions we charged for the night was young.

Drawn into Dogenzaka by the pavement's thud underfoot, we scoured nightclubs lining each side of the block for a vibe to suit our mood.

Two babes passed on thin, tanned chopstick legs. Tight-fitting tube-tops clung to small perky tits and left exposed for our gaze, delicate shoulders above, and flat, firm midriffs below.

'What up, dancing queens?' Dallas had a go.

They looked us over, giggled into bedazzled cupped hands, and tottered off in melodious taps.

Dallas flashed me a wide wild grin. Two years I believe it'd been, clearly, Tokyo had him. Under two weeks, and its glimmering hooks, like a Shibuya gal's extravagantly long nails, were sinking into me.

We settled solo in a popular British pub, Dallas with a couple of numbers in his phone already. After a quick scan of the joint, we approached a pair of half-cut cuties and had them simpering and swooning in no time.

According to Dallas, 'Always try to bring a couple of hotties to the club with you – that's why ya hit a foreigner-friendly bar first. In da club itself, you hafta compete with local gangsters or low-rent celebs, like some limp-dick trance DJ. This is just the way to go, bro, rather than deal with the algebra and unknown variables of picking up there.' He threw his arm around my neck and pulled me into a playful headlock. This intricate theory of the Tokyo pick-up was one of many Dallas had developed and explained to me on the sly as we stumbled with our new lady friends to a local nightclub. Under Dallas' tutelage, I was to become a first-class (perhaps no-class) Tokyo cocksman soon enough.

We moved from club to karaoke, where we intermittently belted out off-key tunes and pawed at the girls. Around 5 am, we headed into the dawn, Dallas and I with our arms around our respective dates, unsure of who was holding up who while swaying in a lustful breeze.

Dallas' call was that we all hop in a cab back to ours. The girls discussed or debated the prospect amongst themselves. I was tempted to intervene and offer my counsel, but Dallas put a raised backhand to my chest and shook his head, already confident in the outcome.

The girls arrived at a decision. 'Great! I'll flag us a yellow cab, easy!' Dallas elbowed my ribs triumphantly with the off-colour double entendre.

We piled out and into the Peach House where the girls turned their noses up at our low-end accommodation. As Dallas was to spell out later, 'What the fuck are they going to do about it then? Ninety-nine out of a hundred will stay.' I wondered if he'd actually run those numbers.

My mate lay on her back, a sporadic 'ooh' or 'ahh' released with a lukewarm breath. Fatigued by the long evening, I'm sure, though I'd hoped she'd have rallied a bit, if even just vocally.

We slept for a couple hours, then I walked her to the station. We passed Dallas' room to pick up her friend, but the sounds of loud rap, ecstatic screaming, and a floppy headboard banging against the wall caused us to exchange uncomfortable glances before we moved on in silence, eyes downcast, wading through a linoleum sky. It was undeniably an awesome evening, yet suddenly, I felt short-changed by the ending.

Maybe I chose wrong. I deliberated, mutely marching my date to the train. *Both girls were up in the air when we met them ... Next time I'll select more shrewdly.*

Or maybe it's me that's inadequate ... maybe I was the cold fish? This more disconcerting thought hit as I remembered the unbridled soundtrack being composed in Dallas' room. Whichever way the bedsheets rumpled, I concluded a mental readjustment when it came to the sexual mores and gender relations of this land was in order.

An adjustment Dallas was more than happy to provide over the coming months. Did I get a slanted view? Mos def! But it was precisely what I was looking for in that city, at that time. I dove into the lifestyle like it was a wave pool in the Sahara.

We'd manufacture stories and facts about ourselves to the ladies we chatted up, and later lay them naked and beckoning upon the bed of lies.

'We're building a beautiful fantasy for 'em to escape into for a night,' Dallas once purported. 'Fuck man, it gets 'em out of their boring-ass monotonous lives for at least an evening. Gives 'em something to brag to their friends about, something to think about when they're tapping the computer keys or ringing up merchandise come Monday morning.' He nodded with serious consideration, and I think he truly believed it was some charitable act to create that web of falsehoods in which to ensnare the woman we approached.

He usually created the backstories. 'Here to box in a K1 match' or 'am producing an album with a Japanese hip-hop duo'. I was assigned things like 'Swedish pro snowboarder' or 'bassist in a touring punk band'. I once told him I wanted something more substantial like a novelist or playwright. Dallas told me to go for it. Which I did, only to be met with glazed expressions. He laughed upon my empty-handed return. I reverted to 'extra in an upcoming movie'.

These personal myths became so commonplace I sometimes forgot what I actually did for a living and why I was really there in Japan. Possibly, the nutso idea of the Beaver Dam beach club was born out of one such spun fabrication. A feeble attempt to drop the 'mis-' from at least one of my multitudes of misrepresentation.

We feigned ignorance of the language. This, coupled with our occupational backstories, according to Dallas, allowed us to remain more exotic, ephemeral or some shit. 'Plus dude, it sets low expectations. Ya know, like it might be an exciting bang with a handsome stranger, but ain't gonna develop into anymo than that.' He'd proclaimed, running his hands through close-cropped hair and exhaling with an authoritative air.

'It's just a game, man. Life's a game; growing up, school, work, sex. Tappin' ass just happens to be one of the more pleasurable aspects of it. They know it, we know it. So don't get bogged down in feelings and guilt. Just enjoy, cheat a little to give yourself an edge, and have fun with it.' Somewhere along our philandering road, I must've expressed some regret or misgivings. So he imparted his view of the scenery as we strut, then trudged, along.

The meaningless sex was fun until the emphasis went off the sex and landed squarely on the meaningless. Too short, too tall, too mousey, too wild, too beautiful or too plain; I searched out extremes. Bowlegged, pigeon-toed, flat chested, snarl toothed, and knock-kneed. Pathologically, I was fed by a belief whereby in those extremes or winsome physical flaws, I'd find a quenching of this mysterious thirst, something to teeter the fulcrum edge, some new quality which would transmute to fill the void inside.

At the station, I dropped off my one-night stand and sealed our departure with an empty kiss on the cheek, the kind you'd give an aged aunt at a family reunion.

I sauntered home over cracked concrete looking forward to crashing for the rest of the day. I probably would have slept straight through the night, but a light rapping on my door woke me just after dark. I got up and answered.

'What up, Freddy B. Get ready bro, round two, party in Roppongi tonight.'

'Are you serious?'

'Hells yeah, "ride or die, I'm dead-ass serious!"' he hip-hop quoted his response.

I was fully prepared to stew in my hotboxed room of cheap draft beer farts. Instead, I cracked a can and figured, in for a penny, in for a pound. Employing one of Gertie's favoured lines made me feel a tinge of guilt for blowing her off the previous night.

Under a cloak of culpability, I crept down to Dallas' room with a road pop for each of us. We listened to a couple of tracks while he finished preening himself. Still feeling like shit and wondering why the hell I was going out again, I asked my burning question. 'How the fuck do you do it, man? No way I can tie on another all-nighter.'

Dallas pulled a small clear baggie of white powder from his jeans and tipped a small amount onto the tabletop. Like winter's first freshly fallen snow, it tempted to be touched, tasted, experienced.

That night I was introduced to the holy trinity of booze, coke and women. I remember well the sensation which came over me the first time I drank alcohol. I felt ten feet tall and as if I could walk on water; I fit perfectly in my skin like it was a handmade suit. Immediately after putting my nose to the tabletop and inhaling through one open nostril, I felt twenty feet tall and as if my feet didn't even touch the wet surface – I glided over it with all the thrust and drive of a low flying F-16. The skin still fit like that tailored suit, except now stitched entirely of pure fuckin' velvet!

'Cool, let's go bro ... drink, dance, fuck; the fuckin' night away, eh' I jabbered, more than onboard – captain of the mother-fucking ship.

'Chill, Freddie B. Put the brakes on that Zamboni,' he teased and gave me a once-over under crawling caterpillar arched eyebrows.

Dallas was a purely recreational user. I, on the other hand, seem to suffer from a disease of more. He'd ration out the nose candy when I hit the proverbial wall. Fortunately, on my meagre teacher's salary and lack of any dealer connection, I was unable to form the habit I'm sure I otherwise would have.

Dallas was in the more lucrative gambit of recruiting, which begged the question of why he was living in a shithole guesthouse and not a proper apartment. His cash came in windfalls, commission made on high-level job placements. These he would summarily blow on blow, Cristal and high-class Russian hostess bars during week-long Roppongi benders.

I'd joined him once for the beginning of one of these jags, but tapped out quickly as it was really not my scene. I failed to see how it could be Dallas'. The Russian girls were cold and standoffish, and the clubs were populated by English bankers in Brooks Brothers suits acting about as self-important and phony as I'd ever borne witness to. Maybe he found some allure in the unattainable, like a ritual of ego-deflation or even self-abasement. Anyone as uninhibited and cocksure as Dallas must have had, in some dark recess, a lurking inferiority complex. But whatever, to each his own.

Dallas' jaunts were an opportunity for me to hop off the debauched Ferris wheel and catch up with Gertie for a sublime night of beers at a local *izakaya* or Shinjuku rock bar. I continued seeing Akiko, even as I went on those all-nighters with Dallas and partook in trysts with untold randoms. We met less and less for a proper date on Friday or Saturday nights. I'm sure she had an inclination of what I was up to, but she never confronted me about it.

In retrospect, I wish I'd have told her about the other women; that in the end, they never meant anything to me. They were only frivolous flings to fill the empty hours and the emptiness. It was only her I held close through the night until morn broke. But I didn't tell her any of it. I didn't see it then, or just couldn't care.

Believe it or not, Dallas had a steady girlfriend, Risa. They'd been together over a year and a half. Mixed, Brazilian and Japanese,

God used all the finest ingredients when he'd put her together; dark complexion with big beautiful brown eyes and the taut body of an aerobics instructor. She was the sexy, outgoing exuberance of Brazil with just the right touch of the demure and cutesy Japanese.

I thought she was the bomb and I told Dallas as much when I asked why he needed to go chasing other women with that on tap. I wondered without judgment and as much to shed some light on my own behaviour. Dallas got that, so he threw a floodlight on his thinking and motivations.

'Never let a beautiful woman into your heart. She'll barge in with heels on and trash the place. If you dote over a woman, if she knows she has all your attention and intentions, she'll lose interest, and you'll lose her.' While he shared this theory on modern romance, he did bicep curls, giving the whole scene a corny macho vibe of excessive Axe body spray and discarded Maxim magazines.

'I don't subscribe to "treat 'em mean to keep 'em keen" school of thought. I treat Risa like a queen on the streets and whore in the sheets. Bitches be lovin that,' Dallas continued his brofication, like a bad 80s beer commercial. 'But ya gotta exhibit a healthy emotional distance. Don't flaunt it, and never voice it, but she oughta know you got game with other women, that you have other options.'

He switched arms with the weight and went on, 'that gets their competitive juices flowing, creates a little fear and mystery, and this combo will always work in your favour, bro.'

It was pretty much the same shallow, sexist shit I'd heard from guys in locker rooms and from bar stools since puberty. Though, I'd never heard it articulated quite so succinctly nor seen the theories executed with such pristine results.

Gertie offered a much different perspective on my behaviour. 'Akiko's a good lass, Fred. Cut the bullocks, if you donna wanna be with her, let 'er go softly.'

'Akiko knows the score. I never made any promises to her about exclusivity, and I don't expect that from her.'

'Listen, Fred, I'm no proponent of religious values, fidelity, and all that crap but she deserves better than this. Aye, she acts cool and distant, but she's not all that tough. And feck if I understand it, but she really likes yer gobshite arse.' She reached across a smouldering ashtray with the open whisky and eyeballed a perfect double into my glass. I'd come to understand this as the Oirish gesture for 'no hard feelings, mate'.

'As long as ya go emulating that chav Dallas, ya goin 'urt er,' Gertie concluded.

I knew she was probably right but feeling cornered, I argued, 'Maybe I'd rather shine brightly of poor character than exist opaquely attempting to walk some moral high ground.'

'Really, is that what you think, Fred? Your character shone jus' fine as it was, ya cunt.' She scoffed and threw back the remains of whisky in her glass. 'One Dallas is plenty enough for this house ... for this fuckin world.'

Months into our dissipated ride, Dallas and I found ourselves back in Shibuya one night, as per usual. After buying a couple pints and turning to survey the crowd, Dallas elbowed my arm and gestured toward a booth in the corner.

Dressed like your classic college girl in knee-length skirts and tight mohair sweaters, they had round winsomely chubby faces and were commonly cute. Slouched on the other side of the booth were two *gaijin* guys. They were in their mid-twenties, English I guessed by the pale skin, shaggy-styled mod haircuts and shabbily dressed by design to affect a sort of Britpop look.

'I don't know man. Let's hold out. We can find better,' I opined, unmoved by the pair.

Dallas shook his head and laughed. 'Oh, can we, dawg?'

'They're already with two guys, and they're not worth competing over.' I couldn't figure out why Dallas was hung up on those girls.

'Fuck, you're thick, Fred. Look carefully at those chicks,' he urged. 'Look familiar?'

'Oh, shit!'

They were the girls we'd met on our first night out all those months back. Shamefully, I couldn't even identify which one I'd bedded that night.

'Fuck Snow Patrol! Let's have some fun wit 'em.' With pints in hand, Dallas led us over. Ignoring the two guys and directing his attention to the girls, he said, 'Ladies, how have you been? It's been too long.' In a rare breach of protocol, he spoke in proficient Japanese.

Both girls' cheeks went even redder than the blush and beer had already rosied. 'We are good,' one of them replied. I identified her as the girl Dallas had previously entertained.

'Cool, cool. Well, you guys have a good night,' Dallas said to both sides of the table.

As we turned to leave, Dallas turned back and threw an arm over the top of the booth where one of the British guys sat. Dallas leaned down and whispered something in the guy's ear before straightening up with a broadening mischievous grin while the shaggy-haired kid shifted uncomfortably on his seat.

As we walked away from the booth, I had to ask, 'Dude, What'd you say?'

'I told him she likes a pinkie up her ass right before she cums.'

I laughed one of those pure guttural laughs, throwing my head back. 'Fuck, man, that's harsh.'

'Yo bro, we don't hafta live perfectly, but we gotta live passionately.' Dallas proclaimed readily as he made a beeline for the night's new targets.

'Fuckin Dallas,' I uttered and chuckled aloud. A nostalgic laugh joyfully shared between just myself and the carcinogens that had filled the confined room. I stared through the glass into the ship's vacant interior and wondered how much of our present reality is furnished with artefacts of our past. Light broke the horizon with a brilliant orange and marmaladed the sky. The sun rose from a shaved zest to full fiery disc in mere minutes, but it felt like a comfortable lifetime.

The final bars of a hip-hop verse played through my earphones, *'it was all a dream, smokin' weed and readin' Word-up magazine, Heavy D up on tha wall ....'* I pushed pause and finished my beer with a wince.

3// Message in a Bottle

I woke up early but stayed in bed until well past noon. My Awamori was running dangerously close to dry. I was at a loss as to how to kill another twenty-four hours on the ship, so I just lay in that half-sleep. Finally, the need to smoke and brush away a layer of fur that had grown on my teeth overnight became motivation enough to rise off the hard tatami floor.

I walked the ship to see if there was anyone of interest. It was the same sausage fest as the previous evening. I stopped by the vending machine for a late breakfast of cup noodles and lemon chu-hi. In the lounge, a working television played one of those Japanese variety shows where a panel of celebrities I was unfamiliar with watched other famous people I didn't know, try food or visit local attractions, and commented on the experience with exclamations of 'Sugoi', 'Oishii' or 'Kawaii' when called for. These shows seem to make up about nine-tenths of Japanese programming. I'd tried watching and was not entertained.

Instead, I went out on the deck to watch the sea and listen if it carried any news for me. The swell was up from the previous night. There was an impressive rising and falling of the ocean surface, the fluctuations throwing up spume as they peaked then receded. To steady myself, I kept a hand to the white wall as I made my way to a bench.

With an angry, devouring sea as the backdrop, I thought of the ferryman's tale and then Akiko. Reinvigorated by the fresh ocean air, my first salty thought was, *if Akiko were here, she'd love to get drilled against that railing.* The turbulent waters below, we'd emulate with our torrent lust – pressed bodies ebbing and flowing, driving against the cold metal rail in waves of pounding passion.

The ferry deck fantasy wasn't me just being a perv, I mean, that was kind of Akiko's thing. It started in the park on that first date, but her penchant for exhibitionist sex only expanded from there. Akiko came off shy and introverted when you first met her, and she was, except when it came to satisfying carnal cravings.

Karaoke booths, onsen baths, back alleys and public washrooms; each offered its own perverse stimuli. She'd grab me for a deep kiss and then swiftly escalate matters. I was usually game, even an enthusiastic participant. Often overly enthusiastic, as the fear of getting caught would heighten my excitement to what was undoubtedly an early release.

Akiko didn't mind, or at least she never complained. Her climaxing was not what she was after with these risqué sexual encounters. I think what she got off on was the degradation, or potential for it. Whereas I was nervous of getting caught, she seemed to welcome it. As if, as an act of self-flagellation, the lash of exposure, humiliation and shame were something she deserved, even hungered for. 'Do you see it now? Do you see my depravity!' Her actions would scream to any chance observers and the world at large.

I had to hand it to her – not much could make me blush. But on more than one occasion, she pushed me beyond my comfort zone and forced my retreat. The first was on a crowded subway car. We held hands, innocuously enough like many young couples, as the train scurried through underground tunnels. Wearing a short black skirt, she took my hand and slid it between silken thighs. I whispered in her ear, 'Do you want this?'

She replied with a breathy, sensual, 'Uh-huh.'

I slid my hand up her thigh, under the skirt and back and forth over the satin cloth. She let out a long low moan, and I felt the fabric moisten. We were surrounded by bodies on all sides. While no one could see where my hand was in the crush, the way Akiko's head was thrown back and face contorted in escalating ecstasy was indication enough of the funny business going on.

A man reading the newspaper next to me cleared his throat, and a businesswoman behind us shifted her body. Those cues unnerved me enough that I slid my hand back down her leg and outside the skirt. She grabbed me by the wrist and brought my hand to her face, holding it there, inhaling deep.

I pushed my way off at the next stop, and she followed me out the sliding doors. 'Fuck, stop doin' this crazy shit!'

'*Gomen,*' she said, yet wore a contrary smile.

'It's just … it's such a fucking cliché,' I sputtered, pissed off partly at myself for not manning up and finger banging her on the train as she wished, maybe questioning my own sexual appetites as milquetoast, but more so flabbergasted with this seemingly unassuming girl always pushing the boundaries. 'Plus, your antics are gonna land me in a world of shit,' I added, on the platform as my official position.

She merely stared at me, like a kid caught with her hand in the cookie jar. Though, I guess it was me caught, with his hand in the honeypot.

I looked from ocean to sky. The clouds above thickened and sky darkened, as did my thoughts.

In all my treatment of Akiko, I was most culpable in my neglect. I either didn't recognize or wilfully ignored how my trained detachment may have been harming her.

After the move from Yorii to the Peach House, we continued to hook up. As much as I tried to pretend nothing had changed, through the distance and over the wall, she began to show her wounds.

I'd first seen it on the shop girl at the local grocery till in Yorii. She was about fifteen and had this standard badass schoolgirl look:

baggy white socks, pleated skirt pulled up well above the knees, costume jewellery, dark tanned skin and thick mascara. As she handed my change, I noticed the red scabs of fresh slashes running across her forearm. I wrote this off as countryside living, boredom and some in vogue rebellion of youth. I took far more notice when, lying in bed with Akiko one night, I saw the same disturbing razor cuts up and down the insides of her arms.

When I put her on the spot about them, she rolled over and faced the wall. 'My cat scratched me,' she mumbled.

I let it die. Besides, that was the sort of indifference she had come to expect from me. If she had wanted to tell me what was really going on, I'd given her an outlet. I was in denial of the easily discernible; her misery and silence shared the same address, probably that of my cramped, musty guesthouse room.

I continued to play whack-a-mole with any concerns my callousness could inflict harm, along with a myriad of other character defects which continually reared their ugly heads. And as my life in Tokyo took hold, Theroux got lost in translation, and I found myself sucking more wind than marrow. Nonetheless, I soldiered on into countless nights, armed with delusions of grandeur, fortified by booze and blow. I'd return home with my spoils, but whether I was victor in this battle against the night was questionable.

As I attempted to float in my solipsistic bubble without it getting punctured and popped, more signs of Akiko in some sort of personal plunge went wafting by.

On a beach in Chiba we relaxed in the sun. I fished for a lighter under the sand packed surfboard, wet and dripping having come to shore following an unsuccessful set.

Akiko was chewing on the filter, teasing to light. I already puffed away on my Marlboro and tossed the lighter on the towel at her feet. She ignored it and continued looking steadfast out past the breaks when she said: 'Let's swim out as far as we can, and when we feel like we cannot swim anymore, push on further ... then stop, and just let go.'

I didn't get what she was on about, I'd never seen her swim. 'I'm pretty beat, let me finish this smoke first and we'll see.'

When I looked over at her, she hadn't really listened to what I said. She stared out toward the horizon, still chewing on the end of her cigarette with an expression devoid of any and all feeling. Thinking of it now, it may not have been so much empty, but an emotion of such depth that it was lifeless, cold and dark, like the Mariana trench.

If there were a limit to the neglectfulness which I could bestow upon her feelings, both of us were approaching that line.

As the nights out and other women continued unabated, I threw more distance between us. To feel no pangs of guilt, I thickened my armour and was often in a state of total oblivion when we met. She'd seen me drunk off my ass many times before, but it was different earlier, partially done for her amusement, and then, she was riding shotgun. But later, it was only me tearing off, tires screeching, swerving all over the road. Akiko left watching from the kerb, burnt rubber and broken glass, an afterthought.

If she ever questioned my behaviour, I was too drunk to remember. There were probably signals in her expression or body language, little messages along the way, but I'd drunk myself illiterate in reading them.

Until one morning I awoke, dull light streamed through the frosted glass and penetrated my eyelids like ice picks. I ran my tongue around a dry mouth; it tasted like I'd inhaled an ashtray. In the indentation on the pillow next to me lay a neatly folded note. It took me a moment to remember who had been there.

It was written on a page ripped from a personal notebook. Canary coloured with borders decorated in yellow chrysanthemums, the paper released a meadow scent when unfolded. The aroma wafted over me as a brief reprieve from the funk of my room.

Gomen Fred, I have to go now, and cannot wait any longer for you to wake up.

For a while I laid here and watched specks of dust dance on rays of sunlight and remembered as a girl when I used to sit on a swing and listen to the cicadas scream. Back and forth I swung, until I was in perfect motion with their song. Later I would walk around the park and look for shells. If I found one, I would carry home the cast-off cupped in my hand, so it won't blow away, but lightly so I don't crush the perfect formation of the thing which once lived in this skin. I'd set them on my windowsill. Eventually, they always break apart into tiny little flakes, I'd sweep off the sill and into the trash, just dust of that fragile thing that once was. When I shook your shoulder to say goodbye, you just mumble something in your sleep and turn away to face the wall. So I'll get up, get dressed, walk through the dust, our dust, and leave. *Mata-ne* ... if I can meet, you, again someday.

Love Akiko

The simple text was cryptic and weighted. I read and reread throughout the morning and poured over it in the afternoon. She'd never levied any direct criticism of my actions, that was not Akiko's way. There was, however, a definite decree in the note, an air of verdict, and I was pretty sure it didn't go my way.

Fuck this bullshit. I crumpled the notepaper and tossed it into the corner of the room, sick of reading those fourteen lines over and over.

I walked to the convenience store for an armful of cans while deflecting all culpability I'd gleaned her dusky sonnet heaped upon me. *You've changed ... Fuck that! I've always been a selfish asshole. Not my fault, you've just realized it ...*

Three tall cans of Chu-hi in the park later, I was devoid of any lingering mawkishness.

I never texted after that night because to seek an explanation or expansion on the note, I viewed as some sort of surrender, tantamount to atonement. Such was the conduct of a stubborn and indifferent man-child.

Aided and unaided, but mostly aided, I remained in a state of detached bliss for about two to three weeks. Then I got sentimental for a split second and nailed the coffin shut.

It all came to a head on a Saturday. With a bottle of whisky in one hand, I rummaged through drawers and pockets for a lighter to no avail. With this excuse, I shuffled sock-footed across the hall's linoleum, space motif and knocked.

The door swung open and Gertie plopped back down on the thin mattress of the simple cot while the springs creaked. She wore what had become her uniform; jogging pants and a baggy T-shirt, crested on the front with coffee stains and jam.

I stepped in. 'Hey, Gertie, could you light me up?'

She pointed to a lighter lying on the desk. I took two steps across the expanse of the Gaijin House room to retrieve it and poured some whisky in the empty glass beside then handed it to Gertie. A book was open on the bed, I pointed and asked what she was reading. She closed it over her index finger, revealing the cover, *Wuthering Heights*.

'Bronte, eh. Never read it. You know ... woman writers are kinda shit.' It was an old taunt, though I was unsure how 'depression Gertie' would take the tease.

She smiled and playfully tossed a pillow at me. 'Ya turnin' in t'more of a sexist cunt each day,' she returned a familiar barb.

For the next thirty minutes we drank and took the piss. It felt like that first long bus ride from Narita to Yorii. We got talking about Belfast and Ireland in general. Gertie informing me yet again that I'd better not go because, 'I'd catch a kicking' as I was too much of a drunken eejit.

I asked her again about the fractious history of north and south, of Protestants and Catholics, the IRA and all that. She shared some new insights and experiences with that as the backdrop of her youth. When I compared it to the Biggie-2pac, East Coast - West Coast rap feud of the late 90s, she again laughed and insulted me suitably. 'Ye definitely 'anging around that American twat too much and look 'ow stupid it's making ya.'

When the conversation momentarily lulled, I tried to fill her glass with another shot, but Gertie declined. I could almost see her slipping back to whatever dark hollow she'd retreated into. The transitory camaraderie we shared during those glasses of spirit was dissipating rapidly. I took leave while a smidgen of lingering joy still clung.

It felt like a night of reconciliation so, half-cut and celebratory, I extended an olive branch to Akiko. *What's up, how you been babe? I miss ya, we should get together … tonight?* I kept the text aloof, much like I'd moulded the relationship.

I wasn't expecting a reply, but an hour later, as I drank alone in small bars around Koenji, my phone buzzed and shivered on a walnut surface. I flipped it open and the screen ignited. *I miss you too! I didn't know if we'd meet each other again, if you wanted to … But okay, I can come tonight after I finish with my friends in Shinjuku. I'll be your place around last train. See you soon.* It was punctuated with an affectionate emoji.

Cool, see you later, babe! I put down my phone and picked up my rum and Coke. The next gulp went down with a burly shudder.

Akiko was free of me, as I knew she should be; then I had to go and ensnare her all over again. When heartache and horniness take form in an errant text, no good can come of it. Fleetwood Mac's 'Dreams' whispered through the bar speakers and cast a pall over my barstool. *Ice clinked, resonating loneliness … heartbeat in my head like a madly beaten tambourine … the tavern stilled, lost in remembering.*

I stepped up my consumption and was drinking doubles, double-time in anticipation of facing my earlier lapse of judgment. Until I forgot the SMS keys punched in fading nostalgia, and the message transmitted from that place of yearning; somewhere between the heart, the head and the base of the cock.

All that existed from that point was a faint menagerie of dancing and singing, lights shimmering off half-full glasses, ashtrays of orange embers and arms thrown around strangers in gregarious gluttony. A garish *gaijin* grandstanding in the fashion of a lowly attention whore.

Emerging from those vague tableaus, I found myself back in Higashi Koseki, lurching the route from station to Big Peach House. I'd barely noticed I was not alone.

They threw an arm around my waist to steady themselves, which all but sent me keeling off the sidewalk. I was in no state to be a steadying force for anyone. I inspected this stranger with whom there seemed to be some established intimacy. Conservatively dressed in a white blouse and black pencil skirt, I must've been testing Dallas' assertion that 'those mousy, pent-up office girls are the keenest, biggest freaks of all, bro.'

I noted through my haze a liberally unbuttoned blouse which was probably the lure; a visible black brassiere underneath, definitely the hook. She had other subtle fashion flourishes, rings on every finger and multiple piercings up each ear, attractively indicative of a possible deviant inclination. A flashback to the recent past saw me sharing an affinity for the Japanese cult band, X Japan. I'd never listened to X Japan, but she would likely be the target of said lie. I could only presume we were heading back to my pad.

We drifted through a gap in the low brick wall, entrance to the Gaijin House property. Stones of the rocky drive shifted and crackled beneath our steps. The marginally unstable ground caused us to stumble and sway even more. The air laced with foolish giggles and drunken babble, we entered the front foyer where the communal shoe racks were.

The X Japan fan removed her black heels. I slipped off my sneakers while an eerie feeling some act of imperceptible brutality had just transpired coursed through me.

On approach, right before I swung open the left side of the glazed double front doors painted with fallen Japanese maple leaves, I sensed a still human figure standing beside and back from the building's edge, just beyond where the light touched. My head turned to look directly at the silhouette in the shadows, and it straight at me. I never paused or even broke stride, though for the briefest of time, a grim recognition seized and sobered me. That silent, ghostly interaction with the figure from the dark hovered until the hand of the drunken office girl grabbed mine and pulled me from the succubus smog and down the hall.

We kissed and pawed at each other in the dark, the foreplay was artless and the sex clumsy. It probably wouldn't have been any good anyway, but throughout a lingering feeling of unease clung to my psyche.

She dressed in the whetting greyness of early morn, buttoning her blouse to the top hole as we bid a hasty and awkward goodbye. For my part, I never even got out of bed. In fact, I lay there until just before noon as an ominous feeling of some nebulous event from the previous night tiptoed about the room.

That lurking sense and a bladder near to bursting drove me from the covers. I took a long piss, made a cup of coffee and walked through the empty house before stepping outside for a smoke and some caffeine to clear my head.

Sat on the dirty bricks of a withered flower box outside the doors, I lit my smoke, took a sip of coffee, and dropped my head. Looking between my knees, little droplets of bright red speckled the smooth curved stones below. My stomach churned as I inspected the area and saw more and more of these red circles splattered on the rocks. I looked up and followed them down the drive as far as my vantage point would allow.

A realization it was freshly shed blood collided with the faint memory of the ghostly figure from the previous night, and they came crashing down simultaneously. What lingered as a vague dream or hallucination, rapidly became a disturbing reality.

The face from the shadows was revived from my muddied memory. It came into view – Akiko – with that same devoid and distant expression I'd seen on the Chiba beach.

I closed my eyes and focused on Akiko's face the way I'd captured it in that brief snapshot look from the previous night. I turned it over in my mind like a polaroid, looking for meaning in her expression. It wasn't shock or disappointment as I would have expected, it seemed more like confirmation. Confirmation of an ugly truth. Confirmation of my callousness and maybe confirmation of deeper insecurities, deeper concerns, and deeper agonies that swam in her head as vicious barracudas.

I stood and walked along the drive, reading each stained stone as a line from some maudlin poem. At the end of the drive, I felt rising bile in my stomach and vomited behind the low rock wall. The retching continued until tears streamed. I stood and stared back toward the guesthouse entrance through a greyish-green watery blur. Beyond that night, I never saw Akiko again, and beyond the morning, I never heard from her.

I texted later that evening, 'Sorry I missed you last night, I got stuck out. I hope you didn't come by after all or wait long?'

I sought verification or even repudiation, but received neither.

For me, the gig was up. Following in Dallas' philandering footsteps was proving to be unsustainable. I didn't judge. Dallas seemed to wear this life like a loose garment. I tried it on, but over time it began to ride up and chafe.

A few weeks later, I cashed in my chips and moved to Mejiro, a quiet residential sanctuary in the heart of west Tokyo, sandwiched between the college town of Takadanobaba and the metropolis outcropping of Ikebukuro.

Before my departure, I said my goodbyes to Dallas and wished him luck. He didn't try to convince me to stay. In fact, he looked somewhat relieved to see me go. I'd framed our friendship as Dallas leading me into temptation. It may not have been that cut and dry. I recall a night stumbling through Shinjuku in a cocaine- and booze-fuelled delirium. Pupils, big, black lagoons of depthless indulgence, looked over for reassurance Dallas was on the same trip, but registered the conflicted expression of a culpable chaperone instead.

Whatever those days were, like most of my life, it felt like I was playing a part. Regardless, the act had come to an end. As the curtains closed, I exited stage left, onto the next role.

The ocean had churned up a flotsam of memories which left me racked with guilt and remorse. I sat on the tatami of the ship's second-class sleeper, staring at lined paper ripped from a simple notebook until the words came. Once written, I walked back out to the deck with the empty Awamori bottle. A piece of paper rolled up and stuffed inside.

Looking back, the whole scene plays out as a farcical pantomime. Like one of those low-budget, cheesy background videos playing as the lyrics stream across the karaoke screen – a biker fills up his hog with gas, then sits brooding alone in a bar, smoking and drinking before getting on his bike and hitting the open road to some undecided destination.

My hammy gestures that afternoon were obviously tailor-made for The Police's 'Message in a Bottle'. I'd heave the Awamori bottle over the rail watching it fall to the tempestuous waters below as the band croons, '... castaways ... adrift on seas ... bottle, bottle, bottle ... sending off this hmm, hm, hmm ...'

The act completed, in silent reflection with a slight sting, I watched as the bottle, for a brief time, rested on the sea's surface before the ship pushed forward and it was lost from view. Only in imagination could I observe the paper-thin atonement float on to wash up where it may.

In finality of that redress fantasy, I see a faceless woman stroll down a sandy beach. She stops at something lapping against the shore, picks up the weathered bottle and turns it upside down. A rolled paper falls into her cupped, waiting palm. Intuitively, she knows it was meant for her as she unravels and reads. Once she ingests the final consonant, some long-forgotten scar magically vanishes from within, and she continues on her gentle amble.

4// Octopus Balls and Tanuki Nuts

The ferry crept through dark seas while I slept.

A gurney rattles down a hospital corridor. On my back pelted by the spasmodic blinking of fluorescent light, I'm deposited in a dark room. I step on the floor. The star-patterned linoleum is wet with an inch of water and small dark whirlpools have come alive where cigarette burns once marred. Stars glow, flicker and fall beneath the surface. The bedimmed walls inhale and exhale with wrestled breaths.

The television switches on, static transitions into a broadcast – an image, the anonymous criminal rants in a harsh dictatorial tone. Driven into the hallway possessed of a stagnant sinister aura, lightbulbs flash off and on with increased rapidity while the painted creatures hung upon the walls breathe in rhythm with the dark. Black-masked faces on the window scenery dart around in the acrylic camouflage and speak in maleficent whispers. Wet footprints leave a trail of my path, which I sense the painted creatures and lurking figures from the pane follow with stalking eyes.

I arrive at the red door emblazoned with the gold fourteen. Skin sizzles as I grab the brass knob. The smell of burning flesh corrodes my nasal cavity. Opening the door a small crack, I push it with fearful caution and am permitted to enter.

A naked body lies strapped to the metal frame of a stripped cot. The feet twitch in feeble resistance against thick brown leather restraints. I scan up from the feet. Pale white thighs highlight each small yellowing bruise, blue vein, and rough red bump. A thick tuft of raven black pubic hair emerges in a round-edged triangle from the meeting of her thighs. Two huge breasts, milky white, and topped with large round ringed areola spill out to each side, as the poor woman lies helpless on her back.

My eyes arrive at the victim's face, and I gasp. Gertie, eyes pried open with steri-strip tape, bears an exhausted expression of terrified resignation.

In some sort of drug-induced hypnagogia, her pupils dilated and rolling, she registers no reaction when I call out, 'Gertie!'

A perverse soundtrack of theremins and loud techno accompanies the central horror of disturbing imagery being simultaneously projected on all four walls and ceiling. Squinting to peer through a thin veil of smoke that permeates the room and limit the assault of light and colour intersecting my sight, I'm able to make out dark silhouettes in back corners of the room – they who orchestrated and now quietly study the whole torturous operation.

The male has long black bangs that sweep over and half-conceal his face. The other, a female, has straight bangs hanging down below her eyebrows and the rest falls as a smooth cloak to her lower back. Lurking in opposite corners, they wear matching black hoodies, black jeans, and dispassionate expressions.

I remain still, my presence either hasn't registered or is inconsequential to them. I look to the ceiling where Gertie's eyes are fixed, powerless against penetration of the ghastly images projected there. A scavenging beast ripping the final piece of flesh off a decaying corpse cuts rapidly to a soldier, his luger pistol pressed to the temple of a kneeling and hogtied, emaciated prisoner; the trigger is pulled, globs of black blood spurt forth through grey space, the prisoner falls, and it cuts to the next atrocity. Escalating horrors of rape, murder, suicide and death, cycle through in an elaborate symphony of gut-wrenching scenery.

I'm shaken taking in these images for even an instant. God knows how much Gertie has endured. 'I have to free her from this mental torture.' The realization snaps me from an agonized daze and I step toward the source, the five-lensed projector in the room's centre. As soon as I move, the male lunges from the corner – grabbing by the throat, he drives me back across the room until I am pinned against the door. He reaches behind his back and when his hand reappears, it's brandishing a large knife. The blade is taken back briskly and thrust forward toward my liver.

I awoke with my face fallen off the thin pillow and resting directly on the tatami mat floor. My skin imprinted with the rough straw pattern, I rolled back on the blanket, lay flat on my back and inhaled deeply of the musty air in those communal quarters. A troubling voice echoed faintly in my ear, 'Ye jus' stood by and let it all 'appen ...'

Hours later, the sound of the ferry's horn blew, indicating we were nearing port. I got up and walked unsteadily toward the deck. The boat shifted. I stumbled, grabbing hold of one of the wide poles stretched from floor to ceiling. My palm brushed round the timber pillar, *it felt like Norwegian wood.*

From the deck, I watched land come into view. Like a phoenix, Kobe's modern harbour rises from the rubble of The Great Hanshin quake. A mosaic of shops and restaurants connect through a network of paths, promenades and waterfront boardwalks, lit by night with old-fashioned gas street lamps and strings of electric light. Metallic white sails and the three-hundred-foot tower wrapped in latticed red steel provides a seismic shift from the surviving 19th-century redbrick warehouses of the old dockyard. The port tower's hourglass shape made me ponder if the sands of time trickled within, counting down to a day when the city's serene beauty would be rocked again.

Beyond the materializing city were the Rokko's hilly backdrop, all cobalt and silver mist sandwiched between sea and sky, as if the

Mountains of Ararat for our Ark to run aground. In the morning chill, I thought, *if Okinawa was my purgatory, then this boatman is transporting me where?*

Upon disembarkment, I half expected St. Peter to be waiting for me at the terminal gates. *What would he ask of me and would I have the right answers? Or any answer at all?*

Down the gangplank and across the vehicle ramp, I kept my eyes peeled for the ferry worker who'd spoken to me. *Charon* was nowhere to be found. Hand in my pocket, I nervously jangled loose change, nevertheless.

An hour later, I walked through the streets of Kobe. My sea legs caused the pavement to bob up and down. I had difficulty making my way in a straight line without swaying or veering sidelong like a common drunkard. The feeling should have been familiar, but to experience it sober felt quite queer.

My stomach, too weak to growl, whimpered for sustenance. A Cup Noodles for the two-day ferry ride was hardly enough now that I was to traverse this land. Red lanterns hung outside a stand on the next block indicated a food stall, and though rarely motivated by hunger rather than thirst, I picked up my pace.

The red awning was decorated with a *kawaii* cartoon octopus, but my only thought was, *I'm gonna eat you, ya little bastard.* I'm unsure about the genitalia of octopi, but they sure have delicious balls.

I ordered a paper container of eight *takoyaki*, which were being cooked in specially moulded pans right before my eyes. The semi-sweet aroma, nostalgic of bread in the oven, wafted over the glass sneeze guard where I salivated like an expectant street dog.

It was served; liberally covered in mayo, sauce and shaved bonito which danced a seductive gyration atop the piping hot treats. About the size of bull testicles, using the only utensil provided or necessary, I punctured one with a toothpick and remembered Matsumura of Okinawan lore. Smiling, I put the whole thing in my mouth. Biting through the crispy battered outside, I was greeted amicably by soft, warm tempura scraps, pickled ginger, and just that little hint of rubbery octopus tentacle. Squid or octopus I usually find offensive in texture. Yet in that packaging, the juxtaposition of textures complimented it perfectly and made the small *tako* chunk feel like the prize in the middle of a Kinder Egg.

I was feeling festive all of a sudden, so I ordered a Sapporo beer to wash down my treat. I figured I would stay in Kobe for the night to recharge my batteries, then hit the trains to Tokyo. I could have caught the much faster Shinkansen but opted for the local trains, remembering this *gaijin* guy in a bar one time telling me about travelling from Osaka to Tokyo without paying a single fare. This kind of grift appealed to me immensely, and since I had nothing but time on my hands, thought I'd give it a go.

I spent the afternoon walking the streets, in parks and out front convenience stores, drinking Chu-hi and smoking; a real culture trip. Once the sun went down, I ventured into a small *izakaya*.

The customary statue of a raccoon dog, or *tanuki*, was just outside to greet customers as they entered. I always had an affinity for these little fuckers, which adorn the stoop of many Japanese pubs. Fittingly, they represented merriment and debauchery. Those of folklore, the *Bake-danuki*, were a sort of supernatural being with human qualities, and some could even assume human form.

With a little smile on their short snout and wide half-crazed adventure-seeking eyes, *tanuki* carry an empty purse and promissory note in one hand and a bottle of *sake* as a road-pop in the other. Equipped with a turtle shell hat, they are short with large beer bellies and massive testicles, like they are ready to blow a most epic load should their spree prove fruitful. Drunken, debt-ridden, horny little buggers, just out for a lash and a laugh, the repercussions be damned.

'Yes, I believe we are kindred spirits,' I said to the statue upon entering the small bar, feeling slack and well on my way to three sheets to the wind.

Inside, I was welcomed with a bowl of *edamame* and cold beer served in a frozen pint glass. The bar filled up. People sat *seiza* on elevated tatami mats around bottles perched on low acacia tables. As the lone *gaijin*, I found myself showered with attention by the elderly and working-class patrons, much like my nights at the small snack outside Obusuma Station.

There was even a chronic karaokeer, who insisted I duet with him on 'Bridge Over Troubled Water', but scolded me when I stepped on his lines. 'Me John, you Paul,' he said like a salaryman Tarzan. 'I'm a Ringo man,' I was tempted to declare and really throw him, but instead just apologized and tried my best to learn my part. The same routine had played out many times in my Yorii snack, except it was a Carpenters duet I kept fucking up.

We crossed our bridge, albeit shakily, and I sat back down to harmonize with my ale.

Being the centre of attention spurred on my drinking beyond its usual pace. After ceremonial *kampai*s with most every patron and getting asked the same five or six introductory questions multiple times, I'd soaked up enough of the limelight. Of attention, I was saturated like the bloated bar rag draped over the draft tower, and so decided I'd excuse myself. I was met with a convivial *'mata o-koshi kudasai'*, but suspected deep down they were happy to see me go and return to their comfortable normalcy.

The wooden door shut with a mic-drop thud and I cocked my head to one side. Studied through a half-closed eye, I gave the *tanuki* a parting nod. That's when he winked at me.

I walked over, set my hands on my knees to steady myself and bent to inspect him more closely. I began speaking as one would to a small dog, 'hows are you doing buddy? Must get a lil boring oot here all night. Yuz wanna come oot partying with me?'

All of a sudden, the *tanuki* became more animated, but then again, so had I. He tilted his head upwards and widened his mischievous grin. I took that as a yes and picked up the knee-high creature, threw him on my shoulders and off we headed into the night.

The ceramic statue softened to a natural form. His sizeable hairless scrotum spilled against my neck, triggering an odd nostalgia. *A departing hug, arms wrap around the deteriorating form of an elderly relative as flaps of loose skin hanging off their frail frame brush the nape of my neck, sending shivers both creepy and comforting.*

From there on, the night became fragmented. It slipped in and out of focus like an old super 8 movie – most of it only coming back a time later as some cockamamie slideshow projecting onto my weary mind.

I see myself getting pulled in and pushed out of bars, by random women and disgruntled bartenders ... Walking down a neon wonderland, my arm slung around a pretty college girl, the purple haze plastered across her profile illuminating a discomforted smile ... Craning back my woozy head, I pucker up to kiss the sky and lurch off into blended halogen hues, a murky mix of happiness and misery. Then on the next slide (or previous), strolling solo down a crowded promenade, half-crazed under a crescent moon ... Moshing up and down in a small club as everyone else is easy skanking ... Screaming off-key, slurred lyrics into a microphone, the salaryman's tie around my forehead fashioned in the prototypical Rambo bandana, while office-worker onlookers wear amused, startled, annoyed and befuddled motley masks, trying to make heads or tails of this unknown intruder – the unannounced *eigo* jester now occupying their private karaoke room. Then out, walkin' after midnight, a Cline kinda crazy running through, *tanuki* held up in the face of a tarted-up club girl, encouraging her to kiss his massive sack, moving it away to steal a kiss of my own as she squeals with laughter and squirms away.

The carousel clicks, projecting off-kilter and ill-orientated

35mms through a dust-covered lens ... Banging against the sides of shelving, knocking off chips as I plough my way to *konbini*-store coolers, for more ... Banging into stools and customers making my way to the bar, for more ... Banging into brick walls and lamp post as I swerve and push forward, deeper into the night, for more.

I came to with my head buried in the crux of my arm. My focus landed on a half-drunk beer in front of me and then the stubbed-out cigarette butts in a shallow ashtray. I lift my face, and the middle-aged woman working behind the counter gave me a placid smile, nonplussed I'd passed out for a time on her bar.

Behind me, on a few couches, in small groups of two or three, local customers drank whisky, talked and exchanged low controlled laughter almost as if they were being careful not to wake the sleeping *gaijin*. I took a long slog of the beer; it was room temperature. Anyways, in the wee hours of that hushed bar, it looked as if I'd reached my final slide.

Two seats down an attractive woman in her early twenties sat alone at the counter. Her beauty was that of a half-moon, it shone most brightly in profile.

Casually dressed for a quiet night alone, she wore a wide neck sweater that showed smooth clavicles, glimmering in the barroom dim. A lit Seven Stars smouldered in the ashtray and a paperback was splayed out, face down in front of her. She looked straight ahead in earnest thought.

Her profile radiated more brightly as she turned the book over and peered into the pages, soaking up words like so much sunlight in the dark bar. Quite taken, I peeked below the counter where the hem of a frilled black skirt rode-up dusky crossed thighs. I felt like Bukowski, drunk, and leering at all that flank.

Lost in literary fantasy, I couldn't resist horning in on that quiet evening in my typical invasive style. A gruff little voice in my head and the prodding of my Tanuki companion egged me on to make a move. It would turn out I already had.

'Hi, sorry to disturb you but I just wanted to say, how beautiful you look, reading all peaceful here on your own.'

She said, 'Is okay,' and flashed a sashimi smile, fresh and glistening. 'We already talk, then you sleeping.' She filled me in, in a lilting voice punctuated by a girlish giggle.

'Shit, I'm sorry. I guess I went a little heavy earlier tonight.' I made a tilting glass gesture and forced a chuckle. The booze must've worn off some during my power nap because I felt my cheeks blush.

'Is okay. It is cute. I hope we can be friend.' She rested her chin in her hand, then shifted it slightly to cover a crooked tooth smile. Movements furnished to appear cutesy and inviting.

'Well, I hope we can be friends too.' I slid one seat over to close the distance.

I asked her what she was reading. She showed me the cover. It was manga, which was disappointing. The whole open book, cigarette smouldering, solitary demeanour was still alluring, but I was hoping that it would be one of the classics like Naoya or Kawabata.

She'd finished work over an hour ago, as a waitress at an upscale steak and seafood restaurant nearby. I talked about Kobe steak and my desire to try. She confirmed that they sold it, that it was delicious, and I should definitely try.

I did manage to steer the discussion from her manga to deceased *Nihonjin* novelists. She only tilted her head with mild interest at my name dropping. With mention of the contemporary writer Ryu Murakami, she leaned in. And when I quoted 'Almost Transparent Blue' she perked up, saying it was her favourite. I dog-eared this information, noting it as a propensity toward a rebellious youth and probable wild child; even though it went against all apparent appearances.

The conversation never became super exciting or established a strong connection. It didn't need to. There was a palpable curiosity, a passing of electric current whenever our eyes met, and so it seemed a foregone conclusion that we would be together that night. We were merely ships passing in the night, to dust off a tired expression, though timely in relation to recent circumstances.

It was almost 3 am, and the mama-san was wiping down counters. A few other tables still had people, but I used this as an opening to leave together. She hesitated none.

I grabbed the *tanuki* and tucked him under my arm. She studied it while scratching her head. 'It's my spirit animal,' I offered, assuming the statue's maniacal grin. I don't think she understood the Native American reference.

As we walked down the street holding hands, I explained I was only passing through Kobe for the night. That seemed to suit her just fine. 'I don't have any place to stay, yet.' At low risk of sounding presumptuous, I asked, 'Can you help me check into a love hotel?'

We were downtown, so there happened to be a five-storey love hotel at the end of the block. After helping me book the room, she accompanied me upstairs. I'd gotten the six-hour time slot, and my new friend seemed in no hurry to get anywhere. I found the contented ease with which she drifted admirable. It was like how I aimed to travel; without the obvious forcing, a constant push and tussle, I couldn't seem to shake.

The second the door closed behind us, we kissed unrestrained, our tongues swirling in amorous exploration. She fell back on the bed and removed her sweater, asking me to hit the lights. She had a soft, plump face, which shone sweet and innocent with a coy smile in the dim.

Ravenous, I removed her bra and skirt, kissed her neck, nipples, and up the insides of her thighs. Before I could lick and taste her pussy, she hauled me up to meet her feverish gaze. Hands glided down my back and seized each buttock, nails pressed against flesh, she guided me into her waiting wet warmth.

Underneath my body, she rolled her hips and arched her back, taking me in deeper and deeper, with a slow, practised writhing.

Ecstasy and escape surged through my body.

I worked to ensure she climaxed, though was operating from a selfish blueprint – a repertoire to work through and scrub the accumulated rust off after my recent sexual drought. But my blueprint blurred, lost as I was in desire to prolong the magnificent satisfaction of slowly suffocating a pervasive loneliness.

Rocking up and down, the surface of her body was a sea of pleasure, rolling me dangerously close to orgasmic shores. I attempted to change course and pulled her arm to drive us to a side position. She staunchly resisted the change of position and pulled away to keep herself breasts up and back pressed against the mattress.

I sensed she was trying to hide something, and even more yearned to explore her full form, in every position.

At last, with a tight hug and body roll, I managed her onto her side. Left leg raised toward the ceiling, I took long deep strokes from my new vantage point, but the suspense was killing me. Manipulating her supple body onto all fours, she squealed a final weak protest and giggled, '*Iie*.'

I seized her hips and positioned to enter. 'Fuck that's hot!' I proclaimed, my eyes met by a tattooed mural covering her entire back.

She lay flat on her chest, hips pushed back, ass up; inviting. I slid in and kissed above each shoulder blade, at faded corners where the tattoo began. The ink there faint, in the process of being erased through some laser removal process, like a love letter a scorned paramour destroys by taking a match to the edges, letting the flames crawl over the document in a futile attempt to erase memory.

It was getting me hot, that lover's revelation. I moved inside of her and ran my hands over the inked art. Black lined lion dogs stretched up the length of her spine, one on each side – guardians of the pagoda temple depicted in the background. One of the foo dogs had its paw on an embroidered ball – *or could it be ... ball of string?*

Struck by a possible enigmatic connection.

The other lion rested a paw upon what looked to be its cub. The rest of the flesh was inked in an Asian design swirling sky. I took a final brush of my hand over the fleshy canvas, with a thrust, hard and deep in appreciation of the illustration.

Having physically and introspectively admired the full-back tattoo, I guided her onto her back once more. Her moaning increased to a steady scream with each succeeding impel as she gripped the sheets with clawing hands. I swiftened my pace and felt the months of pent-up sexual energy rushing to my loins, I held back with all my might, finally, pulling out in a low roar of frenzied bliss. Holding tight to my cock, the ejaculate spurt forth on her chest, shoulders, and bedding beyond.

I took the love hotel bed sheet and wiped her clean. We lay shoulder to shoulder on our backs and lit cigarettes. In silence, we inhaled sweet relief and exhaled spent pleasure. Wispy grey curls danced the air above. Finally, I addressed the elephant in the room, or more aptly, lions. 'That's a sexy tattoo. Must have taken hours to get done?'

With a bashful smile, she explained, 'I used to be a little bit bad girl.'

Well, I met you a couple of hours ago, and I just blew my load all over your chest. I wouldn't say you're entirely reformed. I thought to myself with a sardonic smile, but instead said, 'Maybe so, but you seem a pretty sweet girl now.' I kissed her shoulder.

I touched below the kiss where the ink lines faded, raised and bubbled. 'Are you getting removed?' I asked to confirm my suspicion.

'*Hai,*' she replied.

Why? was the obvious question but my consideration strayed elsewhere. 'Is it possible ... to erase your past like that? Aren't there some choices we are destined to carry for life?'

She shrugged. I thought she hadn't understood, and the shrug was all I would get. Yet, after a two drag silence, she answered, 'I don't know if possible. It hurts, it takes much time and maybe always be there a little, faint and distant. But some things ... you must try remove.'

We slept until the phone beside the bed rang to give warning that in thirty minutes my time in the room expired. I looked at the sexy badass next to me in bed and thought about round two. Instead, I got up and rushed to the sink and vomited. I looked around for any stray cans. No booze in sight, so I vomited again.

The ex-*yakuza* lover from the previous night had woken from the call and witnessed my retching. She looked a little insulted and hurt. I tried to explain. 'Sorry babe, I just get a little sick in the mornings sometimes.'

Her index finger tugged down on her lower lip, as she fished for the meaning of my words. It would seem the Tower of Babel cast long shadows in a low hung morning sun, with the booze and lustfulness subsided.

We dressed and left the love hotel together, an immaculate establishment for such a sleazy concept. The sun's rays were a shock to both our systems, and we reared back as they hit.

Outside the hotel's exit, I spotted a *tanuki* statue lying on its side; lipstick stains on the white of his belly and black markered pubes drawn on the oversized ball sack. A vague recognition returned as I thought, *looks like someone had a pretty berserk night!*

I kissed the girl on the cheek as she got in a cab. She smiled sweetly in what now seemed mock innocence, or innocence reborn? I think her name was Sakura, at least that's the way I remember it now – fitting, like the tree, whose flowers bloom ever so briefly, bringing much-needed beauty and respite to the dreary, hectic lives of the multitudes.

Sanguine in my *hanami* hangover I hustled groggily, dry heaving and eyes watering, to reach the nearest convenience store. Swathed in a chilled blast from the open cooler door, my arm cradled two tall cans of Kiwi Chu-hi, as I reached inside and gripped a third with my free hand. I debated, then pulled it out, splurging on the seasonal flavour before they disappeared like the Central Park ducks in winter.

I arrived at the station, anxious to start my journey back to Tokyo. The first leg would take me from Kobe to Osaka. I entered the platform gates in that first station with a sly bum-rush, running up the backside of a paying customer as they slid their ticket through, and the automatic gates opened. It was the tail end of the morning rush hour, and despite the crowds, the businessman, who was my first patsy, seemed to sense the intrusion on his personal space. He shot a scowl in my direction and went on his way.

Having performed the same procedure to-and-fro stations ample times during skint days in Yorii then Tokyo, I thought, *Shit, must be losing my touch*.

It also may have been my aroma of stale beer, body odour and fermented sex offended his senses and tipped him off. Either way, with about twenty of these manoeuvres in front of me before I arrived in Tokyo, I was going to have to step up my game. I headed straight to the station toilet for a quick sink bath.

Cosmic Pachinko

A man who has been through bitter experiences and travelled far enjoys even his sufferings after a time
—*Homer,* The Odyssey

This fat fucker – I'm assuming he's fat by the loud rustling and creaks made as he stirs. Foghorn snores and vacuum sucking breaths emanate from his side of the partition and have been since he moved in next door eight hours ago. I think he rubbed one out to internet porn in his first 20 minutes; typical Japanese, pubics blurred, office molestation shit, or something. Anyways, he has been sleeping soundly ever since.

I, on the other hand, have been up all night due to his racket, hiding out and writing; rambling prose – madness, like so much spilt absinthe. At least, for now, I got this fat cunt to blame.

A week ago, it was Yukie who sparked my inaudible wrath – though, caught in the crossfire of stupidity and jealousy, bore collateral damage in petty words fired upon my cowardly retreat.

I'd walked her to the bar where she works. Well, the vicinity, she was careful to kiss me on the cheek and bid farewell before I could identify the exact establishment.

I know too little about this woman, I decided, walking away. Especially for the amount of time she occupied my thoughts.

To be fair, she knew as much about me. It had been a bit of a game of emotional hide-and-seek between us. For my part, I'd been careful not to lie, not wanting to fall into Dallas' and my old game of fake personas and utter bullshit. It was like walking an identity tightrope, trying to withhold enough so as to not scare her off yet reveal just enough to keep her interested. And I suspected Yukie a worthy opponent in this game of evasiveness. At first, it created an air of mystery, but by that time – for me at least – the air had dampened toward frustration.

Naturally dishonest, I behaved just so, rounding the corner before doubling back to follow Yukie to her place of work.

Two hours later, after drinking in front of a Kabukicho 7-Eleven to solidify my determination and hatch a plan of attack, I was ready.

I popped the collar of my lightweight jacket, ducked my head low and rapidly entered the club through a tinted glass door. I walked swiftly around the establishment, scanning the pretty hostesses on couches and sashaying throughout the bar. None of them was Yukie.

The presence of this skittish *gaijin* immediately aroused suspicion. The barrel-chested bouncers began to stir. At the back, past the stage where a hostess in a floor-length sky-blue evening gown sang *enka* on karaoke, was a drawn red velvet curtain. My breath caught, and I made fleet-footed for it.

I perceived the suited *yakuza* thugs rise from their stooled perch and close in. Arriving first, I parted the curtain and stuck my face through the gap. It was Yukie, and not alone.

A salaryman sat on a simple desk chair and leaned all the way forward, so his forehead almost touched the tabletop. With his back to me, I couldn't make out his features or age. Yukie's back was to me too, but I knew it was her from the blonde-streaked, flowing curls of her hair, and an indiscernible allure which radiated from her form. Karaoke continued to warble from behind, but a different melody hit me head-on. Mesmerized, I started to step through the red curtain, but caught myself and stayed put.

The man was motionless. Yukie sat next to him, elevated on a bar chair. His suit jacket was off, but he still wore his white dress shirt and slacks, while Yukie reached down with her left hand and sketched swirls on his back with an extended index finger. It was like the game you play as kids, where one traces a picture on the others back, and they try to guess what was drawn. This man wasn't guessing anything. He seemed to be in a deep meditative state.

Suddenly he reared up, his head thrown back and face bent into an expression mixed of agony and ecstasy. He convulsed a few times like he was experiencing a small seizure. Yukie drew back a steady hand, placed it on her lap, then sat still and upright.

I was seized from behind by the upper arm and dragged through the bar. 'Sumimasen, sumimasen ...' I repeatedly apologized in a hollow and befuddled recital, clutching the image of Yukie with some man in a bare-bones backroom as we went. I was tossed into the buzzing blaze of Kabukicho's neon night with the club door slammed in warning behind me.

Back at the 7-Eleven, I continued drinking until around 4 am when I returned and hung back from her club's entrance. Pairs of drunken salarymen and unaccompanied hostesses began to trickle out in stumbles and teeters. Then Yukie emerged and turned left down the lane.

I swayed into action and followed. 'What the fuck do you do, eh?' I called to her back.

She turned, an expression of shock overtaking her face as it registered who was accosting her there in the Kabukicho glow. 'What? Why you here, Fred?'

'A hostess I was okay with,' I garbled. 'But whatever that was ... In a backroom getting guys off, like a common hooker.' I spat with cruel intention.

The nervous edge in her voice was supplanted by sheer indignation. 'You came to my work ... you're spying on me! And then you have the nerve to judge me.'

She turned and walked briskly down the street against a stream of retiring hostesses and unbuttoned salarymen.

I should have chased, but didn't. Instead, I tossed a half-drunk beer can against a brick wall, it made a crunching sound, hissed and spat foam. A few passersby looked quizzically at the fuming *gaijin*. I wished it were a bottle for the desired effect.

* * *

My brunch beers became breakfast whiskies as I set out on a two-day bender where I wrote not a word and stumbled through the streets, on and off trains and through unknown thousands of convenience stores, parks, bars and nightclubs.

I finally came to in the internet café, unshaven, unshowered and unsure. Smells of piss and vomit mingled round the cramped space. I hoped the odours were brought in with me and not generated in the cubicle, though failed to see how it was much better.

I paid up for my previous stint and checked in for my next twenty-four, unable to make eye contact with the young clerk behind the counter.

Walking in the autumn air and drinking a third can as my laundry dried, physically I was on the mend. Mentally, I was still in shambles. Back in the cubicle, I fished through my backpack and pulled out the Okinawan glass-bead keychain bought on a whim. Dipping into my diminishing supply, I grabbed a ten-thousand-yen note and subconsciously pocketed the two names which the old man had written down at the bull sumo.

I arrived and walked up the McD's stairs with a Coke, just a Coke. She was there, sitting in her regular spot. I approached sheepishly and took the stool next. Yukie looked at me and then back through the large window at all those souls with neon halos, traipsing the Shinjuku sidewalks below.

I launched right into it. 'I'm sorry,' I said, and let it stir in the icy quiet.

'I acted like a total jerk,' I continued. 'I shouldn't have invaded your privacy like that ... Seeing you in that environment, I became jealous and possessive, even though I had no right to be.'

Still, she stared straight ahead through the silence, hung like a mistress's panties drying on the family line.

'I was stupid, and what I said was stupid.' I tried to catch her eye by the window's reflection to see if my words were penetrating. The 'I was drunk' approach occurred to me, but in my case, not much of an excuse.

'You see, I manufacture these expectations in my mind ... like designs on people and places or events. And when they don't come together just as I carefully assembled 'em ... well ... I guess, I react like a petulant child or simply retreat.' I finished breathless and shut up.

'Yes, you were a jerk.' Her head turned a slow forty-five degrees to look at me with a glacial expression, though, at least she was looking at me. 'Yeah, I work in hostess bar, sorry to disappoint you! You should already know that, so why you need to spy? Then you call me prostitute. Why? Because I do my job. I work hard to pay rent and save for school.' She crossed her arms which might've indicated she had said her piece and was done, but I suspected there was more. 'You judge me! ... And you don't even work at all, just live in an internet café, like a drunken homeless.'

There it was, the retaliatory dig – well deserved and well played. I could tell she was still hurt by the incident, a cracking in her voice indicated such, but also her expression when finished showed relief.

My apology moved to phase two. I placed the *chura-dama* keychain in Yukie's palm. 'I got this before I left Okinawa. It caught my eye because it's unique and beautiful, like you.'

She peered down at the cheap trinket, the small turquoise ball with its polished, shiny exterior. Her expression remained blank, yet as she squinted and studied the interior – with its misshapen bubbles, those little eccentricities that took in the light and seemed to effuse it all around – a Mona Lisa smile spread across her face.

Her hand rested on top of mine, and she gave a light kiss on my cheek. It was the subtlest of romantic gestures. Though in that moment, the gentle peck felt more stimulating, more substantive, than each and every lubricious ride atop the feminine flesh combined.

I asked her out for a proper dinner date, stage three of the apology, and why I'd dipped into my dwindling resources. She didn't have time that evening due to work, so for the next three-quarters of an hour we talked there in McDonald's with the Beatles discography softly playing in the background.

'I feel like there is this invisible thread, out there in the cosmos or whatever, that connects all the events in our life: past, present and future.' I spilled forth as conclusion to why I'd left Okinawa, lived broke and jobless in an internet café, and spent days and nights writing to reconstruct the events which had led me here, blindly groping for significance and direction.

'Back in Okinawa, I felt like I grabbed hold of it. It led me back here, to Tokyo ... Shinjuku specifically. The thread led me back here for a reason, I can't shake that feeling.' I finished the burst of revelation and hid behind a cigarette.

Yukie lifted a perfectly painted eyebrow. 'If the thread led you here, then it has served its purpose. You are done, *ne*?' She had followed my words, but they'd left her understandably baffled.

'I fear not. Leading me here was only the beginning. Somewhere along the way, this string got snagged on something like splintered wood, an event maybe. Now I gotta find that snag and fix it so ... so ...' It was my turn to look lost out the McDonald's window, tripping on the merry-go-round of Shinjuku's whirling night. 'It's just a feeling, but a strong one ... that, yeah, this is why I'm here.' My face went flush. Explaining my theory, my murky mission as it were, I could hear how self-important and basically nuts it all sounded.

An index finger tapped her glossy pursed-lips, as though she were considering the matter seriously. 'Maybe you aren't supposed to follow the thread, maybe it was presented to you ... to be cut.'

It was a valid point, and I had no real argument against it. My thoughts had offered this same scenario of aborting the whole obscure search. 'But then I would be holding on to nothing at all.' I gave as the same weak retort, I'd given myself many times.

I went on to tell her about the Big Peach guesthouse. How I'd sought it out by wandering the streets of Higashi Koseki, yet it seemed to have vanished into thin air. I talked a little about Dallas and Gertie, how in the course of my travels I'd been reminded of two very good friends. The mysterious phone calls by which I'd been contacted were not mentioned, as I was still grappling with their absoluteness.

I'd laid bare as much as I was comfortable with, nay more. I could only hope that my explanation of where I was at in this life hadn't jolted her to her senses.

To my relief, it didn't scare her off. On the contrary, she reiterated her offer to help in any way, if I wanted.

'It's unrelated, but I met this guy in Okinawa. He did me a favour, and I promised to do him a solid in … I mean, to return the favour.' I produced the two names Hideki had written in *kanji*. 'It might be impossible, but could you find out the whereabouts of these two people? They went to Tokyo University around the mid-1960s and were involved in an anarchist group responsible for the seize of its clock tower. Maybe there are archived newspaper articles about it.'

She cocked her head like a perplexed kitten at the background info provided, perhaps daunted by the task I'd laid at her feet.

'If you cannot, it is okay,' I said, giving her an out.

'Yes, I'll have a look,' she said, taking the scrap of paper from my grasp. I spotted again, the nail with the ellipsed eye. It reminded me how desperately I still wanted to know what exactly was going on in that backroom, behind the velvet curtain. No longer in a jealous way, but with a deep unsatisfied curiosity. I didn't ask. The time wasn't right.

Yukie prepared to leave for her shift at the bar. Needless to say, no invitation to stop by was proffered. I felt the momentum had swung in my favour, so went balls out and suggested I meet her after. She didn't protest, instead said she usually went to a café to kill time before the Yamanote line fired up just before dawn. 'Yes, it'll be nice to have company to wait those couple hours.'

'If anyone knows how to waste away the hours ...' I said with a self-deprecating smirk.

**

I slouched against a convenience store wall, three blocks over from Yukie's work, as per her instructions. She arrived at 3:30. I wasn't totally sober, but as sober as I could remember being at that hour in a long time.

We got two drinks from inside, her lemon Chu-hi and me the standard grapefruit, seasonal pear had already passed, much to my chagrin. If she was looking to slum it, I was definitely giving her the full experience: apéritif drinks à la Macdonald's, and nightcaps at the *conbini*.

A drizzle began to fall in the crisp autumn air. We both started to shiver. I pointed out a noodle shop across the way. We downed our beverages and entered.

My *tonkotsu ramen* arrived, I leaned over the bowl and let the steam wash over my face warming me to the core. I breathed in the aromatic blast of onion, garlic, ginger, and a savoury, almost buttery pork marrow scent.

From that first blast of steam and dip of the soup spoon into the unctuous milky broth to the liquid touching tongue initiating a taste sensation which sends my buds abuzz, dancing like eckied-up rave kids; the noodle dish induces a holistic response. The intangible effect it has on me is inwardly recognizable, yet hard to depict. To start with, perhaps due to my natural disposition, my *ramen* experience always felt uniquely more palpable. Those initial sensations bringing me wholly present into the moment. The outside world, with all its worries and distraction, just vanishes.

While making small talk with locals, in particular young women, their most common pet peeve was that of salarymen making slurping sounds as they ate their noodles. I'd never noticed their slurping, I never noticed if I slurped – I was too absorbed, maybe even transported.

As I made my way through the bowl – stretchy yellow noodles clung to healing broth, hearty chunks of *chashu* pork and poached egg holding tight it's golden runny yoke – I was further transplanted, then embedded in the serene tranquillity of being.

'I thought I lost you!' Yukie commented with a laugh. 'You were like in a trance or something. I never see you so quiet and concentrating.' She studied me with an inquisitive eye.

I set the spoon down in a shallow pool. I placed the chopsticks side by side on top of the bowl, ends facing away from Yukie, toward the sliding entrance door. 'Man, I needed that! I was pretty hungry,' was all I could articulate in response.

And yes, there was something else I needed, though was still contemplating how to acquire it.

Walking through the Shinjuku night, I veered us toward a clean, discreet love hotel I'd made a mental note of earlier. It was closing in on first train, and Yukie made no protest about us heading further away from the station. When we were in front of the hotel, I asked, 'Should we go in … hang out for a while?'

I was kicking myself for not being more direct, for not saying something more tantalizing and memorable. But it got the job done.

'Okay, let's spend a little more time,' Yukie said, seizing my hand and leading us in.

It unfolded slowly, we touched cautiously and kissed soft on waiting and expectant lips. All tethers of hesitation severed, we unravelled into uninhibited passion. Not rushed nor ego-driven, there was a heaviness in each caress, a purpose behind every push and pull.

I lifted her top over her head and brushed aside the long gold-woven curls fallen forward over each shoulder. The room's amber light traced pastel lines down the side of her neck, along her clavicle and down the smooth outline of her slender frame. A black brassiere cupped her supple breast, pushing them together and up, tops exposed and tan lines teased with mocha hues. I pulled the fabric aside, suckled and licked the exposed nipple, letting it swell to a protruding mahogany nub with the warmth of my mouth.

I walked her back until she fell upon the love hotel's heart-shaped bed. While Yukie lay splayed on top a shimmering pink bed sheet, I stood over her and allowed my eyes to crawl up every inch of her silky copper skin. Until our stares met, bore pleading into each other, and I fell upon her with a rapturous splash.

We gyrated rhythmically and built toward climax in fervid thrusts. I'd take myself to the precipice of ecstasy then retreat, viscerally calculating to prolong the union of pressed bodies, of being submerged in her natural spring – wet, warm, revitalizing.

Yukie's neckline flushed scarlet, her breathing deepened, the flowing movements became unbridled thrashing as her moans transformed to impassioned shrieks. We intensified our pace to a rapid pelvic pounding. The interlocking fingers of our clasped hands tightened as we reached the carnal summit in unison and collapsed in waiting arms.

***

Lying in our postcoital bliss, I ran my fingers through her hair and gazed into those chestnut eyes. Intermittently, I'd lean forward and pepper the silence with a planted kiss. Nuzzling my face in the nape of her neck, I inhaled deeply of her ambrosia aromas while she rubbed a hand through my hair and down my back.

It was then, she revealed herself to me.

Halfway down my spine, she curled her index finger in – the nail with an ellipse eye touched my skin. Warmth radiated from the point of contact. She traced her finger in a circular motion of swirls, something like van Gogh's Starry Night coalesced in my blurred vision. My eyelids grew heavy and closed.

Sat on a train heading into the mountains, my head lay on my brother's lap. His hand rest gently upon my head while I slept; our hair, so blonde in our youth. I slept peacefully as my brother peered out the window at the passing scenery, with an ethereal air.

A fresh winter's snow blanketed the ground and weighed down the branches of the passing pines. There was a blinding innocence about the whole scene; in the blonde of our hair, the freshly fallen snow and the purest of light cast across our trolley bench. All was remarkably hush, except for a low pulse like a distant drum or a mother's heartbeat as heard from the womb.

All the sudden, the majestic scene disintegrated into a million shining particles; they spurted and flew off in all directions. Then, there was only total darkness before the breaking of a golden light with the warmth of a thousand sunrises.

My body seized, lungs constricted, and eyes shot open wide. The paralysis lasted only a moment, and I relaxed again into the mattress sheet.

'I'm sorry,' Yukie said, teasing a satisfied smile. 'I should have asked first, but I didn't know what other way to explain.'

'No, I'm sorry,' I said adamantly, and felt even more guilty for earlier assumptions and accusations made. I just figured the dirty bastard was getting off on it, you know, the Japanese and their odd sexual proclivities. Though, it wasn't sexual, not in the least. I could see that now.

The lure of the bottle had long been predicated on its ability to get me out of myself, remove all insecurities and deposit me in a wonderland of carefree and careless revelry. This thing, though, the polar opposite really; drawn deeper and deeper inward – more centred, more quintessentially whole than I'd ever felt – then cloaked in a pure, spectacular peace.

'What ... was that?' I asked.

'I don't know,' she said in earnest. 'No one ever explain clearly to me what it does to them.'

That made sense. I wasn't about to take a stab at it – too personal, too perplexing.

'Once I hear ... *eto* ...' she paused in search of the right English expression, 'ultimate *natsukashii*.' She offered up a hybrid phrase.

I searched my Japanese vernacular, picked up in dribs, and drabs along the way. I located it kicking around my subconscious somewhere, *natsukashii*; nostalgia or feeling of pleasant memory.

'Yeah, that's actually pretty good,' I said.

'Whatever it is they get out of it, I just know in a very small circle of powerful men, this thing I do, it fulfils a need. It is something no one else can do, and so I can work in hostess bar and make more money than all the other hostesses, without the flirting and singing. Which is good because I don't like flirting with salarymen and I'm a terrible singer.' She shot me a wink, playfully.

She stole my move, I thought, laughed and tickled her bare side. Yukie squealed and squirmed away.

Once the horseplay subsided, I asked, 'How'd you realize you have this superpower?'

She giggled and slapped my shoulder. 'Not a superpower ... maybe a little bit gift. *Eto* ... like how a piano player or singer brings goosebumps to members of an audience.'

'That sounds a fairly accurate comparison. But still, I think your thing is more powerful.' I lay serious in my assessment, then asked, 'But, like, were you born with it?'

'I'd just started working as hostess,' she said her voice faraway and searching. 'I didn't like it. I always felt awkward and nervous, lighting their cigarettes and laughing at jokes I didn't even think were funny. But I never finished school and was a little bit pretty, or at least knew how to do good make, so it was about the only thing I could do.'

'You're very pretty, with or without makeup,' I said and took my move back, giving her a pronounced wink and adding an impish grin for good measure.

'I'm certain I was going to get fired. Then one day, the chief technical officer of a big electronics firm came in with his colleagues. I liked him because he was uncomfortable and out of place surrounded by the *sake*, music and woman. You could tell he wanted to be alone, back in front of his computer. There was something authentic about him, different than most customer.' Recounting her first, she sported a subtle reminiscent smile.

'I don't even know this matters,' she threw in, before a digression. 'As a little girl and even as a young teen, I liked drawing. Pictures of unicorns and rainbows then little comics, school girl dramas in manga style. I wouldn't say I was very good, but I enjoyed. It relaxed me and allowed me to express myself. I was a little bit, lonely and shy child.' She looked down at her dainty feet protruding from the covers as she related this background, and for an instant, I spotted the re-emergence of that shy little girl. I exhaled thin circular smoke towards the ceiling, rolled my head on the pillow, and admired the beauty that effused effortlessly from her form.

'I sat on the arm of the couch next to the CTO,' she said, bringing us back to the club. 'Normally, I don't ever touch the customer, but he seemed very uncomfortable, which was sweet. So I start to doodle on his back, hoping it would relax him. I traced a swirl, like a poster of a famous painting I might've seen earlier that day in Tokyu Hands. Then it flowed, my finger roamed independent as if an enchanted painter's brush, it filled that white cotton canvas.'

Yukie shifted and propped herself up on an elbow. The bedsheet slid off her shoulder, exposing breasts like swollen peaches hung firm and tempting off her lithe frame.

'Then, he shoot upright and ridged,' she stated, breaking my luring gaze. 'He stared across the bar, and beyond ... like through the wall to some other scene, some other present.'

She blushed and revealed, 'I got worried. I think maybe I hurt him, or worse, is making him *hōnī* ... um, excited sexually,' she whispered. 'Finally, with his head rest back on the cushioned booth, he drew a long sucking breath, like that last bit of water as it goes down the drain.'

'Did he say anything?' I asked, all jealousy long supplicated by pure fascination.

'No, he only stood up and rushed out of the bar without even paying. My boss was *cho* angry, "why'd you scare him away?"' Her voice lowered to mockingly imitate a severe boss. The little impression was very *kawaii*. In reality, I suspected the boss was a seriously serious man, and there was little *kawaii* about him in an angered state.

'Lucky for me, he came back the next night. He requested my company again, but this time in private.' She went on to explain, 'My boss arranged the card table and chair in the backroom and a simple stool from the bar for me to sit on. The businessman sat on the chair, pointed at his back, and requested, "Again, please."'

I pictured anew, as viewed through a small crack in the red curtain, Yukie and the salaryman with their backs to me, occupying two simple seats in the barren backroom. What was previously a whole perverse scene, now looked benevolent, almost benedictory.

'After that, about every second night, a man of great stature would come in. I never advertise my thing, whatever it is. But still, word got out, and they come.' She flashed a bashful smile, though I detected a glint of pride in her eye for the complex role she held at the hostess club.

I fished through the millions of questions which had formed in my head for the most pertinent or at least most coherent. 'Was that when you painted the design,' I ventured the long percolating question, 'on your fingernail?'

'I never painted.' She gave as her straight-faced, straightforward answer.

'Huh, whatta ya mean?'

'I woke up the next day, and it was there. The black line. Later, I add the bluestone.' She cracked a small embarrassed smile and added, 'you know, for flare and make *kawaii*.'

In disbelief, I recounted, 'You woke up one day, and it was just there?'

'*Hai*, the next day, after the first time at the club,' she clarified. 'And it can't be removed, I tried with polish remover.'

If I thought I was flooded with questions before, they just increased exponentially. I now understood when she had first discovered and practised this alchemy, but it had to have originated from somewhere, something?

'So that night your ability revealed itself. But, don't you think it manifest, like it was somehow implanted, in you earlier?'

'What do you mean?'

'Like did you get hit by lightning or ...?' I scratched the back of my head, searching for another universal example.

She laughed. 'No, I wasn't hit by lightning.'

Yukie lay down flat and pulled the blanket over her shoulders. She closed her eyes as if to sleep.

I lay on my back and lit another smoke, content to let my many questions rest as well. I was halfway through my cigarette and figured Yukie had already fallen asleep.

'In Nebraska, I guess,' she said, surprising me with the revitalization.

'Oh yeah?' I took another drag and waited with bated breath for her to elaborate.

'I was sixteen, and my school had an exchange program with a high school there. Here, you have to wear school uniform every day, so I do the same there,' she began. 'If I didn't, my report would say so, and I'd be scolded when I return to Japan.' She shook her head in disbelief. I guess at her own obedience to societal norms, even a couple continents away.

'At school, in my plaid skirt and white socks, the boys had their fun. Lifting it as I walked by, telling me to spread my legs in class or pretending to speak to me friendly, as one of them crawled behind and look up; then they burst into laughter at their cunning. Of course, the girls then dislike me, saying I enjoy the attention and if I didn't I wouldn't wear the uniform. They say I'm a slut.'

'It sounds awful, teenagers can be such cruel assholes,' I offered whilst reddening with recollection of my own actions.

'Yes, but they got bored. And so then I was just alone. That was okay, I've never had much need for friends.'

That surprised me considering how she dressed, all dolled up with an eye for fashion. But maybe she did it out of genuine interest and to feel good about herself, a foreign concept for me, always seeking the approval of others. Until I was blind drunk, that is, then I couldn't give a toss what ya made of me.

I also wondered, even worried, how she separated me from all those corn-fed white boys who'd given her such a hard time. *A grudge fuck?* The repulsive concept, and even worse prospect, flitted through my warped imagination.

'The real problems started at my homestay. It was a husband and wife and their daughter, who was in my year. She never called me names or teased me, just ignored and stayed away.'

'For fear contact with you might lower her already meagre social status,' I said, showing I was wise to the intricacies of high school politics.

'*Hai,*' Yukie said with a conceding smile. 'Because they lived on a farm, a grain farm, they had others there to help. Especially during harvest. The brother of the dad, the uncle, *ne?*'

I nodded.

'He was the only one kind to me since my arrival. He would ask about school and joke, getting me to teach him funny phrases in Japanese. Perry,' She said his name with some reluctance, 'was a bear of a man, a hundred and ninety centimetres, and well over two hundred and fifty pounds. He usually wore a tank top cause he was always sweating, and thick hair grew on his shoulders and back.'

She paused and lit a smoke. 'Maybe I should have been

suspicious of his attention toward me, but being Japanese, was maybe a little bit naïve at sixteen.' She seemed to check herself here, like to confirm she'd shed this naivety.

'One day, while the family was out at market, I wandered the property and fed the chickens some grain through a wire mesh on the coup. I liked the chickens, they were simple and easy to understand. I was surprised to see Mr Perry drive up in his pickup since it was a Saturday. He was taking the combine out, "ta get a jump on the harvest." He asked if I wanted to come along and see how the wheat was cut.'

Don't go! I wanted to shout like you might at the screen of a horror movie. Instead, I shifted under the satin sheets and felt the static against my skin.

'Being from the city, the farming was interesting to me. So, I agreed and went along. I needed help to climb onto the thresher. Mr Perry pushed me up from behind; his hand clenched too hard against my bum, and what felt errant, invasive fingers slipped between my thighs.'

Dirty feckin, cunt! Gertie's voice shot to mind, and boy, was she right.

'He climbed up easily and took the driver's seat next to me. There was no room between us on the narrow seat. I felt *cho* uncomfortable after the climb. His face was beet red and sweatier than usual. When he calmly said, "Let's get to work then." I felt *chotto* better.'

Yukie turned over and stubbed out her cigarette in the glass ashtray on the bedside table. She remained facing away but continued talking.

'He drove a straight line down the field, explaining how the wheat was cut and threshed by the turning blades and kernels stripped from the stalks. Then, halfway down the row, he cut the motor, and we stopped dead. The thresher continued to spin and spit grain, but we no longer moved. I knew immediately that this wasn't supposed to be.'

Because she'd rolled onto her side facing the love hotel wall, I couldn't read her expression and her voice gave away nothing, projecting deadpan and detached.

'He turned to me, eyes crazed and bloodshot; "None of 'em taking good care of yuh. Uncle Perry, gonna take good care of ya, girlie," he said, or something like that. Then he lean in and kissed me with a wet mouth. He smelled of sour milk and Bourbon. I leaned back to get away from his pressing form and hot breath, and barely caught myself from falling right off the combine. Then he placed a huge hand with hair growing from every knuckle, hard on my upper thigh. I wore jean shorts, and he worked his hand up and under the cuff. I froze with fear as he moved a fat finger onto my, ah, *manko,* and tried to push it in. "You got a tight little Asian pussy," he breathed heavily into my ear.'

Her practised detachment started to betray her in a quickening pace and added edge with each next detail.

'His gross words awoke me, and I struggled free. I climbed off the large machine and ran, but only made it as far as the back of the combine. He had hopped down the other side and rounded the rear in time to block my path. "You, fucking little chink," he swore over the running thresher.'

Fucking redneck, too ignorant to even get his racial slurs correct, was my thinking. Of course, I said none of it. Yukie rolled back to meet my sheltering stare. I was relieved to see her face soft yet stoic and took it to mean the worst of the ordeal was over.

'Suddenly, he lunged at me to grab my arm. I moved in time, and he fell forward.' She broke off and was lost in thought, like one trying to figure out where the final pieces of a puzzle should fall when none of them fit.

'Truly, I can't recall, and really I don't care either way,' she began. 'He may have fallen directly into the blades …'

She paused, bit her lip and a foreign, vengeful look overtook the ordinarily sweet, placid demeanour of Yukie. 'or as he stumbled, I grabbed his arm and directed it straight into the turning blades?' She finally admitted, kind of ... or didn't. It was still very much a question in her mind, and now mine.

'I'd hope it was the latter,' I weighed in. 'If he'd done to me what he tried on you ...' I cut myself short realizing the crazy equivalency I was drawing.

She neither smiled nor frowned at my opine, just fashioned a blank stare as if she were still seriously considering the matter, unable to decide. 'I've played it over a thousand times in my mind. And seen it both ways, I honestly can't tell which one is the reality and which is make-believe.'

'Either way, he deserved what he got,' I added as an armchair judge, jury and executioner.

'Yes, either way, the arm went into the thresher,' she unambiguously concluded. 'It had remained on but with no wheat to cut, hummed a continuous empty whirl. Add Mr Perry's forearm, and it sprung to action, shifting to a loud grinding and chopping sound before the metal chute above spit out a cloud of red mist speckled with chunks of white bone and gristled flesh across a clear blue sky.' She coughed. It wasn't a gag, on the contrary, she seemed to enjoy recounting each detail of his maiming.

'He fell back onto a golden carpet of fallen wheat, and a darkening crimson patch spread around his collapsed body.'

'Did he die?' I tossed the premature prompt into the air where Yukie let it hover and fall.

'You'd think I would've run back all hysterical to the house, but I walked, calm as could be, beside the uncut row, brushing my hand through the soft heads of wheat stalks as I went.' She gazed at the ceiling, a perplexed look upon her face. Yukie's fingers ran over the ripples of the bedsheet as if to capture the mellow manner of that day.

'Probably, you were in shock,' I offered.

'*Hai*,' she agreed. 'I was curled up in a ball on the porch rocking with my knees tucked to chest when the rest of the family arrived home. "Where's Uncle Perry?" my host mother asked, her voice already on edge as if she sensed something a matter.'

'Mute, I pointed to the field. They didn't know what, but they knew something bad had happened. And so, they ran to the parked combine. He'd bled out a lot, but lived,' she said, resurrecting my question from the love hotel's shag carpet floor.

'Lost his arm to the shoulder,' she added, matter-of-fact, and used a flattened hand to indicate where she assumed the amputation began ... or ended.

We both lit smokes, with some of the tension of her tale lifted. Still, the birth of her strange gift had not been explained, I considered with a long inhale.

'It was decided, best I go home.' As if she'd read my mind, Yukie launched into more. 'They were protecting Uncle Perry more than me. No report was made. They declared it a farming mishap, common in those parts. I doubt he admitted to what he'd done, but you could tell they knew something.'

'Must've been hard those last few days after all that shit went down.'

'You would think, but not really. Little changed. Since I wasn't welcome in the house, I spent whole summer nights out on the porch. I loved it out there, under the stars.' Reminiscent, she gazed upward, toward our starless mauve ceiling.

'They just left you on the porch?' I was aghast and was tempted to add 'like a mangy dog' for emphasis. Though I wasn't sure how that comparison would resonate with the woman, I'd just made love too.

'I'd already spent many nights on that porch, looking up at the myriad of stars,' she said, far less aggrieved than I. 'After the incident I did the same, only all night, every night, for a week straight.' Showing true resilience, she squeezed out a smile at the whole ordeal. 'I'd look to the sky, and count the stars. There were millions, too many to count, but the process made me feel small, insignificant, and safe.'

'Yeah,' I cut in, 'I know that feeling.' I did. The insignificant and small part, at least. Yet in my case, I shuddered under the vastness of it all.

'After I tired of counting, I'd raise my arm in the air and extended the index finger of my left hand.' She pointed her finger toward the love hotel ceiling and mimed the childlike caper as if back on the Nebraska porch.

'I started by drawing straight lines, connecting one star to another, this eventually evolved into sketching imagined pictures and intricate designs up in space.' A lingering tinge of wonder twink'led in her eye.

'That's cool. It sounds meditative.' That, I figured, was the origin. She didn't say it outright; I was supposed to connect the dots – like stars in the night.

For good measure, Yukie added, 'In that simple make-believe, where I became architect of the cosmos, I found my peace.'

Nearing the end of our six-hour stint, with the sun already well and up, I felt something else begin to rise. I thought of waking Yukie and giving her another throw. Rain tapped at the love hotel's small window, and water rushed through the eaves and gutters with a benign shush. Yukie's hair curled and flowed across my bare chest. I stifled the urge, realizing, right then, everything was perfect just as it was. And I didn't want to move an inch at risk of toppling the whole magical chimera.

* * *

The fat bastard in the next cubicle makes a choking sound. One of his inward sucking breaths must've collided with an audible outward snore. Nonsensical murmurs abscond as he gets his bearings, followed by the click, click of a mouse. I lean back in my chair and revel in the crisp quietude.

I try to return to that tranquil scene Yukie had conjured, but it's impossible without whatever power possesses her touch.

Instead, my thoughts wander to an image I can conjure of my own capacity. I think about arriving back in Tokyo a few weeks ago on a northbound train – chasing shadows of a neon dream.

Rainy Day Ramen

PART THREE
Tokyo (Tonkotsu)

When in my present lonely lot,
I feel my past has not been free from sins which I remember not,
I dread more, what to come, may be.
—*Murasaki Shikibu*, The Tale of Genji

1// Hachiko on Earth (aka Tokyo Love Letter)

Riding into Shibuya from Yokohama, the skyscraper forest becomes dense old growth.

Earlier, outside Kyoto, the treed hills traversed by train were *hanabi* explosions of auburn, orange and reddish hues bursting forth on a canvas of deep green cedars. The journey had taken me past meadows of tarred and shingled rooftops in small metropolis outcroppings, through lush chartreuse tea fields and labyrinthine rice terraces and past, of course, majestic Mount Fuji. He appeared out of a morning haze with a fresh snow cap starting to form as if the hand of God had come down and sprinkled a light frosting atop the great basalt giant.

I'd made it to the last leg of my slow ride without incident. Getting on and off all those unpaid fares, I'd bum-rushed many an unsuspecting stranger, like some queer sodomizing phantom. My streak, though, was about to come to an end.

It was after work rush hour at Shibuya station. I marked a middle-aged salaryman who moved towards the station gates with a flourish. I swept in behind his cheap suit, but couldn't close the gap in time; my finesse had waned, and the long hours of sitting had stiffened and slowed my legs. The man was through the gate, and the thick plastic barrier had closed. I hadn't made it.

Caught in the turnstile, within seconds, a queue of impatient commuters formed. I squeezed back out. Once the clog was removed, they streamed through to freedom. I thought about having another run at it but detected the station guard had eyes on me. Instead, I stood back from the gates, in view of the agent sat behind his viewing window and launched into my best Stanislavski performance.

Rifling through pockets, pausing flummoxed and searching my wallet in disbelief; I finally concluded my scene by approaching the booth, faux-flustered with an apologetic façade.

'*Sumimasen*, I lost my ticket. I bought but … *ima wakarimasen*,' I spurted, in hopes the frantic miming and my muddled mix of Japanese and English would adequately unsettle the elderly clerk.

I don't believe he bought my act, but I'd put him in a situation where he was anxious to be rid of me. He asked where I had gotten on: '*Doko de kaimashita ka?*'

'Yutenji.' I went with four stops back, one-stop and I could give away the grift. Plus, the poor bastard deserved a break. I paid my hundred and fifty yen and exited into a teeming Shibuya station.

Autumn eve, still breeze
Through the crowds' Milky Way Stream
Hachiko greets thee

With a few cans dangling from my wrist in a plastic shopping bag and one opened touching my lips, I leaned back against the double metal resting railing with the crossing on one side and the famous dog statue on the other. Not a more perfect place on earth to idly sit and watch the world go by than right there.

Perhaps I'd met Saint Peter after all, and just conned my ass in, I speculated, taking in the vibrant atmosphere. There was both punk rock and poetry in the air.

Shibuya crossing rhythmically pulsates the life-blood of the city. Each switch from standing red to blinking green man pours massive throngs of citizens and visitors flowing through its arterial paths.

On my right, erected on a simple pedestal sat expectantly, Hachiko – the iconic bronze statue of a famed Akita-dog. While it is rather unimpressive in physical stature – being of basic design and not much larger than the actual breed themselves – the spectacle of human nature which is on display in the vicinity is what I found awe-inspiring.

The area is imbued with the joyous atmosphere of an airport arrivals lounge and functions much the same. Then, there was the sweet story of the dog himself, which lent to hosting these mini-reunions.

Every day, Hachiko would wait outside Shibuya station for his owner, a professor, to return from his day of lecturing. When the man died in 1925, in exhibition of the loyalty we assign to man's best friend, the dog went to the station and waited, each day for the next ten years, until his own death.

After leaning back and lighting my smoke, I was blessed to witness that celebration of human togetherness which permeates the place as two young women met and greeted. They cried out in zealous screams followed by holding hands and jumping up and down in a slow circle, blathering on high pitched and unrestrained for a minute or two, before they scurried off in giddy C-flat taps.

They may have seen each other earlier that day for all I knew, or that reunion could have been decades in the making. It didn't really matter, it was the purity of feeling, the unabated outpouring of conviviality, comradery and love which I found intoxicating. Scattered similar scenes were improvised in succession around the station courtyard. All under Hachiko's approving gaze.

Then, of course, there were the women. Dolled up in styles ranging from the outlandishly inane to the downright seductive, predominantly leaning toward the categorically sexy. Japan's four seasons could be experienced as much through subtle shifts in fashion than the changing of the leaves. I'd left Tokyo in early summer, it was now autumn; the skirts stayed just as short, but the high heels had transformed into thigh-high boots, like seasonal Chu-his, each treat offered its own craved delights.

I sat for two hours in the early evening hours soaking in the Shibuya scene. I'd emptied the plastic bag and then refilled with emptied cans. The rapid beat of greeting friends and lovers began to peter out, and I, at least for that evening, was saturated with mankind's capacity for zeal and goodwill. In fact, it was starting to have a corrosive effect as I thought: *in a world overflowing with affection, I ain't gettin a fuckin drop.*

Luckily, right when the predictable self-pity kicked in, so did the rains. Hard and cold the precipitation beat down on the moving crowds and seated observers. The populace I'd been observing were immediately concealed under a sea of umbrellas. I rose and picked my way through, frequently dodging to avoid losing an eye to one of the tips. It seemed to me that every person in Japan had an umbrella stashed on them somewhere, at all times. When with the first felt drop, they all go up, the already crowded metropolis pretty much doubles or triples in density.

Both eyes intact, I found myself in a cosy *ramen* shop directly under the Yamanote line tracks. While I waited for the *miso ramen* to warm my soul, I couldn't help but fret over the immediate future.

I sipped my beer and peered into the night. Condensation, created by the cauldrons of cooking noodles playing off the cool rain outside, covered the shop's window. Blurred lit signage pulled through the obstructed view like brush smeared acrylics on the windowed palette. When the door swung open, I'd glimpse a Blade Runner freeze-frame from the street beyond.

The shop trembled as trains rumbled overhead. I found them comforting, a reminder that if it didn't work out, I'd simply cut and run. The prospect of perpetual motion always appealed to me. Erroneously idealistic, I longed for the bygone days of hobos and starry-eyed young men riding the rails in search of life's true meaning.

The Shangri-la notion of indefinite movement as an absolute answer was hampered by a two-pronged problem of finance and egocentrism. It cost money, and I was generally broke. Moreover, there was that guy who always followed, whom I could never seem to outrun. He was proving to be a bit of a pain in my ass. Yet, despite our tangled subjective schemas, we struggle to exist in harmony.

The bowl was placed before me, and not a moment too soon; I longed to escape into it and away from those weighty thoughts. I bowed over and soaked up the therapeutic aroma. With chopsticks, I cut through the dark-skinned egg, releasing molten yoke into waiting broth. Face bathed in the warming steam, I tasted.

Sheltered from the rain
Soothing train, *ramen*-numbed brain
I reap contentment

With the Zen meal consumed and consumed by the Zen meal, I exited back into the chaotic Tokyo night.

The rain had slowed to a misty drizzle, so I decided to walk. I set out with no clear destination but decided to make my way to Shinjuku, I figured I would find cheap lodgings more easily there.

Shibuya turned into Harajuku, in which the girls dress in gothic maid and Lolita fashions, though I'm certain most have never read Nabokov. On weekends you can spot these creatures as they pose in feigned melancholy, flashing dour peace signs on the bridge to Yoyogi-koen or, in matching pairs and triplets, wandering the boutique shopping streets.

On past Yoyogi where in spring, when the cherry blossoms bloom, the park plays host to *hanami* parties. Salarymen loosen their ties, turn red-faced with drink, toss aside shackling mores and vent into the night ... because under those blooming pink-white flowers of the sakura trees, it's permitted.

Finally, I entered Shinjuku. Clouds of the earlier rain still clung to the skyline, illuminated from the city below and moon above they hung dense, low and spectral. Glass towers shot up all around, stiff sentries of modernity, tensed against remnant traditionalism cloistered in the streets below; ancient temples tucked back between high blocked buildings ... the postwar yakitori shops of piss alley where workers continue the timeless rituals of drink, eat, gossip and love ... silent parks which house enormous elderly oaks. And finally, in the hearts and minds of those below still beholden to the Bushido code.

I made my way from business district to entertainment area, to walk under the halogen marvels which spattered the neon night.

At Shinjuku's East Exit young hustlers in knock-off, three-piece suits chased evening butterflies into nets of materialistic deceit. A black van parked near the circular square barked nationalist political propaganda at impervious passersby. While in station tunnels below, four-fingered failed punters drank One Cup Sake, struggling to resurrect long-departed dreams.

Shiki no Michi, a quiet tree-lined path shrouded from Shinjuku's neon barrage, acts as a chance oasis in the swarming metropolis. Trapesing the small path between Golden Gai's closet-sized coin bars and the roguish pleasure ground of Kabukicho; I was conveyed to another time and place.

The mosaic-patterned, flagstone path transmuted to a forest floor. It crackled and squished underfoot with fresh fallen and decomposing foliage. The Japanese oaks became thin white birch trunks, turned grey than black as night fell on the New Brunswick wood of my youth. Out east, our backyard ran into the Acadian forest, and in the late light of summer, I'd wandered further into the woods than usual playing imaginary soldier, or some other such childish pretending.

When I hadn't come home at dusk, and long afterwards, a search party had set out to find me. My parents and neighbours approached, shouting and waving flashlights through the darkened wood. Circling spotlights danced on a leafy canopy above. I didn't call back immediately, but clung to a soft mossy log. I considered hiding, saying nothing, staying lost forever.

At last, I shouted, 'I'm here,' in a calm, controlled little boy's voice like I was up playing Lego in my room and just got called for dinner. They had expected to find me beside myself with fear, crying hysterically. But as my mother would relay the story in the years to come, I was found looking as peaceful as a lamb.

Where the tranquil path turned to bustling Shinjuku sidewalk, I emerged from my flashback, blasted by a flash flood of Yasukuni-dori's incandescent night coursing down a glass and concrete chasm. Physically, I knew exactly where I was but had no idea where I was going or what the future held. Lost in a sense, I felt much like that six-year-old in the woods. Perhaps, in the end, I'd gotten my wish, thus winding up endlessly adrift.

While Kabukicho is nicknamed the town that never sleeps, I myself was fatigued and fading fast as I neared its bottom border. Interlaced fingers and both arms stretched over my head to touch an illusive Shinjuku moon, I twisted and unleashed a long 'yurg'. Physically I walked a little taller, yet my restless soul remained hunched, darting in furtive bursts to each suggestive aberration.

That's how I found myself walking trance-like beneath a grey *torii* gate and stood between two lion-dog statues atop concrete pillars. I looked right then left at the mythical beast, reminiscent of faded ink on the recent lover who'd blown across my path like the pink petals of spring during the nautical stopover in Kobe.

Who'd sent the fleshy facsimile here, and why? Is it meant as a reminder or warning? Or the Universe jus fuckin with me – bouncing at random, off of one protruding manifestation after another?

I took two hesitant steps toward the hybrid lion on my right. In the still of the night, an odd sense chafed my state of mind that it could spring to life, lash out with her concrete claw and strike. The carving remained inanimate, as I reached out and ran my fingers over the granite mane, rutted and darkened by a fine film of moss. I wondered if I'd located my feline after all. It wasn't in the form I'd been seeking, then again, things rarely are.

In front of me were three steps leading to a modest shrine. Even the foliage which lined the cobblestone walk was out of place within the neon decadence this quiet relic was posited. It confounded me the little shrine had never registered during previous jaunts through the Kabukicho bramble. I'd been down that street many times. My guess, while I'd have been seeking, it would've been synthetic and self-serving, for the sensual rather than sacred; divination wasn't on my radar, and so unless wrapped in fishnets, would've passed me by.

I wandered around the grounds, read what I could, and deciphered the rest. When I learned that Inari Kio Shrine was erected to house a demon king, it felt fitting the temple be nestled in this cosy corner of Kabukicho.

From the shadows, a waist-high ogre grimaced at me while he balanced a massive weight upon his head. 'Ain't that the truth,' I mumbled, considering the futility of it – those attempts to shun the evil which lurks in the hearts of men.

'Best be getting it kiddo. I'se essential as the stars in yer sky,' the ogre replied, in a gravelly voice, weathered and worn. 'I'se carry me share of life's load, and it ain't getting any lighter with each passing day. But mark me words, they'll come a day when I'se can shoulder no more.'

I shambled away, unsure if the auditory phantasm was a product of lack of sleep, excessive booze, or something more, like a long-harboured hatred or fear. My fingers ran across the surface of a half-buried boulder, and I awaited blessings on my return to Tokyo from the *kaeru-ishi* stone. If they came, they came in unheard whispers muffled by the night.

I believed not in any god or all. Nonetheless, that night they were busy in my head, contorting in an orgy of straight-up fuckery. And so, before leaving, I walked up the three stone steps, grabbed hold of a thick rope, and rang the *suzu* once. I bowed deep and clapped twice in imitation of what I'd seen locals do. As the clang reverberated into the night, I closed my eyes to summon friends and lovers dispersed and disappeared. I wished them well, wherever they may be. Under the brass bell, I remembered Kiyohime's lore and used the final line of my makeshift prayer to grant all release from personal prisons in which they were held. But mine ... it'd be pointless, I knew this much. So, I simply clung to the bars and plotted escape.

I left under the same Shinto gateway and looked up at the thickly braided rope strung across the length. Splashed in neon, the *shimenawa* appeared weaved with red thread, and *shide* dangled lazily from the line as pink, paper zigzags swinging to and fro, lost on the threshold.

Back in the realm of the profane, saturated with symbolism, it spilt over, and a single tear ran down my cheek. I wanted a clear answer as to the forces which had conspired to draw me back there. Yet all I was getting were enigmas trapped in riddles.

Further down, the alleys constricted and darkened around me as I wandered and mingled with strong-jawed trannies who patrolled outside cheap love hotels, in service of men who harboured secrets too dark for the shadows of the red light. On the main street leading from Shin-Ōkubo station, I smoked and drank outside a *conbini* watching the dwindling passengers of last train trickle home. Until a passing cat conspired with the drowsy night and ordained I'd bunk down there.

2// Tatsuya, Machiko, and the Emo Fascist

In front of Studio Alta, as strangers we amassed, invisible brushes and red paint cans in hand. An email from Yukie earlier indicated she'd found something on the names I'd given her, so we arranged to meet at Shinjuku station's less storied popular meeting spot.

Yukie showed at five after eight and we greeted with a hug. 'So where are we going?' I asked, anxious to fulfil my promise to Hideki.

Yukie filled me in on her research. She'd found some old articles from the 60s about their arrests during the student protest movement, and one in the 70s on a protest turned violent over the expansion of an American military base. Then there was nothing for decades, but in 2003 they were profiled, all rosily, because of their ties to the Zengakuren. Due to the Iraq war protests happening around the world, even Tokyo had a resurgence of anti-war demonstrations.

'That's like almost a decade ago,' I touched two fingers to my forehead and rubbed.

'Yes, so in the article, it said they still held to their roots and led a movement fighting to close down US bases, but also ran a Shinjuku nightclub frequented by the coalition members. I checked, and the club is still there.'

She was clearly excited by her sleuthing. So was I. She'd accomplished more in two days than I had in over a month. 'You're a regular Nancy Drew,' I said, but of course she didn't get the dated cultural reference. I kissed her cheek. 'You did fucking awesome babe.'

The club was close by, on a main street which ran right beyond where Kabukicho petered out and Okubo began. On the other side of the road was a famous budget department store whose mascot looked like a cracked-out blue penguin in a red toque.

'*Don Don, la la la* ...' I sang as we walked by, and Yukie laughed. It was a catchy jingle. You'd go in for cheap booze, a rug or some sex toys and it'd be stuck in your head for a week.

We arrived at a portable lit business sign, simple black with yellow Japanese writing shining through. An open door introduced a narrow staircase leading to the basement club.

Yukie looked pensive and nervous.

'You okay?'

'*Daijobu,* but when I read the article, you could tell they still hold really radical anti-foreigner views. Not only American military, expulsion of all foreigners in Japan.' She shifted uncomfortably on her heels. 'I don't know how well you will be received ... or me with you.'

'Don't worry, we'll just pop in, find the couple, I'll give them the old man's message, and we can leave. Unless it's a cool scene, then we can bust a move.' I did a little raise the roof dance move while sporting a corny smile.

As soon as we descended the stairs, I could tell it wasn't going to be cool, at all. We were met with sharp glares of disdain by the twenty or so patrons inside. The music was a menacing mix; the monotone drone of a low guttural voice, as if it were reciting an antagonized doctrine, interrupted periodically by black metal shrieks and the antithetical vocals backed by a repetitive, oppressive trance track.

There was a DJ stood behind a mixing board in a small booth by the back corner. He didn't seem to be doing any spinning, or much of anything, maybe sliding an equalizer knob to fade in and fade out the conflicting voices.

I tried to lighten the tense atmosphere and whispered to Yukie, 'Is this what passes for music these days?'

My attempt fell flat. 'It's ugly,' was all she replied, on edge.

I made my way to the bar with Yukie glued to my side. We didn't order any drinks, it was clear we wouldn't be staying long.

'Sorry, are these two people here?' I shouted above the music and brandished the paper with their names written.

He completely ignored me even though I'd spoken in Japanese. Yukie shouted the same and held out the paper to the agitated bartender. He ignored her too but glanced briefly at the paper. He then wordlessly walked from behind the bar and through a black door in the back right-hand corner of the club.

I scanned the joint while Yukie looked at the floor. The patrons were mostly in their twenties, the odd one possibly in their forties or fifties. They unanimously dressed in black. They all had straight black hair, the men's longer than your average Japanese; shaggy, shoulder-length and a sweep of bangs covering their faces. The few women wore it long, linear and squared off mid-back. They bore no fashion flourishes or logos on their clothing. Yet, some of those who wore black outerwear, hoodies or military-style jackets, had a patch or insignia on the shoulder. Squinting I made out Rising Sun flags and what I would later research to learn were Tohokai symbols. Basically, the crowd looked like a gang of emo fascists, and the whole place had an eerie Nazi after-party vibe.

Yukie and I continued to get eyed hatefully as we waited by the bar. If it were Sesame Street and they were playing 'one of these things does not belong', Yukie and I – the mixed-race couple, her with expressive, colourful style and me with my blond hair, blue eyes, and pinkish pigment – would be an easy-peasy selection amongst the drably dressed Japanese nationalist. Though this clearly wasn't Sesame Street and certainly didn't feel like a game.

After a few minutes, the bartender emerged, followed by an

elderly couple. Everyone stopped to watch as they strode the short distance across the small club floor. The patrons stood at attention and even looked as if they were about to salute. The couple, thin and serpentine, moved with purpose and a quiet authority. The lady had long grey-black untreated hair, like rotted straw, and both an old hippy complexion, naturally weathered – theirs, by an enduring and shrewd detest.

When they reached where we stood, the old man spoke. 'Yes, you asked for us. Who are you, and why are you here?' he demanded of me in Japanese.

'I met a friend of yours in a park in Okinawa,' I started in a forced friendly manner. 'We talked about when you were all in university and how you seized the tower that day. Well, after the arrest, he felt bad about taking the deal to stay in university. He didn't turn you in or anything, they let him off because of the rugby … anyway, that's me saying that, not him.' I slowed to ensure he was understanding my words and gauge a reaction, a softening, but got none.

'The message I'm to give you is that "Hideki has found his way."' I got to the point, and let that soak in for whatever it was worth. 'I think what he meant was that he is part of the movement in Okinawa and still active in …'

'I don't care,' Tatsuya cut in. 'Hideki is a coward and traitor any way you slice it. The simple fact he sends you, a *gaijin*, here to grovel for him, is proof enough of that.' His words flowed smooth and effortless, like tainted molasses. Not surprised or inspired, but like he'd been rehearsing the harsh rebuff of his old comrade all those years. It was delivered, I noted, in rather proficient English for one so anti-foreigner. I decided not to comment or compliment on that.

'Hey, man, I'm just doing a favour for the guy, cause he did one for me.' I tried to sound blasé and brush off his passive aggressiveness like dirt on my shoulder.

'Hideki can hold his little hippy sit-ins. Our movement is beyond that now, our scope broader and tactics more shrewd, as you may well find out.' He punctuated this veiled threat with a corrupt little smile. 'So you can tell your friend Hideki that the next time you play in the park together.' He unleashed a hyena's cackle.

'Now, you must leave my bar.' Concealed beneath bushy black eyebrows, his dark, deep-set eyes bore into me as he added, 'and if you know what's best ... my country.'

Machiko, who had remained quiet, but stared with a spiteful squint at Yukie throughout, broke her silence, saying something quick and jarring in Japanese, after which her thin lips easily exercised into a sneer. I couldn't catch the meaning, unpleasant I gathered, by the venomous tone and Yukie's reaction.

She dropped her head and hurried toward the exit. At the same time, the DJ began to chant into a microphone some similar-sounding phrase or slogan, inciting the assembled faction to join the jeering. Like bullets fired at the backs of retreating refugees, they chanted the verse as we rushed to the door.

I followed close behind Yukie in case anyone made a move to physically lay hands on her. Not a tough guy by any stretch, but my adrenaline was pumping, and I felt ready to throw a punch if necessary. However, no one advanced on us. Theirs was purely an attack on the psyche.

Back on the street, Yukie moved quickly from the doorway of the basement bar and was halfway down the block before I managed to catch her by the arm and spin her around to face me. Initially, she pulled away in fear. When she saw my face and took in the street noise surroundings, she unstiffened somewhat. Tears streamed down her face. I pulled her to my chest, enveloped her slender shoulders in a towering embrace, and held her tight.

'I'm sorry ...' I cooed, 'I never would have brought you if I knew it was going to turn out like that.'

Still holding onto her upper arms, we separated, just enough for the night's neon to shine through. Inspecting her face in the glow to see her tears had dried, I asked, 'Are you alright?'

'You couldn't know. They're just awful people. I am so sorry.' Why she was apologizing, I couldn't understand. Cultural ill communication, I guess.

I knew I probably shouldn't ask. 'What'd she say? What were they chanting?'

'White devil whore!' she answered in a keck and again began to sob. I pulled her close once more and held her, feeling both warm and cold simultaneously.

White devil sounds kind of badass, I thought, careful to conceal my sly grin from Yukie as we walked toward the outskirts of Kabukicho to find a cosy nook for the night.

3// Dallas in Detention

After our second stay in a love hotel, I was filled with a mix of joyous satisfaction and utter fear. I played the experience over in my mind and even weighed it against a catalogue of other sexual encounters. This only confused me further as to what it was and what it meant.

With most others, it was just playtime, a dive into the cool-watered pleasures of the flesh when the fervent heat became unbearable. You'd splash around a bit, have some laughs, maybe even take a few laps; then you get up, towel off and move on.

With Akiko, it was a raw, pent-up sexual energy that needed release, and when it came, it was explosive like pez in a pop bottle. Though with Yukie, it cut deeper. It was more repressed feelings that needed to be expressed, could only be expressed in the physical; making each kiss, caress, roll, touch and thrust – a communication, even a confession.

The fear arose in a feeling that by pulling Yukie closer, I was only more forcefully pushing her away in a very near future. This had always been my modus operandi. Maybe I could change, but the arch of personal history and my chaotic present only supported this inevitable.

Either way, I was resolved to try. Perhaps in confronting the muddled past, in finding and fixing that frayed end of the followed yarn, there was a new beginning for me. No matter how spurious my logic, it encouraged me to redouble my efforts, to seek out the answers that would lead to a taut and linear path forward.

The time for perpetual reflection and mining memories had passed. It was time for action. *'Objects in the mirror are closer than they appear'*, the stencilled warning on a car's side-view mirror flashed to mind with all the amplified gravity of a dharma doodle, and for some reason, I was inspired to seek out Dallas.

With the vanished Peach House and extensive Google search of Gertie's whereabouts, I was at a loss as to where or how to locate her. I thought Dallas might be easier to track down. I'd only be partially correct.

He had been pretty stable at his recruitment job. I searched for the address of the firm. 'Talent Stars' was located near Roppongi station on the Oedo line.

I found the office using a crudely drawn map sketched on the back of my hand with a ballpoint pen and entered. There were just over ten cubicles and slightly fewer young men in shirts and ties typing away or talking rapidly on the phone. Each looked alternately like they were either hungover or still tweaking. One of them rose suddenly, grabbed his blazer from the back of a swivel chair, and hurried past me out the door, his seat still spinning in slow revolutions.

After a quick scan, I couldn't spot Dallas, but three or four of the cubicles were unoccupied. No one paid me any mind or asked if they could help, so I approached the nearest guy asking, 'Um, sorry to bother you ... I got a friend I'm trying to find. I think he works here ... Do you happen to know an American guy named Dallas?'

The young Brit removed his hands-free headset and looked at me quizzically.

'And who, may I inquire, are you?' he asked in a posh London accent.

'I'm an old friend of his, but we lost touch about a year back,' I said, hoping he wouldn't smell my breakfast Chu-his, though doubted it would matter in this lot. 'Sorry to barge in on you guys at work, but it's important I get in touch with him.'

'Shit, sorry to be the bearer of bad news, chap ... but Dallas is either back in the U.S. or still in prison.'

'Prison?'

'Yes, well, not prison exactly ... I heard he was moved to the Foreigner Detention Centre in Ibaraki a month or so back after his girlfriend dropped the charges. If he hasn't been deported yet, I imagine that is where he still is.'

'His girlfriend dropped the wha ...? Charges?' I stammered. 'Ya ... You mean Risa?'

'Yes, Risa,' he confirmed with a smug-shit smile. 'Well, the Yank really fucked things up with that stunner, now, didn't he?'

'Yeah, thanks,' I said and headed out the door. Dallas had mentioned that he worked with a bunch of assholes, there was case in point.

With Dallas's predicament and pending deportation, it became even more urgent to talk to him. Somehow his fate aligned with the course my life had taken; messy. I had to find out how and why.

On the way to Ibaraki, I double-checked the validity of my visa, listed on the *gaijin* card I'm required to carry with me. Unsure whether I'd even be allowed to see Dallas, I hopped in a cab at Ureshi station and headed to the immigration detention centre on a wing and a prayer.

The outside of the centre looked a little bit like a local high school. There weren't any high walls or turrets manned with armed guards, just a security gate and parking lot out front.

Inside was far more prison-like. I went to the service counter and showed my *gaijin* card. The uniformed officer behind the desk wrote down pertinent details in a logbook, which made me nervous. I really didn't want any record of my being there.

I was in luck. Visitors were permitted to see detainees until 3 pm, and it was five after two. I was told I could meet with Dallas for a maximum of thirty minutes. I nodded my approval and added '*Hai*' with an unnecessary bow.

I was required to leave my non-functional phone and was patted down before being let into a communal visiting area. The security door closed and locked with a resounding clang.

I sat on a stool that was attached to the table and then into the floor through an all-in-one grey metal frame. The other four tables were empty, as was the room, empty and bare. A single long rectangular window let in daylight and grey sky.

Dallas was led in from the holding cell area by a different uniformed guard, who closed the door and stood at attention beside it. The guard was armed only with a nightstick and walkie talkie device. Dallas sat on the stool opposite me. He wore a white T-shirt and jogging pants. I wasn't sure if it was an assigned uniform or just his own clothes that adhered to some loose dress code.

I began the only way I knew how. 'What the fuck man?'

'What the fuck indeed,' he replied, his expression changing from the look of shame he'd entered with to a familiar friendly smile. 'I know it's bad, but it could be worse. My JP days be wearing the fo-five like Jordan ... they've got a lawyer working on my deportation, and so I'll be heading back to the grand ol' U.S. of A. I won't have a record, but I won't be allowed back in Japan anytime soon.'

'Why would you have a record? What happened?' I pressed him unintentionally.

'Long story short, I done fucked up, son!' He said with a cool air of acceptance. 'I know everyone says this, but it wasn't my fault, or not totally my fault. You might not buy it, but I hope you know me well enough that when I explain, you will take me at my word that it was a huge mistake ... a horrible accident.'

'Yeah, of course.' I didn't know if I would yet but needed to say so.

'Okay, so after you left and then Gertie got hauled away ...'

'Wait, Gertie got hauled away? What ...'

'Later,' he informed, '... Risa had been pressuring for us to get a place together for a while. I was pretty fed up with The Big Peach

Guesthouse, and after trying to keep up with you for the last ten months, I was looking for a break from the whole party scene ...'

I was thrown by the implication that he was trying to keep up with me. I had always thought of it as me as a hanger-on. Or at least the blind leading the blind, or maybe, sprung leading the sprung. Rather than interject, I carried on listening, dumbfounded.

'A couple months after you left, we got a crib in Hiroo. Fuckin dope pad, especially after she added the feminine touch,' he said, with an appreciative smile. 'I should've had you over man, but we'd lost touch, and at the time, that was probably best, yo.'

He looked over his shoulder at the guard. 'Spot me a smoke, will ya?'

I was surprised we were allowed to light up, but it was Japan, after all. 'Yeah,' I said and handed him the fag.

'Thank fuck, you showed. We're only allowed the one a day usually.' He shook his head, still in disbelief at this predicament. 'Anyways, I got the pad, and Risa, fly as ever. But I'm like in this constant fuckin' depression. I'd get these fucking migraines that wouldn't go away for days at a time and am having these vivid nightmares. Sometimes even awake, I'd get these tracers, see like a figure that wasn't even there run across the room, 'n shit.'

Dallas puffed furiously on his smoke, and I fished through my pack, ready to hand him another. 'So in an attempt to get rid of the headaches,' he explained, 'I went on this massive coke binge, which was probably just adding fuel to the fire. At the time, though, it seemed like the only way out.'

'One night, in the middle of this binge' – his voice lowered and eyes drifted to the dark grey chain-link covering the window – 'I was at home ... I never went out to party anymore. I'm not sure if I was sleeping off the coke and vodka or if I was awake and having massive hallucinations. Anyways, I was trippin' balls through one of those terrible nightmares when Risa comes in. She sees me; standing, sweating, pale, and in a state of extreme agitation. The sweet girl that she is, she moves toward me to console and calm.' He coughed to clear his throat, or maybe something more.

'But I didn't see sweet Risa. I saw this fucking demonic figure advancing on me. I threw a punch, acting purely out of instinct. Risa screamed and hit the floor, where she held her face and cried.' Dallas stubbed his cigarette into an ashtray attached to the table's underside.

I stared at him, transfixed and silent. No judgment was being passed, yet I couldn't understand. The Dallas I knew wouldn't hurt a fly.

'Just as suddenly, the nightmarish vision vanished, and I only saw Risa – lying on the floor in pain. I didn't know what had happened, but knew I was responsible. The previous nightmare was supplanted with this far worse one.'

I slid the pack with the readied smoke poking out toward him. He waved it off, explaining, 'Trying to quit. Might as well put this shit show to some good use.'

He went on to cover the repercussions. An ambulance came, and he was arrested. Her jaw was broken, and worse yet, legally speaking, the piss test at the station showed cocaine in his system. He'd spent over a month in jail before charges were brought. Risa visited him often and fought to get the assault charge dropped.

'She forgave me,' he said with a wince. 'I was sick with guilt as she sat across from me and, like a fucking angel on earth, asked if I was okay! Fuck me, it hit hard how unfair I was to her, not just on that horrific day where I threw the delirium left hook. More so in other times with the cheating and keeping her at a distance in some sort of petty powerplay.'

I studied him with a new scrutiny. His confidence evident in a slouched swagger, yet dulled, or just different somehow. Like a boxer sat on the stool between rounds, beat but not beaten, he looked through the prison wall, envisioning how to stand strong at centre ring when the bell dings once more.

'What about all your little brofications?' I asked. 'I always thought you were pretty comfortable with how we were rolling.'

'Sheeeit, them just some bullshit I be spitting, to cover up what I didn't know ... or couldn't admit to myself.' The left corner of his mouth drew up in wry rumination. 'When you're fighting scared, ya dance around the ring bobbing and weaving, guard up, afraid to strike and leave yourself exposed ... but sooner or later you're gonna get tagged or lose by decision.'

Scared of what? I thought. *Scared of love ...*

Dallas was always this fearless figure in my eyes, in how he tore through life and made no apologies. But I guess we all conceal our fears behind a myriad of masks, some more convincingly than others.

He went on to explain that with the assault charge dropped, he didn't have to do time in a Japanese prison, but because of the coke, they were able to deport him.

'Shit, Dallas, I'm so sorry ...' I was at a loss for words.

He'd let it out. Then, shrugged it off.

'What about Gertie?' I returned to his earlier mention in selfish pursuit. 'What happened to her?'

He seemed unaffected, happy actually, to shift the focus off his acts. 'So one afternoon, this real old school Irish-looking guy gets outta a cab, short and stocky with a big red, ruddy nose and pronounced Guinness gut. I'm out front, and he asks, "Do ya know if me lass Gertie is in, where can I find 'er?"' Dallas recounted in a pretty decent Irish accent, though more Bostonian.

'So I say, "room twenty-three". No *thank you* or anything, he just pushes on by me. This old guy had seen a pub brawl or two, if not the ring back in the day. When you are a fighter yourself, you can tell, yo.' He threw in, harkening back to his boxing days.

'Anyway, he was on a fucking mission.' Dallas continued his recount of Gertie's exit. 'Comes out a minute later dragging Gertie by her greasy black hair, and she's screaming, "Da no! I can't be going … I wasn't gonna do it …"'

'Like off her fucking head, hysterical! But you know,' he said, tossing me a solemn nod, 'by that time, she was already gone.'

'Since it was her dad, I didn't intervene. I figured he had good reason. He threw her in the back of the cab, and off they drove; to the airport and then on to Ireland, where I hope she's getting some help.' He paused with a look of genuine concern for Gertie's fate. It confirmed my belief that there had always existed an affection between them.

'A little while later, I went to her room to collect her stuff to send home. But the Peach house staff, they'd been through already and swept the place clean.' Dallas leaned back, arms crossed and chin up in examination, like a detective mulling over an uncrackable case.

'Staff? How'd they get there … How did they know?'

'A group of 'em were living there … you didn't know? They were like those weird Japanese loners you'd see in the kitchen or pass in the hall when you went to the can at night. Always looking morose and suspicious; dressed in black, never made eye contact or smiled. The nightwalkers, I used to call 'em … yeah, they were like company employees. You don't remember them?' he asked, looking at me like I was the most oblivious idiot. 'You were probably fuckin' pissed blind whenever you passed 'em since they only showed their faces in the wee hours,' he added with a light chuckle.

I was disturbed by the fact I never recalled seeing these supposed residents and even more disturbed at how the description fit the figures revealed in my recurring dream. I mentioned none of this to Dallas but broached the topic still.

'Do you ever think that the Big Peach Gaijin House is at the root of it all?'

'What do ya mean?' Dallas asked, intrigued by the left-field question.

'Like Gertie going off the rails and being dragged home

to a mental asylum. You and all this,' I said, with an instructive sweeping hand. 'Couldn't it all have come to be from something that happened at the Peach House? Because of the House?'

He smirked, but I could tell he was seriously thinking it over. 'And what about you?'

'Well fuck; I'm broke, unemployed and living at an internet café,' I said light-heartedly. Then, I got more serious and introspective. 'It's like, I've gone from a contented aimless amble through life, to being stuck on some macabre carousel and now twilight's setting in and I got no fuckin idea how to get off.'

'Shit Fred, you always were one for melodramatics, dawg,' he chaffed in captious jest. 'I think it's called growing up!'

'True dat!' I fell back into our old repartee. 'But still, the Peach House, the more distance between me and its doors, the more I'm certain there was something heinously fucked about that place.'

'Well shit man, I've got no answers for you.' Dallas looked at me as if it were debatable who should be locked up. 'Maybe it was us who were heinously fucked up?' He peered down at the open ashtray with a wistful smile and kind of shrugged.

My pained contemplation, wrinkled brow and features mangled like a Picasso portrait prompted Dallas to expound.

'Ya know Gertie and that home she worked at for troubled girls?'

'Yeah?'

'Well, before she got better and worked there, she was a patient, because of like a mental breakdown, depression or some shit. Gertie was one tough chick, but fragile all the while too.'

'How do you know all this about her?' The question came inadvertently framed in an accusatory grain.

'Gertie was my homegirl. She'd have my ass if I said that shit to her.' He let slip a quick, affectionate scoff. 'Yeah, we liked to argue and talk shit about each other, but at the end of the day, she was my mate. I'd stay up late talking with her after you passed out or in a Shinjuku pub when you were off your face on the dance floor. She was under stress with the job losses, homesick and straight-up lonely. It took a toll. I think in a moment of clarity, Gertie reached out to her Fam. She'd been down that path before and knew enough that the help she needed wasn't here in Japan. Not in me, and certainly not in you, Fred.' It was his turn to give an accusatory look. 'She found herself in a dark tunnel with a train a comin' ... so she reached out to the hand she knew could save her.'

'A train's coming ...' I repeated beneath a whisper.

'Thing is, we can always blame something outside ourselves for our troubles. I've done it, and you're the fucking *sensei* master of it. The Gaijin House was a shithole, yeah, but to think that it was some kinda living entity set on destroying our lives is fuckin nuts, no offence.'

He was probably right, so I let it drop. Besides, a glance at the clock, and it read 2:35 pm. I had another five minutes with Dallas and some pressing issues yet.

'What did you mean when you said, "trying to keep up with me"?' I asked hurriedly, having kept that one on the back-burner until then.

'Yeah, dawg, I was fuckin' burnt out.'

'But, I always thought I was the one trying to keep up with you,' I said, realizing right there how petty the whole questioning sounded, given everything.

'Whatever, bro,' Dallas began, obviously finding my whole debate kind of trifling as well, 'we had some laughs, but were probably kinda misguided as well.'

So that's that, I thought, then pressed forth with the final detail I needed clearing up. 'Did you call my *keitai*?'

'Ha, I'm not allowed to use a phone. And sorry bro, I luv ya, but you wouldn't be my first call.' He cracked a broad smile while I caught his drift.

So, as I thought all along, it was only my mind playing tricks on me. I gave a nervous laugh and was ready to drop it.

'Although, you know ... I did think about you out of the blue one night, over a month back,' he added, crow-footed crinkles cropping up at the corners of his squinting eyes.

I straightened in my seat as my ears pricked up.

'Yeah, I'd just been moved here from the local jail,' he began in a kind of Bronx-Texan drawl as the memory coalesced. 'I was lying in bed the first night and slipped into sleep. Then I had this weird dream. You were adrift at sea in this little dingy, yelling into the sky some shit about the sea being your master ...' He trailed off and shook his head, smiling to himself as one might do with recollection of an odd creation from the subconscious.

'At first, I thought, fuck me, I've spent too much time in jail already if I'm thinking about that pretty boy punk. I shoulda been dreaming of Risa or a hundred other birds.' He spoke it animatedly of old, and we both had a much needed hearty laugh.

'Then I got all sentimental and shit,' he went on, 'a little nostalgic for those nights out. I lay there thinking how great it would be to be out of the cell, call you up and have one last tear on the town before I got deported ...'

Time was up. The guard approached to lead Dallas back to holding and left me there to wonder what it all meant.

I stood and shook his hand one last time, the guard eyeing us closely to make sure no contraband got passed.

Dallas headed toward the metal door flanked by the uniformed officer. A meter from the exit he turned, an urgency blazed in his eyes. 'You know Fred, dem nights ... Well, there's no such thing as eternal happiness. And that's probably for the best. Imagine how colourless that would make a life,' he said placid, but with a smouldering intensity underneath, while looking straight at me.

'Now and then, though,' his gaze shifted to the lustrous grey poking through chain-link on the long window over my shoulder, 'occur moments of pure joy, and they'll transpire eternally. Recognize and savour those; slip into them like a winters *onsen*, warming your soul to the core, bro.'

He flashed one more winning Dallas smile before dropping a final bar on me, 'stuck in here I remember something my man Pac said: "through the darkest night emerges a brighter day," so ya know, keep your head up, mofo!'

He turned, broad shoulders rolled and receded. The heavy iron door closed with a finite clang, and he was gone.

4// Devouring
The Manky Peach

Yukie wore a pair of faux suede platform boots and a blue denim mini skirt, showing just that luscious ribbon of flesh mid-thigh. It drove me wild with lust. I planted my hand right on the alluring real estate and desperately wanted to have her back on the love hotel bed, boots on, lights low, bodies pressed ...

'What?' Yukie asked with a flushed giggle.

'Nothing ... um, sorry,' I said, catching myself and softening the lubricious leer.

We relaxed atop our swivel stools and lit cigarettes. Yukie handed me a photocopy of a short newspaper article. It had a stapled sheet attached, a translation she'd completed for me.

'You mentioned your guesthouse in Higashi Koseki had disappeared when you went to revisit. I did some research to see if I could find out what happened. I hope you don't mind, I know you didn't ask.' She looked strangely nervous like she'd overstepped a boundary. Or it could have been that in giving me this information she was uncertain as to whether she would be pulling me out the muddled waters I wallowed, or plunging me deeper into the riptide.

'No, this is fucking great, thanks,' I assured.

HIGASHI KOSEKI GUEST HOUSE CLOSES
AMIDST GOVERNMENT INVESTIGATION

The Big Peach Guest House closed its doors last month and is scheduled for demolition in the coming weeks. The 40-year-old building with single occupancy rooms rented predominantly to short-term residents and foreigners is located in the heart of Higashi Koseki, along the Chuo line.

What is unknown to many but was uncovered by our investigative reporters are the conditions that led to the closing of the residence.

The Public Security Intelligence Agency (PSIA) began investigating the property after suspicions of cult-like activities were raised in documents turned over to the PSIA by the Tokyo Metropolitan Police. Officers had been called to the residence to investigate a suspicious death of a guesthouse staff member who boarded in one of the rooms.

The cause of death was later deemed suicide by self-poisoning in a coroner's report. Police discovered sedative drugs, barbiturates, and scopolamine in the man's room and a toxicology report showed the opiates in his system at the time of death.

Material recovered during a search of the room motivated officers to alert the PSIA. 'We found pamphlets, documents, and other paraphernalia in the employee's residence which called for alerting the proper Agency for their discretion on whether it warranted further investigation,' reported Mr Yamaguchi, one of the investigating officers of the crime scene.

The PSIA did indeed deem the material significant enough to open up a case file on the Peach House, its controlling entity and staff. The investigation was carried out over six months, after which time controlling officers of the company agreed to terminate the employment of all staff and close the property. It should be noted that the Peach Guesthouse was one arm of the company's business. They continue to retain and run other interests.

Investigators stated that, as the only mandate was to investigate this particular property and staff, with the sale of the property and termination of staff, they consider the case closed.

Local neighbours contacted for comment had no knowledge of the investigation but expressed positive sentiments over the dismantling of the property. 'There were often residents returning home in the very late hours of the evening, yelling and laughing as they walked down this quiet residential street. It was not respectful,' said Mrs Ito of the closure news.

'The property was never well kept. The grass was overgrown, and the surrounding wall was overrun with weeds and crumbling in parts. Besides that, there were the rowdy *gaijin*s with their loud music, littering and noise,' explained Mr Tanaka, aged 60.

The Yumori Shimbun reached out to the parties in charge of the company which ran the guesthouse, but they have yet to respond to our request for comment.

'What does that tell you?' Yukie asked when I finished reading the article a second time.

'A fucking lot! Even though I don't know what any of it means exactly … it definitely gets me closer to some answers,' I said, looking contemplative out the McDonald's fourth-floor window.

'*Gomen*, I have to get going.' She kissed me on the cheek and headed off to work.

I retrieved a pint of whisky from my pocket and poured half into my paper cup. Then I sat in the smoking area and poured over the translated words.

I remembered that dead body, I'd seen it. Well, not it specifically, more the plangent of its decay.

I was brushing my teeth at the communal wash basin and looking out the bathroom window on a Sunday afternoon. Over the rocky, weed-covered courtyard brightly splashed with midday sun, I peered through hungover, pin-prick pupils.

The house was laid out like the bottom half of a capital H. Co-ed toilets and shower stalls connected as a short corridor the two separate hallways with rooms situated on either side. As far as I knew, everyone lived in the front hall. I'd never seen anyone emerge from the hallway which ran further back on the lot. Gertie's window faced out that way, and in all the hours I'd spent in there never even seen a light on.

So when I saw a slight shifting movement through one of the inward-facing rooms on that hall, it caught my attention. I squinted to make out the source, and it wasn't actually behind the window, but directly on it where the movement was occurring; shifting black shapes, like animated inkblots. But if it were a Rorschach test, I was failing miserably.

I knocked on Gertie's door and asked her to come have a look at the odd altering image. As we stood by the window inspecting, Dallas arrived on the scene. Just up, shirt off and ready to shower at noon having been, like me, up until the dawn.

'What you fuckers looking at? You're rapt like it's the second coming of Christ,' he said hoarsely.

'Come look at this, man. What do you make of it?' I said.

So Dallas joined our viewing party. He nailed it pretty quick. 'Aw sick, those are flies.'

'Aye, the thick cunt's correct methinks,' Gertie concurred.

Dallas elbowed us both playfully, celebrating his small victory.

'What are they doing there?' I went on, befuddled through a hangover fog.

'It's either like a load of shit or a mass of rotting meat,' Dallas deduced again.

A Dutch couple none of us knew, temporary guests of the Gaijin House only staying for a week or two, passed by and peeked out.

Dallas again played the instructor, telling them it was, 'flies, thousands of them, must be something rotting up a storm in there.'

The girlfriend said something in Dutch, and they hurried away. As for the rest of us, we didn't put two and two together too well. I went back to my room, grabbed a few cans and a copy of Camus' *The Stranger* Gertie had lent me. Then, I headed out to the nearest park to drink and read my hangover away.

I got back after the cans were emptied and I was tipsy with prose. There was a single police car parked on the rocky drive before the entrance of the Peach House. Rather than head in and investigate, my overactive angst bred cowardice and I passed straight by, down to the convenience store where I had two more cans. When I returned, the coast was clear.

'Yeah it was a scene, bruh,' Dallas began his update that evening. 'There was like a coroner's van, and they wheeled out the body under a blanket. It was either one fatass fucker, or the body was bloated to shit, cause it was like a massive lump of white cloth on the trolley. I caught a whiff and fuck man, it fuckin' stank! Gertie was watching with me, but she got freaked the hell out and took off to her room before they lifted him in the back ... took like three of them plus the coroner.' He shook his head in macabre disbelief.

Not knowing is Buddha, so I never thought much about the incident and went merrily on my way whistling through the dark. There in McDonald's, questions around what led to the debut of the obese corpse were resurrected. *Was he murdered and it made to look like a suicide? Did he martyr himself to renounce some immoral deed he was party to? Or maybe he was just depressed and took a hell of a lotta drugs ... But why in possession of all those drugs in the first place?*

The opening of a cult investigation needled me even more. *What would they have found that led to getting the Public Security Intelligence Agency involved?*

The Tokyo subway serum attacks still weigh heavy on the Japanese psyche. The reverberating effects of the Aum cult and tragic events that Monday could have led to an investigation had anything in the man's possession indicated involvement in a political or religious movement construed as having calamitous intentions. *Something like recruitment pamphlets, manifestos or the makings of a plot? But what were the specifics, the intentions and targets?*

I was slipping deeper down the rabbit hole, grasping at the edges but only scraping off crumbling earth and unable to find a sufficient grip to stop my descent. Suddenly it hit me, there was one obvious hold. It'd been there in front of me this whole time, I only needed to grab it and set about clawing my way out.

To seize it, I'll need to find her. In this city of 30 million, finding a single soul is like pinpointing a lone particle in the bright. My final haul from the wax-paper cup, as the whisky had settled, sent a shudder.

5// Cosmic Pachinko

The crack of a bat drew my attention to a row of batting cages, the most ill-fitting of Kabukicho's diversions. *Guess even hustlers and pimps need to blow off steam with a little wholesome recreation once in a while.*

The batting cages and dense block of love hotels mark the bottom fringe of Shinjuku's red-light district. I emerged from the carnival-like atmosphere of Kabukicho's libertinism and entered Shin-Ōkubo where it becomes clandestine, existing as necessity more than luxury.

I'd just left the Beatles McDonald's. While I'd have liked to have met Yukie again after work, and make love until sunrise, it had become impossible to ignore, once again, I was financially fucked. With barely enough left from my bullfight winnings to purchase the requisite Chu-his to get me through another day, I was in no position to be shelling out for love hotels.

Already, I'd resorted to bringing Yukie back to the netcafe to fool around. In the end, we decided not to fuck ... Well, she decided, and probably at the beginning. Jeans unbuttoned, her hand thrust below the band of my boxers ... I got off, which was good ... but there'd been this pervy desire that her mystical unguis brushed against the erection would ... *I don't know? I guess it doesn't work that way.*

I walked her to the station. Sodden and sticky underwear clung to my restful, drooping cock. By the time I'd gotten back to the cafe, my shorts had adhered entirely. Grabbing a handful of denim and the cotton boxers beneath, I yanked outward. Feeling the fastened fabric peel off the smooth rounded helmet, I cracked a warped smile; besmirched and becalmed.

Though, the smile faded as I thought back to Yukie behind the velour navy-blue curtain. While I lounged in my recliner and zipped up, she hurriedly smoothed out the skirt portion of the one-piece dress my forearm had just been crammed up. I caught her eye and flashed a meek, appreciative smile. She gave a counterfeit, uncomfortable one back. As far as love nests go, I decided then and there, the Genki Netcafe was out.

As I ruminated on money woes and when I'd get to be properly intimate with Yukie again, Jae-hyun rounded a Korean BBQ joint on the corner and headed my way.

'Been keeping busy these days. Things must be progressing well for you.' He noted my frequent absences from the café of late with a prideful gleam in his eye.

'Yeah, things have been going okay,' I admitted. 'But, you know what they say, romance and finance, the scourge of a man's existence.'

'Ah, and which is getting you down?'

'Surprisingly, the romance is on pretty good track. But financial difficulties are starting to hamper that,' I said with a pathetic self-pitying pout and hoped he didn't think I was about to hit him up for a loan. But there was a favour I'd been wanting to ask him, something that could help my money troubles as well as scratch a long nagging cultural itch. 'Hey Jae-hyun, can you teach me to play pachinko?'

'I thought you'd never ask,' he replied, breaking into a broad smile.

Jae-hyun briefly stopped by his cubby and emerged donning a baseball cap pulled low and a bulky black jacket. We walked the streets of Okubo past several loud cajoling shops. For reasons, personal or professional, we couldn't patronize any of those. Finally, we arrived at a rundown parlour off Okubo's main drag.

'You want to avoid the new bigger parlours, they rig the machines more and pay out less. They think they can get away with it with all that glitz and theatrics. They practically do, but us old hands know,' he said, with an old cocksureness coming to surface.

Stage one, as Jae-hyun explained, was to walk around the place to find a machine that spoke to you. He said the pros study the machines for hours and see which ones are paying out, then snag them. We didn't have time for that so were forced to go on feeling alone. It was a bit like being at the track, watching the horses as they were paraded around the paddock, and betting on a hunch the one who catches your eye.

The parlour still dinged and binged like the others, there still hung in the air a thick cloud of second-hand smoke and gentle whiff of fatalism; it was just the machines were a little bit older, the lighting drabber, and the carpet sullied with cigarette burns, old stains and sticky underfoot.

My sole peeled off the floor, and I seized Jae-hyun's arm. 'This one!'

A chair, padded with red vinyl covering like all the rest yet in the distinctive disrepair of the joint had rips in the covering and yellowing foam protruding out. It was the rips that caught my attention. There was one extended tear, and beside it, a diagonal cut intersected by a horizontal and that sliced through with another short vertical – making a distinct number fourteen.

I approached and swung the seat toward me, just to confirm, then sat. Jae-hyun seemed to approve of my selection as he walked to my side and stood ready to instruct. We put a five-thousand-yen note in the machine. 'Okay,' instructed my coach, 'press the *tamakashi*.'

Inferring, I pressed a little red button and a bin which stuck out like a pouty bottom lip flooded with silver ball bearings. As instructed, I turned the handle on my lower right side, twisting back and forth.

'You can't manipulate the ball once in motion, just set it on the correct path,' Jae-hyun told me as, by instinct or conditioning, his busted hand reached for the knob, and then retracted as if from a flame.

It was a delicate craft. If you turned the handle too sharply, the balls went right into the losing shoot at the bottom, if not enough, then they fell short of the goal. There were also pesky little pegs on the board, which would knock my ball off course if hit at the wrong angle.

'Aim for the gap,' he said. 'Seek the clearest line to the winning holes.'

'I am!' Frustrated with my ability, I snapped. Thus far, I'd lost all balls down the losing side shoots.

'You're thinking too much. Forget any schemes or systems, find the feel and go with it,' he directed in a firm whisper.

There's some of that Zen shit I've been waiting for. I closed my eyes, took a deep breath, and opened them to the machine's bongo beat blast of blinking lights. Calmly, I adjusted the knob; based not on thought, but through sheer sense.

With my newfound rhythm, the balls started to fall into the winning destination, one after the other. It was like finding the g-spot, challenging to get there but once you had it, didn't want to lose your place as the rewards came fast and furious, and felt pretty damn sweet.

Silver balls spilled forth from the base and collected in a plastic basket below. So much so that one became filled and Jae-hyun needed to grab an empty one to replace. Somehow the impossible happened and the parlour's constant clangour faded away, only the sweet, steady sound of cascading ball bearings, like monsoon rains against a corrugated roof, could I hear.

When my touch waned, Jae-hyun would jump in with more eastern visualization blather, like reading from a sutra of eerily relatable aphorisms. 'Stars falling through the cosmos, guide them through this muddled universe ...' or 'don't struggle against the current; find the centre, relax and flow with it.'

'*Sugoi, aotari*,' Jae-hyun exclaimed excitedly as a waterfall of little silver balls filled an entire basket with a single pour. I didn't know what it meant but knew it was good. The way the machine screamed and lit up, I figured I'd hit some sort of jackpot.

At that point, I wasn't sure if we were making any money. It sure felt like it by the baskets of ball-bearings being set aside, plus Jae-hyun's beaming smile was a pretty good indicator. Despite my ignorance of the rules and results, I could see the appeal. The randomness of outcomes, all the variables and obstacles encountered along the way. The parlour sets the pegs, so yeah, it's rigged against you, that's life! But you determine the course, and that sense of control – the gambler's hit – permeates the player's mindset so a belief prevails; *I can beat the game, with just the right touch*.

It felt like I'd only been playing for thirty minutes, but when closing time rolled around close to midnight, it meant we'd been there almost four hours. We exchanged our many baskets of balls from a kind of gift shop near the front. For my efforts, an alarm clock, teddy bear and handbag were handed over the counter, like if I'd rung three bottles at a carnival. In exchange for this newfound armload of crap, I tipped the attendant with a baffled expression.

Jae-hyun was unfazed. He led me outside and around the corner to a small kiosk, the TUC shop. I handed over my random objects, the officious gentleman did some number crunching, and stone-faced, he handed me a thick wad of crisp bills.

I counted our winnings as we walked back to the main street, just under a hundred thousand yen.

'Thanks,' I said, handing Jae-hyun his half.

He waved it away.

'No, I insist. My first pachinko ... it was something. I've wanted to try ever since I arrived, but never knew how.'

The money hung from my arm in the air between us. 'I've got no need for it.' He glanced at the cash and then away with a kind of disdain. 'The experience itself was all the payoff I require,' he added with the jubilant smile of a travelling Mormon.

I procured us a couple of tall cans from the nearest *conbini*, and without any explicit plan meandered past Don-don Quijote. Across Syokuan-Dori, and tilting at windmills, I pointed out Tatsuya and Machiko's bar. 'Had a pretty fucked up time there the other night.'

'How so?' Jae-hyun enquired.

I gave a brief backstory on Hideki, the names he'd written and then said, 'We were not welcomed, to say the least. All but chased out of the bar by an unrelenting bitterness.'

'Hmm, sounds uncomfortable,' Jae-hyun said, and I could almost see his thoughts hopscotch down a memory lane where every square was a far more significant occurrence of undue prejudice. 'But consider it a peg.'

'A what?'

'It's an obstacle in your path, but how you rebound or bounce off of it will ultimately determine where you land.'

'I've landed on fuck 'em and fuck it. I did my part and delivered my friend's message,' I said, my feigned indifference gnawed through by a persisting ire.

'Forgive us our trespasses as we forgive those who trespass against,' Jae-hyun continued, seeing through my wispy emotional smokescreen.

'Are you a Christian?' I asked, recognising the line loosely from the Lord's Prayer I was required to learn somewhere in my youth.

'Not particularly, I adhere to a meticulously sewn patchwork of theology,' he said, tipping up the brim of his cap. 'But in the end, they mostly overlap and intertwine. So "to understand all things is to forgive all things" if you prefer.' Jae-hyun shrugged.

That one I didn't recognise. 'You forgive your pachinko bosses, for your hand and Eun-ae? Or Kim Jong's regime?'

'All of them ... wholly! I had to. It was impossible to forgive myself until I learned to forgive others. My freedom was found in that forgiveness.'

Freedom? He lives in a fucking 2 by 2 closet, I thought. But we'd been down that road before so I shut the fuck up and listened.

The bottom hemisphere of Kabukicho was in full swing with all the usual suspects drifting through the streets and alleys, like hungry Pac-Man looking to satisfy insatiable appetites. Jae-hyun and I walked void of destination, yet veered deeper into the red-light maze, and who was leading who remained unknown.

I stopped in my tracks and swung the back of my hand in front of Jae-hyun's chest to halt his progress. There, before the Robot restaurant, in front of an old-school *izakaya* situated on the street like an Edo era abode rather than your usual garish Kabukicho establishment and next to a potted gumtree plant, the elegant fingers of a pianist played the single string of his silent instrument. 'Check him out,' I pointed with excitement.

'The kite-flyer of Kabukicho, *ne*!' His eyes squinted and lips curled into a subtle smile. 'Quite a character.' He shook his head with undiminished fascination at the specimen. 'Oh, so you can see him? That's good, most don't or simply choose not to.'

'Yeah, I noticed he goes largely ignored by the masses,' I said. 'Stumbled upon him a few times now but I'm still trying to figure out why he does it ... like a ritual or something? But for what?'

'Yes, a ritual sounds about right. I don't really know, I imagine so he can see ... Above it all, beyond you or me, and all the rest.'

I mulled until my head hurt. 'You ever see what's on the other side?' I stared up at the dark blue underbelly. 'The design that faces the night sky?'

Jae-hyun flickered a puckish smile. 'Now you're thinking like me. Many a night I wandered these streets pondering the same. Even asked Kai about him on a number of occasions. He wouldn't tell me much, just flashed me a knowing grin,' he chuckled with a light-hearted frustration.

'Hold up. Kai knows him?'

'Yeah, Jun and him go way back. Seen them chatting away, on anonymous corners all over Kabukicho through the years.'

This blew my mind. First that Kai ever left the vicinity of our little netcafe and secondly he interacted with someone willingly. 'So they like friends, family, colleagues?' Come to think of it, there was a likeness. If not in appearance, then the way each, in his own way, was too strange for this world.

'Damned if I know.' He tipped his can and drank. 'Partners in some odd scheme, acquaintances at best maybe,' Jae-hyun mumbled.

His bulbous head emerged from the wide teal lapels of that night's leisure suit. He paid no mind to the gawking strangers down the block, but bore a concentrated look as he fixated on centring the rhombus at some specific point in the sky. 'You got any theories?' I asked. 'On the design.'

'More than you'd want ... how much time you got? But I'd like to hear yours. Get a fresh take.'

I stared up, took a drink of grapefruit Chu-hi then let the can fall and dangle by my side. 'It just came to me now ... but like an ancient symbol of some sort, an Aztec eye or something?'

'The Ollin. Hmm, very nice.' His head nodded in slow motion. 'Movement, shifting shapes, Gemini, and Venus, the evening star – pulsating hearts, and the earth quakes, a beat of butterfly wings or undulating motion of weft as the loom weaves,' he spat like Twista. Off the top of his head, the string of connections came as if a computer crunching complex formulas. I understood none of it, but the words individually hit my subconscious like pinpricks.

'It'd answer a lot but raise just as many questions,' Jae-hyun finished, lost in contemplation.

I feel that. 'Your theory? Just give me the top two or three.' I smirked up one side of my face.

He was in good spirits, took two long drags and laughed

heartily. 'That I can do. The first ... You ever read the Iliad?'

'I like dead writers but not that dead,' I smiled back.

'Well, really intricate and busy, like the shield of Achilles. A universe unto itself, an alternate reality, soaring above it all, under Jun's watch and control.'

I looked at the kite-flyer of Kabukicho, Jun, as I guess he goes by. Rooted to the pavement like the potted plant he stood beside and just as unassuming. I discounted Jae-hyun's first theory, out of hand.

'Or if you like, some incarnation of the yin and yang ... the kite sways in constant deliberation. Would explain the location. Kabukicho after the gloam fades, what a better place to gauge the duality of man?'

Each theory came with a gleam of the eye. I sensed he was holding out on me. There was a final, a favourite yet. 'Come on, one more. You're saving the best for last, eh.'

He glanced over with a conspiratorial smile, as if about to share a thought that shouldn't be shared then looked back up at the kite. 'Just black,' he said. 'Pitch black.'

The hairs on the back of my neck stood up. On we sauntered in reflective silence, reviewing each step of the personal journeys which preceded us.

6// Rainy Day Ramen

For the third day in a row, I was back at the small park off the pedestrian shopping street in Kawagoe, drinking and waiting for her to enter, blindly hunting a corrupted facsimile of our first meeting. After several hours observing the steady stream of shoppers, students, shop girls and elderly flowing past, I spotted a heavily made-up girl walking by in a pink shirt and tight stretched stonewashed denim. I stood and moved toward her. I squinted to study her plain painted face, searching for a name I had stashed way back in the messy draws of my subconscious.

Her thin legs balanced in two-size-too-big must-have heels; I caught up easily and called, 'Naoko?'

She turned to look at me, confused before a wash of recognition came over her.

'Fled! *Genki desu ka*?' she asked with a friendly smile.

'I'm okay. Actually, I'm looking for Akiko.' I rushed to the point after a three-day wait. 'I recently arrived back in Tokyo, and I really need to talk to her. Do you know where she is?'

As I spoke my request, her face concealed a frown, but she couldn't hide her worried eyes. I assumed Akiko told her about my behaviour, maybe even warned her not to speak to me if I ever showed up. The kind of negative PR campaign I was familiar with scorned exes propagating.

'Can we go sit and talk?' she asked, sweet and sorrowful.

I nodded, instantly anxious, knowing it was much worse than my ego's contrivance.

She led me into the park. We sat on the same low brick wall at the rear and both lit a cigarette.

Naoko, perhaps because she lacked the English ability, sugar-coated it none. 'Akiko is dead.'

The news was a solid blow to the gut. Though inexplicably, I knew it was coming; from when I can't say – a ways back.

'Oh god, I'm so sorry. What happened?' I asked, my face ashen.

'She fell on the tracks and hit by train. They say fell, but everyone know probably jump.'

It wasn't enough, I needed more. I agreed with her conclusion, 'probably jumped' … *but why?* … *and who pushed her?*

'Where did this happen?'

'On Seibu line. Morning time, on way to school or maybe coming home after all night.'

I didn't think about it, the next question just came blurting out, 'What station?' But I already knew the answer.

'Seibu Shinjuku Station.'

Permanent dawn … the red yarn … the black void … my bird's eye view; directly adjacent to Seibu Shinjuku Station. *And I?* Lured back to bear witness?

'Was there a note or any clue as to why she might have jumped?' I asked, frantic for answers, desperate for clemency.

'No she don't write note. But she have a diary. After the funeral, her dad ask me to read for him to see if she give reason. For him too hard, also he want … *eto*, respect, Akiko privately,' she explained. 'But, I am girl. He ask me to read and tell anything important to him. I have copy. Do you want?'

I didn't want – but needed, in the tactile experience of holding the page and consuming her final thoughts.

We stubbed out our smokes on the low wall behind our legs, and I followed Naoko out of the park to retrieve the entries. We made our way through the residential neighbourhood of low-level apartment buildings and skinny houses situated on tiny lots and made small talk. I told her that her English had gotten very good.

'Thank you, I have study at my school,' she informed, chipper I'd noticed and unburdened by the past and what may come.

I waited outside on the road as she went into one of the skinny two-storey homes. Her family's house, I assumed. It had a small, well-kept garden out front with some colourful flowers and a single bonsai. I wondered if Naoko tended to the garden. It was a pretty little garden, but all just a bit too pristine, it lacked character.

The bonsai though, well, they had always fascinated me for some reason. Carefully cultivated, cut and pruned, so they'd maintain the miniaturized form and appearance of a fully grown tree. Maybe it was that – the art and ingenuity of stunted growth.

After about ten minutes, she came back and handed me an envelope with the pages folded and slipped inside. 'Thanks. Um ... am I mentioned?' I forced out the question which had weighed on my shoulders like a Sherpa's load the whole time I'd been pacing the small plot.

'No,' she said. 'But I have only copy of final four entry. Sorry, I never go back further than this.'

'This is great. Thank you so much, Naoko.'

'Okay, bye-bye,' she offered in the typical overly cutesy and cheerful style of young Japanese women.

It struck as oddly misplaced, given the circumstances. *Just habitual*, I figured, as I gave a solemn wave and walked away.

I'd gotten what I'd come for, but not at all in the way I had wanted. I carried the closure sought in Akiko's words, wondering, *would they exonerate me or levy an even harsher sentence.*

As if reading my mind, Naoko called out, 'Fled, wait.'

I'd only gone a handful of steps, stopped and turned. The sun at her back and right in my eyes, I listened as her words poured through a dark silhouette. 'You need to know it's not your fault. Yes, you hurt her,' She searched the pavement for more words, and I waited with bated breath. 'Akiko get over it. She like you, and when you cheat, she feel betray and upset. But she know before your heart wander, you want out ... your freedom.'

I wanted to contradict, tell her she had it all wrong, but bit my lying tongue and let her go on.

'When she keep hold on, she thinks it makes you push her away so hard. But, is true ... *eto* ... her heart heal from this wound.' She looked up from the cement and met my eyes, perhaps, to register if I were released.

However, I couldn't force the requisite mien. I nodded, turned again, and walked down the quiet Kawagoe street. I don't know if it helped, or was even true. Still, I was glad she said it.

At Kawagoeshi station I opened the envelope and took out the four entries photocopied on two pages, each sheet containing both sides of a splayed open diary. The words written in neat *kanji* characters, like so many small poignant pictures. Left in the envelope were two photos.

I pulled out the first, which must have been taken at least five years prior when both Naoko and Akiko were girls not even out of high school. They were smiling excitedly in front of the fairytale castle at Tokyo Disneyland, carefree and brilliantly pure.

The next photo was a shrine. The little temple, no bigger than a garden shed, was set back in the far corner of a stark park. It had a flowing gabled roof made of dark green clay tiles. The ornamental roof offset by four plain boarded walls with a rectangular space cut out as an entrance. Above and just before the onyx gap hung a simple golden bell on a frayed twine. Alone on the stoop sat a small emerald urn – Akiko.

Holding the photos side by side, it epitomized how she'd been taken far too soon. *If only she could have held on through the pain a little longer.* A single tear of contrition rolled down my cheek on the slow-moving Tobu line train.

Back at Shinjuku station, I went straight to the McDonald's to see Yukie. It was an hour before her work, so I figured I could catch her there. She had written me a message two days previous, but I hadn't responded, I'd been so wrapped up in my daily pilgrimages to Kawagoe. I hoped she wasn't too pissed about freezing her out.

Probably, it was not the ideal time to request another favour of her, especially one involving reading the last confessions of my dead ex. But I needed someone to translate the entries, and she was the only one I could ask.

A girl was sitting in Yukie's usual spot at the window with a smouldering cigarette in the thin tin ashtray. I had to do a double-take to recognize it was her. She was dressed in jeans and tight grey T-shirt. Her hair was pulled back straight and tied in a ponytail. That evening she had put on only the simplest cosmetic touches. Unvarnished how she rolled, and radiant still, when the natural beauty was permitted to shine through.

'Hey, sorry I didn't get back to your message.' I hopped on the stool next to hers mid-blather and fished a cigarette from my mangled pack. 'I've been super busy, taking trips out to Kawagoe trying to meet someone I used to know.'

She looked icily in my direction then back through a concrete dusk to the tracks beyond, her expression pierced with a palpable pain.

Oblivious to the atmosphere, I let the blundering train of thought carry on. 'I've been meaning to tell you ... well I didn't think there was a need, but now I should explain. I need just one more favour, if you could translate this ...'

'*Uzai yatsu*,' she swore under her breath.

Basically, it translates to 'pain in the ass guy'. I know, it doesn't sound too hardcore, but definitely showed she was pissed; the acrid delivery, indicated just how pissed. Unlike myself and other westerners, the Japanese don't swear much. They don't even have many curse words. I once saw two drunk salarymen in a slight physical altercation outside an *izakaya*. They were fired up – over a woman or business deal or something. Judging by how angry they were, probably the latter. Anyways, the best they could come up with as they pushed back and forth was repeatedly calling each other *baka* or idiot. Basically what Gertie used to call me endearingly on a daily, even hourly basis.

With this lack of selection in cursing vernacular, the tone carries a lot of weight. Her tone, essentially told me to, *'Get the fuck to hell you shit-eating, fucking asshole, bastard son of a whore.'*

The verbal slap awoke me to the many cues served up and mounting on the counter of our smoky McDonald's. I inhaled of the aftermath: menthol, grease and cooked ground beef. A blackbird sang from its wall-mounted nest, coaxing forth the dead of night.

'Sorry again about ignoring your email,' I began, attempting to mend a broken wing. 'Like I said, I've been super busy with this ...'

'Yesterday was my birthday.' The pronouncement made colourless and vacant, filled the smoking section air with more bad chemistry.

Shit, it was. October 21st, Libra, Blood type O. I'd asked her birthday the second time we met, an old pick-up trick to make up some bullshit about her star sign, ramble off some positives about her personality and nonsense about our compatibility. Tacky yeah, but as gold today as it was back in '69. The blood type, it's a thing here. Mine's B and Aquarius to boot. The main thing about B personality is selfishness. So yeah, check and check.

'That's why I wrote,' she vented with a huff, 'it didn't matter if you remembered but at least shown up or replied.' Yukie peered out the large window again, too pissed to look at me directly. There was a stain on the glass, like congealed spattered milkshake. Her gaze fixed on it, never making it to the city beyond where Shinjuku's nocturnal soul dreamt in slumber, before her darkening dawn. 'But you get so involved in yourself ... In your little invented dramas and it's like I disappear from your world.'

'Fuck, I'm sorry,' was all I really had at that point.

'Sometimes I feel like I'm only a convenient diversion as you careen through life. Do you even like me?' Her eyes welled up with salty tears as the anger migrated to frustration then sadness.

Did I even like her?

Never had I been more desperate to make clear my true feeling, to adequately communicate just how much I liked her, needed her, wanted her holding me at the centre of this crumbling life. If I could only invite her into my mind to view as gallery paintings the thoughts that occupy when we're together, she'd have no need to question my devotion.

'Yeah, I like you. I like ya so much,' I stammered and stumbled forth. 'I mean ... you are like ... you're my rainy day *ramen* ...'

'*Nani?*' Her reflected expression, distorted and perplexed, confirmed the rocky start.

'What I mean is when I'm with you, no matter how disagreeable life gets, when the elements of it bear down cold and unfriendly, I might lean over and get a whiff of your hair or come up behind you and sense the aroma off the nape of your neck. It makes me feel warm inside ... contented.'

Her tears had dried, and the corners of her mouth curled upward ever so slightly.

Reassured I may have been starting to make some sense, I spilled forth. 'I admit, my mind falls easily into a state of flux which begets a tumultuous self-seeking – but if I can just taste your essence, hold you close and kiss your lips ... then in that moment, I exist in this world as if afloat on serene seas ...'

I trailed off. It had been laid bare. I'd invited her into my thinking, but could she comprehend the quirky notions which furnished it? Were my words adequate to erase her uncertainty? I sipped through my straw and swallowed hard, awaiting her response.

Together in the settling quietude, we captured the moment where dusk turned to dark. All the neon luminosity of permanent dawn and the stretch of Yasukuni Dori leading to it came alive, like a colossal psychedelic chandelier hung from the night had suddenly been plugged in. Yukie's face, splashed with coloured cosmetics of the metropolis night, shone anew. Wishful thinking imagined her savouring my words.

'That's sweet, I'm flattered by your phrases and the pretty pictures painted by them,' she reacted after digesting my little spiel. 'But I worry, that will be it. They'll end up just brushed up scenes of us which exist only on the canvas of your mind or on a page somewhere.'

'I'm sorry, but here's the picture in my mind,' she continued on her soft insightful assault. 'You're a passenger on this speeding train, then come upon this stop ... you get kind of stranded there, miss last train or something. As you wander the low lit streets, you kind of like the place. It's comfortable, and yes, you might even feel a peace there. You talk glowingly of the place but make no effort to stay, to make it a home. Deep inside you know, at dawn you'll be back on that train, because you won't be satisfied until you reach some obscure destination at the end of the line.'

Yorii, I thought, and then stupidly mumbled under my breath, 'It began at the end of the line.' I hoped she wouldn't hear. Though the exasperated sigh she expelled, said no such luck.

In the wandering narcissism of my mind, I all but confirmed her reservations about me; about us. She was slipping away, that much was clear.

'I understand, but for now, it would mean the world to me if you'd let me enjoy the beauty of this place just a little while longer,' I said in a last-ditch effort to hold on. 'At least for tonight. I missed your birthday, but I'm here now, let's enjoy.'

She'd said her piece, though I feared a definitive decision had been made, her hospitable eyes told me she was going to grant my desire and give me tonight.

'*Ramen*, really?' she said sardonic.

'*Hai, ramen,*' I said, and we shared a light-hearted laugh.

We flew into the light of the dark black night and landed in a

7th floor karaoke booth. Spotted pink and green by the cheap disco lamp, I sang a schmaltzy version of Clapton's 'Wonderful Tonight' as a play on earlier compliments. After Sinatra and Manilow, Yukie clapped in appreciation of my grizzled crooner impersonation and laughed a little at how out of tune I was. She sang R&B and a couple of Japanese songs I'd heard somewhere along the road. Whereas she had said she couldn't sing, I found it heavenly and was drawn closer to her with every note.

After two hours we'd run out of songs to sing, so made out in the faux leather booth while an empty orchestra played in the background. Following the prolonged foreplay, we naturally gravitated to a love hotel.

We kissed and clothing fell to the floor like plush droplets in a spring rain. I kissed Yukie's neck and lips, entered her and moved in a slow circular grind. A familiar euphoria surged through me. I closed my eyes, and that's when Akiko appeared.

From there everything went south. A perceptible distance arose and only widened as Akiko crept through my thoughts. The incursion was not sexual, that might have worked. It was the imagined sight of her pacing the platform and those final tortured seconds where she concluded it was all to fractured to be fixed.

Mid-stroke, I wondered, *did she believe something was waiting for her on the other side?*

I grabbed a clumsy handful of breast, but the reality of flesh slipped from my frustrated grip. *Or was it merely choosing darkness over whatever adumbral future she foresaw?*

Gone flaccid, I violently stroked the limp dick. *The train approaching, your head turns to view its flat, metallic face in the distance.*

Turgency returned, I slid into the farcical routine once more. *As the city behind you reflected in the conductor's window grows larger and looming ... Is there a moment of doubt? Or was it already written?*

With each frenetic, futile thrust, my steely focus waned toward wet noodle shame. *The first car has entered the station ... you can still change your mind. Change your mind ... change your mind ... change your ...*

Grunts, sweat and cerebral curses oozed from my flailing form. *One bounding step ... and you're gone.*

I pulled out and blew soft.

The final feeble drips fell to the love hotel sheets. I laid on the mattress and stared up at the ceiling, plotting my defence. In the end, I just came clean. 'Sorry, I've been really distracted by something that happened today.'

'Was it me? Did I do something?' Yukie asked, obviously contemplating the source of our deed's decline.

'You? Of course not.' I rolled on to my side and looked at her lips. 'It was earlier today. I went to see about a girl I used to date and got some tragic news.'

She fashioned a pout but listened still.

It took me the next hour to explain a roughly edited version of Akiko and me. How we'd met, the drifting apart in Tokyo, even lightly touching on my philandering exploits with Dallas; lightly like a brick becomes a feather. I skirted the absolute dissolution, merely saying that I had treated her unfairly and felt the need to apologize. That brought me to the visits to Kawagoe, and tragic revelation it bore.

'That's horrible,' she said, after processing the whole convoluted story. 'I'm sorry I didn't let you tell me earlier.'

'No, it's for the best. Tonight was your belated birthday celebration, it should be a night all about you.' I rested my hand and stroked her kneecap. 'I'm sorry I couldn't give you a proper birthday, rogering.' I added, applying a shitty British accent and gave her leg a playful squeeze, hoping to erase the whole embarrassing scene.

Before our short-term stay ran out, I rallied to give it another go. It wasn't much better. I stayed hard but was marred by a cold sense of urgency as Akiko's spectre teetered on the platform's edge of my mind.

We exited the love hotel onto a sleepy Sunday sidewalk. A triage of the evening army marched on in stumbles and limps, lusts quenched or rampant still. The colour had drained from the evening ambience, as from the faces of those who passed, and all was grey and stark. Yukie and I fell in line with the dawn procession toward Shinjuku's East Exit, but she had other ideas and detoured off the path. 'I have something I need to show you,' Yukie explained as we cut across the stream.

I followed in silence, happy for her to lead me but anxious as to where we'd end up. After a pedestrian underpass with the Seibu tracks overhead, Yukie slipped through a gap between a concrete wall and chainlink fence. I looked over my shoulder as I was pretty sure we were trespassing and sidled in.

About ten feet back from the walkway, Yukie lifted a piece of plywood and picked up a purple spray can. She shook the can, soft 'tinks' from the ball inside echoed through the morning air. A few steps up a grassy incline we climbed, and there, concealed behind a large shrub, a six by six graffiti mural adorned the concrete slab which sheared down from the tracks above.

With a light press, purple mist sprayed an illuminated dusk over a slice of Shinjuku skyline. I stood back and watched her at work. The paint fumes' sweet hydrocarbons induced a dream-like euphoria. In a drowsy daze I said, 'I always thought these were done by like packs of skater kids or something.'

'Well, things are not always as static as they appear.' She looked back at me with a mysterious semi-smile.

Bright coloured buildings bubbled and bent, in a surrealist cityscape. From a mass of Kabukicho rooftops emerged a wavy channel of yellow butterflies who flew into the night or cascaded into the alleys below, I couldn't really detect the direction.

'I like the butterflies,' I said.

'Maybe you're not the only one Fred, who feels led by forces beyond their grasp ... I imagine most have that sense at some time or another. And we all have our trails to follow.' Was all she said on that. I wasn't sure how to take it. Was it an insinuation, advice, or maybe a revelation?

We parted ways in the waking hours outside Shinjuku East Exit. 'I'll do the translation for you,' Yukie said as a terse declaration.

7// Lost Letters
of Eleanor Rigby

I came out of the toilet stall, fastened the lid on my Coke, slipped a mickey in my backpack, and took a long drink through the yellow-red straw. I could barely taste the cheap whisky so moved my straw in a counter-clockwise movement to mix. Another sip. The makeshift highball packed a decent punch, at least a triple but probably should've been a quadruple to adequately calm my nerves.

Yukie hadn't arrived yet, and I was getting worried. In giving her the diary entries, I was essentially playing relationship Russian roulette. I'd inadvertently gambled with our burgeoning romance before in my stupid and selfish actions, though this was the biggest punt yet. I feared what the entries might reveal about me, either explicitly or in reading between the lines with a woman's intuition.

Yukie arrived, high-strung and hurried, twenty minutes before her shift at the bar was to begin. She lit a smoke and sipped her coffee. '*Gomen*, I know I'm late. Morning I had appointment and wanted to make sure to get the translation finished before we meet.'

'No problem, thanks so much for doing it. Hope it didn't take too long,' I drawled, trying to read her demeanour and see if it betrayed any change in comportment toward me. In the end, all I saw was an attractive, rushing-to-work young lady.

I accepted back the original envelope, figuring the translations were tucked inside. 'So, was it kind of intense ... like to read the last thoughts of a dead girl?' I asked of her in morbid projection.

'Not really. Because I didn't know her.' The answer simple yet punctuated with a searching pause. 'But I feel like I know her a little bit now. Like, I know her deepest pain, and I'm in on the biggest decision she ever made ... that anyone can ever make – to end it all.' She stubbed out her half-smoked cigarette in the thin metal ashtray. 'I could tell she's a nice girl, interesting and intelligent.' She kissed my cheek and stood. 'I have to rush off to work.'

'Can I meet you after?' I asked, foreshadowing that I wouldn't want to be alone.

'Tonight cannot, sorry.' She bid farewell with a gentle, parting smile.

With Yukie's departure, it was only me, the pages, the whisky and my thoughts. The thoughts got busy. *Why couldn't she see me after?* I fretted.

Was it something Akiko's words revealed or was it from mulling over last night's conversation when she concluded our relationship was like an eki, and me a passing train? Or was it the lousy sex? Of course, it could have been as simple as she'd had a tough day, was tired and wanted to go right home. The flaw in that theory was it didn't directly involve me.

I lit a smoke and removed the envelope's contents. Inside were four lined sheets carefully torn out of a small notebook neatly scrawled with roman characters; Akiko's final thoughts in Yukie's handwriting. It felt strange, that symbiotic clash of flames.

Looking out the third-floor window, my eyes trained directly at the approaching elevated tracks and entrance to Seibu Shinjuku station; it dawned on me, I would be reading the confession at the scene of the crime. That felt kinda weird as well.

Perched above and beyond, I watched a yellow-grey train chug down the tracks; in the pellucid aquarium scene, it flowed muted into the station like a submarine. *Is it the culprit ... the exact weapon Akiko used to exit this world? She wore a yellow top the first time we met ... Was she wearing it on that fateful morning? Did she hope the train would absorb her and she would exist forever in constant motion, thousands coming and going from her life each day?* I finally contemplated, and those thoughts were definitely fucking weird.

Enough procrastinating, I told myself and let my eyes fall from the windowpane to the letters waiting below.

May 10/10
When I look into my past, I see only wrong paths chosen.
Fallen branches, potholes and perilous weather obstruct
the way. Hurt and loss have befallen me at every turn, and
yet I walk alone this same meandering road ...

'Eleanor Rigby' played in the background as I read Akiko's words. *Whose sick goddamn idea was it to play this now!* I wanted to cry out. Though not crazy or drunk enough to scream out in a McDonald's, yet.

This first entry, a week before the irreversible act was committed, seems to be where the seed was sown in her troubled mind.

May 11/10
Hurt. Unwanted and abandoned, over and over, the
loneliness is an inescapable cell. I have found escape in the
hearts of men and in their beds. In the end, they all reject
me. I'm scraped and wiped away, like dog shit from the
sole of a shoe.

Fuck, what a harsh view, I thought, then, couldn't deny I'd contributed.

The entry went on in a similar vein describing the arrows of love endured and the weeping wounds they'd left. And always, after each she, *'sunk deeper in an ocean of loneliness.'*

The first specific reference sounded a recent hurt. When it spoke of *'bearing the beatings and bruises'* I fear she wasn't speaking metaphorically. *'But even he tired of me and moved on to a new punching bag'* it ended.

I unscrewed the small black cap and had a long haul straight from the mickey bottle, gave a weak cough and wiped the back of my hand over my lips. *Was it me … us?* I fretted over her next account of harmed heart.

> *Foreign men who seemed unique and free of our silly rules and norms. Unique and free … maybe I was viewed the same? Though only briefly, and then I was no more than another dish on the kaitenzushi conveyor belt.*

Foreign men? I pondered the plural. *Was it a mistake? A small concession from the translator? Or really, were there others before or after me?* I used it nonetheless to share blame with these invented others.

The entry went on to describe a short litany of other slights and romantic mishaps: the rugby guy, an older man perhaps one of her profs, a high school sweetheart and a molest in adolescence by an unnamed assailant. She'd been unlucky in love and unequivocally hurt, it was all there in black and white and underlined with faint blue lines.

I'd have to accept my share of the blame, whether parsed out to another *gaijin* or not. *Mine was just one of many assaults, the tiny stab of a single thorn on the wilting rose of her romantic life,* I tried telling myself. Though, I'd rather not have been a thorn at all.

May 12/10
Why not, when I've terminated a life more deserving than my own already …

Shrouded by shadows of the past and fed by lacrimal tears, her poisonous thoughts grew like carnivorous weeds. In the second to last entry, they began to bear fetid fruit, as she leaned toward the act itself.

While never explicitly mentioned, I thought it spoke of pregnancy and subsequent abortion or miscarriage. *'When the little light inside me had burned, blazed and extinguished all too quickly, like a match in the wind ...'*

May 14/10
When the life had drained from her every expression, she held on. When at last all love for herself, her kin and of living itself had drained from existence she decided it time to let go.

From the final entry, I gleamed the decision crystallized in memories of her mother. Everything for her culminated in that single abandonment. There was a long likening, which argued her, and her mother were one in the same and thus, *'Of the same blood, same weakness, same sorrow and of the same fate.'*

The entry concluded as close as it could to a proclamation: *'into each new day's rising sun, I squint weakly through an enduring pain. Maybe, there's solace in the darkness of eternal night.'*

My eyes lifted from the ink to the window as another train crawled into Seibu Shinjuku station. And then, to an oddly conducive Beatles background, Shelly spoke from a Lit lesson long ago.

Life, like a dome of many-colored glass,
Stains the white radiance of Eternity,
Until Death tramples it to fragments.

Gazing through the glass, suddenly, permanent dawn lost all luminescence. A single spotlight shone through the night and landed on Akiko's body laid lifeless in a sea of psychedelic shards on the crossing below. I shook my head and sipped at the whisky-Coke until the lights returned and reality set back in.

I folded the sheets once more and slipped them back into the envelope, vowing never to look at them again.

8// End of the Line

Two hours after boarding at Ikebukuro, I cracked a late-morning beer on the Yorii station platform. Looking up at the glass seven-storey Board of Education building looming over the rural platform, I was moved to decry, *why'd you bring me here!*

After a few sips in the quietude, I decided the extended stay on those five islands was full of experience, regret, pain, joy, loss and love; essential ingredients of a life. Instead, I stood and gave a short bow of gratitude.

Walking on the road's shoulder past scattered homes, small orchards and open fields, all was silent and tranquil. I fell into a comfortable trance. In a cluster of houses where Gertie and I first stayed with the Americans, Akita dogs barked their balls off at me. I scoffed, knowing there was no bite there.

There wasn't any movement inside the house. Assuming the current teacher occupants were all at work, I didn't knock. I paced out front for a while and considered where all its former residents were now. Gertie, sadly I knew. The Yanks, I hypothesized, were all back in their protective bubbles of small hometowns, TV dinners, and two-car garages.

I walked around back for a final peek at the communal garden, the daylit pachinko parlour next to the byway like a roadside mausoleum, and the rice paper sliding door of my old room, its busted-out squares now repaired. I pondered precisely what it was I thought to discover there, then walked on to the station.

Sat on an old wooden bench of the desolate platform at

Obusuma, I envisaged a long wait for the next train. Assessing that I'd come full circle, I tried to determine what had been revealed. There were the influential figures who'd entered my life along the way: Dallas, Gertie and Akiko, and their fates of jails, institutions, and death. Yet destiny had offered me salvation. It lay before me in a life of freedom and love. Nevertheless, I'd spat in the face of it. Perhaps deep down, I felt undeserving, like the universal scales of justice were all fucked up.

With an approaching rickety train, on that rustic platform, I resolved to accept it all, tossing aside the apparent arbitrary merit. I entered an empty car and sat on the faded beige cloth with the sun to my back.

At Kawagoe, an intimate, magnetic force pulled me through the opening doors and onto the platform.

As the train took off and left me standing there, I pulled a picture from my pocket. The shed-like temple the urn was placed on, I was pretty sure, was in the small park next to Akiko's family apartment. The temple tucked in the back corner, I didn't remember seeing the time of our first hot fuck against an old oak in the chilled night air. Though I'd been preoccupied with more pressing matters that evening.

Undeniably, certain aspects of the urn photo sparked my memory, so I found the bar we went to on our first date and was able to trace my way back to the park. There it was, in the back corner behind a bright yellow-leaved ginkgo tree. A cool wind blew and an empty swing rocked back and forth on its rusty metal frame. A cicada shrieked, but it wasn't the season. The sound must've manifest from within. I walked past the tree, over a carpet of fallen leaves which covered the ground like snips of a maiden's hair. An ivory green urn stood on the temple's top step, looking very much like an empty flowerpot – a simple design on the outside of a cherry blossom tree branch with a few budding flowers and the whole container covered in a glossy finish. I sat and considered the sparsely blossomed branch's symbolic relationship to Akiko's life.

'I'm sorry,' I said, 'I know, I should have treated you better. You were so smart, beautiful and kind.' The words came simple and easy as if we lay naked on the old cum- and sweat-stained futon of my Yorii room.

'Couldn't you see you deserved better than me, than this … If you'd just hung around you would've found it, I'm sure of that,' I said with sombre contrition.

'I don't pretend to know your pain … I never asked … I should've asked! Like, what you were thinking about in those moments of introspection. Was that you sinking deeper into the quicksand, or were you searching for a low-hanging branch by which to pull yourself out? I wish you would've talked to me, someone, anyone … then I could be looking into your beautiful brown eyes, watching you nervously chew the end of your cigarette.' I ran a finger down the smooth curved surface of the urn and added, 'that's how it should be … instead I'm here talking to ash and bone.'

I can't well explain what I did next. It wasn't premeditated but occurred as if I were possessed. Picking up the urn, I carried it behind the small temple and with both hands carefully placed it atop a grey wall six feet above the cornerstone, so she rested at eye level. Shielded from the street, though anyone who lived in one or more of the apartment windows which looked down on that back corner could've observed my act.

I unzipped, pulled my cock out, and staring intently at the urn's exterior, I stroked larghetto. As Akiko's sorrowful brown eyes appeared out of blossom buds on the branch, I peered deep into them, attempting to siphon her pain away. Intensifying, both stroke and stare, her whole winsome face began to form around bistre eyes until it encompassed the urn's exterior.

Fixed on the form, I closed my eyes, and we were whisked away on erotic make-believe to the top of Mt. Fuji. Alone at the summit, I slid off her jeans. The top of the mountain strangely warm, becoming even warmer as I entered her; my cock radiating an unnatural, passionate heat. Her body reacted in ecstatic spasms, while her face remained static as a lifeless mannequin stare.

The masturbatory mountain top fantasy, my eulogy, I guess. The thought being: perhaps if I'd exposed her so bare to the heavens, she'd have chosen to remain here on earth. I knew I was committing all kinds of sacrilege but felt no guilt, as something told me it was exactly what Akiko would have wanted from me.

The climax built rapidly not of pleasure but penance. My requiem concluding with hot cum spewed in a thick milky mucus stream against the grey brick wall, as I released a baritone groan skyward. I leaned forward with my forearm pressed against the brick and let the last drops fall. A final circular glob landed on the dirt below, forming a Hokkaido shaped blotch and completing, in opalescent juices, a bukkake cartography of *Nihon*. *Weird*, I thought, wiping my hands on my jeans. I carefully cradled the urn and returned Akiko to her sleepy step.

An afternoon crowd was headed into Ikebukuro. I travelled, physically drained, and emotionally spent. Stood in a crush of bodies, I began to feel light-headed. My breathing became short and rapid, but no air was getting in. A cold sweat broke out on my brow and vision blurred. At the next stop, I heaved myself through the doors to arrest the panic attack, or whatever it was.

The fresh air immediately remedied me. I inhaled deeply and felt strength return to my wobbly legs. I wasn't up to getting on another train just yet, so I left the station and walked the streets of Shiki.

It was pretty much indistinguishable from all the other communities that spring up around stations on the outskirts of Tokyo. As I plodded along, I realized that though upon first glance they all looked the same, if you got up real close, these communities were as unique as snowflakes; each its own extraordinary collection of individuals with their distinct little dramas, dysfunctional lives and crucial connection of trivial relationships.

I nursed a can of Chu-hi and studied the façades of buildings passed by when a particular house grabbed my attention. Overgrown grass along a gravel drive led to the brown, stucco one-floor building. I was baited by the atmosphere to peer over a dried, chest-high hedge and enter the lot. Immediately, I took notice of the frosted glass front doors painted with fallen red maple leaves in the right corner.

In a hypnotic daze, I entered the building and found myself enclosed in a communal shoe-storage space. The strange vibe grew oppressive as I walked the halls looking aghast at wall paintings of mythical beasts and blue linoleum floors, decorated in a cosmic milieu of Milky Ways and white five-tipped stars.

A tall, heavyset white man with a military-style buzz cut walked down the hall. He had big bags under his eyes and a vacant expression they call in vets 'the thousand-yard stare'.

'Hi, you live here?' I asked, friendly enough, but unable to hide a nervous edge.

'Yes, I do,' he answered with a German accent.

'How long you been here?' I inquired my voice low and rushed.

'Four months now,' he answered cold and dead-eyed.

He seemed so emotionally bloodless, I would've thunk him drugged or lobotomized. However, it might have just been the German.

'How do you like it? You moved here from somewhere else or been here the whole time? Like, how long you been in Japan?' I was really giving him the Spanish inquisition. But with good reason, I sought indictment against the house.

'Umm, I guess it iz okay. Yes, four-month, I have been living in zee Mango House all this time.'

'Wait, this place is called Mango House?'

'Yes, it is the name,' the hefty German confirmed.

'Okay, okay ... What do you do here?' I went on, 'Shouldn't

you be at work on a weekday afternoon?'

'No. Shouldn't you?' He aptly rebutted, showing the first tinge of emotion, which was understandably annoyance.

'So you going out today?' I flipped back to a convivial manner. 'Maybe we can grab a beer, and you can tell me about this place.'

'No, I won't go out today.' His eyes shifted rapidly from ceiling to walls and floor, before adding, 'There are perils beyond the refuge.'

What the fuck does that mean? I thought, and noted the even greater listless manner of his delivery.

'Listen, I'm thinking of renting here. Do you think I could get the number to inquire about availability?'

He shuffled the opposite direction back down the hall without a word. I had no idea if he was coming back but stood waiting anyhow. Observing the hall's decor, I remembered how ghetto-chic the Peach House seemed when I'd first moved in.

He returned and robotically handed me a sheet of paper with a phone number and address. 'I booked here. They have office in Shinjuku.'

Back on the line to Ikebukuro, the address continued to administer little stings like short electric shocks or thumbtack stabs, as it pressed against my thigh from the pocket of my jeans.

I told myself to leave it. All was resolved. I had no need to visit. Yet, when I reached into my denim pocket and held the torn corner, wanting to pull it out and toss it on the floor of the moving carriage, my arm became paralyzed – *by fear or fortune?*

To counteract the temptation, I needed to see Yukie. She wouldn't have to lecture me with words. In fact, I didn't plan to disturb her with the discovery at all. I just knew; if I could find her, sit on my adjacent stool, perhaps rest my hand in hers on a sultry runway of flesh, and look into her eyes, then it would convince me I'd already found all I needed.

Sat finishing off a can on a circular guardrail at the smoking area out front the Seibu Shinjuku exit, I peered down the boulevard of lambent reverie. A stream of cars like the Kuroshio current cut through a sea of people occupying Shinjuku sidewalks on either side of the wide *dori*. High buildings formed borders and stretched down the street, massive walls of a blazing canyon. And I another negligible speck in that Shinjuku sea, another molecule in full flight through the cosmos.

I lit a cigarette in hopes I'd burn more brightly. The first drag hit the back of my throat with a chemical smack. Drink and inhale, drink, inhale, until a comfortable nebula settled around my cranium. Removed from the tributary, I watched them scurry; the office workers and waiters, students and pensioners, the indistinguishable shop girls and bar hostesses, the music makers and the dormant dancers, the forgone and the forgotten, the seeking and the found. Watching this river of humanity pour past, I waited on my smoky shore for that perfect opportunity to jump in, go limp, and let the current carry me away.

Turning my attention to a gazillion molecules of light frolicking in the Shinjuku night, I arched my head way back. If I was sucked a hundred feet up from right where I sat, I could see it all. Kubikocho's sleazy maze and the special glow of a particular love hotel, the aberrant nationalist nightclub of Tatsuya and Machiko, the Beatles themed McDonald's where Yukie and I smoked, laughed, fought, reconciled and grew close. And yeah, the fuckin' Seibu platform that stole Akiko from this world. All of it overseen from the vantage point of the dark void's destination, where I'd floated in the Okinawan dreamscape ... suspended in the sky, holding the frayed end of red yarn.

The overactive voice in my head was silent momentarily, then whispered, 'drop it.'

Pinched fingers in my mind's eye relaxed, small fibres brushed the tips, running down ridged prints. Except then, looking to the fourth-floor window of McDonald's, I saw Yukie. It was a fair distance from where I sat, but I could definitely see a figure in Yukie's usual spot. Behind the window pane, with long flowing hair, she brought a cigarette to her lips. I would have been overjoyed to see her there, was it not for the man approaching in a confident saunter from behind.

He wore a shimmery black suit with the heavily moussed, extravagantly coiffed hair of a Shinjuku host. The woman got up, and they embraced. That cleaved me hard in the sternum. I squinted in disbelief but couldn't make out the facial features, especially the eyes. *I need to look in her eyes and reveal the truth.*

Keeping my sight fixed on that fourth-floor window, I moved quickly across the paved courtyard, over the zebra crossing and along a sidewalk blasted by pachinko machine screams. I lost view of the window on the other side of the intersection but was rapidly approaching the entrance to the McDonald's where short lines formed at three tills.

I passed right by the orderly waiting crowd and bounded up the four flights of stairs. Peering over the restaurant's seating, my sight landed on two empty stools. I surveyed the floor and took a frantic walk around the interior, then ran down a level, stood at the entrance and sent darting looks in all directions. Running down the staircase once more, I neared the bottom flight and spotted the backs of a young Japanese couple.

'Yukie!' I called out hoarse and breathless. The woman did a half turn in reaction to the shout, revealing just the outer edge of her profile. The hair and build were similar, but in this teeming metropolis, I really couldn't narrow down the odds. *If I'd only seen the eyes.*

I started to chase, but stumbled in my stupor and barely caught the railing. By the time I'd rushed out onto the street, they'd already disappeared into the Shinjuku evening crowd. I studied faces flooded in fluorescent light as they approached and departed. None of them was Yukie's.

I tramped back up to the fourth floor, mulling the figures over. The area was empty but for a lone salaryman reading the paper and smoking. I looked to the uncleared ashtrays on top a trash can. Of the four deposited there, I zeroed in on the one containing two stubbed out Seven Stars, half-smoked with lipstick stained filters.

It made sense. She had cautioned before her intention to pull herself out of my dysfunctional orbit. The translation of Akiko's diary may have been just the evidence needed. If she aimed to break free of me then latching on to that cheap-suited, gelled-hair, low-level Yak-looking mother fucker had done just that.

I tried to feel comforted that I was back on my own flying solo once more. 'It's less complicated this way,' I muttered to myself in a restless tromp.

'Ya got yourself some girl troubles, stud?' came a familiar husky voice.

'What ya fuckin ... ?' I returned fire bitter and blind, then looked up to see the heavily painted face of an Okubo ladyboy.

'Just saying,' she said, 'you look a bit out of sorts. Could only mean one thing – woman problems. Don't worry, you won't be having those with me, honey.' She let go a low laugh.

Turns out, I'd walked myself all the way to the side streets of Okubo in my resentful stupor and found myself in front of The Dodgiest Little Love Hotel in all of Tokyo. 'Yeah, I'm a bit preoccupied,' I said, 'just life and shit.'

'I got something that'll take your mind off these troubles,' she purred with an exaggerated wink and puckered kissy lips.

'Oh yeah,' I replied dismissively.

'Oooooh yeah, big boy, better believe,' she said, her flirtation becoming comically exaggerated. 'Yours in my mouth, or mine up your ass!' A shriek of glee filled the alley as she stomped her size ten heels up and down on the cement.

'Fuckin hell!' I exclaimed, not easily shocked, but roused to blush and reluctantly crack a smirk with that little gem.

She playfully slapped my chest with the back of her, dead giveaway, massive mitt and red-painted nails. I wasn't offended by the graphic advance, nor was I intrigued. But I was genuinely touched. That this shemale streetwalker would, to no personal gain, take a moment to cheer me – a kind of dickish and at that moment, miserable foreigner – was a remarkable moment of unadulterated brotherly love.

'Tempting offer,' I began, finally finding my composure, 'but tonight, I'll have to pass ... and pass.' Meanwhile, I slipped the filter end of a cigarette out of the pack and was offering it to my old buddy.

'Well at least I get to put something of yours between these lips,' she said, teasing an air of rejection.

I reached out with my lighter and ignited her smoke. 'Bit early?' I noted of her pounding the sidewalk in the post afterglow. 'Where's the rest of your crew?' I asked gesturing with my cigarette to the Y chromosomeless stretch beyond her post.

'Early bird catches the worm,' she said, 'and worms, are exactly what most these Johns are packing.' She held up and wiggled her pinkie while flashing me a mischievous smile.

As much as I was enjoying her bawdy humour, it was getting a little too comfortable there. I missed stewing in my private sento of anger and stale self-pity and worried if I lingered any longer, it would go cold. I stubbed my smoke on the brick planter attached to the love hotel and threw the butt under a shrub.

'Hey, thanks for taking my mind off shit for a second there,' I said with a timid, appreciative smile and slow nod.

'Hey honey, we all on the same trip here,' she said sans off-colour humour. 'You know, dear,' and the forced lilt suddenly dropped from her voice as he added finally in a relaxed baritone, 'only you choose if you're lost or not.'

Cosmic Pachinko

Part Four
Molotovs of the Mind

... There is the heat of Love, the pulsing rush of Longing,
the lover's whisper, irresistible—
magic to make the sanest man go mad.
—Homer, The Iliad

This will be my last entry. A sense of dread hangs heavy over the cubicle. I fear I did something unhinged and irreversible.

Just now, after running to the bathroom sink to vomit, I inspected myself in the mirror. My face looks like it did ten rounds with Tyson. I have a black eye and split lip, a golfball-sized lump has formed on my forehead right below the hairline. And its twin can be felt on the back of my head, when I rub it, maroon flakes of dry crusted blood powder my fingertips.

It hurts to breathe, *cracked a rib maybe*. According to the time stamp on the computer screen, it's the middle of the afternoon. To the best of my recollection, it has been three days since I last sat here. I've blacked out hundreds of nights, but as far as I remember (or don't), I've never before lost three whole days and nights.

I'm fighting to call to mind any events which transpired during those dark days but am irritated by light typing and war sound effects escaping from the consoles of these fucking gamers who infiltrate the café each afternoon. Muffled gunshots and soft explosions from whatever war fantasy they're engaged in, echo and reverberate through my fragile mind, fry my last good nerve and cause me to flinch repeatedly.

A crucified bottle of Nikka Black holds my saviour in a thin golden crown – millimetre dregs shining through the glass. I reach for it with a shaky hand. *A nasty case of the Joe Blakes*, as they say in Cockney slang.

Cockney slang!

... Kai ... the cat ...

Kai was the cat. That's it! The spark which ignited this epic bender. It was Kai, Jae-hyun and that fucking mangy tom.

I'd left the ladyboy and continued to brood, less so but still, as

I trudged back here before the witching hour.

I sat with drinks and wrote. *But what?*

To Yukie. Yes, I wrote her an email. *Shit! What did I say …*

Dear Yukie,

I went to see you tonight at our Mac's. I'd had a bit of an epiphany, as I rode the train home from what I decided was to be my final self-searching excursion. I'd chosen to stay. Get off at your stop and set up shop!

As a gesture of my intentions, I stopped at Don Quijote. I bought a cheap collar shirt and tie and threw them on. It was kinda meant as a joke. But yeah, I hoped you'd get the meaning.

The little get-up, barely intact, is draped in tatters over my bruised and battered body. The white shirt is open to my navel, with all but two buttons ripped off. The exposed curly black hairs of my chest barely conceal scratches long and deep which run the length. An uncomfortable bulge I've been sitting on, reveals itself to be a bunched up, striped necktie. I pull it out and toss in the corner of the cubicle, feeling the hollow gesture meaningless all of a sudden.

I fish into the breast pocket of the white shirt. It's been ripped from the seam at the corner but still holds a soft pack of Marlboros with two burrowed, bent cigarettes tucked inside. I coax one out and light it, before reading on.

But when the doors opened, and I stepped over the gap onto your platform, I looked into a distant window and saw the fantasy *Ku* constructed around your metaphorical stop reduced to rubble by seismic shocks in the form of that young host.

It doesn't really matter … I just hope he treats you right.

I guess what I want to say is, I don't blame you. I should've

known what a good thing I had. You were kind enough
to not let me pass it by, but then still I hesitated ... and I
must've missed my stop. So, I'm back on the train and then
a rainy sidewalk, free to wander, roam and stumble, alone.
Which I guess, is where I'm supposed to be.

I wish you no ill will, no heartache or scorn; only happiness.
I don't know if this will make much sense, but in a way, it
says it all ... I'm sorry I lost you but glad that you're gone.

Fred

I wish I could say it was still in draft mode.

* * *

It was shortly after this gaff – a lack of restraint with pen and send
– when I heard them.

Thing is, I'd never heard Kai and Jae-hyun in any form of
conversation at the café. As far as I was concerned, Kai didn't
converse. Perhaps it was the first time, or maybe they'd done it often
and that evening assumed I was out.

They began in hushed tones; however, it was the dynamic which
really caught me off guard. Kai spoke copiously rather than in his
usual simple enunciations, and Jae-hyun gave short obsequious
answers. They were speaking in Japanese, but it sure sounded like
Kai was reprimanding Jae-hyun in a rigid, measured timbre.

I snuck under my cubicle curtain, as Jae-hyun attempted to
mount a defence and Kai's voice rose to neutralize it. By the time
I'd crept over to Kai's stall, the conference was downright heated.

Sneaking forward, I began to hear it, '... blah, blah, Fred. Blah,
blah, Baka!' My name kept popping up in a string of indistinguishable
chatter, like tripping on shrooms in a crowded theatre. Though in
this case, I was just tripping on the whole weird scene, and I knew
they were talking about me.

No stealthy tiptoe this time around, I took a different approach, threw the curtain open and barged in.

'Fred ...' Jae-hyun's head swung, his expression written with concern and punctuated by panic.

'Wha tha fuck's going on here ...' I spurted, shocked senseless taking in the array of stimuli displayed on the computer screen and partition walls behind the two men.

It was me! My face superimposed in the centre of the screen while a black background filled top to bottom with a complex algorithm scrolled, each new line written with more incoherent code. The walls held the real mindfuck. The web of images I'd observed before, registered this time like a sumo smack between the eyes. My life, my journey, posted and connected by a red yarn on Kai's cubicle walls. From the FamilyMart stoop to the ferry, the evaporated guesthouse to Permanent Dawn and too many other flashes of familiar faces and scenes to take in during the brief sweeping glance I was permitted before Kai lashed out.

'Ye, fuckin' cunt,' he said, levelling me with a steely-eyed stare. 'A Scarborough warning on t' bonny snoopin' arse. Have ye skeg, 'n chuff off mate.'

Well, that's a fucking shift, I thought, rooted to the spot. Fear and confusion turned my shoulders to the open curtain, a double shot of anger kicked in, and I stormed across the internet café.

'Fred!' Jae-hyun called out, pushing through the exit door, into the narrow road. 'Fred, wait! Hold up!' Rubber soles beat the pavement, following me down the street.

'What the fuck,' I swung around like a fastball strike, 'was that shit in there?'

'Listen, it's hard to explain.' A streetlamp shone a spotlight on Jae-hyun from above, and the row of vending machines discharged a dissolving aqua gleam over half his body. 'I'm not even supposed to ...'

'Well, fuck you then, don't!' I started to storm off again but Jae-hyun grabbed my upper arm with his functional grip and spun me. He had the ground in strength you find in middle-aged men, and I was facing him again wearing a scowl of betrayal.

'I'm sorry. I told you as much as I could. I left out either what I didn't know then or couldn't reveal.' His voice was calm, though his words came rapid-fire, fearing I'd take off again and maybe this time put up more of a struggle. 'But, yes, you are Kai's subject.' He looked me in the eye, as the news dropped like a feather from Tokyo Tower and finally landed with a thud.

My eyes widened and I attempted articulation. All that came out was a breathy expel as if punched in the gut.

'When I figured it out or confirmed a supposition, well, yes, I asked to help. I needed to learn ... to participate. It's like ... my reparation.'

He hadn't said much, though his words and revelations bounced around in my head and collided like heated molecules. Then, I reacted. 'So I'm the pawn? Or in your case, just another ball-bearing to steer and manipulate. And for what? Your amusement?'

'It's not like that,' Jae-hyun said, more hurt than sorry. 'Kai's kind have no agenda, not with individuals the likes of you,' he explained back in his pedantic groove. 'But they are tasked with the preservation of a grander scheme.'

He paused, folding in his thick eyebrows, considering how best to explain what he, himself, didn't yet fully comprehend. 'And you were thrown into the mix somewhere, somehow ... Now, I imagine, you have a role to play ... a purpose in Kai's overall plan.' Jae-hyun reached out to rest a hand on my shoulder, but I pulled away. His arm fell back to his side. 'You need to trust me on this Fred; we're on your side, we're working to help you.'

'Well, you're doing a pretty shit job!' I lashed out. 'Why me anyways? And why the fuck are you involved? I thought you were my friend, Jae-hyun.' Neither of us were the sentimental type, but it would seem the emotion of anger had left the door open and other feelings were sneaking through.

'I don't know. Maybe you required an intervention. Like if there's a disruption in the natural lineage, that's when Kai or one like him gets called in – to fix the flow.' He nodded to himself, satisfied with this summation.

'Untangle ...' I mumbled my disgruntled contribution. Jae-hyun raised an eyebrow but I was unwilling to elaborate.

'The argument,' he said, looking at me straight, 'well, this was Kai telling me I was too close to you ... "the subject". I needed to distance myself and work the board from afar.'

Kai's analogy did not sit well with me. I spat in anger, saliva landing at the base of an adjacent beer vending machine.

'So it's a big fuckin' game to you then?' My voice raised and quavered. I clenched a tight fist tempted to strike but was hindered by natural cowardice. I struck out verbally instead. 'You couldn't wait to get in there and fuck up my life, eh?'

'When you arrived, I suspected you were the new subject,' he began, not penetrated in the least by my petulance. In fact, more resolved to justify his role. 'I understood this because I was once Kai's subject.'

'You?'

'Yes, me. And like you, I had no idea why or how. Perhaps, it was the propaganda I was subjected to under Kim or going to war with the pachinko mafia? For whatever reason, I ended up here; confused and searching, like yourself.'

He paused, pursed his lips and perused the path which brought him there. The familiar row of lit vending machines throwing a dull reflection off his dark, flat features while all was speculative and serious in the quiet alley's illumination.

'So I waited,' Jae-hyun revived from his rumination, 'then I came to understand more about it all and finally accept. As it ... as it was always meant to be.' He paused and looked at me with an imploring look – not for forgiveness, that was clear, but maybe, of my own understanding and acceptance.

Though, I couldn't accept, nor understand. 'You're both a couple of fucking loonies.'

'If that's where you're arriving at, so be it, Fred,' he said in an easy air. 'I never meant you any harm. I've waited a long time for my answer to come. Well, it finally did, and happens to be you ... Kai's new subject. That's what I'd been waiting on. Cause I only get to keep what I've been given, by giving it away ... working with the likes of you.'

'But you got shit-all. I mean, look at your life, Jae Hyun.' I'd meant for it to be biting, though not to sink my teeth in so deep; as my eyes flashed from the internet café home to his tattered cardigan, then travelled toward the crippled hand dangling dispossessed of function by his side.

'I've no qualms with where I'm at.' Jae-hyun punctuated the proclamation by pointing two rheumatic fingers down our sleepy side street. 'I've been through the penthouse and left as empty as ever. Here I've gotten something I never owned and couldn't buy. I got peace of mind.'

'Well, you've done a shit job of giving it to me,' I said, a self-pitying snigger added for effect.

'It's not something one can just hand you. Never was and never will be,' he explained, with a dismissive shrug of my complaints. 'As far as Kai or me manipulating you, we just showed you the steps. You took them of your own free will and desires. True, the journey was mapped, but you travelled it, Fred.'

Streetlamps reflected off smooth pavement, the dull glow like a smuggler's runway. My head throbbed in a high-strung trance beat, and all I wanted was to sprint down the alley, take flight and soar away. But my legs were paralyzed. I remained frozen, rendered powerless by an oppressive anxiety until the next question percolated through my confusion. 'Why here?'

'There is always someone behind the curtain feeding us

direction.' Jae-hyun spoke with an eerie authority, his voice landing on my consciousness as a sonic boom. 'Most never see it or take the time to look. They never imagine it's any other way, because they don't have to.' He scanned the street for any roving ears, lowered his voice and went on. 'Though some people – like you, Fred – need to be shown they're not in charge. Only then, can they turn it over and live free. That's my guess as to why you've been brought here.'

When he finished, I was abandoned in a silence as deep and empty as a dry well. His words offered sustenance for a wayward soul, yet I was unable to reach the rays from those depths I dwelled in. All I could grasp was the murky bottom, and sling mud. 'There's been no working with me, just a working on me ... and a fucking with my life.' Having felt the sting of betrayal, rational or not, high on resentment, I vented on. 'Hey, I've been waiting for an answer,' I said, attempting a scornful impersonation. 'Guess what? My answer just came in ... it's FUCK OFF!'

That should have been my dramatic exit. I guess Jae-hyun thought so too. As I turned to leave, he made no effort to stop me.

I took two steps, but something was still eating at me. 'And that fucker Kai ... spoke English this whole goddamn time? What, he'd been saving that? Until it would really fuck with my head?'

Jae-hyun almost broke a smile, but he must've sensed I was in no mood to see that. 'He doesn't, not really, what you heard was only mimicry. A hard, little Yorkshireman was once his assignment. He can probably rifle off some North Korean tough talk as well.'

'Whatever,' I said, careful to hide any appreciation for the explanation. 'And don't think for a Tokyo second that like you, I'm gonna end up being Kai's little bitch.' I felt it essential to end on a confrontational note.

'No one's expecting you to,' Jae-hyun offered before his concerned tone hardened into a final staunch declaration. 'You'll end up where you'll end up.'

I walked briskly toward the FamilyMart, chewing on Jae-hyun's words like bitter pink ginger. Nightmares, visions and *natsukashii* woven together and sewn through life's fading fabric. I swallowed hard that final conclusion while the invisible garment thrust upon me prickled mercilessly.

Betrayed, abandoned, manipulated; I was at my end. Unlike Akiko, the thought of leaping from the platform into an oncoming train never crossed my mind. No, I sought drink and revenge; on the city, the world, and life itself.

***

Headphones on, The Pogues play in homage to me mate Gertie and empty bottles of whisky. I turn over my forearm to read more carefully the writing I'd noticed scrawled on the pale underside. The ink has bled and letters smudged, but the black marker words can still be read. They say, '*Son of man, you live in the midst of the rebellious house, who have eyes to see but do not see, ears to hear but do not hear; for they are a rebellious house.*'

I'm no biblical scholar, in fact I've never even read it, but this definitely sounds like some Old Testament shit.

A quick type into google confirms the verse from Ezekiel 12:2. Knowing this tells me little. The more significant questions of why and when, if I wrote it or it was written on me, what it meant or means and where the hell I came across it in the first place are all still a mystery.

Closing my eyes, I see myself – the sole customer in a dimly lit bar. I'm either the first to arrive or last to leave. A single beer comes into focus through blurred vision. It sits half full and headless, surrounded by numerous overlapping residue rings on a dark oak counter. I lift chin from chest and in slurred speech ask the bartender for a pen. He hands me a black jiffy marker. I roll up the white shirt sleeve and scroll something on my arm, zombielike.

My pulse races. To steady my hand, I grip the mouse until the plastic creaks as I search my mind for more clues. I check, again, my emails. The first offers me part-time work at a local language school. Good news, though I fear it won't matter much now. Next is a response from Yukie.

How had I missed it, I'm thinking, head heavy and slowly spinning.

Ohayo Fred,

I just saw your message. I'm a little confused and worried. I don't know who you think you saw with a host, but it's not me. You may not have noticed this; you have a habit of imagining things to suit your own contrived narrative. Like self-sabotage for anything good that gets in your way. The shirt and tie is a sweet gesture, I wish I could have seen :) Please don't think you missed me in some fabricated window, and don't try to convince me I'm better off without you, it's not true. But maybe the problem is you've always viewed us through a pane of glass, or in some distorted reflection thrown back, only now you see the cracks, that were there all along ...

If you want to see me again, you know where to find me ...

Fred, don't let your illusions get the best of you.

Love Yukie

Love. I flinch at the word.

Well, to write and to voice are objects of much different weight. Nonetheless, I've shied away from both. And reclined here in my black leather chair, her words ring like a standing eight count through my ears.

After reading, the memory persists of seeing Yukie through the fourth-floor glass, but upon reflection, there's no way I could be sure it was her. *What then had swayed me so convincingly to just toss us away?* Unless she was right, I'd been looking for an excuse to cut and run. When I couldn't grasp any concretely ... *had I simply invented one?*

After the windowed forgery, a short exchange with my ladyboy pal and the confounding incident with Kai, I took to the streets shitfaced, maudlin and raving. From there I'll have to piece together the nicotine-stained snippets of events, half-remembered and half-constructed.

Observing lit city streets through a veil of anger, confusion and fear, I trudged the Shinjuku concrete like a cocked gun. In the circular park at Shinjuku's East Exit I found myself, as the night's party-goers stumbled to snatch the first Yamanote line train rolling through the predawn.

'Hey, it's party time ... come 'n tha night ish young.' I slurred out ill-timed, jovial greetings. 'Com' ere and let's have a drink ... Yeah?' Passing by my sorry sight, men clutched their dates to their sides, single women twitched polite wary smiles or wisely ignored the drunken foreigner and one young *gaijin* gave it to me straight, 'go home, mate'.

Across a carless street and above the empty entrance of Studio Alta was the giant, black screen. Silent now, it struck me as ominous and Orwellian. 'All transmission to tha masses have subsided, yer free to think freely.' I screamed blindly into the coming day whilst pitching to and fro on a drunken concrete sea. The incomprehensible maniac quite rightly steered clear of by all.

My lunacy ebbed and I simply swayed, strung-out, looking through the somnolent screen. I blinked thrice, there behind the vast black Alta monitor mingled a collective of silhouettes; lean, squat, feline and feminal. They milled about as if occupying a control tower, staring out at the populace below, pulling strings and plotting their next move. I thought back to Kai's cubicle and all the shit on the walls. *A chessmaster you say, eh?* I mumble incoherently to the concrete. *Then, He must be playing someone ... something ... some force or foe like him?* The thought sobered me momentarily with a shudder. When I looked back, the shadows were gone, but the watchful black pupil remained.

The first green-grey train crawled into Shinjuku station from the west, and just like that the cogs of this great city began to turn. Seated on the tiled steps of the small pedestrian island, in the gutter looking down, I drank in tepid superiority as more and more sheep streamed out of the station. I started to recognize the other homeless drunks amongst the congregation; we were solitary, stationary anomalies, and eyed each other suspiciously over a rushing stream of black-suited, briefcased salarymen.

Well after the morning rush, I finally stood with a heap of cigarette butts at my feet and moved on to the nearest convenience store to procure more supplies to fortify and fuel the coming madness.

***

Fishing through the pockets of my filthy jeans, I retrieve a handful of change – lazy drunks being fond of breaking bills. The coins are mixed with pocket lint, broken cigarette butts, and bits of dried tobacco leaf. A crumpled piece of paper stands out. I unwrap it and with logistics out of the way stare at the address in forced, fractured recall.

The Peach House, its dizygotic twin the Mango guesthouse, and the blitzed out German come flooding back from recent memory. Then there was the firm resolution to let it be, yet for that to take hold, I would've had to have seen Yukie. But then, I peered through a distant window, adjusted the corny clip-on, and promptly whisked away all the little fantastical hopes and dreams cultivated trekking back from the end of the line.

Shortly after I passed Ringo on the Abbey Road intersection in the McDonald's lobby, I pulled the address out of my pocket and read carefully. *Fuck letting it be, I want answers*, I concluded.

Slipping the piece of paper back into my jeans, whispered words of wisdom melted like hot wax; Mother Mary's mask splattering the pavement behind me in blood-red dots.

The pieces are falling into place, not where I want them to but where they belong. I can see myself before the office entrance baffled and apprehensive, yet somehow vindicated. Because, you see, it was one floor above Machiko and Tatsuya's bar with its shitty EDM and sadistic nationalist clientele.

I triple checked, and the office was on the second floor of the same slim eight-storey. I didn't go directly in but needed a couple of walks around the block, drinking and smoking, to muster my courage and hash a flimsy plan to confront what or who I might find.

In the early eve, for fear it might close, I finally went up. The hall was dead quiet. I clenched the address and walked down three doors until I was before a crudely painted red door with the number 14 written in faded gold lettering. My stomach churned as I gave a slow turn of the knob and pushed the office door open with a cautious hand.

Two persons dressed all in black sat side by side at desks. They had outdated IBM computers and stacks of paper on each. Other than their casual dress of black jeans and black hoodies, it looked like any other small Shinjuku office. I was greeted by blank stares and two slight sneers.

'Hi, sorry, I've been looking for this office. I saw your guesthouse in Shiki the other day,' I launched into the prepared performance. 'I've been looking for a place to stay, and it seems perfect.'

They eyed me with suspicion like they recognized me from someplace before. *The club, the Peach House?* I conjectured. *Gotta play it cool.*

'It full,' they replied in unison.

I knew they had lied and pressed on, 'In Shiki? I was just there inside ...'

'You were in Shiki guesthouse?' The male asked, shifting his posture, sitting upright and attentive behind the desk.

'Yeah, I saw the place from over the hedge and thought, wow that place looks cool. So I went inside and with all the crazy paintings and funky decor,' I babbled on feigning a loose attitude. 'I thought this fucking place is like really hip and avant-garde, I gotta get a room here. Gotta say, looked like there was lots of free space.'

It might have been because I was speaking to them so freely and informally or that I was sort of jumping around and flailing limbs as I spoke; but, throughout my spiel, I noticed them exchange uncomfortable looks. Which was as I'd expected and just as I'd planned. Expelling my boozy, tobacco tinged bouquet while I metaphorically prodded their nutsacks was like a clumsy tribute to Matsumura lore.

'We don't rent to foreigners,' they lied again.

'It's a *gaijin* house, of course you do,' I said with a fake chuckle. 'It's kinda your whole business model. Besides, I met the German. You know ... he acted kinda freaked out, like he was on drugs or otherwise altered.' I then lobbed them a leery glance.

'New management rule,' said the woman after an awkward pause, 'too many problems with foreigners.'

My comment about meeting the German had clearly perturbed them. The male stood and asked me quite plainly, 'Now, please leave.'

I threw up my arms in feigned exasperation and exited.

While I had been standing inside the office, performing my little ignorant *gaijin* act, I'd been casing the joint and noted a door between and behind the two desks. I guessed it led to another office. I sensed that after my exit they would then retreat to the backroom, and intuited whatever was behind that second door, I needed to see.

After two minutes of waiting down the hall, I cracked the main door mere millimetres and peeked in. The two desks were empty. I crept through the front office and, without warning, threw open the back office door.

A single desk lay in the back corner with four figures huddled around; two sitting and two standing. Familiar clutter was strewn all around the office floor and propped against the walls; *Kappa* and other strange creatures painted on wood framed five-foot boards. Electric circuitry ran throughout the boarded backs of these paintings. Amongst all the wires and paintings were two or three projector type contraptions with lenses pointed out in all directions and cylindrical reels of super 8 film stacked in leaning towers from the floor.

The two employees spoken to in the front office startled and looked up from the desk they stood over, engaged in warning discussion. Behind the desk was an older, gothic-looking couple: Tatsuya and Machiko.

Tatsuya leaned back in his office chair, calm and composed. As before, he handled the English conversation and addressed me. 'Well, well … look what the cat dragged in.'

'Yes, indeed,' I responded, sensing an odd, fuzzy connection to the common idiom.

'I'm not sure what you are still doing here,' he continued. 'Like a mosquito in the dark, you invade the ear canal and disturb all opportunity for slumber. But, seeing as how unrelentingly you refuse to be vanquished, an anomaly to our methods or perhaps just lucky, I'll give you one more chance.' He interlaced his fingers and wore a confident, off-putting smirk. 'Rather than hunt down and squash you with a firm hand, we'll leave a window open … meaning, you vacate this office, and never set foot in our houses, offices or clubs ever again … in other words, you disappear. Just fly into the night and be gone.'

His little diatribe-cum-ultimatum made little sense to me at the time. I made out the threat with an uncomfortable familiarity implied but was unable to piece it all together as I stood frozen by the door. I searched for what recourse I had but came up with none.

So, I reverted to a territorial battle over that small patch of office and said, 'Fuck you! I'm not going anywhere you bitter, burnout, hippy mother fucker.'

'Get him out, he's done!' shouted Tatsuya to his minions. The young female and wiry young man advanced.

Drunk and in pretty shit physical shape as it was, I relied on adrenaline and threw a wild punch, catching the man on the forehead but without enough power to knock him out or even stifle his advance. A kendo stick was swung, catching me behind the knees.

Next thing I knew, my body was crumpled at the bottom of a flight of stairs.

It's a bit blurry, what happened next. After coming to in the stairwell, I'm pretty sure I struggled to my feet and went back.

Yes. I sat upright, grabbed the railing behind my head, and pulled myself to my feet. In my inebriated state, I felt no pain. The bannister held hard for support, I climbed the stairs once more. The red door was locked. I kicked and pounded it. The iron reverberated with dull clangs as I hammered its exterior, shouting insults and slurs.

Worn out from the tantrum; I bent, opened, and peeked through a mail slot. No one stirred within, and all lights were out. I wondered how long I'd been knocked out.

Stood on the sidewalk in front of darkened stairs leading down to the fascist club, I must've decided against trying to go in since I can't recall another ass-kicking.

I conclude this is where I received my beating and it well explains the state of me. However, digging a little deeper into memory, I'm inclined to think this was only the beginning.

***

I light a smoke and pursue another drink from the empty whisky bottle yet get only a single drop and fumes. Attempting to trace my thinking, I inhale deep with a mule's kick.

The fact that Tatsuya and Machiko were owners of our *gaijin* house all along, I couldn't fully grasp what it meant as I walked away, past Don Quijote and its crack-addled penguin (holding his shit together that evening better than some). *If it were mind control experiments carried out in the Big Peach Gaijin House, then they must be doing the same at the Mango house. The brainwashed German? Drugs, a doctrine ... evidence of some psychological torture scheme discovered in the deceased employee's room ... was that what led to the cult investigation and the Manky Peach getting swallowed whole?*

More questions that swirled in the aftermath of the confrontation, filter from memory and bombard me through the stale air and swirling smoke of my cubicle. Why waste time on us lowly teachers, engineers or recruiters? Weren't we an odd and paltry target for such a scheme? Were they testing their methods on us? Honing them?

Who then? Probably, who it'd always been; who it began with and who it remains. Could it be that the larger target is the US military?

Then what? An ability to infiltrate base barracks? Employ similar models on the soldiers there? The end game, I can only guess, is by penetrating the psyche, cracking and polluting it, the soldiers are driven to destroy themselves, or simply go insane.

Was that Gertie? Dallas?

... is it me?

Fondling the fringe of Kabukicho in a stomping retreat, I inspected what recourse I had. *Could I report them? Would anyone listen to me?*

With Machiko and Tatsuya's office interior fresh in mind, my thoughts strayed down dangerous avenues and wreaked havoc along the way. My feet followed physically as an enigmatic magnetic force drew me deeper toward the effulgent filament of Shinjuku's Red Light.

Engaged in a state of frenzied drinking, I nurtured perverse notions of vigilante justice whilst my head furiously swam, then drowned.

I patched it together madly, and everyone became suspect. Hideki sent to drive me back with his talk of mask, bullfight bills and the cult leader names. Even Yukie, planted on the fourth floor MacDonald's, knowing I'd be drawn to her, ravenous, like a *yokozuna* to the buffet. *Hadn't she found the address of the cult's hostile club and brought the Big Peach Guesthouse article to my attention? The whole translation a fabrication ... They weren't successful in destroying me at the Peach House, so they sent Yukie, a covert soldier, to draw me back into their web of influence and finish the job.*

I can see how insane this thinking is now, sitting here half sober and a couple of days removed from the frenetic flicker of those neon notions. *But could I at the time?* I'm sure I couldn't.

Another deep drag, fingers poised on concave keys; reluctantly, I follow that night's thought pattern deeper and deeper, down the spiral.

I see myself in evening fallen, pacing madly in front of a convenience store shaking my head in a slow metronome to clear away the accumulating speculation, piling high like a blizzard snowbank. I puff furiously on a cigarette and take rapid hauls off a tall-can Chu-hi under an illuminating FamilyMart awning, pelted by conjectures driving me further down an esoteric rabbit hole.

Not a cult, not a plot, not Yukie ... None of it, none of them ... ever existed at all. I paced, inhaled and drank.

It was always Yukie and a host at Mac's. Then there's me; sitting back from the window with a whisky and Coke, smoking – secluded, silent and enviously observing ... Dallas, only a hip-hop verse heard from a cracked door ... Gertie, no more than the cover

of a classic novel, observed on a stranger's seat of a limousine bus
... The Peach House, its office and the club just some black van of
a right-wing political party barking its manifesto outside Shinjuku
East Exit while I pass through into the lambent labyrinth.

Perchance, I'd been travelling solo from the very beginning.
These compatriots and companions only fanciful constructs, like
a child stuck at the bottom of a well or man adrift and lost at sea
creates in their solitude and dwindling sanity.

All of them, merely buds, fed by chemical sunshine, bore false
fruit off the branches of a poisonous tree. Quenched by liquid derived
of the fallen fruit, fermented and distilled into strong spirits – simple
strays; old men on park benches and bar hostesses, morphed into
signposts, symbols and sages. Figments hatched, taken to flight then
soaring; weary of the journey and lost, they have come home to
roost.

*And what of me? Was I corporeal ... did I truly exist in this
place?*

That little mindfuck prompted me to storm the Shinjuku streets,
can in hand, seeking proof. Proof, I was not just another photon
floating in the neon night; I had self-determination. I had agency. I
had form.

Somewhere along the way I deduced that the best way to prove
my physical manifestation of self, of my existence in this world;
was through experiencing pain – real, physical pain. Through the
night, led by a cigarette's glowing orange ember and froth of a fresh
cracked can creating a wake of dissipation behind, I embarked on a
night of masochistic illustrations.

A *yakuza*-run hostess bar was my first stop. I burst in and
lurched toward one of the sofas, where I flopped ass to back. A
short, broad-shouldered man, built like a bull terrier wearing a
three-piece suit was on me promptly.

'You can't drink here. Japanese only,' he stated with gruff
authority. What stood out, because it didn't, was a wide flat nose

that spread across his face, a little like it had been punched so many times it now sat there two-dimensionally.

'Get fucked! I'm staying,' I replied to the flat-faced bouncer.

He obviously was in no mood for debate. I was wordlessly hauled up in his powerful grip and punched hard in the gut, knocking the wind out of me. Incapacitated, I was summarily dragged to the door and tossed onto the street where, on all fours, I drooled over concrete in anticipation of a rising vomit.

I lift my shirt to check out a large bruise to the right of my belly button, so yeah, the story checks out.

Provoked by the Yukie illusion and a simmering resentment reaching boil, I jumped an unsuspecting host and battered his shimmery blazer with dull blows. Others in the gaggle pulled me off and delivered pointy-toed kicks with their polished knock-off designer shoes. They sauntered on, laughing off the recent chaos while the assaulted host fixed his coif and brushed any residue of the deranged *gaijin* from his suit.

Next, I was confronted amicably by a tall Nigerian the next block over. 'Yo my brotha, how you doin' tonight?' he approached.

'I'm fuckin' great. Having an awesome night, my brotha,' I responded in mock enthusiasm, taking the piss whilst playing along.

He didn't catch on and figured he had a live one as drunk as I was. 'You comin check out my club, bro. We gotta the most sexy girls, big titties, nice pussies, they waitin' fo you bro. You come up 'n have a drink!'

I knew the con. I'd fallen for it clean once before. I'd go up and be knocked out halfway through the first drink. An hour or so later when the roofie wore off, I'd wake up with a couple of, yeah, big tittied – but also massively thighed and beer-gunted hogs snuggled up to me on a cheap sofa, an open bottle of Cristal in front us. They then slap me with the bill, which would be in the ballpark of a cool grand.

I played the dupe. 'Sounds great, you lead the way, friend!'

An hour later, I woke up groggy with fat foreign chicks of undisclosed origins on both sides. The recently placed bottle of Cristal was open in view, though I only tasted stale beer in my mouth. I was told my time had expired, that I got too drunk and should leave. Then I was handed an eighty-thousand-yen bill. I just laughed and handed it back. The Nigerians didn't see the humour.

'Wat so funny Motha Fuker?' The friendly demeanour used to lure me in had abruptly disappeared.

'Well, you forgot to include the pill you drugged me with, you fuckin crooks,' I said, emerging from the induced fog armed with righteous indignation and an overall instability. 'And I ain't paying a fuckin dime to sit and drink with those fat whores in your shitty fucking bar.'

A long argument ensued. They were confused at how ineffectual the intimidation of two large black men was in my case. My apparent lack of self-preservation and the way I maniacally laughed off their threats of physical reprisal, finally wore them down and broke their resolve.

At an apparent impasse, 'Yo, dis white boy crazy,' one of them remarked. When they finally realized that there was no way of getting blood from a stone, they hucked that stone down the stairs.

I repeated these types of escapades throughout the night, but after a while, I was too beat up for anyone to even let me in the door. When I became more often met with kind words of concern and a gentle prodding to go home and sleep it off, it became harder to press on with the bitter buffoonery.

I continued to drink, wander, and blindly push my Sisyphus' stone through an endless Shinjuku night. I walked for miles over hundreds of blocks but arrived nowhere.

***

Reclined on the soft black cushioning of my cubicle chair, I stare at the gypsum rectangles of the net cafe's false ceiling and sense I've not yet journeyed to the end of the night, more mayhem lays in store. Two more scenes settle on the scarred, excavated ground of my mind. At first, when I retrieve from the soft mush, they're unseen and inseparable. Like pages of a magazine stuck together, I pull apart to access two torn images.

A horseshoe-shaped wall eight feet high blocked my view of what existed yonder the black tarred roof. The ledge lay behind a bay of ventilation units on an upper shelf. I walked towards the wall, and the drone of the units grew loader like a hive of angry bees. My hand gripped the third rung of a metal ladder hanging down from the second level. I climbed cautiously, feeling the aches of the night, but deeper and more pronounced were those pangs of nights past.

After stepping atop the flat white surface of two industrial air-con boxes, I arrived. Only a low wall to my kneecaps and a foot-wide ledge separated me from the great beyond. I peered down the façade. Nearest my viewpoint were the protruding exterior letters, SHARP, and on either side SONY and TOSHIBA; deities in their own right for an electronic empire.

Below was white siding broken by a fifty-foot wrap-around screen. The form was familiar, and the long curved Yunika Vision screen midway up clenched it. I was fourteen floors up on top of the Labi Electronic store. A building Yukie and I stared across at when the conversation lulled, and we sat in serene silence our evenings in the Beatles McDonald's.

Dormant tracks lay to the left of me, Yasukuni-dori cut in from the right, and scattered buildings in the distance sprung skyward under the dome of light emitted from the permanent dawn. Extended in front of me, crawling upward into the night at a gentle slope, was the red yarn.

Spattered traffic and those who forewent last train for a bit more revelry ambled in slow motion on the streets below. I touched the red string. In reality (*was this reality?*), it was thick, more like the *shimenawa* draped across a *torii* gate, and though it connected to nothing at either end, hung taut through the air. I stepped up on the thin ledge, placed my right foot on the rope, so I straddled the two worlds, and with great care transferred my weight. The mammoth strip of yarn held. I dragged my left instep over the ledge, it floated in mid-air and landed firmly behind my front foot.

Hundreds of feet up on no more than that inch of manila hemp, I stood. Placing one foot ahead of the other, I inched the length like Philippe Petit traversing twin towers. A gust pushed against me, I swayed and gasped before finding my footing to manoeuvre again toward the radial tip, which touched the roofed dome of luminosity encasing East Shinjuku like a psychedelic snow globe. When I reached the frayed end, soft fibres splayed out and projected their essence in all directions; caressing, all I'se been, and all I'se seen.

Stood at the destination of my mind's eye, my memory, *or madness*, crystallizes to portray an image of self, paralyzed with fear as my heart pounds like a *taiko* drum and a single bead of sweat, cold as a mountain spring, slips slowly down my spine.

'Ye almost there, get ta steppin' ye gormless cunt.' A biting wind whispered in my ear, my legs flexed and shaking, braced against the push. I inhaled of the photonic air; it went down frosty, and my exhale's condensed cloud was burned with prismatic pastels of the neon night.

But he's right. I'm yet tethered to the red thread of my mind's eye, not afloat ... where's craved, where was dictated. It was just two steps away. The first dangled my left leg eucharistic to the universe while I wobbled on the other – waiting to be held, bracing for the fall.

Nothing more is permitted; my mind goes blank. *Did I fall?*
Yet I'm here. I'm there.

On the next torn page, in the middle of the street, arms spread, head back, under a late morning sun screaming delirious and incoherent toward a cloudless blue sky.

I'd been stumbling around the area right before where the road underpasses the tracks, searching the sky to locate the exact location where the red thread had ended. When I felt I'd found it above a white painted line of the wide crossing, I unleashed on the fateful spot. 'Why'd you bring me here? Fuck this place! Why didn't you take me? Take me!' I hollered.

Two elderly policemen arrived on either side and led me to a nearby *koban*. They took my ID and jotted down some details. 'I'se had a few too manys drinks,' I slurred. 'I juz need to get some shhleep.'

The cops were kindly, and I managed to convince them I was no threat to myself or others. Something about police custody, it certainly sobers you up in a hurry. I was given a final sceptical eye and released with the ironic request, to go straight home.

I didn't, of course. I went, probably, to another convenience store. By that time a complete lack of sleep and gallons of booze had taken hold absolutely. Which it seems has stifled this nice little flow of recall I've had going.

***

Again, inspecting the writing on my arm, the furious search through mangled memory has not revealed when and why I inscribed the verse. It isn't exactly stigmata, nonetheless, I know it holds meaning.

'I am the son of man' sounds like I was in the middle of a messiah complex.

'You live in the midst of the rebellious house' must reference the Peach Guesthouse.

'Who have eyes but do not see, ears but do not hear' the implications of which, as I think I'm coming to understand, disturb and dismay.

Could it imply, orchestrating some form of retribution on the rebellious house? *Re bellare*, an attack on the Peach House – on Tatsuya, Machiko, and their underlings.

Was that what happened next?

Sick with worry, I'm thinking, *if I did act on this mysterious pronouncement, what if I'd interpreted it all wrong.* Maybe I had it ass-backwards, and I'm the rebellious house; unseeing and unhearing. The son of man tries in vain to provide guidance toward a contented life ... Yet, I do not hear, I do not see, for mine is a rebellious house.

If the latter is the case, all my answers could be found by looking inwardly. And yet, *is it too late? Have I already fallen victim of impulse and insanity?*

A picture of horrific consequence starts to form in my mind. I search myself over to find startling evidence of the crime.

The white sleeve of this cheap dress shirt is either ripped and dirty or it could be slightly charred. I take a sniff, it smells of smoke and grain alcohol, although I'm not sure that's indicative of anything abnormal. Turning them over, my hands are caked in black-brown stains of dirt and grime. Scrapes mar the upper and lower palms from bracing myself against frequent falls to the pavement below. Nails stained yellow, and black gunk like Lebanese hash has collected underneath, yellow pus-filled blisters bubble inside the first knuckle of my index and middle finger from letting a cigarette rest between burn too low. And then there's another broken, red, raw blister on my right thumb from frantic flicking and spinning of a lighter wheel.

What did this all add up to and where does it lead?

Closing my eyes, I force a picture to form, then hope against hope it's only a splintered fantasy.

Dirtied hands carry two bottles of whisky up a narrow staircase. In a hallway under long, spasmic, fluorescent tubes; torn cloth is fed into the bottlenecks. A tiny metal wheel madly flicks the flint and sparks, until comes a lambent flame, then from the lighter's glow, the fabric ignites. A red iron door swings open and an arm hurls the flame topped bottle. It flies with a low arc before smashing against the back wall and exploding. A fire erupts from the point of contact, moves down the wall and spreads across the carpeted floor as blazing roots of an unshackle resentment. The second bottle is picked up and process repeated until it too smashes in scattering flames.

Possessed hands close the metal door and jimmy the handle with a waiting broomstick. White-sleeved forearms swing back and forth in front of a moving form. The final image; dirtied and dusted Adidas, carrying the faceless, expressionless assailant of my mind down brown boarded stairs, through a swinging glass door and out onto a Shinjuku sidewalk.

With that final chilling vision, I desire only to shut down the mind's reel. I surrender in my struggle to retrieve any more recollections from this black sea of memory. And in a dark daze, I stare down at my feet and the muddied Adidas that don them.

Forged? Real? Or some warped and misshapen concocted in-between? I am too close, and yet, also, too far away to decide.

* * *

During the agonizing reminiscence through those blacked-out days and nights, a new message has arrived in my inbox.

Shit, it's from Yukie ...

You haven't come to see me ... Did you get my email? Don't always trust your perspective, Fred. Like skewed skylines in mirrored glass, it has a tendency to betray us. I'm on my way to see you, don't go anywhere! And please, don't do anything rash ...

The message was sent from her newfangled phone. She said she was on her way, meaning she could be here any minute now.

A sense of relief comes over my weary being. At times, I fancy myself a bit of a lone wolf, a solitary survivor; like a solo pilot shot down, boldly making his way to safety through life's jungle. But right now, more than ever, I need saving. Only I fear, I've already advanced beyond rescue territory.

I take off my headphones. The gamers are still at it. My ears are met by an echo of faint explosions, rejuvenating that cascade of opaque recollections whispered through a whisky elegy.

A deep, authoritative voice at reception seizes my attention. Peeking over the cubicle partition I see two large Japanese men wearing overcoats talking to the teller. Their black-jacketed shoulders are darkened further with damp, and one slips an umbrella into the rack. Clearly not salarymen, I presume they are detectives. Fear grips me, spiralling disillusionment, *they're here for me*. My eyes move madly over these cubicle walls, but I'm all hemmed in here.

My mind races. With each rusty revolution of the hamster wheel, an arcane revelation chirps. *All phantoms are just ghost of memory ... life lived like a lazy slalom toward a platform's precipice ... a cautionary tale perched on every lip and redemption in each heart ... loss is a kindness of the cosmic condition ... the destination is always love ...*

However, I'm too frantic, too frayed, too lost and too disoriented to hash them out. Too many paperbacks cracked in lonely little parks and pirated tunes blown through waxy earbuds on arbitrary, aimless treks. So many lumbering Chu-hi afternoons following wasted whisky nights ...

One final squeaky turn, *idle time is the devil's playground, as it's down of an Angel's broken wing.*

I stoop nervously in the smoky paranoia hovering above my computer terminal to follow the men's movements. The girl working the desk gestures in my direction to the stone-faced detectives. They begin their advance, right as another figure enters and slips a pink floral umbrella into the rack.

371

I see only flaxen-striped flowing hair and wide searching brown eyes. *Yukie's.* They frantically scan the netcafé, darting from desks to cubicles. I duck down before she spots me. *If those men are truly here for me, I need to spare her any association.*

Unsure who will arrive at the cloth curtain first, I swallow hard and stare at the keyboard, uncertain of my next move. I've packed these breadcrumbs into an email sent to self, my scream into the void as it were. I sense footsteps nearing ... Hands shaking, I press each keyyh ...

Someone stands at the curtain behind me ... time is almost nigh. Before I swivel the chair to meet fate's hand, I enter one more address. An echo will no longer suffice, there's another soul to whom I need to declare this confession.

A hand grips the curtain's edge. Like the crawl of a departing train, it slides slowly open.

In a plea to destiny, I whisper my order as a final fox hole prayer, just three syllables

...

It's done,

Grab the mouse,

And click ...

Epilogue

RAINY DAY RAMEN AND THE COSMIC PACHINKO

Is he not sacred, even to the gods,
the wandering man who comes in weariness?
—Homer, The Iliad

Dripping wet with sand between my toes, I walk back to the shack. Every day, I swim out as far as I can, trying to touch the horizon. Each new day, I feel like I get a little bit closer, and yet a little bit farther away.

Am I happy? I sometimes ask myself. Well, not eternally. But like Dallas pointed out, that's probably for the best. And so, like the Okinawa Ocean I've finally soaked in, it comes in waves. I feast on those small packets of contentment like a steaming bowl of *shoyu ramen* served up on the somnolent countertop of a rickety shop. Then sit back, surrender and wait for the universe to serve up its next portion.

Sometimes, I spend time in morbid reflection thinking about Akiko, or longing for Yukie. As Karr famously said, 'the more things change, the more they stay the same.'

Yeah, in some respects ... I don't know. I have, however, experienced one seismic shift. I mean, it seems simple, and no one else could even notice, but for the first time I can remember, I can be alone without being lonely. So perhaps, I've arrived at the destination I was meant to all along.

And maybe, permanent dawn and all them nights served a purpose. Long a bonsai pruned by whisky shears, perhaps, despite myself, I've grown a little – photosynthesis under Shinjuku's synthetic skies

***

The Beaver Damn is up and running. More out of lack of anything else to do than a realization of some great ambition. I got Coltrane, not reggae, spinning at the moment ... 'a little Sax on the beach', as I like to joke with Hideki. It's not a customer favourite, but if I'm alone, I'll toss it on. In case an old friend is cruising by and needs a little comfort.

The bar's at the front of the hut, two tables inside and a couple more under an awning in the sand. I got my computer here in the back. A shitty secondhand laptop I bought at the recycle shop, though it gets the job done. Almost makes the tiny bedroom feel like my netcafe cubicle, and that's strangely comforting.

I drink less, a lot less! Perhaps in expectation of Yukie's return, then again, maybe for myself; to get comfortable in this skin rather than lubing up and slipping out all the time. Also, could just be lack of necessity, I'm sedentary, so there's no need for the metho fuel of my mad seeking. Kinda funny, here I am running a bar, liquor galore, but I hardly touch a drop.

Ironic too, that girls come by, usually just on sunny weekends, some of them pretty cute too, but I don't got much interest in them either. At least Junichiro enjoys ogling the eye candy, the ol' perv. 'Living up to his Tanazaki name same,' I often jest of his *hentai* ways.

He's handy though. While Hideki and I pour over the fight forms, Junichiro handles the food and drink orders. He makes a pretty mean takoyaki poutine and always pours generous doubles. Often needed after the fusion cuisine.

Once I reconnected with Hideki here on the island, I told him I managed to track down Machiko and Tatsuya and relayed his message. Then I told him the rest, at least what I perceived it to be. He listened with a pained expression and summed it up with a calm resolve. 'Some of us get lost on the journey, while others know exactly where they're going, but traverse too far along the path in their decided direction.'

Beyond the end of the line. I'd gulped, but said nothing.

* * *

An email arrived the other day, just an image, like a homemade e-postcard. Dallas, standing in front of the Statue of Liberty, smiling ear to ear with his arm around a tidy, professional-looking Asian woman. Underneath in bold blue letters it read, 'Hood forever, New Sinatra, Welcome to NYC ... Peace Brotha!'

I smiled, but haven't written back. I think Dallas woulda wanted it that way.

Every once in a while, I scour Google looking for Gertie. She hasn't turned up. I even phoned a couple of institutions around Belfast, but they couldn't or wouldn't say if she was a resident.

Sometimes when I close my eyes at night, the waves whisper a wishful whereabouts. I see her sitting at an old Remington with lush green hills of the Irish countryside rolling behind. She looks peaceful there, typing a story. Though I can't see myself, I hear my voice call from across the quaint quarters, 'Oy Gertie, What ya doing? Didn't I tell ya, women don't make good writers.'

'Feck off, ye sexist cunt,' she answers with a genuine smile, as a cushion is flung in my general direction.

* * *

I haven't heard from Jae Hyun, although I wasn't really expecting to. He's not the type to write or call, more one to materialize out of the night under a pachinko sky of ball bearing stars – right when I need a smack in the right direction.

In fact, the last I saw of him was that night on the street in a vending machine phosphorescence.

After two days in jail, my release was orchestrated by a mysterious benefactor. When I got back to the netcafe, I found two thick wads of bills stuffed into my backpack. A note placed in between said 'CHECK'. I had no clue what that meant, still don't. Though I somehow knew it was from Jae-hyun, yet no idea why.

I went by to confront him with an apology, but both Jae-hyun and Kai had cleared out. I took their cue and did the same.

A backpack slung over my shoulder stuffed with a change of dirty clothes, a few paperbacks and Jae-hyun's cash, I ran into the last remaining regular. Weepy, in a full suit and tie approached me head-on and placed hands on both my shoulders. For a second, I thought he was going to administer a definitive headbutt. But smiling broadly, he said, 'I go work now, then home.'

'That's great,' I said, genuinely pleased. '*Gambatte*, yo!' I called at his swiftly retreating back. He turned, gave two thumbs up, then made his elated exited.

I've danced with the modern Moirai, I briefly considered at Weepy's triumphant departure. *Hmmm, they who weave with shuttles of adamant and duet with the Sirens.* I searched the empty air above Kai and Jae-hyun's cubicles. *Masters of all that was, are and will be ...*

What tracks have you sung in the celestial karaoke?

Fuck off, Homer. I shook my head with a chuckling scoff at the absurdity of it all, then basked in the comfortable wooziness which descended in the aftermath of my exit.

A few days later I showed up at the police station to meet with the same two feds, though I'm sure they're called something different in Japan. Anyways, some sort of large and intimidating plainclothes cops.

Grainy black and white security camera footage showed me with a bottle of whisky in hand pacing in front of the office door just before the arson occurred. But the bottle didn't leave my hand. Instead, I stepped toward unit #14 and opened it, after which the two flaming Molotov cocktails soared over my head and into the office. An arm entered the frame and yanked me back, to fall against the corridor wall. As I scrambled up, you could see the mysterious figure close the door and jimmy it shut with a wooden handle. The popped collar of a black blazer obscures the person's face as they plod off down the hallway.

They hit pause. 'Who was it?' the men asked with gruff

authority.

'I don't know,' I proclaimed.

They asked me the same in various iterations several times. To each I declared my ignorance. The feds moved on to what I was doing there.

'I wanted to rent a room,' I reverted to my official line.

Sweat beaded on my forehead, though I avoided wiping it away in case any touch of the face would act as some sort of tell to the two detectives. My mouth had gone too dry to swallow. I asked for water, but they ignored me and pressed play to resume the tape.

I chased the black blazer down the hallway but must have thought twice about it as I returned to wrestle the broom handle from the door. The next scene showed me dragging two willowy bodies from the office as smoke billowed out the top of the door frame. I dropped them there in relative safety and hit the fire alarm. Tatsuya, in a semi-conscious state, extended a wiry arm and said something. I don't know, nor remember, what it was.

I'd looked back and mumbled words of my own. Then two dirtied Adidas carried me off screen.

The cops let the video play on for a couple more minutes. Tatsuya struggled to his feet then helped up his lifelong comrade and companion Machiko. Together they lurched off down the hallway, supporting each other's mass as they went. As I watched their escape, my mind wrestled with what this new version of events meant, and how it meshed with what had flooded through my ruptured recall at the net café. *Manufacture dissent? An attempt to knight up and be more than a pawn in life's game? Forgiveness foisted upon me in an elaborate hoax? Or simply insanity – a psyche gasping for air beneath the bell jar?*

The broad-shouldered men in black suits lobbed a few more questions my way. Of which I evaded or pleaded ignorance. With my interrogators, I sensed there was an existing relationship or awareness of Machiko and Tatsuya, but never really found out what that was. In the end, they wrote me off as more of an annoyance than criminal mastermind. I wasn't charged with any crimes, though it was suggested it might be best if I left Tokyo since it seemed I had no real purpose there anyhow. *I've got no real purpose anywhere,* I'd thought with a self-conscious shrug, *and now more than ever.*

* * *

For another two weeks I hung around, went to the Beatles McDonald's every evening and drank whisky-Cokes until I fucking loathed every ounce of lyrical genius from the Fab Four. At closing time, I'd lurk around her place of work, but Yukie never showed at either.

At dawn one morn as Shinjuku's signage forced their final photons into the ether, I crawled through the gap between the tracks and chainlink fencing. I trudged up a short slope to admire her beautiful mural one last time, and in hopes, just maybe, I'd see her there. I was met only with dismay as neither Yukie, nor her art, were found.

Yukie's cityscape now lived under a six by six, matte black oval, which had been spray-painted over the top, obscuring it entirely. I reached out, half expecting my arm to be absorbed by the blob, but just touched brick and black. With spread fingers and palm pressed I felt the vibration of an approaching train. When I retracted my hand, a powdery paint residue remained. I huffed the dust hard, inhaling the aerosol scent, in hopes it would hit like a fresh cut line of blow, but it only marooned me momentarily in a glue-like stupor. During this brief high, the silly notion of taking a run at the wall like a prepubescent Potter persisted. Though I was still nursing the injuries of my recent bender and decided against the wacky test.

Instead I stumbled around and searched the ground for any messages she might have left for me, lifted the board to find all the paint cans gone, and looked again at the concrete slab, into and around the dark mass. Then it struck, though I had no fucking idea what it communicated, the blackened wall was the message all along.

Taking a final glance at that blank, black canvas, a discussion I had with Jae-hyun in my early days at the netcafe came to mind. "Be that as it may," he'd said. "Destiny isn't to be discovered, but defined."

* * *

My final break from Tokyo's warm embrace, came that same evening when the neon glare burned once more, and speckled the streets anew.

I approached him with the nonchalant familiarity which comes after a few drinks. Looking down at the portly fellow, his triple chin and single line, I asked, 'Come on buddy, can I have a go? Just for second or two.'

Under the glow, his pale skin was almost translucent, as he peered up at me like a dim sum dumpling and broke into a wide maniacal smile. 'Nine seconds,' he said and handed me the string.

I set to work, toggled the line and navigated the night. The kite steadied in a spot above the buildings of our alley. I felt a surge of energy course through me and everything went black. When my vision returned, I was no longer holding the string, I wasn't even on a Kabukicho street. In fact, as I stared down, those weren't even my hands.

They were smaller, softer, more feminine. Around her, low sloped roofs piled high with snow, and frustrated breaths escaped the form whose perspective we shared. I listened, and though she said nothing, an adrift, dreamy aura permeated the scene. A yearning was palpable; to be elsewhere, to be found.

The disco nails of her slender fingers fiddle for a Marlboro Red and the white backdrop of the rural town closed in, shrouding everything. A flash of blinding light eclipsed the scene, before Kabukicho's chaos coalesced around me once more.

Old frog-face had retrieved the string and was back in the zone, flying away. Maybe that was nine seconds, though it could've been nine minutes, hours or days, for all I knew.

'*Arigato*,' I said in a nebulous stupor.

'Good, good. Yes, yes, goodbye,' he replied with smiling, beady eyes.

I marched on through halogen caverns, a sense of relief and all new confusions butting horns as I went.

After that, I threw in the onsen towel. Took it off my junk and tossed it on the tiles of destiny.

I've ended up back in Okinawa of my own design, with no idea where else to go. As far as I could tell, there were no planted premonitions luring me back. And there has been no word from Kai in the form of enigmatic signs since.

***

Then there are days, *yes those days*, where I float between notes, slip into syllables and live between the letters.

The Beaver Damn has three stools pulled up to the tiki bar. That's where I see her. As I enter through the sandy threshold and glimpse tanned, delicate shoulders protrude from a cascade of wavy locks. *C, B-minor, E7, A-minor, G and F,* plucked on a Celtic harp break the silence of the empty bar. The music doesn't play in the background, it exudes from her form, sung out to me as an enchanting aria. I'm drawn nearer and nearer as all my troubles start to disappear, until I find myself run ashore and seated on the stool next to hers. I take a deep breath and look sidelong to request a *raita* for my unlit cig. But all that's there is empty air where the music once stirred.

Lifting myself off the stool, I reach over the bamboo bar and grab our cheapest bottle of whisky. A four-finger free pour fills half the waiting mug. I pause, in a single swift motion bring the glass to my lips, and drink in two long, languid swallows.